EDMU
KINGDOM

– PART 1 –

ADVENT OF WOLVES

ANGIE SEYMOUR

Produced by Softwood Books, Suffolk, UK
www.softwoodbooks.com

First Edition

Paperback ISBN: 978-1-7384628-0-3

Published by Stonhams Kiln Books

Printed and bound in Great Britain by
TJ Books Limited, Padstow, Cornwall

FLEGG
ISLE

Holt

Weallesham

Smaleburgh

North
Burgh

Bauburgh

Caistor

Wimundesham   Hethel

Yaremouthe

The Breedon

Burgh   Gurlastuna

Bunincga-Haye

Elmham
South

Telvetaham

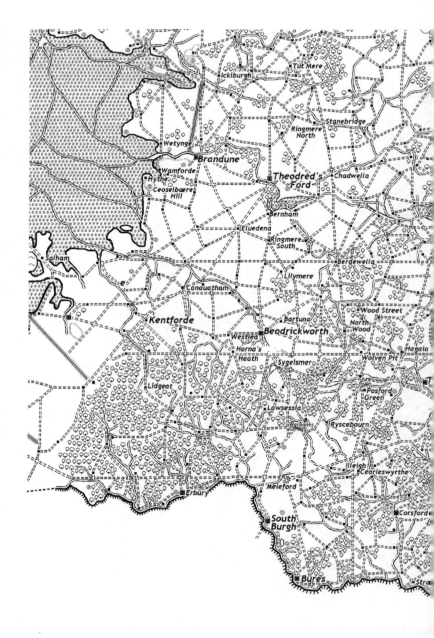

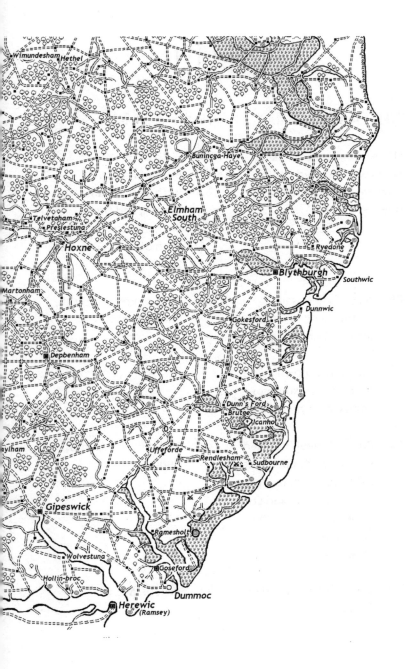

TIMELINE

EVENTS IN VIKING WARFARE

(There were several Viking fleets which raided and/or were mercenaries for various rulers in Europe.)

841   Asgeir's fleet sailed up the Seine River and attacked Rouen 14/5.

843   Hastein occupied Ile de Noirmoutier, south of Loire estuary.

845   Ragnor's fleet attacked Paris on 28/3. Charles the Bald paid them to leave. They then attacked Louis of Germany down the Elbe before returning to pillage along the Seine.

846   Danish pirates invaded Frisia.

EVENTS IN THE TALE

834   Birth of Osketil.
835   Birth of Kadlin.
836   Birth of Guthrum, Gragus, and Greg.
838   Birth of Aesc.
837   Birth of Ærnbjörn and Sæwara.

841   Birth of Edmund, Frith, Will and Valr.

845   Birth of Lee, Pip and Lindi.

846   Birth of Win.

848	Northmen besieged Bordeaux.
850	The Northmen were reported to be fighting amongst themselves. Godfred moved into the Seine and formed an alliance with Charles the Bald. Rorik was hired by Lothar.
851	London and Canterbury attacked but the Viking marauders were defeated by Ethelwulf of Wessex.
852	Godfred's fleet of 250 ships were bribed to leave Frisia. Godfred raided along the Scheldt and then sailed down the Seine in October with Sidroc.
853	Sidroc moved on to the Loire. Godfred's fleet made camp near Nantes. Danish pirates, perhaps under Sidroc, burnt Tours and the church of St

848	Birth of Eth.
849	Birth of Branda.
850	Birth of Æthel.
851	Meeting of Guthrum and Gragus. Birth of Fred. Kadlin is washed overboard along East Anglian coast.
853	Sæwara captured by slavers. Guthrum left the household of Gragus and returned to Hastein.

Martin. They encountered opposition at Orean and returned to the Lower Loire valley before they attacked Angers.

854 Sidroc returned to the Seine.
Many Danes returned to their homeland to fight a civil war. The king, Horik, died and many ruling families were wiped out. A Viking fleet overwintered on Sheppey.

854 Kadlin was found by Weland.
Gragus returned to his homeland but fled when his family were wiped out during the civil war.

855 Sidroc's fleet returned to the Loire. Failed to get past Poiters.

855 Erik, son of Weland, took Kadlin to Halland.
Edmund crowned king of East Anglia at Bures.

856 Hastein raided up the Severn River into Mercia. Late in year the Seine pirates under Sidroc and Bjorn attacked Paris.

856 Gragus is betrayed and three of Weland's sons die in Mercia.
Gragus joined Weland's fleet.
Kadlin's son died at birth.

857 In the summer Sidroc and Bjorn attacked Paris. They made camp at Oissel Isle next to Rouen. Sidroc left with his fleet.

857 Birth of Bjórstein.
Ærnbjörn joins Weland's fleet.

858 Bjorn was joined by Hastein.
Charles was weakened by internal power struggles and failed to defeat the Seine pirates.

858 In the autumn Guthrum summoned Ærnbjörn.

859 The Seine Viking fleets continue to attack settlements along the Seine. Bayeux, Laon and Beauvais are all attacked, and their bishops killed. Hastein left to raid into the Mediterranean plundering as far as 'Pisa'.

859 Stein, from Hastein's Camp, joined the Scandinavian traders in East Anglia.
Birth of Mundi.
Kadlin married an East Anglian.

860 Weland, leader of the Somme Vikings, was recruited by Charles to drive out the Seine Vikings. While Weland waited to be paid, he attacked Winchester in Wessex.

860 Ærnbjörn joined Stein in East Anglia.

861 Weland with 200 ships besieged Jeufosse and the rival Seine Vikings withdrew. Weland sailed to Melun to winter there. Meanwhile, Weland's

son along with the Seine
Vikings who decided not
to withdraw, ravaged
the Forest of Brie and in
December burnt Meaux.

862 Charles went to Meaux.
He surrounded Weland's
men who were forced
to release their captives.
Weland made a deal with
Charles but later died in a
duel.

862 Frith is injured at Meaux.
Gragus takes him to East
Anglia.

863 Civil wars in
Northumbria.

863 Birth of Sæbjörn.
Ærnbjörn returned to
Hastein's fleet.

864 September. Young Fred
confronts two 'oarsmen'
at Holy Cross and the tale
begins.

EDMUND'S KINGDOM

BOOK ONE

ADVENT OF WOLVES

PART 1

MAIDEN OF THE HELLESDEN

CHAPTER ONE

OARSMEN

At Hellesden Hall the oaken barn doors were shut fast. The harvest was gathered, and the workers had dispersed to pursue their trades, the men to the woodland coppice, and the maidens to their distaffs and gardens. But not Lee. She bounded through the meads towards the woodland pasture where cattle fattened themselves on lushness that befitted May rather than September. The beasts, destined for winter slaughter, neither looked up nor lowed to warn those isolated from the herd. They had grown accustomed to her ways.

As had the King. He knew the maiden of the Hellesden liked to run as free as the horses he had placed under her care. She would never conform or bend to rules without reason. Following the death of her parents the king had provided her with a guardian from the Wuffingas royal line. The two had bonded with ease when, without warning, Gisla abandoned Edmund's Sutton household and Lee returned to her home at Hellesden Hall. She was safe enough living on his royal vill. And, in her own way, diligently watched over her young brothers who were the keepers of his woodland coppice.

Lee approached a broad ditch, danced across the narrow bridge, squeezed through the stile wedged like an oar between two woven hazel panels and reached the summit of the massive wood bank. Overhead, the clouds, like heaven's lambs, hastened on their way. She paused to watch them. They reminded her of the heathland flocks in May when Edmund's cousin Osmund, had tried to gather them for shearing. Without warning the tightly packed flock had spewed forth like water from a breached dam. Os had commanded her to be silent. Until then the whole party had delighted in her laughter which sparked much merriment and bonded their brotherly fellowship. But their high spirits had startled the sheep. The faint-hearted beasts squeezed through hurdles, jammed themselves under the furze and headed for the miry creeks.

"Quieten yourself Leoba!" Os had bellowed. "Remember this is how it will be when 'they' arrive in our kingdom. At their advent, we will be scattered across every hill. And our flock will fall into miry pits – pits of filth you cannot comprehend."

Lee shivered. It was a reprimand she would not forget. Osmund never used her birth name. His mother did. She was pious and had once tried to send Lee to a nunnery to follow in the footsteps of Leoba, the much-proclaimed saint. However, Edmund had rescued her and from that time she was always called Lee.

Standing on the wood bank Lee continued to gaze at the clouds. They were a fledgling heavenly flock, fleeing from unseen wolves; sea wolves who harassed them from the north and east. Os was right, Edmund's peaceful reign may come to a sudden end. It was four days since her brothers had met with their kinsmen to discuss all the familiar post-harvest rumours. Northern raiders: the heathen Viking oarsmen, were prowling the grey seas, waiting for opportunity. Yet Edmund had said fear must not squeeze their hearts or distort justice.

The remembrance of Edmund's words restored her hope, and she leapt down the bank into the meadow nestled against the coppice. She laughed and danced around the stormy sea of berry-laden branches. Edmund delighted in gathering blackberries and hazelnuts - but Edmund had not yet returned. He had gone with Hunberht to negotiate with the other bishops - the ones the Mercians had thrust upon them when Edmund was a boy. He had reigned for almost ten years and was the bravest of warriors, the most steadfast of scholars and almost as wise as Solomon in his judgements.

Edmund, however, was conscious he had not yet witnessed the chaos and destruction which had fallen upon Francia where, since his grandfather's days, many oarsmen bands wreaked havoc wherever the wind blew them. Edmund was determined to defend his people and had prepared his kingdom as a good shepherd would prepare a safe fold for his flock.

The king had accompanied Os during the summer shearing though neither had gone to the northern heathlands to chase sheep. They had been aiding their kinsman, Will, who sought news about his aunt Gisla. While the royal party searched for her, Edmund learned much about the kingdom's defences - and weaknesses. His Lee was more discerning than the thegns who accompanied him, for she saw that certain men honoured their trade above kinship and loyalty. She had warned him about the Mercian churchmen who saw him as the latest usurper in a land once ruled by their lords. Inside sacred halls they whispered a higher obeisance to a ruler far away.

Edmund knew her words were true for years earlier Bishop Æthelwold had seized control at Elmham North - though his Bishopric was at Dummoc. Reports from the northern thegns never varied; the Bishop was content and had no allegiance to Mercia. But at Easter their veiled words were proved false for Æthelwold's Mercians had barred Bishop Hunberht's men from Elmham North and Dummoc. His reforms were not welcome there. In response, Edmund had given the faithful Hunberht the royal vill at Hoxne and commissioned the building of the new Minster, Elmham South. Hunberht's sudden influence was like a beacon driving into darkness and the rulers at Elmham North shuddered.

Lee turned her eyes away from the blue skies and continued north to where her brothers, Pip and Win, worked. The sun was already in decline. They were certain to complain about her lateness.

However, the two young men were frantically dismantling a charcoal barrow and gave no thought to their sister's slackness. When they heard her merry call, they shooed her away from the smouldering mass. Lee looked at them and laughed. They were almost as black as the berries she intended to gather on her return journey. Her mirth irritated them. Their scolding was singed with sternness which might have struck down the faint hearted, but Lee did not give way. With great deliberation she took the cloth-wrapped lunch from her basket, threw it towards them and ran.

When she was out of sight, she remembered the bunch of teasels she had left in the meadows beyond the barrows. Hilde, the wife of the household steward, had been asking where they were for days, and she had forgotten them again! Lee took a coin from her purse and prepared to throw it. If the horse landed uppermost, she would turn around, run past her brothers, collect the abandoned teasels, and return by way of Riscmere Hall where her older mares grazed. They were beautifully sleek like the image on the coin she had found weeks earlier near Gisla's Hall in Hunestanestede. It was where Edmund had recounted ancient tales about the horse god of the Iceni and his ancestors the Wuffingas.

Lee hoped the coin would land showing the horse but when she looked amongst the grass a cruel face stared upwards. It was not the terrible Iceni god of war she saw – the image was an oarsman. A bloodthirsty heathen - forerunner of the many who brandished brutal swords. They wore leather riveted armour –

so she had been told - and cursed all they fell upon. She looked again at the wild man on the coin and laughed. He reminded her of Pip dancing on the charcoal barrow. He would be fuming if the cloth had caught fire, and his loaves were cinders. She would not return that way.

Lee lingered in the broadest of the woodland rides where butterflies wavered before resettling on late summer flowers. Swathes of arrow scabious grew there. As blue as the ocean Will once said. She had never seen any sea the colour of the flowers which surrounded her for their sea was grey. Once more her thoughts turned to wild warriors; the terrible Viking sea-wolves. Edmund preferred to call them oarsmen. Their gentler kin, the Scandinavian traders rowed their merchant vessels everywhere, bringing prosperity to his kingdom whilst extending his influence. The king hoped they would keep the wilder bands from landing on his shores.

Edmund's advisors were divided concerning his favourable treatment of the Scandinavians. Some feared the same men who traded cloth and combs were also trading children and women - including Gisla.

Lee did not believe the rumours. Gisla knew more about Scandinavian languages and precepts than either Will or Edmund realised. She had told Lee many tales about her work with the traders from Flegg and Weallesham. Her traders were more important to her than her court duties. The Danes respected and valued her. Lee looked to Gisla to intervene if any of the Sutton household were captured and ransomed. But Gisla was missing.

Lee sighed. She wished Edmund would hurry back. Perhaps her Will would return with him. Lee sat down on a dry gean stump to weave a posy of arrow scabious. She would dry it above the hearth and give it to Will as a love token - then he would have to tell her why he turned from his search at Hunestanestede.

Lee placed the posy in her basket and continued to where

her willow grew. The tree had blown over during a fierce storm the year following her birth and eighteen summers had adorned it with a new flush of branches all at a different angle to the older ones. It was like a spiky bridge spanning the damp ride which oft flooded. Lee climbed up the trunk. Soon she was above the height of the two-year coppice. Peering through slender sallow branches she could see as far as the wild apple perched on the massive boundary bank. Its branches were weighed down with glistening yellow fruit. Lee decided to gather some windfalls to bake with her berries.

As she began her descent a jay's alarm call echoed above the coppice. Its pinions flashed blue as it flew away from the apple tree. The beautiful sight was soon gone but before she turned to complete her descent Lee saw another flash. It was reflected light from below the golden laden branches - from a sword perhaps - catching and throwing back the sunlight to warn her. Without hesitation she slipped to the ground, caught up her basket and squeezed between the roots into the dense bramble thicket. The hole where the roots had once grown was like a den and she settled herself until she was as still as a night watchman. Along the ride someone was singing and another laughing. The merry sound grew louder.

Through a gap between the dry, fibrous roots Lee saw them approach then veer towards her hiding place as they stooped under the willow arch. They were playacting and shook the hair from their faces as they straightened up again. Lee hoped they would move on, but they tarried there to eat apples. A knife fell to the ground and lay glinting in the sunshine. It was a middling, single bladed domestic knife, not a sword or seaxe. Lee was overwhelmed with relief.

"Look a maiden has lost her flowers." The darker-haired man threw the arrow scabious posy to his companion.

"These are no flowers, Frith. These are the blue eyes of

Freyja." He feigned being attacked by them and Lee almost laughed aloud. "They seek Odin to the ends of the world."

"Or are they the blue eyes of Gisla searching for Alcuin?" Frith responded. "I wonder where he hides today?"

Frith snatched the posy from his friend and proceeded to search all the crevices in the willow trunk. Lee overheard him whisper, 'no, not there,' several times before he turned and faced her hiding place. She froze.

"I doubt she will ever find the wily old bard," the fairer man said.

"Which is just as well for he is more treacherous than she understands. Revenge is dangerous."

"Revenge? And why, Gragus, would your poor Gisla take revenge? Has her Bard written an unfavourable saga about her latest cheese?"

As he laughed, he threw the posy high in the air where it was caught by a gust of wind and landed amongst the brambles above Lee's head.

"Leave it," Gragus whispered. He looked at the posy far out of reach.

"It was beautifully woven. The poor maiden will never find it up there. Let me get a stick to pull the briar down. You're tall enough to unhook it."

"I will not linger here."

"Why not? Are you angry because I mentioned Gisla?"

"No. Though the day she left I felt a black shadow pass overhead."

"Is there something I do not know? Come on Gragus, share the tale with me. We are as close as brothers, aren't we?"

Gragus stood with his back to Lee, and she saw waves in his sun-bleached hair like wind-blown sand on the distant Hunestanestede shore.

"Another day Frith," he murmured. He began to walk away.

"Let's not spoil the memories of this place. There are myriads of flowers for scores of maidens to make posies. We have apples and hazels in abundance - and *he* may be waiting at the barrows ..."

Their voices faded, and Lee wondered if she had dreamt it all. But overhead her flowers swayed in the breeze. Was it her Gisla they had spoken about? It could be no other. Gisla had blue eyes and was a cheese maker. And Alcuin the Bard? Alcuin the play actor! He had fooled Will and thrown him off track. Alcuin had clearly stated he had never known anyone called Gisla or Issy or Gis. Yet Frith, a stranger, had called him 'her Bard'.

Lee stomped away in disgust. Will had been so close to the truth. Alcuin had lied. But he was not pursuing Gisla, she was chasing him. And for revenge! Gisla had taught her never to take revenge because reprisals often recoiled like a bow string. Lee recalled blackened bruises on her arms when she had learned to shoot arrows. She grew more troubled with every step. Gragus had mentioned a black shadow and refused to explain what it was. Did he know Alcuin?

Alcuin the Bard was esteemed for his music making, poetry and lavish entertainment. He was at a banquet when Will caught up with him in Hunestanestede. Will had stumbled, overcome by bitter memories of his mother's disappearance from her hall there, he had succumbed to fear.

At the time, Lee thought Alcuin was no more than an entertainer who created sweet legends in cruel times. She had not accompanied Will to the banquet and supposed the Bard's sentimental ballads had dulled Will's senses like drinking too much sickly mead. What had the Bard done, she wondered, to cause Gisla to seek revenge?

Deep in thought, Lee arrived back at her hall empty-handed and ill-tempered. She threw the willow basket upon the table so fiercely the handle snapped. Hilde began a lengthy homily complaining about the thoughtless young. Lee stormed off to the stable shelter and climbed the ladder to the half-loft. It was her place of refuge.

"What did you say to Lee?" Hilde enquired as soon as the two weary brothers returned home. "Though the skies were fair beyond noon, she returned under a black cloud. Did you complain about your lunch? It was my fault she was late."

"We said nothing, and she said nothing," Pip replied.

"Then ask what troubles her," Hilde advised. "She left the hall merrily enough, full of wit and singing but has returned with a heavy heart."

"She has been variable since Os brought her back home," intervened Win, the younger brother. "I should have gone with Edmund's thegns; her roving has unsettled her mind."

"I don't think Will has sent word to her," Pip added.

"Her heart is broken." Win mimicked his sister who was fond of tales of tragedy.

"These are not days to make attachments of the heart," Hilde muttered. She walked towards the doorway where she paused and bellowed. "Hurry up with the soap Lee! They are blacker than ever tonight."

Lee emerged from the hut across the yard and when she did not look up Hilde sniffed and left. Win took the bucket and walked away leaving his brother to ask the difficult questions.

"What's wrong Lee? I'm sorry I was short-tempered at the barrow. The whole thing overheated, and we were afraid it was about to ignite. We don't want any extra work – we have too few workers to get the supplies to the forges as it is." Lee remained silent and Pip paused. "Have you received ill news from Will?"

"No, I have received no news at all." Her tone was very matter of fact. "What did those fellows want?"

"'Fellows'?"

"Those two men on foot – they were meeting someone at

the barrows they said."

"Were they woodsmen?" Lee shrugged her shoulders which annoyed Pip as it was one of her ways of intensifying a tale. She had used the word 'fellows' to begin her intrigue and he did not want to be pulled in. "Didn't you think to ask what their business was? They might have been sent to order more charcoal."

"Well, they couldn't have missed your smoking pit, could they?" She paused and looked up at her brother and whispered. "If they were monks who wanted charcoal, then Win's cursing frightened them away."

"Were they monks?"

"I don't know," Lee teased. "They were so tall I couldn't see the tops of their heads."

"I have no time for playacting, Lee. Tell me what they wanted," Pip scolded.

"How would I know? I was hiding. It's the safest thing to do these days. Or do you want me to end up like Gisla?"

"Lee!" he exclaimed, "You've filled your head with nothing but fanciful tales for weeks. All your adventuring in the coastal wilds with Will..."

"And Os," she interrupted.

"And ....and I don't know who. If Elweard or Cenhelm had been here, you wouldn't have been allowed to go at all. They were sorely vexed when they visited and discovered you had gone roaming. It must stop!"

"What's got to stop?" Win asked as he returned the empty bucket.

Lee did not answer but Pip continued his objection.

"She's begun another of her mysteries."

"Who's disappeared this time? Will? Edmund? Æthelric?" Win laughed. "Or is it more than one person this time? 'Two fellows' perhaps?"

Lee ignored his comment and no more was said about her

encounter with the two strangers in the Hellesden Coppice.

Four days passed before Lee and her young friend Æthel returned to the Bramble Mead to gather blackberries. They also picked up the best of the golden windfalls before returning to the kitchen hall to do their baking.

Lee had not long removed the fruit loaves from the iron when armed thegns from Horna's Heath arrived at the outer gates. Hilde watched their yelping hounds with increasing dismay. Her husband ushered two thegns into the hall. Lee followed. There was no introduction.

"I understand you reported seeing two strangers in the Hellesden last Friday? Which fell were you in? And where were the men heading?"

The thegn was abrupt, and though Lee found his manner offensive she brushed his coldness aside.

"Who has told you such tales?" Lee's voice was warm and merry. She intended to breach his aloofness. "Would you like a bramble loaf?"

"We have no time for cakes."

His haughtiness disturbed her. She had not seen the man for three years. His manners had not improved. Though once a close companion of her brother Æsc she had never liked him. He had advised Edmund not to educate her at Sutton because she was a maiden. And now he was their Chief Thegn.

The Thegn's recent success as an enforcer of the edicts of the realm deepened his conceit and even Edmund questioned his manners and methods. His lack of concern for Gisla, who had failed to attend the Easter Courts as was her custom, had unsettled Edmund. Lee convinced him his Chief Thegn had refused to investigate Gisla's disappearance because she was a woman and, therefore, worth little in the Thegn's small mind.

"Your brothers reported you saw two men in the Hellesden."

"Only two?" Lee mocked as she turned to leave.

"Well, did you see them or not?" The beast pressed.

"When did you speak to my brothers?"

"I am the one who is asking questions, now answer me plainly."

"I will not respond to discourteousness."

Each time he came closer, Lee stepped back.

The older thegn, Wiggi, smiled. He knew Lee was fond of playacting and decided to intervene before she maddened the Chief Thegn.

"Dearest maiden, have you considered the possibilities? What if these men are oarsmen spies? There was an incident about a week ago. Some produce, including a fowl, was stolen from the hall near Chad's Spring. Young Fred challenged the two men, but he gave way because he was threatened with a knife – one which, he swore, had enchanted oarsman runes on it."

The Chief Thegn was thwarted by old Wiggi's disclosure of confidential information. Lee saw his officious anguish and burst into laughter.

"How long has poor little Fred been able to identify runes?" Her voice remained merry which irritated her inquisitor. "Æthel saw him two days ago – he was well enough."

"Was he?" Wiggi continued. "The poor lad was cornered at the Holy Cross and bowed to their demands; he didn't want his throat slit, so he let them escape before we arrived. We were almost upon them for another had reported they were making enquiries about the way to Theodred's Ford. The Blackheath Thegns were quicker than us and intercepted them before they reached the highway. But in the confusion of our arrival, we lost the two vagrants again. Then we heard someone had frightened the flocks at the old barrows beyond the Mardlandr Bourn – one of them was certainly heading towards the Hellesden."

"And the other one?"

"He made a desperate dash towards the old road. My fellow thegn here is convinced they are hiding in the Hellesden thickets. Were you in the thickets?"

"No. I was in Osier Ride. You know wicked oarsmen run like wolves when they are hunted. They will be far away by now. Do you have men stationed along the highways and at the borders to intercept them? Have you sent men to Theodred's Ford?"

"Of course," he added without consulting the Chief Thegn.

"Then why, if they are so dangerous, haven't you sent word to warn us? Edmund will not be pleased when he hears of your neglect."

"Say no more," the Chief Thegn growled. His gloved hand grasped Wiggi's shoulder. "Now, my churlish maiden, I order you to answer my questions with greatest care. What did these two men look like?"

"Are there oarsmen in Theodred's Ford?" Lee feigned alarm, but he ignored her.

"I command you to describe their likeness!"

"What?" Lee responded in an incredulous tone. "I was at the top of Osier Ride. I heard them laughing and whooping a league away. I thought they had been drinking so I ran to hide in Ramson's Fell."

"Did they use our Angle tongue?"

"Yes. They were singing our songs - one of Alcuin's lays, *The Willow Song*. It's his latest. Do you know it?"

"I know neither the song nor the bard," he muttered.

"But you must know him." Lee insisted. "He has grown very rich and famous through his ballads – I thought you marked all who ascend to distinction."

The Chief Thegn looked alarmed and took his companion to the far end of the hall where Lee could not hear what was said. When they returned, the older man remained silent.

"What did they have with them?" The Chief Thegn

27

continued.

"I did not see. I was hiding, sir. If you were a lowly maiden, such as I, would you have risked discovery by gawping at two drunken men?"

"If I were a maiden, I would not be alone in a place like the Hellesden. I would keep to my household tasks."

"And if I were Chief Thegn, I would occupy my time by uncovering what the Bard Alcuin has been up to. Have you found Aunt Gisla yet?"

"I have no evidence she is missing."

"Then you must be blind!" Lee shouted. "I am certain Alcuin has sold her. And Os is determined to discover who informs Alcuin's slavers."

The older thegn coughed, and the interrogator turned away from the maiden. No further questions were asked.

"I remain convinced you saw them, but I will take my leave. If you fail to report such matters again, I shall arrest you," he threatened.

Lee ignored him and asked Wiggi if he would like her to send refreshments to the men who waited beyond the outer gates. She glanced at the Chief Thegn who bristled with anger.

"Very well, Leoba. If you have nothing more to say I will summon your brothers," he warned. "Your older brothers – not Pip and Win who know no better than to trail behind you."

Lee sat down and looked miserable as if he had defeated her.

"Well, perhaps they were not drunk," she began. "But I was hiding sir. I was returning from delivering my brothers' lunch – I was alone because poor Hilde cannot walk as swiftly as she used to. I did hear them approaching. They were singing. I thought they were on their way to see Pip. Did he tell you he had to pour water over the barrow to cool it? No wonder no one else heard the men – or saw them. The water choked on the heat and spewed forth great clouds - like an angry dragon."

Lee looked at the Chief Thegn with contempt. He was a brooding dragon himself and she laughed at the vision she had conjured in her thoughts. His inner fury threatened to burst forth, so he turned away from her and abruptly ordered Wiggi to dismiss any thought of refreshments. He would not be laughed at by some spoilt maiden who thought she was beyond the law. She ought not to have been raised in the royal household amongst æthelings and thegns, for it had made her wild beyond redemption. A woman should not be given too much freedom. He was a man – a thegn - and had authority to uphold the law.

Lee watched in disgust as he took the whole party of thegns and hounds to search the out-buildings. And without her permission! She left the hall and stood amongst her ponies watching the Chief Thegn with rising resentment. The man had infringed her rights. She was furious.

When he realised how carefully she watched him, he smiled. He would let the foolish maiden stand in the rain if she wished. Without looking back, he led his thegns into the Hellesden Coppice to continue his search for the oarsman spies.

Since being observed by Lee in Osier Ride, the men had spent three days in the immediate area of the woods, but heavy rain had driven them to find better shelter. It was six days since their flight from the thegns on the heath and they waited and watched. Gragus had been too hasty at the sacred cross where he had drawn blood from the lad. As soon as the lad swooned, they had heard horses fording the stream. The great tumult reminded him of rolling breakers on the shore where he should have been. They ran back the way they had come. A cloud of dust beyond the heathland edge warned them another mounted band of Anglian thegns was approaching. The two men separated, but it was not their tactics which had furthered their escape. When the rival bands of thegns merged, many rough words were exchanged, and the two strangers slipped into the shadows.

The woods south of the heathland were on high land and were the wildest and most extensive they had discovered in Edmund's kingdom. Frith insisted the gods would watch over them if they bathed themselves in the beauty there. Gragus laughed for he was thoroughly soaked.

Later Frith tried to persuade him to enter a low thatched building encircled by a massive bank. It was an ancient place surrounded by coppice fells; a place where woodland spirits had been appeased before the Christians placed their marks upon the gates. Gragus would not enter the sacred hall but agreed to seek shelter from the rain inside a small hut which stood beyond the earthen amphitheatre.

The hut was filled with baskets which they squeezed between. Both wondered what they might contain and opened one. To their great delight, they found two woollen coverlets which they wrapped around themselves.

Frith pondered their route to freedom and construed all ways began there in the woodland and spread out towards the sea. If they followed any of the water courses, they would reach safety. But which one should they choose? A drip fell from his wet hair, and he shivered. It rained most of the night - and wet ground betrayed strangers.

"Light at last," whispered Frith. "Would you like an apple or stale bread with your wood fowl bones?"

"I can hear dogs, and I don't like dogs," Gragus replied.

"The dogs will be chained. They're at the farmstead to north."

"We will stay here until dark and then move on."

"Stay here all day? We need to be out exploring the byways. He's not coming to rescue us. It's too open between here and those barrows. I will not return there."

"You found the wrong barrows. I found some too – they

were more like the ones he described. We will go back at dusk."

"Do we really have to stay here all day?"

"What do you suggest we do? The ways to the west and north are swarming with thegns. We need to get to Gipeswick and lose ourselves amongst the traders again."

"Easier said Gragus."

"I wonder. If we had travelled further south and then east from the sacred cross instead of going north, we may have found a way to Gipeswick. Perhaps we are closer than we think to the place where Gisla purchased her baskets – which was upstream from Thorney, wasn't it? You said all streams start here. But I will not venture out until dusk."

"Then you have time to tell me more about Gisla and why she is going after Alcuin for revenge."

"I've told you before, Frith, I don't know."

"At least go over it again. You met Gisla at Gipeswick?"

"Yes."

"She sold you some cheese?"

"Yes."

"And some roasted hazelnuts?"

"Yes."

"You fell in love with her?"

"No! When have I ever pursued love? You know very well I was with Weland when I first met her. And I never left his side – would he let me become prey again? And at North Burgh you never left my side when she introduced us to all those traders. They've been very useful, haven't they?"

Frith nodded and hoped Gragus could take a bit more teasing.

"And you must take care, my friend, for you have a rival," Frith paused. "Alcuin wrote a love ballad for her. Her own words, remember?"

Gragus groaned and pulled the blanket over his head. He

did not want to discuss Alcuin. He had first encountered the man at Dummoc many moons ago. Weland had made a secret arrangement to meet him to sell some fine silverware, but a young monk warned Weland not to trust Alcuin, for the Bard had ways of recovering his purchase price whilst keeping the goods. Weland wisely weaved his escape from the gloomy religious halls which Gragus feared more than the thick of battle.

In the land of his birth, his father had protected him from the ways of priests. They had their sacred groves and pools, but his kinsmen had barred every one of them from entering the royal hall. Then, at thirteen summers he understood why, for the arrival at their household of his sworn brother, confirmed everything his father feared. The young refugee had trembled for days in throes of forebodings. He was certain the temple guards would find him. Many years later his oath brother told him the reason for his flight from the priesthood - but by then his warning was too late. He had lost precious companions because of a maiden's intrigue. Frith had been thirteen summers when his older brothers had perished – and all fell without honour. Gragus clenched his fist in despair. He had been willing prey. For nine sacred years, the woman's enchantment had haunted him!

Although Gisla was not like the woman who had beguiled him he had kept his distance. His willingness to aid her against the intrigues of the priests at Elmham was nothing to do with affection he reasoned. She had been no more than a ray of good fortune lighting the way for his intent. However, the light dimmed when he discovered Alcuin was Elmham's man. Gisla spoke of him as a friend whereas he knew him as a traitor. He saw at once the Bard must never know Gisla knew him - or Frith - or she would perish. For her sake, he had withdrawn from Elmham. He had no idea why Frith thought it was love.

Rumours about raiding parties abounded and Gisla may well connect the fragments for her openness and honesty had made them feel too much at ease. She would warn her king if she discovered news which threatened their borders. Edmund was an inspiration in times of peace, but how would he fare in darker times? If he could speak to the king face to face, he would urge him to leave his Christian ways and take up the demands of the warrior life. True brotherhood and honour were found on the battlefield not in temples. Edmund appeared to be no more than a dreamer, writing plays, reading his sacred books; always trying to impart unfathomable wisdom to his flock. His forefather Sigeburght had been the same. As a Christian he had not been man enough to fight. His thegns had implored him to lead them into battle and when he appeared with a staff instead of a sword all his enemies ridiculed him. He had worn no armour and died straightway. Many songs of derision had been written about him. If Edmund followed his ways, he would be dead soon enough. But was that what he and Frith desired? They both admired Edmund's honesty and fairness. He stirred the hearts of those who served him, so they soared like eagles. The loyalty he inspired was exceptional for he honoured his subjects and they in turn made great sacrifices for him.

The longer he stayed in Edmund's kingdom the more Gragus felt compromised. He was an oarsman who had fought on many battlefields. Raiding, extortion and lies had been his way of life. Until now Edmund's kingdom had been overlooked but raiders needed somewhere to raid.

He had lingered too long in a kingdom where people were remarkably joyful without battle. Where men were content to settle in front of a hearth with wife and children, rather than yearn for the excitement of the hunt and the hoard and high seas. They sang thanksgivings to their god, rested in partnership with one another and were at ease. And he was not. He missed his longship and his lith; his family of warriors. But Weland would never command another fleet. He had fallen, and his liths were dispersed. Frith's injury and long recovery had isolated them from past fellowship. They simply had to get back before they were forgotten.

There was one who sought to reunite Weland's liths. It was he who called them to the barrows. A missed gathering would have sent him back to the port to await their arrival. They must not fail him. They must escape.

Gragus could not rest. The air in the hut had grown stale and he felt hemmed in by his confinement and his thoughts.

"Let's go and explore then," he murmured, and the delighted Frith sprang to his feet.

They returned the way they came skirting around the rough summer pasture, abandoned to the snipe-fowl and hares, until they reached the dense coppice. Not far away a wagon driver was urging his oxen to pull through the muddy ride towards the charcoal barrows. They had come up from Elm Green and others were ahead and behind. Frith and Gragus patiently waited in the gloom. When all was quiet, they darted across the ride, scrambled up the far bank and found themselves in a small bracken glade. To the south was another broad ride which they thought best to avoid so they turned north, reaching the arrow-like head of Lee's Bramble Mead.

Frith turned south, and they zigzagged between the blackberry hillocks passing the stile where Lee had paused to ponder the clouds.

"That's east," Frith pointed. "The way to Gipeswick."

"It's too open," Gragus complained.

Frith insisted it was good enough cover but further on, the woodland narrowed to a thin belt. His mind, however, was firmly set on getting to Gipeswick, so he went ahead leaving Gragus trailing behind. At the eastern edge a deep ditch ran towards another section of coppice. Hazel adorned its western bank, and a stock proof weave obscured the view to the east. Frith was unstoppable and slid into the gloom.

Gragus hesitated and gazed to the west. A well-trodden track ran along the southern edge of the vast woodland towards two or more halls. It was all too open, so he too plunged into the ditch.

Frith was waiting below the log and earth bridge.

"Are you mad?" Gragus demanded. "Did you see how many halls there are to the west?"

"But there may be none to the east," Frith whispered before he sprang from his companion's grasp.

The ditch soon shed its protective woven hedge and they wrenched themselves up the wood-bank and entered a stand of high coppiced hornbeam. Dogs barked in the distance. Gragus feared they would be discovered and moved into the shadows. Frith saw him drop into a hollow and followed.

They were in a hollin grove and barely a stone's throw from a grand hall enclosed by ditches, paled banks and fortified gates. Gragus backed away. A pack of yapping hounds emerged from the hollow way and scattered across the open green. The grazing stock panicked and thundered away. The thegns called the hounds back while their leader demanded the gates to the hall be opened. The gatekeeper, an old man, leaned over a rail high up in the wooden tower. He made no reply and in time rattled the heavy bolts. The leading thegn swore and complained about the delay.

"They know something Frith. Perhaps someone saw us."

"We haven't been anywhere near this hall so don't worry. Perhaps there has been a murder; nothing to do with us."

Gragus watched the hounds as they passed through the gates. He knew it was the same wretch who had almost caught them a few days ago. Frith refused to move. It was safer to remain in the dense cover of the hollin grove. It was the right decision. The Thegn did not tarry long at the hall. He took the same path back and kept his hounds on their leashes.

When the rain eased to drizzle, the two oarsmen retraced their route. At the hut they wrapped themselves in the blankets and planned an early escape. However, dawn's grey skies did not wake them. A twig snapped and both sat up as the door burst open.

CHAPTER TWO

SEAXES

Hilde's husband warned Pip not to intervene as his sister appeared to have brushed aside the Chief Thegn's contemptuous accusations. Lee, however, remained furious and vigilant. She was determined to find the two strangers before the Chief Thegn flushed them out. She found work cleaning the leather straps on the lunge harness and watched for his return from the vantage of the stable loft. When the light began to fade, she thought the Chief Thegn must have captured his quarry and taken them to the holding rooms. She descended the ladder, crossed the Long Mead and slipped down into the hollow way. Boundaries were always in dispute she reasoned. And Pip did not state exactly where she must not go.

The ancient track was a little used tunnel of hazel and thorn, but its depth indicated it had been the main thoroughfare into the woods for many distant generations. Halfway to the earthen bridge Lee heard horsemen approaching and climbed up the bank into the hornbeam coppice. Dogs were under the bridge and their frenzied sniffing alarmed her. What had they found? A pair of waterfowl broke cover causing Lee to flinch but not enough to give away her position. The Thegn soon bellowed orders to his men to call in the hounds.

From the wood bank Lee observed the sodden thegns turn south. They had no prisoners. At the rear the arrogant Chief

Thegn held his head high untroubled by the driving rain and chill wind. She knew he would not give up.

Lee rose early to complete her chores before her brothers came tobreakfast. When they did, she left to tend to her mares. Pip sighed for he had no time to follow her. The Chief Thegn's visit lay heavy on his heart, so he gently ordered Hilde to be cautious. She promised to send another with their lunch.

But Hilde had no time to act. Lee left but a breath behind her brothers. Her mind was consumed with her plan to rescue Gisla. Lee had already packed bread and pies – enough to feed her brothers and the men if she found them. Once they were occupied eating, she would bribe them with silver. She and Edmund had hidden a quantity of buckles for such times and Lee hastened to retrieve them.

At Alder Fell she deposited the basket of food in a hollow high in an oak pollard and crossed the bronzed bracken towards Furze Fell. The coppice abruptly gave way to wood pasture and from the fenced bank Lee glanced towards the ruined Wæccan Hall where she later hoped to find the two men. She dashed though the open pasture and rested in the coppice. At its southern end lay the eastern extremity of Bromes Lane. It was as old as her Hellesden Lane and less frequently used. From there Lee hastened towards Sutton Church.

Lee was drawn back to her childhood. Much time had been dedicated to rehearsals at Sutton Church under Gisla's guidance. The cheering crowds seated along the banks inside the enclosure stood as she led the opening procession. Lee had danced while her friends sang and played flutes. But today the place was silent, and Lee's vision faded. The hut was the only thing left there from those energetic days when the king's youthful household had been schooled at Sutton Hall. She and Edmund had packed away all the props and hidden the silver inside the mud bricks used for Jericho's walls.

Lee noticed the latches on the hut were adrift. A wild fury took hold of her. If the spies had stolen her silver, her plan was ruined. She wrenched the door open, and her play act began.

"Don't move or I'll set my dogs on you!"

Before they blinked, Lee grabbed the blanket which covered Frith along with a seaxe in its holder decorated with jay feathers. She threw the blanket down behind her, put the seaxe belt over her left arm and held out her own knife towards the two men. Bleary-eyed they stared at the young maiden.

"What do you know about my Aunt Gisla?"

"Your dogs are very quiet," Frith whispered.

Bemused, and still smiling, he stood up. Gragus was more cautious.

"I know how to use this," Lee growled as menacingly as she could. Gragus watched in silence. The maiden's hand did not tremble. "Where is Gisla?" She demanded.

The eyes of Gragus were fixed on his seaxe. The jay's feathers trembled as the maiden took a step backwards.

"I don't know where she is." Frith said and asked his companion. "Do you think 'Aunt Gisla' is hiding in the basket over there?"

His mirth was short lived as Gragus impatiently rose to his feet and deliberately pushed against him.

"Here we are," Gragus said. "Two men with swords by our sides and you, with a mere knife, dare threaten us? Rather than 'who is Gisla?' I demand to know who you are."

"I did not ask, 'Who is Gisla?', for you know very well who she is. I overheard you talking about her blue eyes - and her search for Alcuin. And, yes, I know Alcuin – he's a treacherous beast! Now, answer me! Where is Gisla?"

Frith knew Gragus was edging forwards and stepped into his path.

"Return his seaxe my fair maiden for I cannot vouch for

your safety," Frith warned.

"Move back! Both of you." Lee ordered.

She knew Gragus was about to pounce and began to move towards the doorway. The distant sound of a hunting horn and yelping hounds broke the tension. Lee suddenly stamped her foot with frustration and threw the seaxe at its owner.

"A knife will not save you now," she warned. "You must get out of here, climb the oak tree and hide in its hollow."

Lee was out in the daylight pointing upwards.

"Stay at my side," Gragus hissed to Frith.

"They're coming up the lane," Lee warned. "He will stop and search this place. I'll take this blanket down the path over there. His dogs will pick up your scent on it. Hurry. I know these dogs; they're good, and their surly master is determined to catch you. If I fail do not resist him, surrender your weapons, and request Edmund's counsel. That is your right."

Frith climbed the door to the roof and then hauled himself into the overhanging branches. But Gragus remained at her side.

"Are you Lee?" He asked, but before she could reply there was another shrill blast on the hunting horn.

"Come on Gragus, we have to trust her now," Frith urged from amongst the branches. "I think she knows what she's doing."

"Leave the door," she said as Gragus bent down from the thatch to close it. He studied her grey-blue eyes. They sparkled with determination. "Yes, I am Lee," she said before she turned and ran.

Gragus was struck by her calmness and without complaint hid himself with Frith in the hollow of the pollard. The hounds drew near and, as Lee had guessed, ran through the open door into the hut and began fighting over the woodfowl carcase. They were uncontrollable. Frith recognised the frantic voice calling the dogs to order. Their handlers scolded and whipped. Even so, it was a long time before the dogs grew quiet. An order to bring out the remaining blanket raised Frith's spirits – the maiden knew her huntsman well and his hounds obediently followed her false trail.

Lee had raced along the paths towards the southernmost hall on the royal vill many times before. It was where she had once lived with Edmund's kin. She crossed the highway, squeezed through a hedge and then another to return to the hedged lane which ran south to Sutton Hall. She laid a false trial to the west and then bounded through a coppice. At the southernmost bank, she paused for breath. Ahead of her lay the common grazing land sprinkled with furze and brambles. She zigzagged towards the bourn which flowed towards the road to Meleforde and South Burgh. Os lived further downstream at the busy port of Bures and was probably on one of his mother's many errands, or perhaps reading a scholarly parable to his four sisters whom their mother never let loose from their hall. For, unlike her, Lee pondered, they were being raised to be submissive and pious.

The bourn was shallow, but the trailing blanket soon became heavy, and she grew weary. However, her escape had never depended upon her strength; stealth would complete her diversion. She hoped the dogs would plunge into the water leading their master downstream as far as the millpond. Spies would head south to Essex he may well reason and his band of thegns would gallop headlong towards the border. Lee feigned a route, retraced her path, and hauled herself up amongst the overhanging branches of a willow.

Win's Wood began as alder carr but further in, amongst the trees, were the remains of boarded walkways constructed by the Sutton youngsters. Lee soon came to the wood bank and dropped down beyond it scrambling northwards until she came to an old black poplar. She deposited the blanket in a hollow where a branch had fallen off when 'Charlemagne was a lad' old

Win used to say.

Lee reached the highway where she sauntered along as if nothing were amiss. She knew it was a busy day for wagons as the charcoal was being measured out and transported to the forges.

"Hello there, young Lee, I thought I recognised you. Do you need a lift?

I'm going as far as the Stone."

It was old Sig, mill owner and healer.

"Have you been up to the barrow?" Lee asked as she climbed up. "I hope my brothers were not bad-tempered."

"Well, they were not as merry as usual, but they have to work twice as hard these days," he replied.

"Hmm, I did offer to help but 'a woman's work is on the homestead.'" They both laughed as Sig joined her in the old saying.

"Why then, dear maiden, are you so far from your workplace?"

"I'm collecting teasels for Hilde's comb."

"Invisible, are they?"

"Have I lost them again?" She smiled and looked all around. He knew her ways and laughed. When they came to the Stone Lee scrambled down from the cart as it slowed to turn towards Ryscebourn. She waved goodbye and headed towards the hop-yards of Linden Pits. Very soon she was back in the Hellesden Coppice.

Lee collected the lunch from the pollard where she had hidden it earlier. Although she was not late her brothers scolded her and ordered her to go home and not speak to any of the wagon owners. Lee shrugged her shoulders for she had no time for conversation. She must return to the hut.

It was deserted. The baskets were all overturned. Jericho's walls were strewn in a corner and using her knife she prised one apart. Inside, like a kernel of a walnut, was a piece of crumpled coarse cloth. She unwrapped what she sought and gazed upon five shining buckles. A sudden thump on the roof made her jump. She had not expected the two men to wait for her return.

"So, you threw them off our trail?"

"Yes, I did Frith, and I've returned here to find out where Aunt Gisla is."

"Will you guide us to the bourn which flows to Gipeswick?" He asked.

There was another thud on the roof and Gragus appeared at the door. He did not join Frith inside for he was uneasy.

"We must go, this place is not safe," he urged.

"But she has brought us some food."

Gragus took no notice and turned towards the coppice. Frith and Lee followed on behind. Later Gragus paused and looked towards Lee.

"If you show us the way to the bourn which flows to Gipeswick then I will tell you all I know about Gisla," he offered.

Frith looked amazed. He had been trying to persuade his companion to tell the tale of Gisla for weeks, moons! At Furze Fell Gragus beckoned Frith and Lee to sit down. She passed the food and drink and waited to hear what had befallen Gisla.

"I am certain she is dead." Gragus showed no emotion.

He had not expected one who had acted so bravely to give way tears. He had never seen Gisla cry. Gragus stared towards the distant birches, his thoughts were far away. Frith was more sympathetic and put his arm around her shoulder.

"The truth is we don't know what has happened to her," Frith whispered. "If Alcuin had her killed then I'm sure he would have delighted in showing Gragus the body - and we have not seen her, so she must be alive. Your Gisla was very kind to me. When I was close to death, she tended my wounds. It was very peaceful in those halls near her dairy. And this is a peaceful place too."

"Why don't you stay and work with my brothers?"

Frith laughed and took her hand.

"Because I must get back to Gipeswick. But I will consider the offer when my work there is done."

"And Gragus?"

Frith prodded his companion.

"Tell her what you mean to do when we reach Gipeswick."

"If we reach Gipeswick."

"I'm sure you will reach the port. It's not difficult once you pass Thorney. Please tell me where Gisla is - or where she was."

"I will." Gragus replied. "But do not play games with me. I saw how well your scheming led the thegn and his hounds on a path to nowhere."

"He should be on his way to Essex. You must head east."

"We were east of the wood yesterday in a hollin hollow close to a gated hall. Do you know it? We saw the thegns and kept hidden," Frith revealed.

Gragus was uneasy. He did not want Frith to say too much and glared at him. Frith immediately looked away and Gragus continued.

"Tell us the way and you will never see us again."

Lee detected his impatience but was unsure where to begin. She decided not to mention the hollin grove.

"Did you pass through a strip of woodland to the east of a narrow mead scattered with brambles?"

"Yes," Frith confirmed. "We turned south at the end of it and crossed a track by going under the bridge ..."

"Did you see the track to the south?" Lee asked. Frith nodded. "It goes towards a hall close to a rookery. If you stay in the ditch along the woodland edge and then climb out onto the track, you'll find the way well hedged. Go straight over the track at the rookery – you won't be seen from the hall. Continue south until you see another track to the east – it's not far. You can cross there into the woodland and go east. When you see a row of low hornbeam pollards find the one which looks like a sunken ship, with its mast all broken. If you stand with your back to the wood-bank and walk south, you will find a way. Follow it until you reach a broader way which will take you to the southern edge of the wood. The track crosses pasture into Brocc's Wood. Don't take the highway south but turn east – there's a path which follows the woodbank. It then turns into the coppice. Follow it until you reach the bourn. The alder carr is good cover until you reach the steep part. There's a hall straight ahead so go east up a ridge, and you'll soon find another stream. Follow it down to where the first stream meets it and then an old sunken trackway will take you to the pool. There used to be a mill beside it and if you look under the branches of the middle grey willow you will see a terraced bank. A small craft is tied up there. It will possibly sink, but that's the way to Gipeswick." Lee paused and Frith repeated her instructions until he was sure of the way. Without warning Gragus rose to his feet.

"We must leave," he urged his companion.

"Sit down friend, and tell her about Gisla," Frith insisted.

"What does she want to know?" He replied in a detached manner.

Lee did not want to throw away her chance to find out more about Aunt Gisla, so she intervened.

"Three months ago, my friends and I approached the port of Hunestanestede not knowing Alcuin was there," she said. Gragus sat back down. He wanted to learn as much as possible about Alcuin. "I did not see him myself, but he told my companion he had never known anyone called Gisla, or if he had he could not remember her. Unfortunately, Will was convinced by his persuasive tongue." Lee sighed. "When you were speaking about Gisla I realised Alcuin had lied. Whatever he did to upset her must have been very treacherous for she always taught us to forgive - and you spoke of revenge."

"Where do you live?" Gragus asked.

"Across the other side of the woods," she waved her hand vaguely in the right direction. But he was not easily put off. Doubt had surfaced in his mind. He feared she had betrayed him.

"Did the thegns visit you yesterday morning?" He demanded.

"Yes – they called at every hall. Which is why I returned as soon as I could. To find these." Lee took the bundle from her bag and unwrapped the silver buckles. "To pay you for information about Gisla - if I found you."

Lee gave Gragus the buckles and he took them willingly enough. He then removed the seaxe from his belt so he could unfasten his purse.

"Or perhaps they gave you these for our heads," he accused. Lee saw her peril and turned once more to Frith.

"I need to know where you last saw her Frith. What had Alcuin done to make her so determined to pursue him?"

It was Gragus who replied. He did not look at her but steadily turned the buckles over and over inspecting them for marks.

"I last saw Gisla in North Burgh. There had been a meeting between some of your Elmham priests. They discussed ways to safeguard their property." He looked up at her with distaste.

"Did Edmund's men know about this meeting?" Lee asked.

"No. Alcuin took many charters to the meeting and then took even more away with him. Gisla wanted to see them."

"And the purpose of the meeting?" Lee pressed as she was determined to learn what treachery had been done.

"I do not know the details. Gisla said it was to do with a property, certain assets, and privileges the priests acquired years ago ..."

"Where was the property?"

"Hunestanestede," he scorned. "And you said you were right there! You must see more clearly than I do for you have known Gisla since you were a bairn."

"Since I was thirteen summers," Lee corrected. "What other assets did they discuss?"

"I do not know, but whatever they were, Alcuin and his bishops were planning to use them to fend off sea pirates."

"You mean oarsmen," Lee interrupted. "Like those Gisla befriended?"

Gragus had betrayed himself she thought. She began to doubt he was Gisla's friend. These were two wanted men and she had helped them escape. Perhaps she had made another of her blunders.

"Is Gisla dead?"

"I cannot say," Gragus answered. "It is not that I will not say for I do not know. No ransom note was sent - so she must be dead don't you think?"

"Have you seen her dead body?"

Gragus was surprised at the maiden's intenseness and persistence.

"No, I have not."

"Then she is not dead. Frith said earlier Alcuin would have delighted in showing you her dead body – and he hasn't because she is alive, and I need to know where she is."

Gragus turned pale. He had not caught Frith's words. Without warning he turned upon his friend.

"Did you say that?"

"Well, yes. He wants revenge. You did try to slit his throat."

"He did not know it was me in the shadows. Why would he associate me with Gisla? Unless ... "

Lee was alarmed at what he said. Then Gragus lost control.

"Did you tell those leeches we knew Gisla?" Frith tried to

move away but Gragus grabbed him. "I told you to say nothing about who we knew, or our business."

His hands clasped Frith's neck. She had witnessed many battles in the Shield Hall where Edmund's thegns practiced - and had trained with them, but she was quite innocent in matters of true violence. She hesitated, not knowing what to do.

"Did you know she had possession of a document he had forged?" Gragus demanded. "She was pursuing the traitor with it to ruin him. But what authority would she have commanded if someone told him she knew us?" Frith could not reply. "I encouraged Gisla to pursue him so we could slip away from this wretched kingdom." Lee edged away. "And I would have done moons ago - but my vow constrained me. How could I leave either of you here? Let's hope he has not been betrayed like Erik."

The oarsman's agonised lament terrified her. His seaxe lay nearby. She picked it up. His tale continued. She did not want to know what had happened to Erik. Lee began to waver between some lost tale and the reality of the oarsman's words.

"I should have slit his throat while I had opportunity," he continued. "I hesitated because I thought I could use him to find Nerienda. She who betrayed our captain! I encouraged Gisla go to Ely to unmask Alcuin. I was to follow. And I would have done so. But another task was thrust upon me. If Alcuin has any evidence that we know Gisla, then I have let her walk straight into a trap. You fool ... " Frith began to whisper like some penitent monk at the feet of his abbot.

"Alcuin was but a bard." He rasped over and over.

Lee slipped away. She did not see the two men embrace as they consoled one another. She was no longer dawdling like a confused calf she was running. As swift as a hart ran from hunters – she must escape. Gisla had gone to Ely. To Ely - Ely of the Mercians.

Gragus came to his senses and stood up. Aware of his vulnerability he fixed his gaze on his quarry as she raced for cover.

"We must catch her before she betrays us."

"But she has helped us. If she mentions what she has done she will bring judgement on herself. Let her go. I know the way to Gipeswick."

"I know when I have been betrayed." Gragus thumped his chest. "She took my seaxe!"

He moaned in great bitterness of spirit. His thoughts raced back through the years and his heart ached. The ruinous turmoil of betrayal swamped him. He sprinted away and Frith, his loyal companion, followed. He was confused. His throat ached. He wanted to be going south but he was running headlong to the north.

Lee's course was clear. She must reach the charcoal barrows. Wolves did not like gatherings of men. As she neared the coppice she glanced back and was alarmed to see Gragus leaping through the furze like some frenzied beast. She took a deep breath, said a quick prayer, and pressed on. In the open ride she ran as far as she dared before twisting through alder and ash coppice to the place where golden tinged birches burst above the dark green hazel coppice like heavenly fountains. It was good cover. She slackened her pace to ensure she proceeded as silently as she could. The wind had strengthened, and many branches were creaking, and countless leaves rustled giving her cover from the wolves.

Lee strapped the seaxe against her leggings and crept deeper into the fell, following a route which would lead her to the perimeter fence and bank. In making such a move Lee was now further from her brothers than her pursuers were. She could hear the barrow workers and so would he – but he didn't know the secret route she planned to take. The fruit laden brambles were dense and dark. If she took care, she could flit from cover to cover like an unseen wren. Her timing had to be perfect.

"I think we have lost her," whispered Frith. "She knows these woods and we do not - but I know the way to our ships. Leave her. It's a risk we must take."

But Gragus did not take risks. The maiden's boldness had entranced him. She had been stealthy and cunning in the way she had outwitted the surly Thegn, but how? Where was he?

The track led to a hurdle gate. Beyond the barrier the way crossed a broad out-mead where cattle serenely grazed close to the wood edge. She could not have passed that way. Yet he was certain she was heading towards the charcoal barrows. She must have slipped past them. In his fury, he turned along a sinuous path which followed the coppice boundary.

Frith remained where he was and signalled his refusal to follow. Gragus retraced his steps, grabbed Frith's tunic and without a sound brought him to his knees. Then Gragus fell. Frith was much his old self and had wrestled him to the ground. Flat on his stomach Gragus gazed through a breach in the woven hazel panel which crowned the wood-bank.

In the mead, crouched behind a bramble clump, Lee's thoughts turned to the teasels. They lay abandoned further on, close to the place where her brothers worked. She must reach the sunken lane, where she had paused a week ago to watch a leveret writhing in the grass. She would be safe there. It was the place she had thrown aside her teasels because a stoat had caught the young hare by the neck. Lee thought of Frith, and then the wicked stoat about to inflict its final bite. Lee recalled how she had stood up and startled the beast, so it let go. But Gragus was no stoat! He was a sea wolf, a mighty hunter. She was the innocent tender leveret, motionless and terrified. It should have run, Lee thought, before the hunter struck. The way of hares was to hide and watch and lay low in a form and at the last moment turn and leap to safety and run. Once freed from the stoat's jaws the little one had run.

It ran until it was lost amongst the tussocks of grass and rushes.

Gragus saw her, in her form. Her watch was perfect. He flinched. Then pointed. Frith saw her. He rejoiced because she was now far enough away to outrun Gragus. Frith loosened his hold and Gragus jumped to his feet. The hunt was far from over.

Lee had neither heard nor seen anything for she was convinced Gragus was far ahead waiting in the thick hedge close to the barrows. Fear gripped her mind and though the hollow way would have been safer, she recklessly took flight through the tussocks.

Her hunter was running along the woodland edge hidden by the woven hazel fence draped with briars and honeysuckle. He swiftly reached the place where the wood bank began to curve into the pasture like a hoo thrusting into a sea of waving rushes. He saw her running like a frightened doe - straight into his snare. Not far ahead the perimeter fence lay decayed, and he caught sight of a gap. He ran towards it like a wild cat gaining speed to pounce. At the point where he was adjacent to Lee, she saw him rise like a black beast about to leap from its stronghold. Instead of bounding away she drew to a halt and turned; her look was stern and determined. He did not pause but charged straight towards her. Like the captivated leveret, Lee did not move. She saw Frith draw to a halt upon the wood-bank and smiled. He wondered how she could be so merry when such a fierce beast was about to fell her. Lee looked down and Frith saw the boggy Gean Mire which separated her from the advancing predator. Gragus had charged knee deep into the mire for his eyes had been on her. Frith drew close to his companion to draw him out but as Gragus looked down upon the black, stinking sludge, a long-forgotten fury rose within him. A stealthy woman was a dangerous one. Was the silence of the grazing beasts a spell from

Freya? He hated the gods. He feared misfortune even more, so he snatched the seaxe from Frith's bosom and hurled it towards her.

Lee moved backwards, startled by the horror of what was happening. She slipped on the wet rushes and fell heavily. A flash passed by her head as if lightning had struck her down. She sat upright and saw the warrior-hunter wading through the muddied marsh, determined to retrieve his prey. For a few seconds their eyes met. His colder than the icy realms beyond the grey seas and hers full of fire. Burning with anger at her own folly Lee sprang to her feet, caught up the seaxe which lay a short distance away and bounded to safety.

Frith stood amazed. He could not grasp what he had witnessed. Gragus had aimed to kill. The seaxe was thrown to pierce her heart. Gragus never missed from that distance. Truly some god had kept watch over the gentle maiden who had risked so much for Gisla. It was not her time to die. She had escaped.

"What have you done?" Frith demanded as Gragus hauled himself from the mire. "You aimed at her heart, didn't you? What if she was found there murdered? What would Gisla think?"

"Gisla is dead," Gragus snarled. "Now make haste and find the way."

Frith turned south and soon they were hidden in the dappled woodland gloom. At the sunken hornbeam Gragus paused to look north. His heart confirmed it was the maiden's hall by the hollin pit. Sudden tears rolled down his cheeks. He did not fear the gods who dwelt in secret groves – he feared his own hand. He would have killed her; he had no doubt about that, for no one could change his course once his eye was fixed upon the quarry. He had shed no tears for Gisla even though he was sure she was dead, so why did he weep for the maiden?

Lee jumped over the low bank into the sunken trackway and pressed on towards the barrows. She did not remember picking up the teasels but at the perimeter bank near the barrows she gathered them in her arms and hid Frith's seaxe amongst them. It was late in the afternoon when she walked into the clearing. Pip glowered at her.

"I thought I told you to go home and stay there?" He launched out in astonishment at her sudden appearance. "Look at yourself. There's mud right up to your braids. What have you been doing?"

Lee did not reply but held the teasels tightly in case he snatched them from her and exposed the seaxe. She stepped backwards and began to circle round towards the direction for home.

"I've had enough, Lee! Do you understand? I can't be your mother. And you ignore all Hilde's advice. I ordered her not to let you near the coppice today. Do you want to be sent to another household? The Chief Thegn has accused you of treason and has made plans to protect you from my carelessness! He is about to confine you to his mother's household. Did you know that? Do you want to be under his protection – as his wife?" Others turned to listen.

"Please Pip. I promise. I will not leave the homestead again. We could get young Fred to help. I'll send him with your lunch - and everything. Please Pip don't send me away, not to him ... " Her words faded. She slunk away like a thoroughly whipped unruly hound.

When Pip arrived home, he found his wilful sister sound asleep. How often had others told him she was out of control? He had taken no action because he loved her. Lee was difficult to discipline for she missed their parents, and he had no heart to be harsh with her.

Pip worried all night about how he would reprimand her but when morning came, to avoid conflict, he left her sleeping. The weary Hilde was incensed because the Harvest Feast was drawing near, and she needed Lee's help with the preparations.

What had the maiden been up to? A whole day to collect teasels and such exhaustion. Hilde was exasperated.

Lee woke with a start. She saw a seaxe cut through the air and a great shadow looming behind as if rising from the mire. Lee soon realised it was Hilde come to wake her by throwing open the shuttering.

"I've made three batches of bread already and have to fetch another from the oven at the green," she began. "You will have to get up now and pin out the covers. Then check the soap and start at least two more batches. Then go down to the hurdle yard to find out why they haven't delivered the fencing yet. No, I'll have to do that – Pip said you're not to go beyond the home pightle today."

Lee recalled Pip's rebuke and her solemn promise not to leave the homestead. She was determined to work with all her strength to make it the best harvest feast since her parents' death. Then Pip would forgive her.

Lee toiled until dusk in the out-shed where she prepared three buckets of soap. When all was completed, she retrieved a bundle of cloths hidden behind a pile of bark strips. Wrapped inside her muddied legging bands were the weapons which belonged to the two men. As she scrubbed the strips Lee stared at the knife which should have pierced her heart. It was the one she had observed as the men ate apples - sturdy but very plain. The other outshone it in every way. It was like comparing a laboriously written parchment with an everyday birch bark note. She marvelled at the blade; intertwining swirls of metal flashed mysteriously. At its widest part she could see what looked like a wild ocean churning beneath an arrow-like skein of geese cutting through billowing clouds. The amber inlaid handle was carved in the likeness of a snake or dragon which uncoiled as it drew along the blade to the point. On the flat edge was writing – runic symbols from beyond Edmund's shores. It was a king's weapon, but no doubt Edmund would prefer the plainer humble one. Did Gragus own it or was it stolen? Young Fred had not lied – the seaxe was enchanting.

Lee knew she must hide it far away from the homestead although she would have to break her word to Pip. Under her mattress was too obvious. It would be the first place the Chief Thegn would look. If only she had not mentioned the two men to Pip. Lee recalled her brother's words and trembled. The Thegn had taken an interest in her! And there was nothing about him she liked.

Her fury brewed like an impending storm, but the sun's rays crept in through a gap in the shuttering. The blade she held aloof flared like an unruly fire. Once more she was drawn to its dreadful beauty. How soon would the oarsman return for it?

There was a noise at the doorway, and Lee dropped the weapon onto the pile of washing. It was Pip.

"I need to talk to you alone; before Win returns."

"I wish I had not mentioned those traders, Pip, for I fear Edmund's wretched Chief Thegn means to trouble you more than he did poor Æsc."

"It was Win's fault. He was set on showing off to his companions and went too far. They were asking how you were, and he said you were unsteady in temper because of lovesickness - you know what he's like. He overheard you mention 'two fellows' and told his friends they had passed this way to tell you Will was off to marry another. And the Chief Thegn was there. Was it fate Lee? Why did he, of all people, have to overhear what our witless brother said? He took great delight in questioning me about the two men. How could I lie? I had to repeat all you said to me. Perhaps I should have denied it all. He is certain those two men are the spies he lost along the heathland edge by Chad's Spring. He fell upon me yesterday in such a fury - I was terrified. He came up from the Warbanks a short time after you appeared muddied, and phantom pale. I'm sure if he's seen you, he would have arrested you there and then, and made you confess. Fortunately, the last cart had gone and there was no one to reveal the state you were in."

"But I …"

"Don't say anything Lee. Nothing at all. Then I can be truthful and say I don't know. Edmund is the only one who needs to hear your tale. You are loyal to him - and he knows the Thegn has not treated our family well. I never want you to belong to him." Pip held his sister in his arms and whispered. "Until Edmund returns, we must be wise in all matters."

At supper Pip had to endure the increasing force of Hilde's scolding. How was she going to do this and arrange that? What about fetching the bread? And the fowls? How could she be in two places at once? Pip gave way and agreed Lee could go on some of the errands. Hilde left the room satisfied the next day would be easier.

And it was. Lee rose very early and attended to all the outstanding errands. She took a slight detour through Hornbeam Row where the broken sailed ship pointed into the dense coppice. She made her way to a long-abandoned hall where she placed the seaxes in the sunken ruins. Lee had wrapped new linen strips around each seaxe, and rolled them up, first in leather, then birch bark with grasses and moss. Had the two men followed her revealed route to freedom? How long would it be before the heartless one returned for his beautiful seaxe?

When Pip and Win arrived home, Hilde was in a much better mood.

"We've sent the last of the charcoal from the barrows for this season," Win announced with great relief. "Every fragment has gone. If they need any more down at the forges, then they will have to wait until we get the Hopyard Barrows going. We will be closer to home Lee - and outside the Hellesden." Lee wondered why her brother had stated the obvious. "He's banned you from entering your favourite coppice until the spies are brought to justice."

Pip kept his thoughts on the matter to himself. If the men were the oarsmen spies, he was certain they would have crossed the border by now. And, if they were the innocent travellers his sister described then they were long gone. Either way the two fellows would not be seen again.

Pip was wrong. Frith and Gragus had been detained at Gipeswick's inner ditches. A group of horsemen surrounded them. There was no escape.

Win was thoroughly exhausted from his work at the barrows and Pip feared he would be easily outwitted by the Chief Thegn. The two must be kept apart.

"You must leave early tomorrow for Meleforde. I've forgotten to send word to Æthelric. Get him to deliver those yearlings he promised."

"Not a chance, brother," Win objected. "I've worked like a slave for you for weeks. I'm taking my ease. My friends will be here at the feast. I'm allowed to spend some time with them I think."

"I think not." Pip echoed. "I think you ought to be feeling ashamed about your loose tongue. Wasn't it bad enough when he hounded Æsc and now your thoughtless boasting has brought him to our door."

Pip's accusation offended Win. Lee raised her head knowing a fight was nigh.

"Brothers, all the tables are set. The confusion over those two men is my doing. I take the blame. I will not go into the Hellesden coppice until the Chief Thegn's accusations are proved false. I don't like him at all, and I fear what he could do to us Win. We don't have Elweard's experience or Cenhelm's shrewdness or

Æsc's friends to aid us this time. Do you want him to take me to his hall?"

"Never! Which is why I must stay here. I'll protect you; he'll have my knife to reckon with."

"But Win, he is cold and calculating and you are full of life and wit. He will make every effort to confound you - I'm not saying you are weak, or you lack courage, or honour, or love. It's him, he cares for no one. He has put duty and keeping statutes before pity or care. Please Win, go to Æthelric. He will be pleased to see you and you can go fishing in his bourn. I will prepare a feast for you at St Clements. That beast will be proved wrong by then – and you can invite all your friends."

"I accept," Win replied.

Pip was relieved and laughed so loud Hilde thought the merriest of feasts had begun early.

High spirits and hearty feasting marked the first day of the Harvest Celebrations at Hellesden Hall. The second day was more sober with reflections led by one of Hunberht's men. Lee's new foals arrived on the Monday with a communication from Win. He had gone fishing with Æthelric. Lee barely had time to inspect her new stock before she had to go and judge the children's fowl competition. Æthel's sister guarded her crate of chicks and passed one to Lee just as a band of late guests arrived. Unseen, they dismounted in the yard. Their leader announced his arrival by loudly summoning the head of the household. It was the Chief Thegn and his dogs.

However, his pretentious arrival was undermined when the hounds caught scent of the parading fowl. Chaos ensued. Even the gentlest of guests were filled with wrath and complained bitterly because their simple pleasures were ruined by the untimeliness of the law.

While one of the senior kin settled the crowd, Pip escorted the thegns to the banqueting hall where the tables were laden with all kinds of delicacies alongside good hearty food. Mead was taken to the Chief Thegn but not by the lady of the hall. Dismayed, he took a single draught then demanded Pip summon Win and Lee.

"The Chief Thegn wants to see you," Pip whispered as Lee pinned a ribbon on Æthel's sister who had won the competition.

"Is he going to search our buildings again?"

"I don't know. Let him go ahead for we have witnesses today. Don't be taken in by his flattery."

"He doesn't know how to flatter," Lee laughed as she made her way towards the hall.

The Chief Thegn, however, did know how to charm his victims and he smiled when he saw Lee. He raised his gold-rimmed cup towards her. It was years since his old companion Æsc had left for Wessex and he saw his sister had grown very comely.

"I hope the mead has refreshed you after your journey." Lee was very solemn though close to laughter at his pomposity. She controlled herself and smiled very slightly.

He was pleased and beckoned her to sit down.

"There's much to celebrate, Leoba," he proclaimed. A cold chill blew across her heart because few used her birth name. "A fine harvest, an excellent firing of charcoal." He looked at Pip. "And I have received word concerning those 'two fellows.' They have been arrested."

Neither sibling faltered. The Thegn was furious.

"And, Leoba, I will not allow you to be called away like your brother. You must remain here while I consult with the Blackheath Thegns about the execution ..." He paused. "... of the law."

Lee was pleased Win's absence had irritated him.

"Where are the Blackheath men?" She asked. "We invited them to our celebrations. Why haven't they brought this welcome news themselves?" He paused. "Do you refuse to tell me?" Lee teased. He then confounded himself by giving too much away.

"They remain at Gipeswick - guarding the spies. We are on our way to meet them and must press on."

"Please let your men share our feast or they will think we are mean hearted. You did not allow them to taste my bramble cakes on their first visit. We can serve you first. Have you provisions for the journey?"

"We have had no time, dear maiden."

"Would you like us to pack some supplies? You have missed two days of feasting. Where have you been?"

"You are so thoughtful, Leoba." He smiled and looked up at Pip. "You are most fortunate to have such a mindful sister. We were called to Theodred's Ford but soon realised it was a ploy to draw us away from our real quarry. And it would have worked but for the Blackheath Thegns. They have shown wisdom at last." He knew the maiden would be annoyed her local thegns had caught his prey for him and hoped she would take his bait and betray herself. She did not. "Now my dear maiden, tell me again what you know."

"I know Edmund values your astuteness. You are reliable and thorough. No task is too great for you, for you do not show favouritism. Is that why you have been so cruel to me?"

"Cruel? I have not been cruel. If my hound is reluctant to obey, he feels my birch twig. Is that cruel? He is happy when he pleases his master. Now describe those men."

"What men?"

"Those you saw in Osier Ride."

"I saw no men in Osier Ride."

"But I have your report."

"You have recorded no more than rumours. I have never said I saw the men. I was hiding in the brambles. I will show you where I was."

Lee turned to leave but one of his men barred her way.

"Will you swear you saw nothing at all?" The Thegn asked. "I think not. Your boundless curiosity leads me to believe you would have peered through the undergrowth to catch sight of the two men."

"As you say – I did glance through the briars. But all traders look the same to me."

"Come now, it was less than a week ago. And I know you can identify a stolen horse in a mead of thirty with ease." He looked pleased with himself. He sensed victory was near.

"Horses are quite different," she continued. "I like horses. Your old master sent me horses as his harvest gift." Lee stood up. "All brought gifts. I must honour their generosity."

The Chief Thegn flinched at her rebuke. He was empty handed.

"I have been generous and reasonable thus far," he whispered. "Perhaps you would prefer me to take you to them, to Gipeswick?"

"My sister is committed to her duties here at the hall," Pip protested.

"Committed to duties?" He echoed. "Where was her commitment when Cenhelm – whom she has not seen for five years - passed this way? Wasn't she roaming the wilds of the northern shores?"

Pip was silenced. Then the Chief Then turned back to Lee.

"Leoba, I will give you a choice. Accompany my thegns and prove your innocence or go with my man here to the holding rooms until I return."

"Do not insult my brother," Lee objected. "You know I was with Edmund when Cenhelm called. I went with him to examine certain evidence which you so freely cast aside."

"Do not digress!" He bellowed.

"I am more on track than you," Lee insisted. "You can

neither detain me nor any of our traders. All you can do is confine me to this hall until all the evidence is gathered. And what evidence do you have so far? A pathetic confession from little Fred saying he was waylaid by a seaxe-wielding wight? A phantom which vanishes like mist? Edmund will not have men charged on such flimsy evidence."

"I could find more," he threatened.

"Well whatever evidence you find, the men still have a right to defend themselves in Edmund's court," Pip reminded him.

"You are wrong, young Pip. The evidence is undeniable." His reply was for her brother, but his eyes were ever on Lee. "And Edmund is not here, is he?"

"What evidence do you have?" Lee challenged. "Real evidence like weapons. Did they resist arrest?" The captive was suddenly freed and as she entered the courtyard Lee whispered to Pip, "He has no evidence at all."

"He has not finished with us yet," her brother warned.

As the guests took their places in the hall Lee and Oswald's kinsman went to serve the folk who had been with them during the outdoor activities. They were soon to disperse. Edmund laws stated the poorest should be shown respect and have some share in the joy of prosperity. When their task was complete Lee made her way to the place where Wiggi sat.

"Has your Chief gone?" She asked.

"He does not give up easily, my child. You have opposed him, which was not wise. He is not used to being challenged and will discipline you."

"I am not a hound," she insisted.

"Indeed not!" Old Wiggi laughed aloud before continuing his warning. "He is a determined man. He is making a further search of your outbuildings. But if he finds the evidence he seeks, I will stay by your side," he promised.

"There's nothing to find," she replied.

Pip returned and was visibly distressed. He had seen the thegns take a coverlet and give scent of it to the Chief Thegn's hound. The dog was infamous for its ability to track down criminals even when given the smallest shred of cloth. Did the coverlet belong to the oarsmen?

"Why are you so solemn, Pip?" Sig's wife asked.

"The Chief Thegn is about to arrest me," Lee intervened. "For aiding spies – oarsmen spies. He's determined to find some evidence to fit."

"Then he'll have us all to deal with," Sig's wife proclaimed. She turned in haste to encourage the guests to give aid to their kinsman's orphans.

The dogs feverishly sniffed the second blanket from the hut which the Chief Thegn had packed away to conserve the scent of the oarsmen. Lee, however, had washed all her clothes and then over-perfumed herself just in case. The dogs continued to sniff everything, but the dense mass of people made their task difficult. It was a timely Harvest Feast.

The Chief Thegn called his hound to heel just as Hilde crossed the yard from the preparation hall. She was carrying a large harvest celebration pie wonderfully decorated with teasel heads which represented birds. Each teasel had a pastry beak and eyes and spectacular crests made from coloured threads. The Chief Thegn's dog showed an immediate interest in the pie and the other hounds heeded the leader of the pack and pulled forward causing Hilde to trip. The pie fell to the ground. The thegns quickly had the situation under control - so they thought. One of the teasel birds had rolled towards the blackest of all hounds and he would let no-one retrieve it, not even his master, the Chief Thegn. The foreboding low growls alarmed Lee, but her guests were laughing.

"Go on boy, it's tasty." A burly man urged.

"It'll peck your eyes out." Another ridiculed.

"That's right boy, keep it in sight or it will fly off."

Lee remembered the seaxes and the embroidered case had been hidden for a day amongst the teasels. Surely no dog could be so skilled. The Chief Thegn retrieved the fabulous bird and looked at it with interest. However, as Hilde passed with the pie hastily re-arranged on the platter, a guest plucked it from his grasp and returned it to its place. Hilde smiled as she bowed under an arch of cheering guests. However, her moment of delight was short-lived as the black dog pulled the Chief Thegn towards the tables. It leapt upon the teasel decorations hanging from the knotted table covers and called to the other hounds. The pack rushed forward in a frenzied attack on the teasels. The guests saw things differently. They saw greedy dogs pulling on the covers in a wild attempt to reach the food. Their food! The crowd commanded the thegns to control their dogs. There were feathers everywhere as the dogs had torn into the cushions as well as the cloths. The guests demanded the thegns leave at once. Kinsmen cried out in defence of the generous and loyal family who were being treated in such an offensive manner. They threatened to petition Edmund.

The defeated Thegn knew he must make a quick, dignified retreat. His dogs and men were soon gone. Lee took heart for though surrounded by chaos and disarray she knew what to do.

CHAPTER THREE
THE BONDS OF LITH BROTHERS

Despite their arrest Gragus and Frith had also fared well. They had been taken to a household where the portions were generous and the beer fine. Frith rejoiced in his good fortune, but Gragus was weighed down with regret. If he had trusted the maiden from the Hellesden they would have been free men.

Frith had followed her directions with ease, and the discovery of the small craft on the terrace behind the willows was a pleasant surprise, for despite Lee's warning, it had been sturdy enough for a whole band of lith brothers. It glided downstream under a haze of moonlight. Rynes and rills rhythmically rippled from the valley sides swelling the bourn and lulling them to sleep. Gragus resisted for he feared he would awaken to discover another terrible slaughter. His wavering thoughts went back to the night when, after a great victory, he had lain down with a maiden; a deceiving lure who had blighted his life forever. So, little by little, his doubts grew broader and wider, until they were a raging river of dread.

He knew silver buckles were common currency and had inspected the smallest notch and every scratch thereon. He could see no secret mark of ownership and yet he could not rest for betrayal haunted him. Perhaps the maiden had arranged for them to be arrested at Thorney. He pictured her there on a bridge, in the arms of the man in the dark fur trimmed robe.

Frith had argued against trading in the buckles for coins because he was certain Lee would not betray them. The maiden's dismay when the Thegn drew close to capturing them at the hut was beyond doubt. She understood the relentless way he hunted - as did he - because the Thegn was the fiend who had chased him across the heath after the incident at the cross where the lad demanded they return his goose.

After their arrest at the port ditches Gragus had given way to bitter self-rebuke. The gods were lined up against him! Retribution, perhaps, for his attempt to take the life of Gisla's ward.

The leader of the Blackheath gárhéap, an armed band equivalent to an oarsman's lith, was Edmund's most loyal household thegn. As steward of the king's extensive royal vill, he was a busy man and chasing two almost unidentifiable traders across the breadth of the kingdom was not his priority. The humble thegn recognised the dangers of arresting unarmed travellers. It would cause unease and resentment amongst the Scandinavian communities. He was determined not to offend the two men he held under house arrest.

"Now, sirs," the Blackheath Thegn said as they sat down to a hearty meal. "We are here to quell rumours which have arisen since a poor lad was attacked at my liege-lord's settlement. Our orders were to stop and search all travellers and you were found to have stolen coinage in your bag."

"I can explain," Gragus began. "We have need to accept silver as payment for our goods but there are many who prefer payment in coinage, so we exchanged our few silver buckles at Thorney. The man and his son looked honest enough."

"I have already followed up your report," the Blackheath

Thegn interrupted. "I believe your story. I had in mind to release you at dusk - but we received an urgent order to hold you here."

"From your King?" Frith asked.

"No, it was from our Chief Thegn. He heard about your arrest. But you must not worry for I have sent men to seek those who robbed you and when they arrive you will be freed."

"Will your men get here before this Chief Thegn?" Gragus asked.

"I hope so. The Thegn has taken his men to Theodred's Ford. He received word from there about his two spies. If the tale is true, then you will be released and if false, he will be delayed. His hound will be wearied ... "

"Hound?" Frith echoed.

"Yes, there is none like it in the whole kingdom."

Gragus could eat no more of his supper. He hated dogs.

"Lovely mead," Frith said rather too merrily. "And the cheese was the best I've ever tasted."

Gragus glared and Frith said no more. Later they slept under the watchful eyes of the Blackheath junior thegns whilst their leader dispatched a further message to the Thorney Ældorman ordering him to transfer the actual thieves to Gipeswick. However, the impending feast days slowed procedures and a waiting game commenced.

As Ralph and Will, the two spies busied themselves chopping wood and filling wattle panels in the newly constructed out barn. A host of other tradesmen were working on the building, some stayed all day and others brought supplies and left. The Blacksmith called several times and spoke at length with Gragus. Frith hoped his two companions would not rouse suspicions for the Blacksmith was adamant they should fight for their freedom and never return to Edmund's kingdom for the wily Chief Thegn had not taken the bait he had lain in Theodred's Ford.

The Thegn, however, had not been wily enough to outwit

the unyielding Maiden of the Hellesden. Having escaped the rising vilification at the harvest feast he arrived back at his lodgings, threw down his heavy gauntlets and glowered at his men.

"Why didn't you hold back your hound until all the guests were seated?" The one they called the Dark Thegn asked.

"Do you place feasting above rule?" His leader growled. "My hound has convinced me the girl and her brother are guilty in the matter of aiding oarsman spies. I tell you, my hound here caught scent of them! If you had held back your curs, I would have my evidence – and her."

"What your dog found were teasel heads. Women use them for combing wool. They had the appearance of fabulous birds and your hound thought he was chasing tardas!"

"He knows a tarda goose when he sees one! I swear he caught scent of the oarsman who slept under the blanket. You must find out where those teasels came from."

"You place too much upon a dog's nose. Stop chasing the wind and let me find the lad. He is the one who has seen the men."

"My hound is never wrong!" The Chief Thegn insisted. "Do you know where the lad is? I am certain you do not. But I know she saw them! We must ride to Gipeswick. My hound will match the scent from the blanket to one of them and the truth will be out! Hand it over."

The junior thegns amongst them looked at each other. In the chaos of their departure, no one had returned to the wood store where the blanket had been left. It was late, very late, before the Chief Thegn was informed all bags had been searched and the coverlet from the hut was missing.

The Dark Thegn was immediately sent to Gipeswick to prevent the men being released. The weary Chief Thegn planned to visit the maiden's hall to retrieve the blanket, teasels and hopefully more. He overslept.

"You were right Lee; your Thegn has returned."

Hilde moved away from the opening where the shutters had been removed. Most of the guests at Hellesden Hall had left earlier that morning. Lee sat in the sunshine repairing the cushions.

"Fetch some mead Hilde, and some of those leftover pies."

Lee was pleased he had returned. She had already guessed why. She too had wondered about the dog's senses. She had heard stories about uncanny, black marsh dogs who long remembered the smell of those who disturbed them; dogs which could wade through waters while holding their victims in a trance-induced stare; dogs which melted into mist only to reappear in places least expected.

"Sir," she said as the Chief Thegn entered the room. "I have sent for some refreshments. Do you have time today to enjoy them?"

"Time is short, dear maiden, but I will sit with you," he sighed. "I have left my men at the outer gates. Is your brother at home?"

"He has gone with Oswald's kinsman - as far as Bourn Street. They are returning the baskets to the miller."

"I hope they were all empty. I believe I may have left a blanket in the wood store. Have you seen it?" Lee looked back down at her sewing.

"I saw it there yesterday lying on the ash logs," she admitted. "But then there was such confusion with the hounds leaping and jumping everywhere. I am having to spend my time making all these repairs. Look at the great pile I must stitch! Hilde said they must be finished before I leave this room - and I am so anxious to inspect the new yearlings."

"My dear maiden, you rarely follow her instructions." Lee was alarmed but he laughed. It was not the soft free laughter she shared with Wiggi, but it was laughter. She looked up at him and was caught in his gaze. "Do you know where the blanket is? Did your brother check the baskets?"

"Yes and no, sir," Lee answered as innocently as a lamb. "I mean 'no', I have not seen it and 'yes' all the baskets were completely empty."

"Perhaps Hilde has put it to one side?" His voice remained carefree and mild. Lee wondered at the change in his manners.

"Hilde washed everything early this morning, sir. Is it out drying?"

It was the Chief Thegn who stumbled. His playact ended abruptly.

"It was my blanket, nay more than that, my evidence!" He rose to look out upon the washing. The blanket was not amongst the drying linen.

"If you ask me politely, I will give your men permission to check the outbuildings again."

"This is a serious matter, Leoba. If the blanket is lost, I shall not be pleased."

"But you are never pleased sir," she replied.

"And if your brother has taken it, I shall arrest him."

"I say one of your men has it! Go and arrest him and leave me in peace. Look, you've damaged all my dear mother's embroideries!"

"I came here today to express regret for the disruption the hounds caused. I am willing to make payment for the damage. Name your price Leoba for I will name mine if the blanket is not found."

He looked at her more intensely than ever and she got up to leave. He prevented her.

"Edmund is far away, Leoba. Yet he will learn how I came to apologise for the events of yesterday. I know how close we came to causing disaster at your generous and well-planned feast. But I withdrew my thegns, didn't I? And without hesitation. You know very well I had authority to arrest you there and then - and your brother."

"You are wrong," she smiled. "Without evidence, you are powerless. We are under the jurisdiction of the royal vill, and I will petition Edmund's Thegn for recompense without delay."

"But I have offered my deepest apologies. All you have done is to behave like the haughtiest of maidens. I will have Edmund - and his Household Thegn - informed about your opposition. You need to be under the care of a worthy lady who will teach you humility and other womanly virtues or you will never be fit to be any mans' wife."

"I have no plans to take a husband." One of his thegns entered the room and heard what was said. He assumed the Chief Thegn had asked the fair maiden to marry him and looked bemused.

Without hesitation, the Chief Thegn ordered his men to make a thorough search of the hall. Chests were unlocked and the hangings and fixtures were all inspected. Lee remained quiet throughout. She did not object to his thoroughness because she was playing for time. She had burned the blanket – every thread of it. And every tooth on every teasel had gone into the same furnace.

At length, the Thegn called off his search and demanded the maiden abandon her work with the yearlings and return to the courtyard.

"I will send for you," he said. "And the lad. I received word he has returned to his aunt. She has taken him to Spring Farm."

"Has no one told you, sir?" The Thegn swung his horse round to hear what the infuriating maiden had to say. "Fred did return to his work but has not been seen since church on Sunday morning. Oswald sent men to make a search for him and ……."

"I am tired of your wearisome tales. Where did Oswald go?"

"Canauatham," she lied.

The Thegn was angry enough to sweep the maiden off her feet and force her to ride with him, but cold reasoning stayed his hand. She would be nothing but a burden and hindrance. And he must put his hound in the saddle sling and ride as swiftly as possible to Gipeswick.

Gragus and Frith completed the wattle panels and later enjoyed an unexpected feast which the Blackheath Thegn had laid out for them. Frith devoured two loaves and a wild fowl while he listened to witty tales about the thegn's eight sons. The eldest, Eth, was away training at the Mickleditch where he had won a prestigious archery match. Gragus was worried Frith might follow with a few tales of his own, but he wisely offered to sing a few songs instead. They were tales but their heroes and victims could be anyone. Gragus relaxed while Frith sang three familiar ballads. However, Frith then announced the fourth, one seldom heard, was about a maiden who loved cheese, Gragus moved away from the hearth to slap a hand over Frith's mouth. Before he reached his target there was the sound of hooves outside. Frith stopped mid-verse and thought the Blacksmith had arrived to rescue them. But it was not he who entered the courtyard.

"Is this what you Blackheath thick-knees call guarding prisoners then?"

It was the Dark Thegn.

"We have worked hard brother, panelling, and chiselling. Come now and take a cup of ale with us." The Blackheath Thegn offered a cup of ale, but it was refused.

"Where are the prisoners you guard so carelessly?"

Frith, who did not want the friendly thegn to suffer shame, stepped forward but had hardly muttered his name Ralph when an unexpected blow toppled him.

"Stand back!" The Blackheath Thegn ordered just as Gragus leapt from the shadows to defend his comrade. "These men are under my protection. They have toiled for days without complaint."

He helped Frith to his feet. The Dark Thegn, however, did not give way.

"My master will deal with these spies. You do not outrank him here."

"These men are not spies. I release them."

"Really? My orders say they are to be detained."

"The port thegns have agreed to let them board a ship before sunrise."

"You are a fool." The Dark Thegn sneered and raised his hand.

Gragus waited for the Blackheath Thegn to act, but he hesitated. Then an older man appeared leading two thegns. All three had swords drawn ready for attack.

"Wigstan!" The Blackheath Thegn called. "This is no battlefield. Go and call up the port thegns and the reeve. They will settle this matter."

The bungling Wiggi had no time to comply. Edmund's Blackheath Thegn was struck and fell heavily against the door where he lay lifeless.

Gragus could have fled into the darkness, but Frith was wounded, and he was oath bound to stay with him. The treacherous Dark Thegn ordered his men to rope Frith and Gragus to the horses. As soon as their riders gathered pace Frith stumbled and fell. Gragus called for mercy and the horseman drew to a halt. He was soon reprimanded by his superior but not before Frith was on his feet again. The horsemen turned into a narrow lane and the party slackened their pace. At first the overgrown hedges obscured the view but before long Gragus saw the river. They were heading straight towards its brown waters. However, when they reached the bank, potholed by the strong undercurrent, the riders veered round the hedge onto a narrow muddy track which led through the margins of the estuary. A foul stench was in the air and thick oozing mud filled their boots. They tripped on rush tussocks and Gragus urged Frith to roll and slide on his good side.

Later the mud gave way to a raised walkway where several torches were set upon poles. The horses drew to a halt. Gragus helped Frith to his feet and, not far ahead, they saw a spacious warehouse with many storerooms. The Dark Thegn had already reached it and a woman ran to embrace him. She was delighted he had brought two more workers. He was pleased to oblige and despite the late hour he ordered his prisoners into the mud to secure alder panels near the staithe. The two were then hauled out and chained in one of the lesser buildings until dawn.

No refreshments were offered, and the pair plunged into the muddy waters to continue the work. When they were beyond the reach of the Swan's whip, she grew bored and joined her thegn in the buildings for breakfast. But there was no opportunity to escape because the Dark Thegn had sent a man to watch over his captives.

"The latrine pits of all the liths in Francia could not wreak like this place," Frith whispered before the guard drew close.

"Keep quiet," Gragus hissed in return although he was glad to hear his friend's wit.

Once the alder wattles were fitted more posts were thrown their way. Gragus pulled himself up the bank leaving Frith to steady the posts from below. Gragus hammered them in with ease and grew warm whereas Frith grew colder. After more pleas for mercy Frith was drawn out of the mire. They were ordered to saw logs for the boardwalk. Each backward movement of the blade caused Frith much pain. Gragus swore revenge.

Before nightfall the two spies were thrown a loaf and secured in the storerooms. Frith shivered as a dull ache spread across his injured body. He could hardly breath. Two weeks earlier when chased through furze and gorse he had ran swift and low like a hare and had led the thegns away from Gragus. Now they were like captive fowl, and he could run no faster than a goose fattened for slaughter.

Gragus lay awake pondering the missing thegn – the one with the dog. Where was he? And the callous Swan? A black swan she was, like those who haunted his rescuer. Where was he? Perhaps she had enchanted him.

The mist rose eerily from the marsh like a veil engulfing his senses.

The gods were urging swan maidens to receive their battle-dead lovers. Their ghost-like forms wavered above the reed-choked margins calling him to their embrace. But he turned his back to them because without a sword to wield he could not die honourably, and they would scorn him. Later he was woken from his night-dreads by someone shaking him. It was the Blacksmith.

"Wake up Will," he whispered.

"What took you so long?" Gragus complained.

"I was told you were free men and waited for you at the ship."

"The wretched man I told you about sent his thegns. And the one who brought us here savaged Frith. I could not abandon him. The reason I came to this wretched kingdom was to restore him."

"So, you agree at last, this is a cursed realm." The Blacksmith hissed like iron plunged into water. "We must go and never return."

"Frith is too weak to run from this place. Let him sleep for tonight. One of the guards is wavering and tomorrow I will bribe him or outwit him – or both. We are being held here until their Chief arrives. He is on his way with the lad -.the one with the goose. You must make sure they do not arrive. Then find the maiden – but take care or she will charm you with her smooth words as she did me. Kill her."

75

"Why? Frith said she meant no harm."

"What does Frith know? Does he ever see danger? He was singing ballads when the one called the Dark Thegn felled him."

"He's already a dead man," the Blacksmith whispered. "And I know how you think Gragus. I have not forgotten."

"Then make haste and do what I say," Gragus insisted. "If my plan succeeds, I will leave word at the forge."

Vows were pledged and Gragus watched his avenger pass between flickering mists and moonlight unaware the bleakest of oaths to fading gods had no hold in Edmund's kingdom.

The weary Blacksmith lay down to sleep in the barn where he had fitted the hinges and bolts. It was his intention to inform the Blackheath Thegn where his prisoners were being held captive. However, the next day he learned the injured man had been dispatched to a healing hall inland. He had no time to pursue him.

While the Blacksmith pondered his next move Frith and Gragus were ordered back into the waters. Frith's stomach heaved with every whiff from the foul stench. And the pain in his side grew worse. Ralph was slipping away and would soon betray himself.

Early in the morning Ralph the trader had gone and Frith the fearless one, struggled as in the throes of battle. He could bear the pain as Frith but not as Ralph. Gragus, aware of what was happening called out. The woman overheard and drew near with her whip.

"He needs some water," Gragus pleaded.

"What do you think that is, out there?" The Swan hissed.

Gragus guided Frith towards cleaner water.

"Don't drink much. Just enough to cool your throat."

"I can't swallow. I'm so cold and the ice is almost to my heart."

"Think back to summer," Gragus urged. "Find strength –for

her. I know you love her."

"Yes, I do - but your maiden was just as kind and warm hearted."

"My maiden?"

"Yes, the beautiful maiden who has your seaxe."

"You are confused my friend." Gragus looked back towards the wicked swan maiden. She had gone.

"It's the smell," complained Frith. "I will pass out if I breathe this stench any longer."

"It reminds me of the cheese we collected from Icanho."

Although Frith did not laugh or show signs of amusement he was warmed inside and his spirit revived. Gragus saw his chance to escape and was about to urge Frith to discard his jacket and swim out into open water when the Dark Thegn appeared.

"He's not far away!" He called to his Swan. "Get out you two!"

The pair struggled to get a grip in the mud and emerged like two ruffled marsh dogs.

"They stink." The Swan held her nose which annoyed her lover.

"Get them to the washroom and make sure they are clean when he arrives. And alive! I'll take your whip!"

"But my love – you said make them work."

"He wants them alive, and they don't look very much alive, do they?"

Gragus and Frith were prodded with a sturdy stick and made their way to a building where two tubs of clean water awaited them. The Swan threw in a generous number of hot stones and passed them a pottery jar of perfumed soap. Later two new sets of clothes were laid on a bench and their old tunics were taken away.

The two prisoners were already dressed when a dark horse with a tall straight-backed rider broke forth from the concealed lane. Two men followed. The black Swan flapped along the staithe and hissed at her slaves to eat their food and finish their ale.

She hoped the Chief Thegn would be satisfied. However, as he drew closer, he grew more agitated.

"I've taken care of them for you sir. They were lazing about in the hall of the man you loathe so I put them to work." She pointed to the new alder panels.

"Those are not the garments they were wearing when I pursued them."

"They requested new garments."

Gragus shook his head and Frith asked when his old shirt – the one his wife had made for him – would be dry.

"Dry!" The Swan screeched. "It was not fit to use in a midden."

"Where are their garments?" The Chief Thegn began reasonably but when she pointed to the blazing fire, he yelled out like a cormorant caught in a trap. "What have you done! My hound would have proved my case. You fools! Have you no wits between you? This hound can track man and beast where none other can. What good are they to me smelling like silly maidens at a wedding feast?"

"But they smelt terrible, sir."

Had the Blacksmith known the Chief Thegn was in the vicinity he could have rescued his comrades, but fate had ushered him inland. He rowed up the Orwella to the crossing at Beleham. The sun was already low in the sky when the vessel moored. The master's wife was waiting at the staithe and thanked the Blacksmith for helping her weary husband.

"There are few who would work with that," she laughed as she pointed to the cargo of midden. "Wils does his best to cover it with wrack."

"I was too late to shovel it," the Blacksmith smiled.

"Make no apologies, sir. Your rowing was excellent. I did not expect to be home today. Show him the washrooms, my dove, before those Scandinavians arrive and declare it theirs – as they always do."

The Blacksmith followed the maiden to the great tavern which stood between the main bourn and a tributary. She asked a few questions which he politely answered.

In the seclusion of the washrooms the Blacksmith slammed his fist on a beam. A dark foreboding had fallen upon him as he listened to the desolate tales Wils recounted about Beleham. It was a place where ancient roads converged; where two former forts lay stripped of all but their ditches and where, under certain moons, a demon horseman rode north with his draco standard screeching so horribly cows fell dead and sheep stampeded headlong into watery mire. He hated such tales for beneath them lay a bleaker truth.

The Blacksmith took no pleasure in ballads and sagas for their heroes deserved no devotion. Frith's stories in verse or prose had hardened him to their misery - which was as well because he might have struck Wils with an oar and left him midstream. Frith had, by accident, taught him to listen lightly and remain outside the tale. It was what he desired to do with Frith's tale about the maiden of the Hellesden. He could see no reason why Gragus would profit from her death.

Later a fair-haired maiden served his ale. He took it to a quiet place behind one of the oaken pillars. The tavern was a rambling sort of place where hall had been added to hall. It was divided up into stalls by way of wattle panels swathed with wreaths of ivy and dried flowers. He shivered again for wreaths were oft woven with strong magic. As daylight began to fade, lamps were lit above the tables and merry travellers soon occupied the remaining stalls. He was not at ease. He longed for the freedom of the sea and yet his pledge to Gragus had to be obeyed – a task which required him to go upstream.

Beyond the partition a tall man sat down, drank his ale, and belched. A dog, lying curled up beneath the trestle shifted and whined. The Blacksmith opened his eyes. Dogs were like sudden beacons in the night giving away position and destroying surprise. He had seen many a warrior brought down by vicious curs. Some could not be outrun. The gods must have looked down on the maiden with great favour he thought, because both Frith and Gragus had told him how she had thwarted the Thegn's hound. Or had she charmed it? Drowsiness has begun its work and sleep would follow. The waves of ivy began to overcome him and once more he shuddered. Between their crests, he saw an elegantly dressed thegn approach the man with the sleeping dog.

"Have you finished so soon?" The tall man demanded.

"The lad will see to the rest. It's what he's paid to do," the older man said. He sat down. The dog grumbled.

"Even so, I will go and check later."

"Your whining is worse than your hound's. Let me explain what happened, it was no fault of mine. Your man dismissed me before we reached his new place. I had no means of preventing what he did. He may have his uses but, as I have said many times before, he's an ignorant brute. It's no use complaining. A mad horse needs more than a bridle and bit!"

"What do you propose then – a spear?"

"Not at all. He did not ruin your plan - it was his woman. I agree your dog has an excellent nose and would have given the men away - if they are the ones we seek."

"What do you mean, 'if'? Are you still not convinced?"

"Where is your evidence? You should have found the lad. He is the only person who has seen them."

"The Hellesden maiden saw them too," the tall man growled. "When she testifies, I will make you grovel."

Beyond the ivy sea, in deep shadows, the Blacksmith froze.

The man had said 'when' not 'if'. Gragus was right; she had to be stopped.

"And just how do you propose arresting Lee? Her kinsmen are already nervous, and they will not be willing to let her go with you. Will you kidnap her like a heartless slaver?"

"It might come to that."

"I will not allow it."

"And how will you prevent it? You owe me too much."

The Chief Thegn hoped Wiggi would give way, as he usually did; but a few reminders here and there should buy his loyalty. He, meanwhile, would provide some temporary evidence. Any engraved knife would do. He could hide it under her mattress and then act swiftly. They sold most things down in Thorney and he had plenty of silver in his bag.

"I will take my leave then," Wiggi said. "I do not like this mission of yours. I am sure she is not guilty."

"Dear Wigstan, you are mistaken. She has the missing seaxe and I will find it."

"Really? I have never known an oarsman to be parted from his seaxe, especially an enchanted one. No, they are not the same men. The Blackheath Thegn knows it, or why was he about to release them?"

"He knows nothing at all!"

"He is like a father to the maiden and will make you pay for your folly." The dog stirred at his feet but only to stretch itself. "Your fondness for the hound has addled your senses."

"Do not fret so. I will deal gently enough with the maiden."

"If you force her to give witness against the men, she will never consent to be your wife."

"My wife?" He laughed. "It is your senses which are addled. Go to your bed and forget what has been done today. Then go home and take mother over to Lidgeat for a few days. I will reward your silence."

The Chief Thegn remained at the table to let his dog sleep. The Blacksmith quietly rose to depart. He had not considered the fate of the missing seaxe; the precious weapon he had helped forge and shape for his friend. Surely Gragus would have hidden it? He hardly supposed the fair maiden had taken it by force. Perhaps she knew where Gragus had left the weapons. If he killed her, it would be lost forever.

Later, the Chief Thegn took a lamp and entered the stalls to check his horse. His hound, now refreshed from a long nap, immediately caught scent of prey. He stood still and growled.

"Is it you, Wiggi? Very well draw your sword if you must. Make a fool of yourself."

He welcomed the challenge and unsheathed his sword. His dog leapt forwards towards the man who stood amongst the bundles of fodder. The Thegn heard it yelp and fall back. Something had struck his dog. Instinctively he bent down and held the lamp over the lifeless hound. Beside its body, in the chaff and dust, a seaxe glinted. It reflected the orange-red light from the lamp. The weapon had broken the skull of his hound in a single blow. It held his gaze for too long. He perceived his assailant was close but had no time to turn before a blow hit him from behind.

He did not know what time it was when his senses returned. At first, he could hear no more than the blood thumping through his head. He lay bound; thrown down on a layer of twigs which pressed into his cheek. A cloth had been pulled across his eyes. Two ivy owls harmonised their calls beyond the shelter where he lay. He was not at the stalls. Sudden grief for his hound welled up and he uttered a cry of remorse. A violent kick silenced him. A light spun downwards as if he was being drawn into hell itself; slowly he drifted amongst spirals which twisted and turned like those fateful swirls and runes on the enchanted seaxe. With deadly accuracy, it had felled his beautiful hound. It had not been

Wiggi in the shadows.

His assailant quietly paced about. Without warning his boot thudded upon a boarded floor. The Thegn curled himself into a ball like a hedgepig.

"What do you want?" He asked.

His captor replied with another well aimed kick but said nothing.

The Blacksmith paid for the horse with stolen money and plunged down the sunken lane without caution, boldly riding towards the hut where he had last seen Gragus. It was deserted. Once more he found himself re-tracing his steps. He wandered for a time until he reached a sheltered mead where he left his horse to graze. He was tired and rested long into the evening before he rode back towards the stench. He did not like the place.

The Black Swan had returned to her nest. He approached with caution and kept his distance. He asked several times where the two men had been taken. She guarded her nest eggs. The man's urgent tones made her think he would pay a good price for the information. His words paced round and round. The same question. Where were the men? He ignored all her smooth words and continued to turn away and back like Reynard waiting to strike. He knew what sort of swan he dealt with, black in heart as well as plumage. She played for time knowing her man would soon arrive to take her to a grand hall – but he was late. Too late; for Reynard struck. The faint sound like two thick-shelled eggs being knocked together was swift and final.

At dawn, not far from a wood store, a jay crossed his path. It remained quiet – a sure sign of the gods' favour. He unfastened the door and offered the Chief Thegn some refreshment. He readily took the drink for his throat was parched. Then his captor slammed his head to the floor.

"I'm not the man you seek. I am just his servant." The thegn cried out.

The Blacksmith paced up and down. Should he question the man and risk being unmasked himself or go to the maiden? He lay down for a while to clear his head. But he found no peace in his sleep. Images of the past haunted him. Black swans swooped down and carried him away. They dropped him in a richly furnished hall where a girl was about to leave. He saw a young warrior asleep amongst gold embroidered pillows. His face was turned towards him; such peace was there. He lay untroubled, but the Blacksmith winced with pain and was roused from his sleep. He knew the place. Those dark swans had taken him back to a wicked place!

He sprang to his feet and paced the boards until, thoroughly exhausted, he threw himself down to rest. This time he was on the floor looking up. The black swans were crouched together high in the rafters. He dared not close his eyes for if sleep took him, they would swoop, their long necks attacking from all directions. But on the dreadful day, long ago, a boar's hide had been dropped upon him from the gods themselves. The vicious pecking of beaks seemed only to tickle him. His tears had given birth to heavy laughter and pleasure found only on the battlefield. The hide had dulled his senses and thrust him into the warrior world.

Morning light held back, and his thoughts rested on Gragus. He came first. The maiden would have to wait. Once more his thoughts drifted. He thought he saw her running away from a hut, this hut. He felt uneasy and leapt to his feet just as a heavy log hit the floor where he had lain.

The struggle did not last long for the Chief Thegn was tightly bound and unable to fend off the blows that fell upon him. When he lay quiet the one who had overwhelmed him spoke. It was only one word.

"Speak."

The Chief Thegn's story did not satisfy, and he felt the wrath of his captor. His tormenter was persistent, and the hardy Thegn gave way. He disclosed where he had sent the two men. The door opened and slammed shut. A wedge was put against it. He tried to move but passed out.

CHAPTER FOUR
THREADS

"Are you asleep? Lee." Hissed Æthel. "Meet me outside by the vines."

They were at Sunday prayers. The visiting priest conducted the entire service in Latin and only a few understood what he said. Æthel did not know how to follow and Lee could not concentrate. She prayed for her friends and then her enemies but did not get further than the Chief Thegn.

"It's Fred;" Æthel wailed. Lee grabbed her arm and dragged her to a secluded place beyond the vines. "He returned yesterday. He said he had been to Canauatham, but his other aunt was worse. She gave him the birch and sent him back to Sigeburght and he was furious too. He set Fred to do all his tasks in one day and poor Fred could not keep up," she paused for breath. "Sigeburght beat him and now he's half dead! He may be gone - gone to join his departed mother." Æthel sobbed.

"Does anyone else know?" Lee asked.

"No. Well, Sigeburght does. I haven't said anything because you asked me to tell you first if he returned and I couldn't get away yesterday, so I've put him in the barn between Hollin Hall and the Slough. Did I do right?"

"Yes, of course you did. I'll come over this afternoon. I'll gather some herbs and you bring the pots and find some wood."

"Do you think the oarsman cursed him with the seaxe?"

"You can't get cursed by a piece of metal. Fred has been treated like a slave for months. It's time we rescued him."

"If he's not dead already." Æthel gloomily added.

Lee hurried home and later crept into the Hellesden as if she were a wicked robber. She blamed the Chief Thegn for her guilty thoughts. Somehow, she had told the truth - Fred had gone to Canauatham.

At Strawberry Bank, she hastily plucked up the last of the woundwort and took the most direct route to Hollin Hall past the deserted charcoal barrows. From there she pushed though the hedge to gaze upon the wavering rushes by Gean Mire where weeks ago she had slipped. Had she not been so clumsy she would, by now, be buried beside her parents. Woundwort would not have healed the piercing Gragus had intended.

"Did you find some?" Æthel called. She was sitting on a tree stump waiting at their usual spot.

"Yes, but don't mention where I found them, or I'll be ... " Lee made the gesture of the throat being severed. They laughed.

"I don't understand why you can't walk through the coppice," Æthel bemoaned. "What did you do wrong?"

"The Chief Thegn thinks I hid the men who attacked poor Fred."

"Did you?"

"No. Where would I hide two fierce oarsmen? I was picking blackberries - that was all. He doesn't like maidens being out picking blackberries."

"I know, he once told me maidens should spend their time inside washing and baking and sewing and ..."

"... Serving him wine," Lee interrupted. They laughed again before slipping down the steep wood-bank into the narrow meadow which separated the coppice from Hollin Hall's extensive orchards. At the far end, they wriggled between ash roots and disappeared into an abandoned double ditched lane. It was often flooded towards the Slough and impassable. However, they were not going that far and left the path through a gap in the hedge. They emerged behind the barn where young Fred lay shivering.

Woundwort had long been used in various forms to soothe bruises and to hasten the healing of cuts and other wounds. Lee wished she knew more about healing plants so she could be useful in times of battle.

Fred struggled to drink the late-season whey which Æthel had brought with her. It was obvious Fred could not remain in the barn so Lee suggested they move him to Hellesden Hall where Hilde could watch over him. It would not be easy to carry him, but it must be done.

The two maidens stopped to rest by Lower Buchan Woods and at once heard approaching horses. They were riding fast and soon came into view.

"Stand next to me in front of Fred. They may pass without stopping," Lee ordered and Æthel obeyed.

Indeed, the horses did pass by, but the foremost thegn signalled to slow down. They drew to a halt and their leader turned his horse round. Lee and Æthel shuffled awkwardly to keep Fred hidden.

"At least it's not him," Æthel whispered.

"Why are you so far from home Lee? What are you two hiding there?"

The Blackheath Thegn asked as he drew closer.

"It's Fred," Æthel cried out. She took a cloth from her bag, stooped down and wiped the boy's brow.

"She's a very tender-hearted girl, sir. I had to help her. And you, my lord," Lee said with respect. "You are injured too."

He ought to have rebuked Lee, but he was delighted he had found the two little birds the other rebellious thegn sought.

"Fred has a headache," Lee sighed.

"The lad has been severely beaten."

"I know - it was his master at the Springs. Poor Fred, first he had to face those two ferocious oarsmen – and now this," Lee dared to say. "He would have been treated better if he had stolen the goose himself. Hilde will take care of him."

The Blackheath Thegn instructed Lee to mount the horse and passed up Fred for her to hold steady. Æthel was praised for her efforts and escorted home by two of his thegns.

"You must take more care Lee," the thegn scolded. He had waited until none could hear. "If he had passed this way, he would have arrested you."

"Who would have arrested me?"

"Our Chief Thegn. Hollin Hall lies within the boundaries of the Hellesden – and you must have met Æthel there."

"You did not say how you met with your injury, sir."

"Do not 'sir' me. I've known you from your cradle Lee. Have you turned from the Way to walk dangerous paths?"

Lee considered his accusation. He was not as close to her as she thought, though she respected his efforts to be a father to her. He certainly did not know her inward thoughts as Edmund did.

"I was just trying to help poor Fred, sir."

"You must take care Lee. Our Chief Thegn is determined to bring those you keep company with to justice."

"Do you mean he is going to make Fred pay for the goose?"

"I am not referring to Fred. You know very well who I mean – those two fellows."

There was a long silence between them as they passed Riscmere and made their way to Hellesden Hall. Lee dismounted at the gates.

"You did not visit us for the Harvest celebration," Lee said. She looked up at him and hoped he would reveal more about his mission for she was curious to know what had become of Frith and Gragus.

"I'm sure you already know why, my child. I was delayed at Gipeswick while investigating a theft – a theft which involved two traders. Traders of cheese, they said, though neither had as much as a crumb of it about them."

As her colour deepened to a fiery red, he knew he had touched upon the truth. The maiden seemed to be familiar with their occupation. Lee turned away and hoped he had not observed her blush. He did not question her further because he was satisfied his Ralph and Will were no more than Scandinavian traders.

"You go straight inside," he ordered. "And do not turn from the Way. It was traders who led Gisla astray - so keep away from their kind. I will take the lad to a safe place – and do not mention your errand today to anyone outside your hall."

"But Fred is too weak sir – let him stay here."

"And have the Chief Thegn find him? He is heartless when hunting. If he should return, then tell him all you know. He is not a man to take your uncooperative behaviour lightly."

"What do I know?" She asked.

"More than you have said, my child. Yet you must have reason – do you not trust me?"

"I would if you told me where you are taking Fred or how you were injured."

"You do not need to know more about either matter – but I will send word concerning Fred, so do not question anyone. And watch who you keep company with. What would your father or mother say if they knew you now?"

Lee ran through the gates straight to her bed where she lay sobbing. No one comforted her. Her household knew the Blackheath Thegn had rebuked her and were certain it was what she needed.

Three days passed. On Thursday news about Fred reached

the hall. He had fought off a fierce fever but remained weak and prayers were requested. Lee re-read the birch-bark message and threw it onto the fire. At that very moment, unannounced, the Chief Thegn staggered into the hall. She looked up and ran to greet him. The message had not yet fragmented into ash, and she wanted to keep him from seeing it. He steadied himself against the door frame and she caught hold of him as he half-fainted away. There was dried blood on his wrists and his hands were swollen with bruises.

"Hilde! Hilde! Fetch some wine." Lee shouted. She helped him lay down upon the longbench.

Hilde had seen the Chief Thegn enter the hall. His arrival aroused her suspicions and she had promptly sent word to Pip and Win.

Hilde poured some wine. Lee's voice had reflected the urgency of the matter and she hoped he had not struck her. However, when she saw the Chief Thegn lying there Hilde was as shocked as Lee. She ran to the north-room to fetch some herbs and bandages.

Lee tried to raise the cup to his lips so he could sip the wine. He was in terrible agony. His eyes closed, and she wondered if he would die.

"Who has done this sir?"

He opened his eyes. He was confused. His wrath fleetingly dispersed.

"I thought you knew."

"No, sir. I understood you had gone to Gipeswick. Are your men safe? Was there a battle?"

"There was no battle," he struggled to whisper. "Look at my hands. I have been bound; hands, feet and eyes - then half kicked to death by one of those men you aided."

Lee paused. How could Frith or Gragus bind him if they were under guard? If they had escaped, they would have gone straight to their ships.

"Do you think I would help anyone who could do such a thing as this?"

"Yes, Leoba, I do. Maidens cannot judge men as thegns can. The man who attacked young Fred and the man who did this are one and the same." He looked at her and raised his hand to her face. "Are you shocked? oarsmen are brute beasts. And you will come with me to identify them."

"Who must I identify?"

"Those two spies you helped escape - I have them under guard. And you will testify."

Lee stood up. The man threatened her. Even though she had shown him pity and compassion.

"You must excuse me, sir," Lee faltered. "For I do not follow what you have said. You say you have two men under guard. Did they attack you thus before or after their arrest?"

"Arrest? I was on my way here to arrest you."

"Was anything stolen from you?"

"Yes."

"We have thieves enough among our own kind. And violent ones too."

He thought back to his confinement in the hut. It was no more than three days since he escaped. He had prised up the floorboards and wriggled his way to freedom. When he had moved far from the hut, he had eased the bands away from his eyes and walked in the dark until he had fallen into a bourn. A felon who was taking fish without permission had found him on the bank. The Thegn pledged his cloak if he would cut his bonds. He felt hemmed in by common thieves. But the man who had killed his hound was no common thief.

"He had the seaxe, the one Fred so eloquently described."

"Seaxes are very common items, sir. And it could not be the same ..." she hesitated. What was she about to say? The same seaxe because she had it? The wicked Thegn was trying to extract a confession! She was cornered. And sometimes innocent prey act in desperation. She bowed her head, kissed his brow, and whispered. "It cannot be the same man because you have him under guard."

He opened his eyes and looked at her in disbelief. Her reasoning was sounder than his. He was dazed, very dazed, and confused. She was right. The men he held could not have been involved in the attack at the stable. It must have been a mere robber. He felt uneasy and frail and was ashamed she had seen his weakness. He was but a fool in her eyes. He needed the peaceful surroundings of his own hearth - with his dog laying at his feet.

"My dog. My poor little Arrow! He's dead!"

His intense cry alarmed Lee. She feared he was about to die too and for the second time she kissed his brow.

Hilde returned to witness the unexpected scene.

"I do not want you to see me like this. Go and find your brother. Hilde can attend to my injuries for now."

Lee ran off towards the Bramble Mead and was about to climb the steep bank into the Hellesden when she heard a twig snap.

"Saved you!" Someone shouted as she was wrestled to the ground. It was Win. "What did the Thegn say? Don't cross the boundary. Don't give him cause to arrest you, Lee. Where is he?"

Pip arrived and looked down on them from the high bank.

"Tell this oaf of a brother to get off." She demanded. "The Chief Thegn is lying wounded at our hall. Hilde is trying to save him."

"What have you done?" Pip asked and scrambled down the bank towards his sister. To her surprise, he kept running and called back to Win. "Come on, bring her with you."

Pip found Hilde binding the Thegn's wounds. The bruises

were severe and his whole chest was blackened. His face was grazed, and his wrists were burned where ropes had cut into them. Pip knew Lee had not harmed the man and he turned away sickened by the sight. Win saw Pip but not the Thegn. He called out thinking Lee had murdered him.

"We can blame those two fellows. Did she use the enchanted seaxe?" The man moaned, and Win realised what he had said and hung his head in shame. Lee smiled, took his hand, and told him not to worry because the Thegn was very confused.

The following day Pip accompanied the Chief Thegn to his Lawsessela Hall where word had been sent to his mother concerning his injury. The journey was made in silence. The Chief Thegn showed little sign of life until they reached the outer gates of his hall. He stoically greeted his steward and told him the wretched fate of his hound. It had been struck down by a seaxe. A wicked, cursed one. Pip was startled by the tale and made a hasty retreat before any questions could be asked.

He returned by way of Ældor Hall, but Edmund's Thegn had already returned to Gipeswick. His wife, Flæ, sent the anxious young man to make his report at the King's Hall which lay a short distance across the heath. Without delay. a message was dispatched to Gipeswick warning Edmund's Thegn to be vigilant. The Dark Thegn had lately been found hanging from a beam in a building by the new port upper marshes and the Chief Thegn captured and beaten. Old Wiggi had also vanished, and two junior thegns were missing. And no-one could be found who knew where the two traders had been taken.

Pip ate at Ældor Hall with Flæ's sons. Their tales were all light-hearted and Pip forgot the murderous beast at large in their kingdom. It was dawn when he woke, and he hastened back to Linden Pits where he had left Lee under Win's supervision.

Lee barely slept as the bed at Linden Pits was uncomfortable; indeed, she hated the place. Unable to rest she began to fret about her mares. One was lame and awkward. Hilde had probably left her in the mead all alone. Before dawn Lee squeezed through the broken wattle panel and raced down Rookery Lane to the Long Mead. None of the mares had been secured.

Lee did not report to Hilde and had in mind to go straight back to Linden Pits once she had checked her stock. She used a good supply of apples to persuade the young mares to enter the stable shelter. The first mare was checked and was so calm Lee risked inspecting the nervous one next. She held the mare's rear hoof towards her, tucked well into her side and carefully prodded with her knife. The horse swerved and she dropped it. Lee was determined to keep hold of the mare's leg and felt around for the fallen knife.

"Can I help you, my fair maiden?"

She did not recognise the voice and let go. The mare remained steady, so Lee stood up and found herself facing a young man whose gentle smile captured her gaze. He held her knife by the blade, and she took it from him and returned it to her belt.

"Who are you?" She asked. "My brother is out in the mead."

"Pip or Win? Don't be alarmed, I'm Ædwine. I was told you needed workers in the coppice."

"Pip has never mentioned anyone called Ædwine. His coppice men are all sent down from the Haugh. Have you come from there?"

"No," he replied. He wanted to be honest with her. "I didn't know I had to be sent." He smiled again. "But now I am here, can I help with these beautiful mares?"

Lee watched him fuss over the awkward mare and thought he was harmless enough. There was something familiar about him.

"Of course, you can - but leave her to settle."

She watched Ædwine coax each beast to his side as if he had

95

inspected thousands of hooves. He was kind and softly spoken and she was impressed. At last, they came to the ill-tempered mare.

"I don't think she will resist," he said.

The other mares were restless, so Lee opened the side door to let them return to the mead. As they did the young mare reared up, taking Ædwine by surprise. He held on, but she twisted round hurling him through the air before bolting through the doorway. The young man lay at Lee's feet.

"Did you do that on purpose?"

"No. I would never hurt anyone."

"Then don't let any out until the last one is checked."

"I'm sorry. I usually work on my own."

She helped him to his feet. It was then he realised the young mare had half wrenched his bag from his belt. Silver coins lay scattered before him, and some other treasure had fallen amongst the straw behind him. He hastily retrieved his second knife and secured it in its place, beneath his jacket. He thought the maiden had not seen it as she appeared to be fully occupied gathering the silver coins.

"I'm so sorry sir," she said. "They have fallen amongst the chaff. Do you know how many you had?"

"Well, I'm not sure exactly."

"You must be very rich then," she teased.

"Yes. Very."

"So why would you need to be working for my brother?"

"Ah, now you've caught me out." He smiled and moved closer to where she knelt on the dusty floor. She was a beautiful maiden; friendly and fearless.

"Do you bring good news? How is he?" Lee asked assuming the man had been sent with word about Fred.

"Good news? Haven't you received word?"

"Just tell me if he is well," she said. The man did not answer. "At least tell me where they have taken him so I can send him some of my bramble cakes."

Her bramble cakes had been much discussed and praised. His confidence grew and he whispered.

"To Dummoc. They've taken him to Dummoc."

Lee thought the man teased her though his tone was suddenly serious - and distant.

"But Dummoc is halfway across the kingdom. Why did the thegns take him there?"

"They had their orders."

"Has he grown worse then? The terrible beast who beat him must be punished. I will tell Pip I must go to him before he dies."

"Don't fear. Will has taken care of him."

"Will? My Will? Is he at Dummoc too? I have waited so long to hear from him. You must tell him not to leave this realm without saying farewell. No, tell him I don't want him to leave at all. It was a misunderstanding. I fear Alcuin might kill him."

"And so do I my fair maiden."

He was amazed at this chance conversation and thought the gods were with him. She loved him!

"Why? What do you know?" Lee asked.

"His agents seek to roam free in Edmund's kingdom. The latest have been prevented from venturing inland and you are safe for now."

"Is Will worried about me? I do miss him."

"Do you love him?"

"Love?"

"He needs your love but knows not how to express what he feels."

"It's the curse of ecclesiastical halls," she gloomily replied.

The man sensed her disdain for the controlling priests at Dummoc and took her in his arms and embraced her.

"Tell me I'm not in a dream," he whispered. He kissed her hair.

"Of course, you are not in a dream," she said crossly. She immediately freed herself from his embrace. "What do you mean?"

"He did not tell me how beautiful you were."

"Will values honesty and brotherhood above all else. A beautiful woman may have a very black heart, don't you think?"

Ædwine could hardly believe what the maiden revealed.

"And a man may give every appearance of being cold and unmoved when in truth he has been smitten by love. Keep safe for him my fair maiden. And don't trouble Pip or he will ask why I have not stayed to help. I must return with this news for it will give him hope and strength."

He kissed her again and left as suddenly as he had appeared.

Lee returned to Linden Pits where she once more blamed the Chief Thegn for her situation. The place was worse than the holding rooms at Beodrickworth. The ownership of the hall had been in dispute for many years but was seasonally occupied by workers at the linden pits. The rope barn was in better condition but two of Pip's workers were sweeping the floor, so she did not tarry there.

The home pightle was dissected by several rectangular pits where bark from lime trees was submerged in water to separate the bast bands, the raw material for making rope and cords. The bark had been stripped from the nearby pasture coppice where the small leaved lime stands had been cut and dried for winter fodder in July. It had soaked long enough and needed to be removed and separated. The outer bark would be dried for oven fuel and the bast bands were spun to make cords which were then twisted on the frames inside the barn to make cordage.

Win was at work opening the drainage channels and stinking waters suddenly flowed from the pits. Escaping the foul odour Lee entered the gardens and then the dismal hall.

"Os!" She cried. She was relieved to see a familiar friend

and threw her arms around him.

"I hear you've thwarted poor Hilde."

Before she could reply Pip appeared.

"Did you know his dog was dead?" He bellowed.

"Yes. He was very upset."

"He is more than upset. It was the best hound ever trained."

"I know. And I am sorry it is dead. Did he suffer too?"

"It was done in an instant he said. And by the same enchanted seaxe which was held to Fred's throat. He was blessed to escape."

"He should have taken more care," Os added. "Oarsmen are apt at hiding in lodging places. Fred said from the start the assailant was not wearing amour or a helm – nor did he have a sword. Take care Lee for these oarsmen look much like their brothers in our marketplaces."

"How is Fred?" It was an innocent enough question which she hoped would steer the conversation away from oarsmen. If Gragus did belong to them, then it was not his seaxe which had killed Arrow for she had it.

"He is improving," Os replied.

"I understood Will went to visit him."

"Did he? I thought Will was on his way to Medeshamstede."

"Medeshamstede!"

"Have you not told her Pip?"

"How could I find the right time when the Thegn is hounding us?" Pip took his sister into his arms and kissed her. "I am sure Edmund does not want Will to go to Mercia."

"Please don't let him go there. Alcuin will kill him."

"He got on well enough with him in Hunestanestede, Lee. There's no need to cry. I will try to delay him until Edmund returns."

"Will cannot express what he feels," Lee repeated. "He is confused Os, and you must not let those Dummoc men persuade him to go to Mercia."

"I promise to do what I can Lee. And I will try to rescue you from this wretched business with our Chief Thegn. You know how dedicated he is to securing our kingdom against the pagans."

"I do not like him."

"I do not like him much either, but it does not make him untrustworthy."

"I did not say he was," she corrected. "But I do not like the way he treated Fred. He is but a poor lad afraid of all thegns, and of course he said he was attacked by an oarsman with an enchanted seaxe. He wanted to impress him. It was an ordinary knife."

"Then why do we another tale about a mysterious seaxe?" Os mused.

"Both stories are from the same man. The man who has driven me from my home and my horses." Lee cried. "I cannot bear living here away from them."

Os was a peace maker. He rarely failed to settle disputes. Edmund said he was like king Solomon and his gentle wisdom was much appreciated as the days grew more difficult. He persuaded Pip to return Lee to Hellesden Hall. Win could take charge of the men at Linden Pits.

When the daylight faded, the kinsmen settled on the longbenches while Lee cracked open hazelnuts by the hearth.

"I would like to see Will before he goes to Mercia," she said as she passed Os a handful of hazels. "How long before he leaves Dummoc?"

"Dummoc?" Os repeated looking very puzzled. "What makes you think Will is at Dummoc?"

Lee was perplexed for she thought Os had confirmed Will was at Dummoc. She did not want to shatter the welcome peace by mentioning the other stranger at the stable so she hastily muttered.

"I thought you said he was there with Fred."

Unfortunately, Pip overheard.

"There she goes again, Os," he complained. "Fred is at Ryscebourn Lee, not Dummoc – so no more of your tales."

"I'm sorry Pip. Would you like some hazelnuts now you are awake?"

She took her seaxe and began to crack more hazels with its blunt edge. It took several strikes to break them open - but poor Arrow had been broken with a single blow. Her thoughts were dark and dreadful. Perhaps she had imagined the seaxe Ædwine had concealed under his jacket? It was so very like the one she had hidden away. The flash of the blade was like the flash of moonlight reflected off water droplets caught on cobwebs. She had seen twists and turns like flames flickering from ashen logs. The handle was familiar in shape and form. The brown amber on the seaxe she had hidden was matched by greenstone all shades of a mead. Her brief glimpse of the knife confirmed the man at her stable was an oarsman. She had embraced a heathen oarsman. He had kissed her! She suddenly stood up and spilled the remaining hazelnuts.

"Lee, look out!" Pip cried.

"You haven't singed your tunic again, have you?"

Lee did not reply to Win but made her way to her mattress and lay down to sleep. She dreamt she was lying under the stars amongst the broom of the northern heathlands. The moon shone down and reflected off ripples gathering speed along the chalk bourn. Soon the waters would meet the sea; the great grey sea where oarsmen roamed.

Lee woke early the next morning afraid the oarsman had returned and stolen her mares in the night. She pulled on her boots and made her way to the courtyard.

"Where are you going Lee?"

"To the stable, Os. I have work to do."

"And so, have I. You must tell me what you know."

"It is nothing."

"Then why do you think the Thegn is being so thorough? Are those men more than traders?"

"How would I know?"

"Sit down Lee and tell me what happened." Although Os sat by the grey embers, Lee remained standing. He looked at her intensely and held her hand. "What are you keeping from me?"

"I must go and check the horses, Os."

She turned away from him and left.

The horses were all well and she sat watching them from inside the shelter. She did not want to return to be cross-examined by Os. As she lingered there drawing patterns in the dust with her foot something glinted in the chaff. It was another coin. How many more had Ædwine lost? What if someone else found one? She dropped to her knees and began searching the chaff and dust - for evidence. It took a long time to check the whole floor, but she was quite certain no-one would find more than the sixteen silver coins. Then her heart missed a beat. Tucked behind the water bucket, a folded piece of coarse cloth caught her eye.

"You have been out here a long time, Lee. Have you dropped something?"

"No. Yes, just my knife."

Lee stuffed the cloth bundle in her purse with the coins and hoped he had not seen it.

"Your knife is here." Os handed her the knife and looked at her once more. "You must tell me everything, Lee. Don't you trust me?"

"Yes, I trust you. And I will tell you this much - Gisla is in danger."

"Are you still pursuing our summer quest?"

"Of course, and I've unsettled Pip a good deal with stories

about Gisla, so I have to take care not to mention her name."

"Go on Lee, tell me what you know. These two men you saw, did they come here with news of Gisla?"

"I overheard them mention Gisla the cheesemaker. They did not see me." Lee looked away again because if she said more, she would have to lie, and to lie so directly to Os would be too much to bear. "I have promised Pip I will tell Edmund more – for Gisla's sake."

"You must tell me what this has to do with her. She is my kinswoman."

"Only distantly. I do not believe your Chief Thegn wants Gisla to be found. He never sent any of his men to look for her and yet he has time to trouble me three times. And he has vowed to return here when he has recovered."

"Did he tell you who attacked him? I do not believe this nonsense about enchanted seaxes any more than you do. Was it his Dark Thegn? Is that why he hung himself? Because he thought he had murdered his master like Judas?" Lee did not know how to reply, and Os thought her silence confirmed what he thought. "He was a rogue Lee. It was he who persuaded our Chief Thegn not to seek Gisla. He probably knew where she is and has taken his secret to the grave."

"Gisla went to Ely to find Alcuin."

"Who told you such a tale?"

"I cannot say."

"Those two men you saw?"

She had strength enough to nod before darting into the mead with the horses. Os followed and they laughed and chased through the galloping ponies just as they had done on the coastal moors near Hunestanestede. The bonds of comradeship briefly returned. And then they were back at the hall. It was Sunday and they had to prepare for church.

"Have I missed Os?" Asked the Blackheath Thegn.

"Yes," Lee said smiling as she stood up to welcome her guest. "Come and sit by the fire. Mind my needles though. Pip and Win have gone with him, but you must have known that if you passed the guard."

"It was you I wanted to see, my child. I'm sorry for my ill humour when we parted. I do not doubt your integrity and I did not mean to accuse."

"I took no offence sir. How could I? You knew very well there were certain things I did not reveal. But I have told Os now, and he will pass them on to Edmund. As for the two traders, I don't think they are spies."

"I reached the same conclusion and was about to send them to a ship bound for Francia when they were stolen away from my care. It was done on the orders of the Chief Thegn, but I have not been able to find a reason for it. To use such violence. There must be some motive I cannot see. The one they call the Dark Thegn - he hit Ralph without provocation. Caught him right under the ribs. Then he pushed or tripped me, well both ... he took me by surprise, and I fell heavily and cannot remember more. But his past has caught up with him. He was found hanging from a rafter in the new ferry building. There was a dead woman with him – her neck had been broken. They think he killed her and in a fit of remorse killed himself. But he has never been a man of regrets, has he?"

"I don't know him, sir."

"He had invested his silver in the wharf where the traders were taken – so why would he kill himself? It was done after his missing juniors had taken the two traders to another location. They were seen leaving but no one can be found to say more. I have searched fruitlessly all week. I hope poor Ralph has recovered from his toil in the stinking mud. That's what they were forced to do, you know. They had to hammer in piles and fit alder hurdles for the wharf. I understand our Thegn rode this way. Did he say why he had treated those two strangers without compassion?"

"I cannot account for his harsh treatment towards the traders. I was unable to question him because he arrived here half dead. Pip says it will be a long time before he is fit enough to return to his duties. But he knows where the traders are hidden because he threatened to take me to identify them - whether I am willing or not."

"Then I will demand he reveals where they are."

"Where is old Wiggi? He might know," Lee mused.

"I've no idea where the woolly-minded thegn is – but if you hear any news send a message to Eth."

"Eth?"

"Yes, he will be joining my company. He must behave himself now he is a trained thegn."

Lee smiled and thought about young Eth, his eldest son. He had lived away for almost a year, and she looked forward to seeing him again.

"Tell Eth I won't ask to borrow his sword again," she said at their parting. "Does he have a new one?"

It was late evening when Pip and Win returned. They had brought Fred to stay. He was well. Lee jumped up and they danced with delight. Long into the night they sang songs and played tunes on flutes and reeds and harps. Pip was bemused and wondered if he and Win had grown up too quickly. Perhaps Fred was what Lee needed; a young ward to nurture.

Lee lay awake. She longed to recapture the days when she had been Fred's age when she had sung and danced and acted. Yes, she would write a play to perform. A play for their times. Fred could make the items she would need. She would memorise the text. Or Fred could read it. His mother had taken great care with his education because he had been a sickly child and she hoped he would find work as a scribe.

Lee pondered the plot. It would have a dramatic final scene – with a seaxe. A maiden dies - with a seaxe in her heart. She had tried to fulfil a quest to save her dying liege-lord - despite opposition from a villain.

Lee was at her writing desk early and half-way through the morning Eth arrived. There was great merriment, but he could not stay long because his father had given him a long list of errands to do. Fred went with him to the outer gates and later, much later, passed on his message.

"Eth said you must send word at once if you hear news or rumours about Ralph and Will."

Lee froze. Eth's father had mentioned Ralph but not Will. Slowly the truth dawned. Lee realised Will was Gragus. If Ædwine had meant Gragus instead of Will, what had she done? He was taking news to Gragus declaring she missed him, worse, that she loved him.

Had Ædwine been sent by Frith and Gragus to warn her about Alcuin's man? But he had said the man had been stopped.

And the seaxe troubled her. Was it possible the gentle Ædwine, who had embraced her, was the one who had brutally beaten the Chief Thegn?

Her heart was tearing apart. Had he not flinched when she spoke about outward beauty and inner wickedness? Ædwine was very good-looking with beautiful dark wavy hair which fell upon his shoulders. He appeared to be kind and gentle, but she had to face the truth. The buckles in her purse were the ones she had prised from the mud brick. Gragus had inspected them. In her vision his pale hair hid his face, but she knew Gragus was Will - and Will was at Dummoc! They had been taken to Dummoc.

"Where is Eth going today – did he say?" Lee asked Fred.

"To Elm Green."

"Then we must catch up with him. I know a short-cut through the Hellesden. We will have to take a chance. I am sure the Chief Thegn will be in bed for weeks. Come on."

"Is it far?" He asked.

"Yes, I suppose it is. You stay here and convince Hilde we are busy working on our script. I'll be back soon."

And so, Fred began to understand what sort of unthinking maiden Lee could be, but he did not mind. She was kind and protective just like his mother had been. Lee loved all kinds of tales, and he forgot his beating and looked forward to a new life under her guidance. Lee, however, forgot how dangerous it was to be drawn into fanciful sagas.

The Gipeswick Ældorman had already been informed that Gragus and Frith were at Dummoc, but no action had been taken to rescue the traders. The Abbot claimed the Church had the right to hold its own trials. However, the Ældorman challenged his presumption for, like the majority in his rank, he did not like the recent edicts about obeying an authority as far away as the Holy See. After some wrangling, the disagreeable Abbot promised to wait until Edmund returned. Until then, the prisoners would be held at Dummoc.

Gragus had feared imprisonment in such a place, but it was not as bad as he expected. He was sent to work in the gardens while Frith rested in bed. They shared the same quarters but dare not reveal anything of their true selves. They were cheese makers and did what cheese makers might do. Gragus cut lengths of osier which he split and passed to Frith who wove the whips into small baskets for holding cheeses. Gisla had taught them well when they worked with her at the dairy. Gragus hoped he would never meet her again. Gisla must never learn that Lee died on his order. She must be dead by now for the Blacksmith was not one who turned back.

"What's wrong? Have you seen a phantom?" Frith asked. He wondered why his companion had suddenly stopped splitting the osiers. Gragus made no reply. "Have you eaten too much cheese?

It gives you bad omens," he laughed.

Frith loved his role as cheese trader, but Gragus did not.

"You talk too much," Gragus grumbled.

"The young maid," Frith began loudly knowing the guard would hear. "Whose aunt made the blue-veined cheese, she will wonder what has happened to us. Do you think we could send her a message to explain why we are delayed?"

Gragus looked at the guard and then frowned at Frith.

"I am sure she will not be concerned.".

"Nay, she will be cut to the heart." Frith pretended to stab himself with the small knife which Gragus had discarded.

It was an unexpected and sudden attack. Gragus pressed hard against Frith's wound. The cry of agony alerted all the guards who rushed in from the doorway to strike Gragus with their staffs.

"Do not be hasty! We are just old friends who argue over the love of a fair maiden." Frith looked at the guards and smiled. "Ask him."

"Is this correct?"

"Yes." Gragus replied as he released his hold on Frith.

"Then you must settle your quarrel with words. A prudent man would ask the maiden."

"But he will not ask her, good sir. He trembles with fear." Frith looked at Gragus. He so wanted, no needed to gauge the depth of his friend's feelings for the maiden. "He fears she loves me."

Gragus did not enjoy Frith's game. He knew it was not aimed at his heart – the very part of him which ached so.

"Yes, she loves Ralph, not old Will here," proclaimed Frith triumphantly. The guards looked at each other and laughed. One of them pulled a birch bark note from his bag.

"I think not," he said as he handed the message to Gragus. "We had this delivered, when was it? Tuesday? It slipped from my thoughts until now."

Gragus read it and re-read it.

"I visited the place, and she says she truly loves you Will, and misses you. So make haste to her embrace. TB"

"It must be the lovely dairy maid of yours, hey?" Mused the guard.

Frith was anxious to read the communication and snatched the note from Gragus. He could not believe his eyes.

"Never." He muttered as he threw the note towards Gragus and lay back on his bed. The watchmen left them to ponder their revelation.

"What has he done?" Gragus groaned when they had gone.

"He found out, what I guessed from the beginning," murmured Frith.

"Guessed what?" Interrupted Gragus. He was feeling very uneasy. Why had his brother in arms not done as he had commanded?

"That you are fickle. You give every indication you love the one, when in fact you love the other." Frith sensed victory in prising the truth from his friend but wondered what had been said to inspire Lee to reply in such a way. Ædwine himself spurned love and knew tender embraces and Gragus did not go together. Frith felt his own ribs and winced.

"I sent him," Gragus whispered. "To kill the girl, not to woo her."

"You did what?" Frith sat up. "You would have him murder her? She was like no other maiden I have ever met – except the one I love."

"I'm sorry Frith. I thought it was best to be rid of her, so we can go free…" His voice was scarcely audible. "These past few days have been cruel, so cruel Frith. I have been washed along rivers full of hidden rocks, and I'm cut to pieces." He moaned with fists clenched in anguish. "It's truly wonderful he did not do it, for she is a beautifully brave maiden."

"I do not understand you. Why would you even send him on such a mission? Is it because you do not want to be loved?"

"I have been betrayed - you know I have. It cannot be overcome. This is how I must live. I must feel nothing."

"She will not betray us. I know it here in my heart."

"I do not share your certainty. I cannot love the maiden."

Gragus looked at the message with a heavy heart. Closing his eyes, he saw the maiden running from the hut, then leaping like a doe through the bracken and finally dashing through the rush strewn mead. Memories flooded his whole being. He was drawn to her, and fate would have its way.

In the morning light Gragus picked up the note which lay beside his mattress and laughed. Frith watched him crush the bark and scatter the fragments.

"Love is gone," he declared. "But it never was Frith. She knows me as Gragus." He said as he threw himself onto his back.

"Perhaps he revealed our names to her before he wrote the note."

"I don't think he did. Cast your thoughts back to our conversation in the glade. Who was she with in Hunestanestede?"

Frith remembered and lay back heavily on his bed. Lee loved another Will, not Gragus.

CHAPTER FIVE

THE TRIAL AT DUMMOC

The Minster at Dummoc was built within the walls of an ancient shore fort which once served as a lookout for Wuffingas pirates. The fact she was descended from pagan sea farers made Lee smile and she added it to her tale. For days, she and Fred lived in the realm of her Swan Princess which bridged the pagan world and Christendom.

They rehearsed whenever they had opportunity which left Hilde thoroughly exasperated. One morning she was driven to distraction by Fred's flute playing and snapped at Lee for parading around in a white gown when the apples needed to be gathered. Lee put her tunic and cloak on over her costume and Fred collected together all they needed before joining her in the orchard. Lee threw down the empty baskets and together they began to pick the lower fruit while rehearsing the lines of the ballad.

Later Lee gently packed the apples Fred passed down. He was good at climbing and slowly they worked their way across the orchard until they were close to the sunken lane which ran behind the horse shelter towards the Rookery. The way was hidden by an inner bank which had been thrown up as a wind break when the orchard had been planted several generations ago. The other three sides of the enclosure were hedged by thorn and holly which kept livestock and deer from browsing the fruit trees.

At length Fred came to the final tree. It was very tall. Its leaves remained green, and none had yet fallen. The large yellow apples were difficult to see, and Fred carefully followed Lee's cheerful instructions. He reached a high foothold where the tree forked and wondered what branch or twig she would have him step out onto next. The leaves rustled wildly as he struggled to reach in the direction she urged. He diligently picked each apple and tucked it away in a bag slung over his shoulder. Then all went quiet. He dared not look down but called out.

"Lee. Where do I go next?"

"You come with me, my lad."

Fred almost fell from the tree in his haste to descend. He saw Lee with a cloth round her mouth and immediately dropped the bag of apples, raced towards her, kicked the Chief Thegn and dashed away. However, another man caught him, but not before he had picked up his two bags which lay close by. In the shadows of the lane Lee's hands were fastened with linen bands and she was lifted onto a horse.

Fred fixed his gaze upon the Maiden of the Hellesden, and a fearless calm fell upon him. Lee had accomplished in five days what thegns could only hope to impart in five moons. Young Fred was loyal unto death. He sat behind her, and she took the reins between her bound hands. They knew where they were going. The detestable Thegn was taking them to Dummoc.

They rode towards Ryscebourn and then along quiet byways which Lee did not know existed. At one point the track turned sharply and they plunged down into an overgrown hidden path. Lee thought it must be very ancient for it was straight, and firm underfoot. It was the route the Chief Thegn had staggered along in his agony less than two weeks before. The way took them to Beleham and the river.

Their captors rested beneath willows until, in the moonlight, two vessels appeared. All boarded - including the horses. Lee and Fred were made to lie down on the deck of the first. The young lad was soon asleep, but she remained alert and prayed for an opportunity to escape. However, she was being closely guarded for she could hear men talking and laughing nearby. It was unsettling to hear the wicked thegn laugh. He and the master of the vessel appeared to be well acquainted. Lee wriggled closer to where the two men sat behind some barrels. They discussed various ways to retrieve the horses if they leapt overboard and then ... Lee shuddered. Their words stung her soul. The spies would not escape, they said, for they would hang at the gallows by Dummoc, trial or no trial. The grey sea which had spawned them would be the last thing they saw.

Lee vowed there and then to jump overboard when they reached Gipeswick. But the Chief Thegn cleverly avoided the port. The vessel drew close to the northern reed-fringed shore where the Thegn jovially embraced the master before mounting his horse and leading the party along a winding path to the highway. His face was set like flint to fulfil his task at Dummoc. Lee thought the river journey would give opportunity to act but as they rode headlong, she knew there was nothing she could do to slow his progress.

Too soon she saw the pale, torch-lit fortress. She scolded herself for not being more alert at the orchard. At least Fred had run. She had done nothing. She could do nothing. Her hands were bound, and her knife was in the bag with the flutes.

Without warning Fred lent heavily against her. She tried to nudge him, and he awoke with a start and kicked his legs against the horse as if to signal a gallop. It was soon ahead by some distance. The thegns did not give chase because the road was a dead end and led directly into the fort courtyard. However, the horse veered to the left and entered the enclosed yard of a large, richly decorated hall. The horse saw a man in the shadows and pulled up tipping Lee and Fred onto a small hay cott. The muzzling cloth was removed and both she and her rescuer smiled.

"My fair maiden, you have arrived too soon."

"I know. I could not stop him."

Lee thought she was dreaming. Why was the oarsman there?

"I could hide you," he offered.

"No. I overheard the Thegn say if we escape, the men will hang without a trial. He is acting on some motive beyond my wit."

"And mine. It has taken me many days to get this close. The priests here are involved, and I don't know how or why. They have the judgement seat prepared - and now you are here they will press ahead."

"But not today, it's the Lord's Day. Monday will be the earliest they can hold a hearing. You must get a crowd. Such things must not be done in secret." Fred kicked her and looked at the bags of props. "We are to perform a play. Entertainment is allowed – encouraged - at a public hearing. Edmund says it focusses thought. You must gather your trading friends - and anyone who is willing to stand up for justice - but no violence this time Ædwine. Ease the bands back over my mouth and go in peace."

"I cannot leave you with him. Has he harmed you?"

"We are both safe and unmolested. Tell Gragus I do care for him, and Frith. I do not want them to suffer because of my foolishness." Her words muffled as the bands tightened.

Ædwine left as quickly as he appeared, an unseen shadow in the darkness where mists swirled. Lee heard the Thegn's horsemen enter the courtyard and she and Fred began to moan as if in agony.

"No need." The Chief Thegn cursed as his men tried to get the pair back upon the horse. "Let them walk."

He dismounted and took Lee very roughly by the arm and when she pretended to trip, he put her over his shoulder. She struggled and moaned but he took no notice. They entered a hall where he discarded her. Although her bands were removed Lee remained quiet. She felt humiliated.

"Take some bread and refreshments. You are right to be angry with me but there was no other way to bring you here. Take care of the lad and remember you are a maiden raised in the King's household. I expect you to behave honourably – this is the Bishop's Hall, and you are under his jurisdiction."

He crossed the room and took a bundle of papers from his pack. Fred swiftly gulped down his cup of mead, but Lee secretly tipped hers away behind the wood pile. Fred looked concerned.

"Am I poisoned?"

"Of course, not. He needs you alive. But only for one more day."

"What are you two whispering about?" The Thegn demanded.

"We feel so tired, sir. Is there a place for us to sleep?"

The Chief Thegn looked pleased. The draft had worked well, and he showed them an inner room where they lay down to sleep. When the door closed, she took an apple from her bag to quench her thirst. Then she found her knife, fastened it to her belt and lay down again. The Chief Thegn checked them twice. They slept soundly, so he thought.

Later the Chief Thegn was joined by two strangers. Lee heard their greeting and moved closer to the partition. She could hear the Thegn and one of the men but the other was too softly spoken to catch his words.

"It was easier than I thought," the Thegn mused. "There was no guard along the lane, and they were out in the fields."

"The heavens smile on you, my friend. You are outstanding when it comes to catching little mares."

"I will prepare her when she wakes. It will be over soon enough." Lee perceived the betrayal of coins. "I look forward to the final instalment on Monday Eve when justice is done."

"They will steal no more of my precious cargoes!"

Lee tried to mimic the gruff voice in her thoughts so she might remember it belonged to a traitor. Then the quieter man gave himself away too, because he laughed, and laughs were more unique than words.

"May they never stalk or fleece the church again."

The legs of a stool scraped the floor and Lee hastily found her bed. This time the Thegn came closer to check his witnesses.

"Sleep well my wild one, for tomorrow you learn obedience. There will be no play-acting here."

Lee did not stir, but her fists clasped in fury; it was not horses the master of the vessel had discussed with the Thegn – it had been her! They had expected her to escape and run but she would not. She must play her part and play it well. He left and it was early in the afternoon when she awoke. Fred was still asleep and so was the Thegn in the adjacent room. She walked right over him and opened the door into the kitchen yard.

"Good afternoon, young sirs," she merrily greeted two junior thegns. "That was some adventure last night. Did you see how beautiful the willows looked when the moon shone through their canopies? I am sure I saw an otter dive below ripples."

"I saw one on the bank chewing on a crayfish. I don't expect they travel up to the Hellesden very often."

"Old Sig sees quite a lot down along the Brett, and Os says they are a nuisance down at Bures. And I have seen them dart across the Carr Meadows in the Hellesden - but not under the moonlight."

"We were blessed with a clear night."

"Is it always this foggy here?" Lee asked.

"It's sea mist. Have you guessed where you are?"

"I knew before we left. Of course, I could walk a few yards into it and disappear." Lee scurried away from him.

"It's a steep fall into the sea," he laughed. "And the path is guarded. Besides the lad needs your protection."

"So, you agree your Thegn's actions are unjust?"

"Who am I to make any judgements? We just do as we are told."

"Why? You should ask more questions. I was brought up to question everything. You must join forces with the port thegns and wash your hands of him. I will speak in your defence if you turn from this folly. Os is already on his way, and I've sent for Will. He knows these churchmen. Do you? Who was the captain? What was the vessel called?"

"Come now. I cannot answer all those questions. My head is in a spin. The boat is known as, I don't know, something to do with seaxes."

"You jest!"

"Do I?"

"I thought the Chief Thegn did jest when he said he would bring me here to witness little Fred's tale about a seaxe. But no. This is to do with more than seaxes. Much silver changed hands last night. Does silver deliver justice? Do you consent to rich men buying a poor man's head?"

"You have lost me completely now, Lee."

"They intend to murder two innocent traders. I would be very careful if I were you, for your Thegn was paid a handsome price for bringing those two men here - those who will be on trial tomorrow. Their fate is sealed unless you act, and I will make sure all who betray their fellow men pay - I was raised in the King's household, and men must give account!"

"What can I do to make any difference at this late watch?"

"They must have a fair trial. Tell the port thegns the truth - money has changed hands. Do not delay – and send word to

Edmund's Thegn. He knows these men are innocent. And do not fear - I will speak up for you and your company. The Chief Thegn has deceived you all."

He was surprised at the forcefulness of her reasoning, and then, by the sudden appearance of the Chief Thegn.

"Come here, you wench!" He bellowed.

"Why are you so ill-tempered sir? You know I must have fresh air. Do you have a headache? How far is it to the shore? I would like to splash my feet in the sea."

He had no choice but to cross the yard and escort her back to the hall.

"Come with me Leoba, we must talk."

He spoke quietly and appeared to be wholly reasonable at last. But she was not! Lee darted across to where the other junior thegns stood. This time the Chief Thegn signalled to his senior men to bring her to him.

"At least let me go and watch the waves sir. Can I? We are so far from the sea at the Hellesden. Perhaps I can spot some real oarsmen for you! Is that where the master of the vessel will take me after the trial? Across the sea? Will you really have me sold as a slave?"

The junior thegns were alarmed by her boldness.

"Go to him, Lee," the one she had spoken to urged. "I will do what I can. Do not cross him. He has the advantage here."

Lee turned and went towards the Thegn who stood by the door which he slammed behind her so all in the yard heard.

"There was no one to hear you out there. Your foolish games will not gain a footing here. You know why I have had to act so, don't you Leoba?"

"Yes, of course," she replied. "However, have you considered what my brother must be thinking? And what will Hilde say when she finds the apples in the mead and not safely packed away in the store? If the mares have eaten them, I will be in trouble. They might get cramps if they eat too many and what about our Holy Mass festivities? They will be ruined if we have no apples. Apples can be used in so many ways, sir."

"There are more important things to consider," he intervened.

"Such as?" She went on. "I have always been told to consider my household first. Which is what I am doing. All the gold in the kingdom cannot make for a happy household at Yuletide if you don't have apples. What if the mares have kicked the baskets in all directions? I packed them up so neatly. It took me all morning. The mares might have trampled on them."

"Made cider of them," added Fred. He was awake at last and took great delight in following her games.

"And what do you think Pip will say when he learns I have been travelling without a guardian?"

"If you had handed over the weapon, I would have no need of you."

"Fred, do I have any swords hidden about me?"

"No, but you do have a small seaxe I think." The Thegn looked disconcerted. It was the signal Lee looked for. She stood up and with great deliberation, drew back her cloak and unclipped the holder from her belt.

"There," she said, "A mere apple peeler."

The Thegn inspected the knife, it was small and plain, an everyday implement.

"Keep it with you," he insisted.

"No. You accuse me of having a weapon - you keep it."

"I am speaking of battle seaxes, Leoba. Do not play games with me."

"But is a seaxe sir. For what is a seaxe but a single-bladed knife? And this sir, as you can see has but one blade. This side is blunt and very useful for cracking hazelnuts and fastening pegs. The point is useful for prising stones from my mares' hooves."

Lee snatched her knife from his hand. "I shall ask your expert here. Fred, is this a seaxe or not?"

"It has the shape of a seaxe. A very small seaxe."

"And now?" She asked as she held the knife close to Fred's nose.

"It's a large seaxe now Lee." Fred could not stop laughing. The Thegn did not understand their jest. All he saw were two silly children wasting his time.

"Leoba, do not try my patience. I expect you to behave honourably tomorrow and tell the truth."

"I will sir."

The Thegn was not convinced.

"I am warning you Leoba; tomorrow I will be watching you. I can read you very well, my dear. I will know if you lie. And you, young Fred; I will be scrutinising every word you dare utter. Do you want to end up in the slave market?"

Fred stopped his playacting and gravely shook his head.

"I will be very serious, sir."

"I too, sir, will be sombre," Lee added.

They both earnestly meant what they had declared. Their play was a tragedy. Death was solemn. Particularly death by a seaxe.

"Now, I must leave, but you may amuse yourselves until I return. My men will be outside so do not leave the hall."

When he had gone Fred and Lee looked through their bags and sorted out the things they would need for the play. They went over the words several times before they were satisfied with their enactment. It was unlikely the Chief Thegn would allow them to take any baggage into the courtroom, so they hid certain items under their outer garments.

"It will all be decided by the tone and suspense created. We must appeal to the heart and create a sense of foreboding and outrage."

"Do you think he will put the sleeping draught in my drink tonight? It left me with such a headache."

"We can get a drink from the kitchen maid before he returns, and I will cause a distraction, so you can pour his poison away."

"Will Edmund rescue us?"

"Yes, of course. And even if Edmund is not here in person, all the good he has done in the last ten years will stand. Most love him and we must pray and hope many people will arrive and insist on hearing the trial."

"And our play?"

"Yes, the play as well," she reassured.

Not far away Gragus reflected upon his latest visitor - the Chief Thegn. He had been unpleasant and attempted to exploit Frith's good nature. Fortunately, Frith had replied wisely and had given nothing away. Gragus hoped the maiden would do the same. Earlier, he and Frith had listened to her merry voice in the courtyard. Her warning about her fate as a slave was timely and Gragus sent word to the Blacksmith to keep watch over her.

Late into the night Lee and Fred talked and lumped and laughed and sang. The Chief Thegn was disturbed and wondered why the sleeping draught had not taken effect. He had lost count of the number of times he had settled, only to hear faint sounds of glee which grew louder until he was fully alert. The girl had grown even more wild and wilful, but he would have her tamed soon enough. Finally, they slept, but the Chief Thegn was soon woken by the cockerel crowing. He had business to attend to and he was very, very tired.

Lee and Fred slept until late. They ate their breakfast and dressed as smartly as possible. Fred wanted a final rehearsal, but Lee insisted they spent their time in prayer.

When the thegns and some brothers called for them, they were still on their knees. They were ordered to take nothing with them. It was a pitiful scene, a fair maiden in a white gown all wrapped in a cloak, and her companion, a weakly looking lad, fair of face but very grave in spirit. Beyond the outer gates people were gathering, Lee turned but could not see who they were, though Ædwine saw her. A gust of wind blew back the hood of her gown and there she was, a beautiful swan princess with hair braided through with silver threads and decorated with a crown of blue flowers interwoven with white feathers. She passed through the gates to the inner hall and was gone. Neither lad nor maiden witnessed the crowd surge forward into the courtyard.

The Chief Thegn greeted her, made a great show of manners, and praised the humility of her attire. Very reluctantly she allowed him to take her hand to lead her to her seat – she feared he would notice her costume. Fred also clutched his cloak tighter and stayed by her side. He had promised – no, more - he had sworn on the memory of the enchanted seaxe: sworn to serve Edmund as his king and uphold his justice.

They were seated facing away from the accused, who sat below them to the side. Gragus could barely see Lee for even when he lent forward the hood of her gown shrouded her face. He longed to warn her to take care. Between her and the Thegn the young lad shook with fear. They were like trembling prey for the black crows to feast upon. Edmund was not there - nor anyone with authority to release them.

The proceedings were about to commence when the port thegns were called away. Everywhere was hushed and people began to wonder what was about to happen. Gragus looked tense. Shouting could be heard beyond the gates and one of the thegns ran back inside and whispered to the clergyman who would make the judgement. Frith looked at Gragus, but he did not respond.

The doors opened wide, and many people were ushered in, reeves, a great many port thegns, traders of all kinds, women, and other onlookers. Some had come to find out why a secret hearing was being held – and in Edmund's absence - which was not the way of court proceedings. Others came because the rights of traders were being undermined and others had learnt there was to be some kind of grand entertainment.

Gragus saw the Blacksmith among the crowd. He slowly made his way to Frith's side and Gragus thought they had some chance of escape even if things went against them – as they certainly would.

The Chief Thegn wondered how all the interlopers had received news of the trial but could not intervene for he was summoned to begin the proceedings. He stated he had brought before them two men who had been spying out monasteries and minsters, and mints and merchant's houses as a means of weakening the defences of the kingdom and threatening good Christian folk. They had been stopped by a young lad at Edmund's Holy Cross – but escaped when they cruelly slashed him. He waved his hand towards Fred.

"Now, young Wilfred, I want you to swear to answer all my questions honestly - on fear of death."

The Thegn spoke in solemn tones which unnerved Fred.

"I do promise, sir, to serve Edmund, my king." The crowd leaned forward to hear the lad who shook in dread of what was to come. Then he remembered what Lee had said about playacting and he grew bold and loud. "To serve Edmund my gracious king, to uphold justice in the realm, to do my utmost to promote peace and right decisions. And, as Edmund would insist, to treat strangers and aliens in our realm with kindness and give them full protection of our laws, including the right to defend themselves."

Gragus was taken aback. The lad showed intelligence beyond his age. The Thegn was equally moved. He had no intention of allowing the spies to defend themselves.

"Now, on the thirteenth day of September, it was reported by your kinsmen, how you challenged two men at Holy Cross and one of them slashed your neck with a weapon intending to kill you. Is this true?"

"I was at the Holy Cross, sir. Two men did set upon me there. Well, I tried to stop them because they had stolen one of the fowls I tended." Fred hesitated and the Chief Thegn urged him to continue. "One of them knocked me to the ground but neither said anything at all."

"Are these the two men, standing here?" The Chief Thegn pointed towards Gragus and Frith. Without faltering Fred looked straight at them.

"No sir, I don't think they are the same men."

"You don't think so! Look again! Are these the men?"

"Well sirs, the sun was low and reflected off the pool by the cross. I was dazzled and more so when a blade flashed out of deep shadow. Then I was pushed aside. I tried to creep away as one man took hold of the other as if to urge him to flee. Then I was grabbed from behind - so I did not see him. But I could describe what his sleeve was like."

The man who was to make the judgement in the case intervened. "Either he can identify the men, or he cannot. Which is it? Do they wear the same attire?"

The Chief Thegn knew it was a pointless question and did not want to draw attention to the incident at the wharf, so he veered from answering.

"Do these men bear any resemblance to the men who attacked you?" he continued. Again, Fred looked at the two men. He left his seat, walked towards the pair, and looked up from below and then returned.

"I cannot be certain. I could identify the knife he held at my neck sir. He held it here, like this." Fred demonstrated and a few quiet laughs sprang from the crowd. "Could I see it again?"

The Chief Thegn was speechless. Ædwine began to enjoy the show but Gragus was gripped by anxiety.

"Well Thegn? Do you have the weapon here?" Asked the bishop's man.

"No sir, but if I may question the girl. I believe she knows where the seaxe is."

He turned swiftly to the maiden to catch her unawares.

"Will you now, in the presence of these honourable lords and bishops, console your hitherto good Christian conscience, by revealing the hiding place of the weapon used upon the lad?"

"Sir, it is unwise to lead such men as these to err in their judgement. Perhaps you will reveal your own description of the weapon - for I understand it was wondrous - the description you extracted from Fred, under duress."

Lee wanted the Thegn to make the first statement about the detail of the seaxe. Then she would demolish the case. However, Fred was already ahead of her and before she could prevent him, he lifted his tunic to reveal his recent injuries. As he bared his thin, scared chest and back, the crowd called out 'shame' and 'justice' for the lad. Lee was not pleased he had wrongly inferred the Chief Thegn had beaten him. As she lent forward to rebuke the lad Gragus caught a glimpse of her face. She appeared to look very shocked at the sight of the lad's wounds and thus fanned the wrath of the crowd.

The Thegn struggled to contain himself and the judge nodded for him to continue but his argument had lost its flow.

"Your description, young lad, was of a seaxe made of swirling metals, embellished with runic characters which you drew for us." The thegn looked at his notes and went on. "I believe they loosely translate as 'goose'."

"Are you saying the boy saw the word 'goose' on the weapon?" Asked the judge who had not quite caught the Thegn's muffled words.

"He had stolen my goose, sir." Fred was also confused. "A young 'un, not yet fully fattened."

The Thegn struggled to remain vague, for he did not want to reveal how the goose had gone into his bag, and exact enough to convince the judge. While he hesitated Fred's enthusiasm grew.

"The handle of the seaxe was carved with a dreadful dragon. It had big bulging eyes and an amber belly."

Gragus grew alarmed at the lad's eye for detail. However, the stony-faced oarsman gave nothing away. The Blacksmith, who had forged the knife and carved the handle, marvelled even more because the patterns described were faint and the dragon indefinable.

"You must understand," Lee intervened. "This lad feared for his life in more than one sense. He was terrified by the owner of the goose and what recompense he might demand. You see sirs, by this time the goose was dead. Fred was all astir, for his master has a heavy hand – indeed it was he who made the marks you saw on the lad, not the noble Thegn here. The goose was lost and yet the men fled empty-handed."

"I was worried about the goose sir. I tried to get it back for I was afraid of getting beaten again. Otherwise, I would not have given chase and risked death. I was trying to get the goose back when I was grabbed. The knife was dark and shadowy, sir, and caught the sun so it flashed me in the eye, and I was dazzled again. I thought if I made it to be an enchanted seaxe which caused even the goose to disappear then my master would not punish me. I am sorry for such a tale. It did not help, but I am tired of all the beatings."

There were more gasps from the crowd, and some began to call out. Fred was carried away by the drama of their intervention and called out he had the seaxe. The Thegn thought the lad was about to reveal the truth and admit the maiden did have the weapon.

From his belt, Fred drew out the seaxe. It was of medium size – a weapon which would have been a useful back-up in battle except it was crudely made from wood. The crowd laughed and it took a long time to settle them. They commented on the beauty of the thing. Had he made it? Fred was anxious to please Lee and urged her to tell them about the play. Lee did not say a word so Fred made his own plea.

"Kind sir," he said addressing the judge, "I did make this seaxe. It is for our play; the one we have planned to perform today. You must remember what Edmund said – 'if good people come to see justice done, they should also be entertained.' We will do our best to obey our king though it is not quite finished for we were kidnapped by the Thegn here and bound across the mouth, so we could not practice our lines – until we arrived here, and then he gave me a draught which caused me to sleep so long. But not Lee, she tipped hers away."

The noise from the crowds drowned the Thegn's feeble apologies and the port thegns had to intervene on behalf of the bishop to demand silence. Lee saw Ædwine lean towards Frith. He was about to take his seaxe from its case when Lee stood up. He saw her and hesitated, and something drew him to look behind her into the darkness. There were many armed men there.

The port thegn thought Lee had leapt up out of loyalty to Edmund and pledged justice would be done and the play would be performed. The judge ordered the Chief Thegn to hasten with the evidence for there had been none so far and Lee sat down again.

"Do you have the weapon?" He asked the Thegn very abruptly.

"No sir, I do not."

"And you lad, do you have the weapon which was used against you?"

"No sir, the men ran off taking it with them."

"So, if there is no evidence in this case, what charge do you have against these men?" The judge was growing impatient. All in the room were eager to learn more and shuffled forward. A few exited the hall without hindrance and slipped away. "You said the girl would reveal where the weapon was hidden." He turned to Lee.

"Were you also there when the lad was attacked?"

"No, sir. I was not. I was with my kin; I did not see the man nor the seaxe."

"Let me explain sir, why the girl is here," urged the Chief Thegn.

"Go ahead then and be brief."

"This maiden reported to me she had seen two strangers in the same vicinity. This was two days later. I have made careful investigations into the matter. Unfortunately, some of my evidence has been lost; lost I must emphasise under very suspicious circumstances. I believe she knows more than has been revealed. Much more sir, I believe she knows the whereabouts of the seaxe – the weapon in this case. I have been unable to persuade her to tell the truth and I was hoping you would do better than I. She is a child who has been allowed to grow wild sir; she has no mother."

The judge asked Lee to tell her story. It was blunt. She made sure he knew she had not reported anything to the Thegn because there had been nothing to report. Two tradesmen. Distant singing and laughter. Broad daylight. No contact made."

"Are these the two men?" The Thegn demanded.

Lee rose to her feet, pushed back the hood of her cloak revealing her fine silver-braided hair, crowned with a garland of blue flowers and feathers. The Chief Thegn was startled and lost faith in his judgement.

"The thickets obscured them sir. Do they have the seaxe?"

His thoughts went back to the night the seaxe had killed his hound. He was tired and forgot his lines. Lee wondered why he paused and asked once more to perform the play. As she spoke many thegns entered the hall and she addressed them directly by saying they could join in the singing of the *Willow Song*.

The crowd took great delight in the thought of seeing the play and singing the song. They applauded the Swan Princess. Gragus thought of deception and dark deeds – she may betray him yet. Frith turned and saw the look of terror in his friend's eyes and held a tight reign over his own merriment. Perhaps one fateful twist was about to be revealed.

Lee coughed and signalled to Fred.

"We begin at an abandoned mill pool where old pollards have split, and branches hang low towards the water. I am sure you will follow. Summer leaves are falling and all else is slipping into winter."

THE SWAN PRINCESS
Cold leaved spears of gold, piercing the still water.
Shimmering sallow; his lowered branches veil
That forgotten place, the bitter haunts of this tale.

Her lord lay death-like; frail on canopied couch.
She, all wrapped in white, calmly waits to depart
At Fate's signal. A test for her loyal heart.

Run to the West, towards the setting sun;
To reed-fringed lodes, which lace the fertile sound,
Where a sword, once lost, will bring healing, if found.

Brave Swan Princess, rise from bended knee,
Leave your solemn hall, where your lord will die,
If you should yield and look into the wolven eye.

Far away the wolf sentry stirred, for he devours
All who venture near the offering to a nameless
And forgotten god. He wakes and is ruthless.

But love moves her, and spurs her into action,
She resigns herself to follow the lonely quest
Retrieve the sword, lay it upon his kingly breast

And all will be restored.

"Without a shield, take nothing but your knife
Fixed at your girdle sewn from silver thread."
She left at dawn, 'neath skies flowing blood red.

Gold leaves of sallow, kissing the still water.
Shimmering reflections; the fair Swan Princess draws near
To release her lord from all sorrow and fear.

Abandoned pool, reveal your hidden craft!
With long pole she stood, through shallow waters glide
Dark mud gurgled while wintry wind-blown reeds sighed,

As if they knew her hopes were all in vain.
For none had ever returned from the uncertain, lonely way
Where the ancient wolf stalked his unwary prey.

She gazed ahead, seeking a landing place
And tied up the vessel where the ancient track arose;
Weather beaten planks, posts in routed rows.

Like broken teeth, from a cruel, gaping jaw
They pointed the way, to the saving blade
Lain in remembrance to those long dead and slayed.

Amongst alder-carr, draped with leafy lichens,
Darkness crept upon her; shadows veiled her sight.
She was slipping towards those black swans of eternal night.

But a light dawned.

The old coppice thinned, reed beds stretched from side to side,
And amongst them lay the fleshless ribs of shipwrecked craft
Except for one, wide it was, with shallow draught

It lay beached and whole, and she thought it strange
That waves and many tides had not prised it apart
As if it were waiting for some signal to depart.

Fierce oarsmen had rowed it from shore to shore
Seeking easy treasure and death with honour and fame.
Wild restless hearts, which only fields and love can tame.

A sudden chill wind caught her cloak and swept her on.
In the lee of the craft she sought shelter from wind-blown sand
And pressed against its warm planks hewn in a far off land.

The wood was smooth, and she caressed its warmth.
She marvelled at the skill and love which had wrought such beauty,
But above on dragon prow, the wolf waited to perform his duty.

Bleached white and grey, he'd seen those warriors drown.
Now silently guarding the way, he let her pass by.
He failed to leap! Perplexed; for he knew not why.

His cold hungry eyes fixed upon her – his certain prey
And ghost-like he slunk down and followed on behind;
No need for haste, he knew what she would find.

Her steadfastness led her to the place where
The planks all failed, and there was no way
To cross the water. Swiftly she knelt to pray,

And pleaded with her god to grant her success, but not
for herself,
For she desired neither fame nor treasure.

The wolf drew back, doubt had pierced his ancient heart.
Her hope was renewed, she would not yield to despair
Hidden below ripples were new planks for repair.

She lay them down and slowly neared an isle
Where distant summer cranes roost on twisted limbed trees.
She heard them call, far away on distant breeze.

Down she sprang, as roving pirates leap from ships,
Crossing sandy beaches to raid unsuspecting halls.
He followed at ease, certain she would heed his calls.

On the far shore, submerged in drifts of sand,
Like a beached turtle, was a coracle and an oar.
Her eyes were lifted in praise, and he was unsure.

Cast to the tide, paddling swiftly across the gap
She passed below the funnelled nets where shy water fowl
Seek refuge from baying dogs. There the wolf's howl

Mightier than any hunters horn drove her towards the snares;
But she neither turned towards him nor to webs of deceit
And landed safely, her costly task to complete.

Back on the path, the fair maiden pressed on
Until the track faded to a thin thread in open water.
It was the place where he should have caught her,

For the track ended where steps led down to murky depths.
Her arm was bared to seek the sacrifice of old;
In worm-infested mud, she drew out the blade, so cold;

Then raised it high, and years of memory ran down;
Flowing like sand, revealing emerald embellished hilt.
Time turned back; age to youth; innocence from guilt.

She did not comprehend the tide had turned.

In the shadows the wolf's withered muscles grew strong,
His eyes flashed with scorn, his heart began to sing.
Impossible now, the task to save her king.

The metal gleamed, runes wildly swirled and framed
His dark form behind her. He was reflected in the blade.
Her warm heart froze, but she was not yet slayed.

With oar in hand she looked down at the sword
Green gems set in gold, shone brightly at her side;
His hot clammy breath so close – and nowhere to hide!

She would not turn. Though dragons upturned her boat
She must return to the king and lay the sword over his heart.
Then he would live, and they would never be apart.

So cold she grew, through effort and ambition;
The wolf watched her slide from hope to despair
And renewed his efforts to catch her there

Where nets entangled. Her oar was lost and she stood still.
Struggling with cupped hands, she barely moved ahead,
She reached up and caught the cold woven thread.

It clung like thorns, but her free hand reached down;
At first touching warm fur, but then cold steel.
The blade cut through deceit. The wolf left her heel.

She landed safely amongst the sandy dunes.
Blood was washed away from where the barbs had clung;
And she touched her neck band where his ring hung.

She rejoiced, thinking she was safe to travel home
For the wolf had vanished and she was warmed in the sun.
The king would live! The evil was undone!

But all had changed except the sand.

Cranes were replaced by crows which sat waiting
For flesh to devour. As they dived down to peck
The crafty wolf snapped the cord around her neck.

And there they fell; her beads and his precious ring -
She must turn back and sift the sand for his love token,
For words and troths must never be broken.

The wily wolf waited but she did not turn.
It must be left; sentiment had no place on the desolate day.
All colour drained, pale she was; shadowed by grey.

Feeble she had become like a lonely star in darkness,
She stumbled on unsteady planks and plunged headfirst
To watery depths. But the wolf did not rejoice – he cursed.

She was his and no water god would snatch her from his grasp.
He plunged in and caught hold of her girdle of silver thread
But with both hands she swung the ancient sword of dread.

He sprang away, and she fell heavily on the boards
Then, with raised head, his howl pierced joints and marrow
The maiden lay trembling like some fallen sparrow.

In her grasp the sword it shuddered, setting gems afire
Illuminating its hidden swirls and sacred runes.
And men stirred upon the age-locked boat held fast in dunes.

Their long wait was over. It was time to raise their banners
To fasten on their swords and helms
And row to plunder divided realms.

The drum beat began and the wolf's howl ceased.

His lith of warriors were too early! For his victim had fled
And he was fading - he was youthful - not yet fully grown
He must act soon. His time for revenge had flown.

She shivered from cold, her wet garments weighed heavy;
Back under the old prow the winds roused and sounded
Ancient chimes revealing how past dynasties were founded.

The proud Wuffingas had rowed with vessels adorned;
Some had dragon heads, this one had a coloured vane
Which captured the breeze and echoed back fear and pain.

She watched the banners float upwards and heard men shout.
Where was she? What battle was about to spew forth?
Peace to war? Were these the men from the north?

The wolf looked up at the oarsmen all set to leave.
He must press on. Why should they wait?
A wolf can fail - but can it turn away Fate?

The Swan Princess came through all those gloomy places.
She conquered weakness, the grown wolf had been defeated
With sword in hand, her weary quest was completed.

Golden leaved branches, now kissed her wet sparkling hair
But she smiled for her king would not die.
She had not looked into the wolven eye.

The sun sank leaving delightful skies streaked with red
All was at peace, until a cry she heard;
Upon the safe bank, some helpless babe had stirred.

All curled and weak, a wolf cub lay pleading.
She coaxed the soft head and looked into its eyes so blue.
He was beautiful. She looked and looked and knew!

They found her there, laid out upon the bank;
Hair all frosted, with garland of golden leaved spears
A seaxe near her heart – betrayed by his tears.

There was a deathly silence in the great hall. Lee was not sure if her tale was liked or not, so she urged them to sing *The Willow Song*. It was a well-known ballad with a rousing refrain.

"*A fair swan maiden lay dying under a willow tree*
A knife in her bosom, her hand on a key.
Sing willow... "

Lee and Fred began, and the crowd followed their version of the long, merry song. When it ended, Lee began her conclusion.

"Thank you, sirs, for listening to our tale – and singing with us. This trader standing before you, has a delightful voice. I am sure it was not he I overheard singing *The Willow Song* in the Hellesden Coppice."

"But you saw him!" The Chief Thegn interrupted.

"The men were far down the ride when I looked - and in the shadows! And Fred did not see their faces either. He has told you he was dazzled by the sun off the lake, and a knife when he encountered your spies. The men fled with the knife and yet you searched my home three times for it. And with dogs. The best dog in the kingdom."

At the thought of his hound the Chief Thegn collapsed onto his bench in despair. Lee turned and addressed the one would judge the case.

"He found my sewing needles sir, and my bramble cakes – but no seaxe. Why does he think I have it? Indeed, the Thegn was recently attacked by a man with a seaxe, a man who cruelly slew the best of hounds. And yet at the time of the attack these two you see in front of you, had already been moved here to Dummoc – and in great secrecy. And I understand the men had no seaxe between them when they were arrested in Gipeswick. Indeed, they are here because they had exchanged their own silver buckles for stolen coins. And you must know Edmund's Thegn found the rogues who stole the coins and deceived these traders. Their confession was made and yet these two were not released but spirited away to this place. Why? You need to ask Edmund's Thegn. Do you know why he is not here?" From the back of the hall men tried to push through the crowd but no one would give way. "The Chief Thegn does," Lee continued. "For it was he who sent him off to the ends of the realm, to Ely I think. And why? Did the one known as the Bard command him perhaps?"

Her revelation silenced all the whispering amongst the

bishop's men. The Chief Thegn denounced her accusation, so she cried out.

"If you continue to object then you must explain why you spurred this case to a hearing – a secret hearing! Have you asked the right questions? Who has those stolen coins? And the silver buckles, where did they go?"

"And the goose?" Voiced Fred.

The crowd laughed for they were on his side. The Chief Thegn pondered the situation and remained silent. Then the Blackheath Thegn accompanied by Os and Will stepped forward. Lee and Fred hugged Edmund's Thegn and stepped down with Will.

"Stay by my side and say no more." Will held her arm tightly. He led her to one side. She was close to the prisoners, with her back to Ædwine.

"Let go, Will."

"What are you playing at?" He whispered as Os began his address to the court.

"It was no game." Lee shook herself free, but Will was intent on passing judgment on her.

"Why are you scantily dressed like a sacrificial virgin?"

"She's the Swan Princess," Fred innocently replied.

He was still impressed but Will was not. The young cleric snatched the veiled feather garland from her hair and angrily stamped it underfoot.

"I did not mean to offend you, Will."

"I have had to leave my studies to sort out this disaster. Os was terrified you were about to be hung in public. Well? You were public enough, weren't you? You could not have thought of a more fitting way to humiliate me, could you? And in this place!"

Lee moved to put some distance between them. The man behind her coughed and she realized who it was and, unseen by Will, he took her hand.

"They loved you. You were pure and honest, and he had too much to hide."

Will continued to shuffle between the bystanders. Lee was slipping away from his command, and he was furious.

"Well? Did you give aid to raiders who want to burn our books and ruin our land. Did you?"

She let go of Ædwine's hand and turned to look directly at Will.

"I will answer to Edmund, not you. Why did you desert Gisla?"

"Gisla? What has all this to do with Gisla?"

"Everything."

Will turned away to listen to the trial summary. No one had mentioned his Aunt Gisla. Ædwine pressed close to Lee again and tried to take her hand a second time but she forced it away. She felt torn apart and alone. She had lied. And the oarsman who had tried to kill her knew it. She wanted no comfort from his wicked companion. She blamed the Chief Thegn for her predicament and raised her eyes to look at him. His head was bent low but not in regret. The bitterness of the girl's scorn had humiliated him, and he waited for his chance to escape.

Os was about to step aside to allow Edmund's Thegn to dismiss the case and he beckoned Frith and Gragus to move to his side. As they passed Frith smiled.

"I think we've won, Lee," Fred whispered.

Gragus looked at her coldly and was gone. Lee squeezed through the crowd. She felt hemmed in and unable to breath.

"What is wrong?" Fred asked as they reached the door. "We did win, didn't we? Os will let them go free, won't he?"

The maiden was overcome with emotion and outside, in the cold courtyard, she covered her eyes unable to stop her tears. Something about Gragus moved her heart and she did not want to be moved. She had lied when she loathed lies. Liars were dangerous and to be loathed. Will loathed her. He had changed; his scorn had crushed her.

The Chief Thegn crept quietly from the hearing but on seeing her he began to shout abuse. Doubt had been cast upon his character and he was wounded. His fiery rage burned through everything Lee had done; layer upon layer was blackened, her innocence, her bravery, her playacting, her compassion, her honour. His words were cruel and desperate.

Ædwine overheard what was said and his hand went inside his jacket where he felt the cold stone handle of his seaxe. Before he could intervene, Will approached the scene and the Chief Thegn let loose another flight of indignant accusations. Ædwine waited for Will to defend the fair maiden but he did not. Then the Blackheath junior thegns brought blankets and wrapped them about the brave pair. Their young leader urged the discredited Chief Thegn to move on, and before the crowd left the hall, he had gone.

Before long Frith merrily burst into the courtyard. The crowd was close behind him and together they surged across the wide space towards the outer gates. The junior thegns proudly stood back from their wards.

"Thank you, Lee," Frith called. "A brilliant performance young Fred. I'll learn the ballad – such inspiration."

Fred laughed with joy and handed him one of their scripts. The men were free he thought and that was what his friend Lee had desired.

Lee watched Frith being carried along by the surging crowd. At the outer gates, he embraced Ædwine and they both turned to await the arrival of Gragus. Though Os had demanded to speak with him in private they knew Gragus would not betray them. Gragus was closed and cold and safe. They watched him emerge from the hall and beckoned him to join them. Instead, he walked towards Lee. Frith's smile vanished.

"Leave her, my friend," he whispered fearing he would insult her.

Gragus stood in front of the maiden and pulled back her hood so light reflected off the silver in her braids. Her eyes met his gaze. His cold blue eyes startled her. All she had done, chilled her heart.

"Did you write the saga?" He asked.

"Yes, I'm sorry. It was for Gisla."

Then in front of the crowd, Gragus whispered, "for Gisla," and he kissed her silver braided hair. He drew back, looked at her and murmured, "and for the beautiful Swan Princess." He kissed her again. He was not aware of how long he held her close. Frith later said time had stood still and it was forever.

Gragus joined Ædwine at the oars of the craft as they rowed out to sea away from the ancient fortress. Frith re-told the trial and the play and made a fair effort at singing the song. Ædwine smiled. He was impatient to hear the real story behind their adventures but for now Frith was in the hands of the gods, telling tales which had some truth in them.

"Your parting gesture was inspired." Ædwine said as Frith continued to sing. "And she clung to you."

For a long time Gragus did not reply. His eyes were fixed on the towers of Dummoc where he had narrowly escaped hanging. Their steady rowing put safe waters between him, and the snare lain for him on the holy hill. It was a distance which healed and wounded at the same time.

"Her old Will had no heart," Ædwine went on. "She knows he does not love her - which bodes well for you."

Gragus looked up again and peered into the grey mists. Dummoc had vanished. As far as he was concerned the greater the gulf between him and the maiden, the safer he would be.

Though Gragus was determined none would stir up what he had laid to rest Frith later passed him a token from the trial.

"When her Will cast down her crown, she lost nothing but him. I have it here Gragus in the folds of my cloak; the blue flowers which grow in the Hellesden and white feathers from a goose. The gods could not have sent you a more obvious sign my friend."

Gragus took the gift but would not discuss the fair maiden.

When they had rested a few days at Flegg Isle Gragus declared they must go to Ely to seek news of Gisla. He sent word to Ædwine commanding him to go and work in the Hellesden until their return. At the trial, the maiden had linked the Chief Thegn with Alcuin and he needed to know why.

News of his companion's imminent departure frustrated Ædwine who hastened to the quayside where the oars of the vessel already kissed the rippling waves.

"Why are you leaving so soon? I haven't told you about the Thegn," Ædwine shouted. "His words in the courtyard were bitter and the maiden was wounded. You need to know what he said."

"It will have to wait," Gragus returned.

"He threatened her in every possible way."

"That's why I am sending you to work with her brothers. Find where she has hidden my seaxe before he does. I want it back!"

"Is it just your seaxe you want?" Ædwine pleaded.

"No." Gragus called from the stern. "I want … "

The rest was lost as the wind slapped the square sail and shoved the vessel onto the open sea. Ædwine was left to guess too much.

PART 2
A NARROW WAY

CHAPTER SIX

ISOLATION

The Dummoc acquittal ought to have been celebrated as a triumph for Edmund's justice and impartiality; indeed, the Scandinavian traders in Gipeswick were much encouraged by the result and several leading kinship groups began to seek more permanent roots in the kingdom. However, those closest to Edmund were left to struggle with many issues. The Chief Thegn remained convinced the two men were oarsman agents masquerading as traders. He felt humiliated. There was other evidence he had not brought into play. He thought he had no need to use it but his confidence in his ability to prise a confession from the maiden had been misplaced. She had not yielded to him, and he felt like a broken man.

Os was perplexed. In less than a season, his sharp-witted and cheerful companion Will had been transformed into a dreary ecclesiastic. He tried to resolve the rift between Lee and Will, both of whom he loved dearly, but time had been against him. The day after the trial Will had parted company with them at Gipeswick and headed for Medeshamstede in Mercia. Os wrote to him encouraging him to reflect upon the years they spent in Edmund's household. He reminded him of all he and Lee had achieved over the years. They had produced many plays, and a few months previous Will would have enjoyed the performance of the *Swan Princess*.

Os wondered if Dummoc had scattered them forever, as youthful friendships were oft doomed to end when each found new ways to tread. He hoped Will would grow tired of his parchments and detached debates and come to his senses.

And what of Lee? Os was certain the rumours strewn abroad by the Chief Thegn were unfounded, but to protect the maiden's reputation he decided to place her with his family at Bures. He was confident she would enjoy his sisters' company.

Lee disagreed, but Os would not give way, so she and young Fred reluctantly boarded a merchant vessel to Bures. When they arrived, Oswald's mother was annoyed her son had not consulted her over the matter of his guests. The truth was she secretly feared her son was too fond of the imprudent maiden whom she did not like.

Lee soon discovered life with the four sisters would not be easy. They seemed to resent her presence for Os preferred her company to theirs. To keep the peace Lee busied herself teaching Fred the Scriptures.

Rumours tickled certain ears at Bures. It was whispered that Lee lacked discretion and had humiliated herself at Dummoc. The two middle sisters were convinced the rumours were true. They thought Lee had arranged to abscond with one of the heathen traders on trial but did not talk openly about it because they feared their brother would hear.

The household may have kept this distant but orderly peace had it not been for the arrival of Drega - a favoured friend of the small-minded third sister, Wulfrune. Drega was tall and thin and very mean. The two girls began to make Lee's life unbearable.

Lee often hid herself in the outer rooms where Os kept his books and papers. There was a beautiful cushioned longbench where she would lay and dream about the Hellesden. She wondered if the winter coppice workers were the same team as the previous year. How had Pip explained her absence? She had never missed the dedication of the new season's work. When she was young her father would take her to the ceremony at the Sutton St Chad's church, on the far side of the Hellesden – the very place she had met Gragus and Frith. Lee recalled how her father knelt in prayer and read from the psalms placing all his workers under God's protection. The simple ceremony always ended in the Hellesden with the dedication of the firstfruits to the Lord where wild game was roasted on spits over the embers of the first hewn logs. Lee hoped her brothers had taken care to follow the family tradition.

It was almost six years since her father and mother had died and her unexpected separation from her brothers renewed her loss. She even longed for the comfort of Hilde's constant scolding. The higher manners practised in the Bures household brought no joy or comfort. Lee could not follow the watching and signalling and the nods of approval or disapproval. She knew her father would have rejected such 'appearances of wisdom', as he was fond of saying, for the self-righteous always thwarted God's ways. He had endorsed Edmund's friendship with the Scandinavian traders because many were separated from their homelands through war and famine. The law of Moses decreed that strangers in the kingdom must be given full rights of protection and access to justice - despite what some thought. The Mercian churchmen had vehemently opposed Edmund's point of view and scorned his mercy. Yet Edmund was steadfast and opposed the rule of their churchmen.

Lee's concern for her king deepened because rumours about his discourse with fretful overlords in the Borders suggested he had made no progress. She blamed the Mercian-appointed bishops, particularly Æthelwold. It was no coincidence that Frith and Gragus had faced trial at Dummoc where Bishop Æthelwold had earlier opposed Edmund and tried to replace the faithful old Hunberht with another dreadful Mercian bishop.

Hunberht had since retreated to Icanho leaving fickle, faceless men to rule the ancient sea fort at Dummoc. Lee shivered as memories of the cold courtyard came to mind. How she wished the fair oarsman had walked past without even glancing her way. She was banished from her own hearth because of him.

One evening in early November Lee and Fred sat in front of the fire, surrounded by illustrations they had copied from Oswald's books. They were both low in spirits. All Saints Day had been a dreary vigil without food or drink or sleep. Lee was accustomed to an evening feast seated around a roaring fire listening to tales about her energetic ancestors; but laughter had been banished at the Bures celebration. Os was absent and she had inadvertently irritated his mother with her constant shivering and endless questions concerning the remembrance of the over-pious.

Fred and Lee became more and more engrossed in their patterns for the scabbards they planned to make later in the winter months and did not notice the arrival of Drega, the 'wispy wight', as Fred later named her. She peered over their shoulders then snatched the dragon design from Fred.

"Look, Fred had drawn your mother!" Drega declared. The two sisters giggled mischievously but Fred looked up in disgust.

"Give it back, walnut face!" He shouted.

"Not unless Lee tells me all about those oarsmen."

Drega held the illustration over the flames.

"Lee doesn't know any oarsmen," Fred declared.

"Yes, she does. She loves the fair-haired one." Lee flinched. She felt ashamed because of the wicked rumours fuelled by repulsive girls like Drega. "Did you like being kissed by him?" She scoffed.

"Don't talk such rubbish, you miserable worm."

"Take no notice Fred," Lee whispered.

However, the venomous snake had no intention of

slithering away.

"Uncle says oarsmen like impious women like you."

Fred could no longer contain himself.

"Does he keep company with oarsman?"

"Of course not, you turnip!"

"Then how is it he knows what sort of women they like?"

"Fred! Ignore her," urged Lee.

"Why should I? Branda told me a few things she said about her and if she will not shut her big mouth I will tell Os - and he will send you away!"

Drega sneered and Fred took his quill and flicked pigment over her. It made a line of speckled dots from her nose to her ear.

"And I'll tell my uncle about you two," she screeched. "He's coming to church tomorrow!"

"Good, I hope he takes you away with him," Fred declared.

"And I hope he flogs you."

"Well, I'm looking forward to meeting your uncle. What's his name?" Lee asked.

"He's called Greg - after the great saint."

"Is he pious like you?" Fred jeered.

Oswald's mother returned, but fortunately, she had not heard what the lad said as she was greatly agitated. Drega was firmly ordered away to wash her face and the sisters were all sent off to bed.

"I have to make provision for a man of high standing tomorrow - and you must behave Lee."

"I will be as quiet as Branda," Lee replied.

"You must wear your new dress and tie your hair back."

"Yes, of course. Drega told us her uncle will be at church tomorrow. Is he your guest?"

"Yes. I have a great deal to organise. He will feast with us tomorrow."

"Can I help?"

"You must ponder all you have learned since you have been here."

"Fred and I will discuss the Scriptures with him ... "

"A maiden should learn in silence. I forbid you to ask any questions at all. I am thoroughly worn out by them."

She left. Fred and Lee each put a finger to their lips.

"Did you see Drega?" Fred whispered. "She was speckled like a toad."

"Don't annoy her Fred. Toads squirt poison."

"Is it fatal?"

"No, it's just irritating."

Their laughter echoed throughout the household and further exasperated Oswald's mother who thought they were being disrespectful. It was about time the unruly maiden was brought to heel she thought. She needed a husband's discipline not a mother's love.

On Sunday morning Fred and Lee busied themselves getting ready. It reminded them of their preparations for the trial at Dummoc. Fred wearily put on the outfit which had been provided, and Lee wore her new gown which was pale and not very practical. They left and arrived early at the church where they knelt to pray. The younger maidens rushed in unaccompanied because their mother remained at the gate to greet her guest. Branda struggled to keep order, but Drega was beyond her control. She called out her uncle was there, and the two younger sisters turned and said how handsome he was. Lee and Fred gazed towards the altar. It was bad manners to stare. They were determined to behave perfectly.

When the closing prayer had been uttered the priest left and Lee turned to see what sort of man Drega's uncle might be. How glad she was Fred could not see over the heads of the crowd, for near the door, at the side of the church, stood a man she knew well. Her heart missed a beat, it raced and then held steady as if she stood on a battlefield.

"What is he like?" Fred asked. "You look worried Lee."

"You must keep calm Fred. Drega's Uncle is none other than the wicked Chief Thegn. And he dines with us."

"I feel sick."

"And so do I."

Without saying more, they made their way towards the man. He had his back to them and spoke pleasantly to people as they left the church. Lee watched as Drega, and the three younger sisters pushed ahead and drew alongside the Thegn. But he did not have time to greet them because Oswald's mother ushered them out into the church courtyard. Even so, Drega turned back to sneer at Lee whose thoughts turned to betrayal and Gragus. He had feared deception, and now she was walking into a trap. Had Os contrived this meeting? He must be familiar with Drega's kin.

The Chief Thegn was uneasy. His parting words at Dummoc haunted him. Years before a similar outburst had cut him off from her brother Æsc and he had never had opportunity to make amends.

"Good sir," Branda's mother intervened. "I believe you are acquainted with my wards, Lee and Fred." Fred bent low in obeisance but later insisted he thought he was going to be sick, and it wasn't a bow at all.

"You are transformed." The Thegn faltered then took Lee's hand and kissed it.

"Indeed, she is."

Lee did not like what Oswald's mother had said. She feared the lady might go into dull detail about how she intended to convert her into a pious wretch. Fortunately, there were many who wanted to greet the Thegn, so Lee and Fred managed to slip away without anything else being said.

"Did Uncle Greg kiss you?" Drega called out. Her intense

sneer caused her nose to crinkle like a walnut kernel and Lee turned to Fred and laughed.

"Yes, he did." Lee said at length and laughed again.

"He will beat you when you're his wife," Drega cried in frustration. Lee continued to laugh with Fred for they saw how it annoyed her. "I'm going to be the maid at your wedding," Drega continued.

"Really?" Lee giggled without restraint. "And Fred's going to be the bishop, aren't you?"

"Yes, and I have been practicing my handwriting and sermons for the last month." Fred caught on to Lee's act and followed her.

"Bishop Fred, shall we go and prepare the guest list?"

"I must fetch my quill so watch out, you horrible walnut," he cried as he sprinted towards the highway with Lee. Neither were seen again that day.

They bounded down the narrow lane which led to Oswald's coppice and paused to look down upon the Hall where their supposed protector had contrived to throw them upon the Chief Thegn's mercy. Lee's mirth turned to anger. The ways followed by the Bures household thoroughly perplexed her. She despised the dress she had been compelled to wear because it was so very difficult to run in and was about to suggest a detour to change into her usual garments.

"I can hear a horse," Fred cried.

"It will not be him," Lee reassured. She squeezed through the stile. "He has too many pious cheeks to kiss. We must go and find our own garments and begin our journey home."

"I'm so afraid. I know he will send me back to my uncle or worse. Remember how he threatened to sell us in the slave market?"

Lee turned and caught sight of the lad as he disappeared through a gap in the opposite hedge. She retraced her steps snagging her dress in the stile. It tore and she rolled into the muddy lane.

Lee was breathless when she caught up with Fred. He was almost at the woodland which crowned the high ridge. Down below they could see the river snaking through the valley; beyond it was the Kingdom of Essex. It was a long time before they spoke because Fred was weeping.

"Even after we won, we must still be slaves," he sobbed. "I wish Frith and Gragus had taken us with them. We saved their lives, didn't we?"

"We don't have to run to them. We will be safe enough at Hellesden Hall but it's a long way. And we must avoid the highways."

They continued to discuss their escape and once they had entered the woodland on the ridge their hearts cheered for the oaks were at the peak of their golden hues. Lee was at ease although the unfamiliar winding paths caused her to yearn for the Hellesden's straight rides and peaceful glades.

They followed the track along the crest of the ridge and reached an area of long tussock grass where they rested for a while. The skies darkened. A storm was about to burst upon them. Lee urged the weary lad to make haste and seek a place to shelter. Her prayers were answered for, beyond an open field, Fred caught sight of a building nestled amongst golden oak trees. It was the sacred hall where Edmund had been crowned. Lee caught up her dress, held it above her knees and challenged Fred to a race.

They reached the shelter of the covered gate moments before the unseasonable storm struck. Lightening flashed over the chapel, thunder echoed across the ridge and then the rain fell. The great storm went one way and then another masking the light of day until dusk. They thought about sleeping in the chapel but when they tried the door it was locked. They concluded they had no choice but follow the way downhill to Bures.

Fred kept hearing noises. Drega had terrified him with her tales about slave traders who frequented the fens along the Stour. Several times the pair hid in outbuildings and behind woodpiles. It was late when they crept into the hall. Os was sitting alone by the hearth.

"What have you been doing Lee?"

"We got lost." She looked down at her ruined dress and tried to explain. "Fred ran off and – and I am his guardian. He is terrified by the man your mother invited to dine with us."

"You have offended my mother, Lee. Now go to bed and we will discuss the matter tomorrow. I must send word to those looking for you to say you are safe."

"But…" Lee began and then stormed to her room.

Early the next day hunger drove Fred to seek a crust of bread from the kitchen hall. He tasted a broken flatbread, then some pottage and was reaching up for an apple from a hanging basket when he heard someone approach. He hid himself in a recess.

"Did you know our Chief Thegn is Drega's uncle?"

"Yes, and I thought you knew too."

"I did not know. My sisters have different guests every week. What must Lee think of me? No wonder they ran. You were not at the trial mother. I saw how he threatened them."

"But I thought you knew," she repeated.

"I did not know. And to think you invited him here to dine with them! No wonder they were terrified."

"I was with him at mass; he did not threaten her. He seeks to make amends for taking her to Dummoc. He searched for her all afternoon. Even the storm did not deter him. He was soaked when he returned to his lodgings. And he made me give my word I would not punish her." She paused before discharging her full fury. "Even though she deserves to be thoroughly whipped!

You brought the girl here. And I've had nothing but trouble for weeks!"

"I expected you to behave like a vigilant guardian, mother. Instead, you have thrown her in the way of the very man who vowed to take revenge on her. I brought her here – to protect her from him."

"He told me he desired to apologise to the girl."

"Of course, he spoke like that. He was going to try and frighten her to make her think it was all her fault."

"And wasn't it? He is a worthy man, highly esteemed by many."

"Only by those who do not know his true nature. Would you think the same of him mother, if he, by his own hand, had kidnapped Branda and taken her bound and gagged to Dummoc? And there forced her to face a trial full of rottenness and falsehood? I brought Lee here for her own safety and you have let me down. You had wonderful opportunity to uphold her noble character – for truly she is noble, even if you do not like to think so."

"You brought a troublesome girl under my roof! But I did not complain. I have shown her many skills and graces. She has put away her knife, hasn't she? I do not want her to have a bad influence on your sisters. Would you be pleased if they all ran away with oarsmen?"

"Lee did not run away – she was abducted by the same man who has tried to worm his way into my household to prise her from my care. I will not be contradicted in this mother. Lee is true to Will."

"Then why has he abandoned her? I do know what happened at Dummoc. And I was told you brought her here against her will. Perhaps you should have let her oarsman take her to Flegg."

"What do you mean? What gossip have you bent your ear to?"

"It is said she humiliated and abandoned Will. How could she embrace an oarsman after all they did to his father – and then his mother?"

"Rumours, mother! And it was Will who abandoned Lee. Your wretched bishops have turned his heart to stone. You are as cold as they are. You have failed mother – failed to comfort her!"

"Perhaps it is time for Greg to have words with her then."

"What do you mean?"

"He has indicated he wants her to be his wife."

"What do you mean? Has he asked her? Is that why she ran off?"

"No. He has hinted he might ask."

"What did he say?"

"He said Will has no intention of pursuing his attachment."

"What exactly did he say?"

"He wanted to know if any other man might ask for her hand. He said he felt great regret the Dummoc trial had caused such animosity between the two. He had followed his duty and is concerned for her."

"Concerned for her? After all the accusations and slurs he made upon her good character, he ought to be concerned!"

"He wants to marry her. It will solve all our problems." Os did not reply. He had quite run out of ways to make his mother understand the deep distress she had caused him. "Do you object?"

"Yes mother, I object! Unto death I object! And you mother, I will have sent to Mercia where you can serve your pious bishops in some nunnery. And I will find the poorest worthy men for my sisters."

At last, he had said something which made her think about the depth of despair she had caused him.

"My son," she pleaded. "I did not mean to upset you, but I beg you - send her back to her brothers."

"No mother. She is staying here with us. So is Fred, but Drega is never to come here again. They will have no visitors without my permission. Perhaps you should choose one of them for the Thegn – if you have such high regard for the man. After all he is of kingly birth."

"They are all too young."

"Branda is old enough."

"Edmund should have found a husband for Lee when she was Branda's age. Who else will marry her, now she has grown so wilful?"

"We thought Will would ask her, but he did not. And I am glad because he was insincere. Lee must remain here until Edmund returns. He will know what to do."

"What is this to do with Edmund? Greg has already made agreement with her Riscmere kin. She ought to be grateful and go to him."

"Ought to go to him? Like a prize heifer? And how has he been able to make any arrangements? Pip had not said a word."

"He does not need Pip's permission. He has written to her mother's kin, and they have agreed."

"But Gisla must give her consent."

"Gisla is dead."

"She is lost mother, not dead."

"Then you must find her before Holy Mass Eve."

"What do you mean?"

"Is it such a dreadful thing to marry a man of such standing?"

"I would rather she ran off with an oarsman."

Os left as angry as he had arrived.

Fred made his way back to his room and told Lee all he had overheard. She feared she would never return to the Hellesden. Os was in his rooms when she burst in.

"Fred overheard your recent discussion," she declared. "I am sorry to have come between you and your mother. Let me go home to Pip."

"Don't worry about mother. I was firm with her. She does not know the true nature of the man as we do. I wanted you to be happy here - but I fear my family have humiliated you. We have too much wealth and have become complacent. Some poverty might do us good."

"Os, you are very wise, but it is not your family who have crushed me, it's those rumours the Chief Thegn began at Dummoc."

"Those with upright hearts know it was all lies. I know you would never pursue the sort of life their women lead."

"I want my old life back!" Lee passionately exclaimed. "I miss Pip and the Hellesden; all my familiar paths and ways. It's not your sisters' fault."

"Yes, it is Lee. You did not miss your brothers when we travelled the coastal heaths looking for Gisla did you?"

"No, of course not. But we had a purpose."

"And I have a purpose now - to keep you safe."

"But I feel caged," she whined.

"If he takes you for his wife, you will be truly caged."

"Why would he want me for his wife? He must be the most foolish thegn in the kingdom if he thinks I will marry him."

"Did Fred not tell you about the negotiations?"

"Yes, he did. Fred tells me everything. I will visit the Thegn myself and tell him I do not want to be his wife."

"You must not meet with him Lee," Os insisted.

"Why not?"

"I neither like him – nor trust him. He will be gone soon."

"He needs to know I will never consent."

"Do not play with fire," Os warned as he left her.

But Lee would not let go. Later she persuaded Fred to take a note to the Chief Thegn. She would be direct and polite.

Dearest G. Even though, my king, Edmund, himself agrees with your request, it is I who will be your wife, and it will be against my will. I do not love you at all; I never have. I long to return to my hall - where I born. My brothers will watch over me and I will care for them – I desire no more. You lured me from there and I did not like the darkness of the cliffs and the raging waters. I was pleased to leave you behind that eve, and I will not change my mind. In those few turbulent days, I understood what you really are, so do not try to persuade me otherwise. I am not some prize to be bought or snatched away and taken to where I do not belong. Besides I have lied to you, and you are not one to forgive matters of deception, are you? I love another and must wait for him. Lee

Fred was brave enough to offer to deliver the letter to the Chief Thegn. Early on Tuesday he accompanied Os by boat to South Burgh and at the Belindune Bridge, he disembarked to peruse the market stalls set out at the crossing point into Essex. He told Os Lee had asked him to purchase certain goods which would take some time to negotiate. He disappeared amongst the booths and at the farthest one he gazed towards the hall where the Chief Thegn lodged.

Fred trembled as he walked up the path and was soon shown to the Thegn's quarters. On entering, he caught sight of the man he feared. He was standing beside a table strewn with papers.

"I am sorry, sir. I was afraid when I ran off on Sunday last. We did not know Drega's Uncle was going to be you, sir. Lee was only meaning to take a short cut back to the hall because of Drega but when I heard a horse, it reminded me of the kidnap, so I ran. Lee would not leave me on my own and followed, and then we were lost and had to shelter from the storm. When we found a highway, it was already dark."

"I searched all the highways my boy and the outbuildings of

every hall around. I could not find you."

"I am sorry you were inconvenienced sir. I have come to deliver this note from Lee."

Fred handed over the note and the Chief Thegn opened it. He showed no emotion as he read it and Fred wondered what Lee had written. He said he would reply without delay, so Fred remained seated beside the fire while the Thegn returned to his writing table. A leash for a hound lay beside the hearth and Fred was reminded of a tale Lee told him about thegns who loved their hounds more than their wives. A new hound might drive away thoughts of marriage he reasoned.

"Did the Ætheling send you?" The Chief Thegn asked as he handed Fred the sealed note.

"No sir, Lee sent me. The lady is very upset with her, and we are trying our best to put things right. It was all we tried to do at Dummoc."

"Well, your mistress says in the note she lied to me. Can lies right wrongs?" His severe tone took Fred back to Dummoc.

"I do not know what was in the letter sir," he faltered.

"Did she lie to me at Dummoc?" He demanded. "Did you?"

"Well, I don't think it was *The Willow Song* the men were singing sir. We put in the song because it went with the play."

"This is nothing to do with songs!" He yelled. "She lied to me about the seaxe, didn't she?"

"No sir." Fred was certain Lee had never seen the seaxe.

"Then what was it?"

"I don't know sir. Should I ask her?"

"I will question her myself. She must explain what she meant. If the maiden admits to telling lies and then says she does not love me, how do I know she speaks the truth?"

"But I know she does not love you sir. She is betrothed to Will."

"You are mistaken, my lad. I spoke to Will the day he left

for Medeshamstede. He told me himself he is not willing to have her as his wife. It was from his lips I learned how the oarsman embraced her after the trial. Her failings repulsed Will, so why would he change his mind about her?"

"I've seen the letter he wrote. He's forgiven her, sir. We were all very tired and confused at Dummoc - the trader was pleased to be free; he kissed the Swan Princess, not Lee."

"Oh, was that how it was?"

"Yes, I heard him say it himself."

"Well tell your mistress I intend to kiss her, not a Swan Princess. Take this note to her. I will call, after noon, on Friday."

The Thegn showed Fred the way out using the side door and the lad leapt away as fast as he could. He had much to do. How easy would it be to find a dog before Friday?

Everything went well for Fred who found a trader and arranged the time and place to make the delivery. However, his high spirits did not last long for Lee was troubled. Fred had lied about the letter from Will. The Thegn was bound to ask for evidence. At length she decided to tell Os but said nothing about the note or his reply.

Leoba I did not understand how much you missed your household. I will speak to Oswald and have you returned to your hall though I fear you are without guidance there and I am concerned for you and your safety. I have known you for many years and your dearest father and mother would be heart-broken if they knew how you have been neglected. The cliffs of Dummoc were all darkness and Will was rightly distressed to see how you behaved with the Dane. Do not give those pagans further opportunity to humiliate you. I have arranged to visit Wood Hall on Friday afternoon. Gregory.

The Thegn, however, arrived very early when both Os and

Fred were absent. He offered to return later but Oswald's mother was determined he and the girl should talk privately and sat them down beside the fire.

"Thank you for sending the note with the lad. Now tell me what it was you lied about. I fear it involves the seaxe which I believe he buried in his bag in the Hellesden. Did he tell you where?"

"I wrote the note so we can sort out our differences - before you do something you may regret."

"Regret?"

"Yes sir. I understand you have approached my kinsmen regarding matters you have not discussed with me."

"It is for your own good."

"Really? Didn't you read my note?"

"I did read it. Tell me plainly what you lied about at Dummoc."

"I told the court you were a noble thegn for truly you are not!"

"They sent a note to you, didn't they? To say they were at Dummoc? Did it say where the seaxe was hidden?"

"I swear they did not send me a note!"

"You are more wicked than I thought, Leoba. How else would you know where I'd taken the men? Do you deny sending word to young Eth?" Lee did not know how to reply. She did not want to reveal there was a third oarsman – one who troubled her more than she cared to admit. "I am a defender of this kingdom. Those men were here to examine our defences. And why? Answer me, you careless child. My duty is to be watchful. Now tell me who delivered the note."

"There was no note." She insisted.

"I do not believe you."

"If I am such a wicked liar, why do you want me as your wife?"

"You kissed my brow. The day I stumbled into your hall. Do you remember? Was it part of your playacting too? You play a dangerous game."

"It was you who began the dance sir. When you came to my home accusing me of harbouring spies and would not let the matter rest – even when you found no evidence."

"I could find no evidence because you are a very cunning wench ..."

"Only a wench today, am I? Are you going to repeat those wicked things you uttered in the mists at Dummoc?"

"Your defence of pagans was a terrible mistake, Leoba. Why can't you see it? I never want you to meet their kind again. You will find shelter enough in my household. Marry me."

"No sir. I will not. Never." Lee moved away from him towards the inner porch where Oswald's mother vainly strained her ears to hear what they discussed.

The first words she overheard the thegn say were, 'I will forgive you' quickly followed by 'Even though you have lied under oath.'

Lee moved from the shadows and the lady feared she might be seen.

"Very well," Lee said. "I will tell you plainly, the men you took to Dummoc were the two I saw in the Hellesden - but they were not your spies. I overheard them mention Gisla. They spoke of her with such warmth and love, how could I let harm fall upon them? They are her friends. That was what I kept back!"

Lee returned to the bench and buried her head in her arms. He sat beside her but did not embrace her. Had he have done so she might have yielded but he was not an affectionate man.

"I warned Edmund about Gisla's lack of judgement ..."

"Has Alcuin captured her?"

"Alcuin?"

"Yes. You know more about the viper than you care to say.

How much did he pay you at Dummoc?"

Lee leapt up and stormed towards the door. He was slow to recover from her blow.

"You are out of your mind!" He yelled.

Oswald's mother winced but dare not move.

"Am I? You did not even begin to ask the right questions at the trial. And I know why."

"I do not have any ... I have not communicated with Alcuin in this matter."

"You lie. I know it. Tell me where she is."

"Gisla is dead – and by the hand of those oarsmen you say are her friends." He looked at her again and knew she did not believe him. "I was acting on evidence and those men were guilty."

"Whose evidence? Where did it begin?"

"I have men keeping watch all over the kingdom. The report was from North Burgh."

"Oh. Elmham men, I suppose! Were they directed by Alcuin?"

"No. I swear not. What have you heard?"

"The same as you - rumours. Is truth ever conveyed upon rumours? You have begun enough of them about me!"

"What do you mean?"

"I mean you have brought ruin to my name. I have been open and honest, but have you?"

"Yes, I have. It is you who is untrustworthy."

"Then do not take me as your wife. It is an impossible match sir, for you find me disagreeable, and I say you are lying about Gisla. You know she is not dead! But she is no longer free, and I will find out what part you played in her downfall."

"I know nothing about her disappearance."

"Then use your men to find out where she is. Do you have any amongst those Mercian bishops?"

"It is no business for maidens. Your place is with a husband, to bear him children and keep busy in his hall."

"I already have my own hall and I will choose my own husband. And with Edmund's consent."

He bowed awkwardly and left without saying more.

Oswald's mother was not pleased with the way Lee had dismissed the Thegn, and harshly rebuked her. Lee, thoroughly exhausted, gave way to tears and complained she had a headache.

On his return Os enquired about Lee. When he discovered the Thegn had arrived earlier than expected he was furious.

"Did you know he would call this morning?"

"Of course, not. She was happy enough to see him. They began in an agreeable way. I left them to discuss what they needed to. Then Lee suddenly called out and ... "

"What did she call out?"

"Something to do with Alcuin and Gisla."

"Say nothing of this mother. Do you understand? Gisla might die because of this. Did anyone else hear?"

"No." His mother wept, and he embraced her. "Please send her back to her brothers. I cannot bear her disruption any longer."

"I will mother, though it breaks my heart to do it. She is my dear friend and out of her depth. And I fear our Thegn has not revealed all. How is he connected with Alcuin? Do you swear you will say nothing?"

"Yes, I swear. Please forgive me Oswald."

Later Fred crept into Lee's room to see if she was awake and found her staring at the roof timbers.

"I've ruined everything Fred. I will never find Gisla now. The Chief Thegn came to see me, and I admitted it was Gragus and Frith I had seen the Hellesden. I told him why I lied. It was for Gisla's safety. He vowed he had no contact with Alcuin, but he wavered Fred. He hesitated and so did I. If I had pressed on, I may have discovered where Gisla is imprisoned. Perhaps we should have bought him a puppy Fred, if only to bribe him."

Fred took courage and hoped the goods would arrive in time to help his friend. He said nothing to Lee about the pup. However, his tales about missing maidens who vanished from the lower meads distracted Lee. The river reeve thought they had been taken by slavers who were skulking in the margins downstream from Bures at the same watch as Lee and Fred had been lost in the ridge coppice.

It was early afternoon when she and Fred went to find Os in the courtyard. Fred listened smugly thinking he was about to solve everything.

"Don't fret Lee," Os said. "I will speak to him when he arrives. It is good he understands your opposition was undertaken to protect Gisla not those oarsmen."

"They were innocent, Os. There was more to the trial than you think. Alcuin *is* behind Gisla's disappearance. Alcuin does know Gisla. And he knows the Thegn too."

"There is much I do not know Lee but your love for Gisla overwhelms me – and mother understands at last - so take heart. She heard you cry out."

"Was she watching?"

"I do not know."

"Did he kiss you?" Asked Fred.

"Of course, not. Why should he?"

"He said he would."

"He did not get the opportunity."

"Good," concluded Os. "I must go and sign a letter."

When the Chief Thegn arrived at Wood Hall he was taken to the outer rooms where he and Os discussed the disappearance of Gisla. Os was convinced the Thegn had not acted upon instructions from Alcuin at the trial.

Before they left the outer rooms Os showed him a letter from Will. It was a request to the Ætheling Os to oversee the betrothal arrangements with Lee's kinsmen, ahead of his return from Mercia. The Chief Thegn made a careful study of the letter and asked if Lee had received confirmation. Os said a letter had recently arrived from Will, but he had not seen it.

"May I speak to the maiden?"

"Of course, come and sit by the fire."

Fred sat beside the hearth anxiously wondering if the puppy would appear in time. Lee had no idea what Os had done so when the Chief Thegn approached her, she expected the worst.

"Os has explained why you lied. I do not think your way was wise, but I will leave without dispute. If our paths should cross again remember I will not take falsehood lightly a second time."

"Thank you, sir." Lee was lost in wonder at the turn of events.

"Lies and deceit are very wicked faults in one as young as yourself."

"I know sir," Lee said as she hung her head in shame.

The humbled maiden with bowed head did not see the look of horror on the Thegn's face when he recognized the man who swept in with a basket full of pups. The sisters had seen him arrive in the courtyard and followed him into the spacious porch. Lee overheard them squeal with delight. Os left his study to see what had caused the disturbance and then the pups all escaped. For a moment, there was complete but cheerful chaos.

"Someone wanted a pup?" Enquired the stranger.

"Yes. I did," Fred whispered nervously. Os looked astounded. "I ordered the puppy of a good hunting hound for the Chief Thegn. Lee thought he would like to choose one since his own has never been found."

"How considerate," Oswald's mother proclaimed with great delight.

The Chief Thegn was overwhelmed at the turn of events and asked Lee to choose a pup for him. Very purposefully she chose one which was not completely dark as a good hunting dog should be. It had a large flash of paler fur on its forehead and two white paws. She was sure the pup would never be a hardy hunter like Arrow, but it would make a good companion for him; something for him to set his affections upon. She passed the chosen one to him and he received it with immense pleasure.

The man who brought the puppies was not in a hurry to leave. Lee did not notice how fiercely the Thegn looked at him for her eyes were on the pup. Eventually the stranger gathered up the rest of the litter and returned them to their basket. Without comment Os paid for Lee's parting gift and he left.

The Chief Thegn remained a while longer completely bewildered by the change in the maiden. She was no longer discordant and rebellious but gentle and compliant. The pup was wholly content in her care. He requested Lee take charge of it while he made ready to leave. Outside she passed him the tiny bundle and he felt his heart soften. The maiden understood his loss. She was not beyond redemption.

CHAPTER SEVEN
FACING THE ENEMY

Lee was straightway aware of her own foolishness. As she entered the hall Branda told her Os was waiting for her in his rooms.

"What were you thinking! I've just lain my reputation in the mire for you Lee. And do you know why? Because I do not want him near you. But what did you do? Why?"

"I thought a dog would be better for him than a wife."

"You thought what?"

"If he needs something to love then let him have a dog."

"Having a dog is the same as marriage?"

"He wanted to train me up so others could admire me. He's better off with a dog. It will learn in silence and not answer back."

Os did not laugh.

"And what if he wants a dog and a wife?"

Os despaired and thought about the vain gesture he had contrived to save her from the wretched man. He was angry.

"If you had let me return to the Hellesden," Lee rebounded. "I would not have been thrown his way by your mother."

"Poor mother!" Os retaliated. "She is worn out trying to guide you. And I am exasperated. I offered my best and you throw it away."

"What have I thrown away?" Lee demanded.

"I was determined to protect you, and it has cost me dear."

He slammed his writing frame onto his table, and she jumped. She had never known Os to lose his temper. She backed away towards the door. He thought she was trying to escape facing the truth and questioned her loyalty. He said she was wayward. Lee saw herself back in the courtyard at Dummoc but this time a friend accused her. She fell under the flash of Frith's seaxe flying over her head. Fred stood by her as she regained her senses. Everyone seemed to be astir, and she felt so dizzy.

"Help her to her feet," Branda urged. "Did she hit her head?"

"I don't think so. She just went down," her brother replied.

"Lee, can you hear me? It's Fred. He took the puppy, didn't he? It will take a lot of training and he won't be back for months so we're safe."

Os at last saw their reasoning. He helped Lee to her feet and sat her at his writing table. While he left to fetch some wine, Lee glanced at the letter which lay unrolled in front of her. The righteous ætheling had forged a letter to save her. And she had ruined his plans.

Lee struggled with her doubts and went to lay down. Later Branda reported to her brother that Lee was asleep. Lee, however, had secretly left the hall. A bundle of clothes had misled the simple maiden who was far from understanding the complexity of Lee's reasoning.

At the chapel gate, Lee recalled the loving-kindness of her father. At Edmund's coronation, he had placed her upon his shoulder so she could observe the ceremony. How proud he would have been to witness all Edmund had done. But her king was away and her father long in his grave.

Lee recalled the day when news was brought of her father's untimely death. And then her mother too. Within a few weeks her older brothers had left for Wessex where dubious overlords were set to claim their father's properties. All three had hastily married Wessex maidens and had never returned. Pip had said he would always be there for her, but they had been separated by the terrible Thegn.

Lee felt alone so she curled up under the covered gate where she and Fred had found shelter from the storm.

As she wriggled to get comfortable a set of keys jangled as they fell to the ground. Lee picked them up and wondered if they would fit the chapel locks. They did, and she found herself standing where Edmund had stood for his coronation. The heavy wooden throne had gone but the humble footstools were arranged around a table where someone had placed a candle in a broken pot. Lee's vision of the marvellous day soon faded.

A soiled mattress on the floor annoyed her. She wondered who had slept there - and why. Perhaps it was the man who had recently replaced the thatch. Lee gazed upwards but could not see his handiwork because the roof space was panelled. Then she saw what appeared to be small footholds in the wall and though they began high up she managed to ease herself upwards. Soon she entered a space between two roof panels which led to the loft. She was inside the small bell turret which crowned the roof.

High above the stars twinkled and the moon dimly outlined the course of the river as it meandered through the valley. She could see out across the lower meads where slavers had captured the maidens. Cattle lowed in the vale, and then bellowed. Lights, like fallen stars danced across the meads. Lee froze. Their torches flickered as they passed below the thatched outer gate. Os must have sent his thegns to find her. She lay down upon floor, pulled a blanket over her and waited.

The door opened and slammed shut again. A light was brought to the table, and she strained to peep through a gap between the roof boards. It was not Os. Three men threw down their packs and sat around the table below her. One was the man who delivered the puppy.

"Alcuin, my friend, I have the gold," he said. They cordially embraced.

Lee peered downwards. The taller man was Alcuin! He was cloaked and his face was all shadows. The man put his booted foot on a stool and unwrapped his leggings carefully removing coins from secret pockets. He counted them onto the table.

"Ten for each gold coin I think was what we agreed."

The third man's voice sounded familiar. It was the voice of an older man, but Lee could not place it. She wondered what the ten were.

"Nay, some are more valuable." The puppy trader interrupted. "The fairer they are the higher the price. We agreed two prices. Same for the maidens."

Lee flinched as she realised what it was they discussed - and it wasn't hunting dogs. They were the slavers! And she would join their captives if they discovered her. When the money was counted out Alcuin divided it into three unequal piles.

The Bard had cast aside his mellow theatrical tones and beneath all his layers showed himself for what he was, a hardened despicable thief. Alcuin without his sentiment. Lee knew he was familiar with Mercia; a realm of usurpers, clawing clergy and conspiracy. But she did not know the extent of his influence in Lindissi, the small kingdom north of the fenland Borders, which many generations ago had been allied to East Anglia. Once a lofty noble kingdom, it had foundered under the weight of Mercian intrigue. During former wars the Anglian minsters at Ely and Salham were occupied by Mercians from Medeshamstede, and latterly Bearddanig in Lindissi had suffered the same fate - Alcuin was familiar with all four.

"Wolf, my lad," the third man said at length. "If you want me to pay you extra for each young maiden with fairer hair - for they are preferred - you must go to the Borders where the mares roam on the chalk hills. I hear they are more common there." Lee realized where she had heard the voice before. It was the way he said mares. He was the master of the boat the Chief Thegn had used to transport her to Dummoc.

"I know where you mean but I fear the black dogs."

Alcuin laughed at Wolf's answer.

"And your own Black Dog? How is he?" Alcuin asked. "This is his share," he said without waiting for an answer and pushed the smallest pile towards Wolf.

"He is well. Very well I would say. He found a good batch for us at Gipeswick. But there were strange dealings there. Someone killed the lovely Black Swan and her master. He was found swinging from the beams. They say it was from his own hand. But it was not."

"Do you think your Black Dog murdered him?" Alcuin asked.

"They were at each other's throats," said Wolf. "But why kill the man who does the hard work for you?"

"If he was the one who killed his hound at Beleham he would have been furious enough to slay him. The beast was priceless," the third man commented.

"Well, I have today supplied him with a new one. It was a gift," Wolf smiled. "As you know Lok, I had been summoned to the Ætheling's hall, and I certainly did not expect to find him there. He was with a maiden!"

"Was he now?" Lok crooned.

"Yes, she chose a new hound for him."

"I hope it was your best."

"He wanted her to choose and what do maidens know? It was the worst!" He laughed.

"And you didn't intervene?" Asked Alcuin.

"How could I? He could not take his eyes off her and he accepted the runt as if it had been from the finest stock in the land."

"So, he has caught his little mare then?" Lok added.

"You two seem to know more than I do. Don't tell me our Black Dog has grown soft," Alcuin laughed. "Who is this little mare?"

"The Swan Princess from Dummoc."

Alcuin hit the table hard with his fist.

"Do not jest! I was at that farce of a trial."

"You were?"

"Oh yes, I would not have missed it for all the silver in Gipeswick. I should have had the oarsman's head and that of his fool. And I would have - but your Black Dog was outwitted by her. She used my own song to delay judgment and the sanctimonious underling here freed the pair! Do you know how many months I have diligently pursued them? But I understand ..." Alcuin paused in a sinister way. "Men are dangerous when struck down by love."

"Very dangerous." Wolf had caught the bitter sarcasm in Alcuin's voice and gleefully fuelled Alcuin's wrath. "But you encouraged him."

"How!" Alcuin exploded.

"He's spent more than his share of our profits persuading her kin to part with her. Something he could not have done, Alcuin, had your woman been there to oppose him. Do you want him married to the little swan?"

"Never!" Alcuin declared and thumped the table again.

"Then let your woman go free."

"I'm biding time Lok," Alcuin said slowly. "I'll send the ransom note soon enough. She was at Dummoc you know. I wanted her to watch Gragus hang."

"Ah, Alcuin, you are a cold, heartless man," scoffed Lok.

"And my Black Dog is all heart," laughed Wolf. "If you hold on to her, he will marry the maiden and she will bring Edmund down on us. You have lost your oarsmen so why keep Gisla any longer?" Wolf asked.

"I'll keep her just as long as I need to."

"Did the Ætheling not search Dummoc?" Lok enquired.

"He did, but I left early. There was no point in delaying once the Blackheath Thegn arrived. I had her taken down the cliff path."

"Did you send her back to Ely?"

"No, she is much closer to hand. I linger here in these infested marshes waiting. When my oarsman does not find her at Ely he will turn around like an angry boar and hasten straight into my trap. She is my lure."

"Then you need better bait," interrupted Wolf. "I understand Gragus is under the Swan Maiden's enchantment and has forgotten Gisla. My poor Black Dog was devastated when he learnt the oarsman had thrown himself upon the maiden. Which is why he has acted so swiftly to secure her."

"The oarsman is not interested in the girl," Alcuin insisted. "He wanted to ruffle a few feathers - and he has. Yet I see his passion has worked to my advantage for it has distracted your Black Dog and kept the Ætheling at home. I must act soon while their eyes are turned away."

"There is nothing here to lure Gragus. He never wanted Gisla," Wolf insisted. "You must risk using the master seaxe as bait."

"What seaxe?" Lok asked. "Our Black Dog was murmuring about a seaxe - the oarsman's seaxe."

"Yes - and he said at the trial, the girl had it!" Alcuin cried.

"Does she? Then the haste to the altar is explained," Wolf howled.

"It's probably under her mattress."

He laughed loudly but Alcuin suddenly beckoned they listen.

"We must send word to Gragus to say his Swan Princess is anxious to return the weapon. If he draws close, we will know for certain she has it. You must persuade your Black Dog to find it -

then it's as good as mine. We must act soon. I cannot keep Gisla there for long. The trees will soon be bare."

"Is she in the depths of the Hellesden then?" Wolf asked.

"I do not frequent such places. She is out in the open – a hunting place all the same. I do not chase bucks, do I?"

Wolf laughed at his master's sly comment, but Lok was sullen because he did not know what Alcuin meant.

"Beware," Wolf said at last. "Those northern wolves may get to your prey before you do."

"Let them *pit* their wits against me," Alcuin laughed. "For I have fixed her in the place."

"He means the lodge to the north of my home," Wolf revealed. "It's not quite as luxurious as the bishop's place, more like a store at the bottom of his garden. It's a crumbling, musty hole but the old lady is as blind as a bat and as deaf as a stone."

Lok grinned as if he had clearly understood now where Gisla was being held captive. Alcuin raised his cup.

"The poor old dear has kept Gisla busy - and we must keep Lok busy.

Raise your cups to the *Green Blade* and all the barrels on her."

"More barrels, more beer," cheered Wolf.

As they celebrated their trade Lee closed her eyes - her fists tightened. How could they jest about broken lives and murder? She had misjudged the Chief Thegn. He was a common slaver who had bought her! A man who walked with the enemy; mockers who were thoroughly wicked. She vowed to challenge him and make him confess. There was much to uncover.

While she lingered in the chapel, she rejoiced she had saved Gragus and Frith. She understood how the net had tightened around them. Alcuin had been behind it all. He wanted Gragus dead, and Gisla to watch the ghastly deed. He must hate Gisla very much but at least she was alive.

Os was about to send a party of men to look for Lee when she boldly walked into his hall. He hugged her and said sorry a dozen times or more. Lee confessed she had slept locked away in the chapel and he kissed her braids. His mother was not pleased to see him with the unruly maiden. She silently vowed to send her home without delay. She hastened her son to an important meeting and when he returned late evening, she told him the two troublemakers were on their way to Hellesden Hall. Æthelric had passed by and offered to escort them, Lee enjoyed Æthelric's company for he was amongst those she had been raised with at Sutton Hall and cousin to Os. She was cheered by all his news, and she revealed to him, at least in part, the true story of Dummoc.

She was free from the suffocating household in Bures and delighted in being out amongst Æthelric's horses at Meleforde. He basked in her exuberance and gave her five more mares to train.

Lee arrived back at her Hall on Monday and penned up the new mares. The older ones, she concluded, were exceedingly well trained so she asked Æthelric to take them to Edmund's Hall without delay. They both marvelled Pip had found time to prepare them to such a high standard.

Hilde laid out a goodly midday feast after which Æthelric left. Later Lee tried to persuade the new ponies to go into the stable shelter but only managed to pen them in the inner pightle.

Pip was pleased to have his sister back at home. Apart from being worried she might be tempted to flee to the traders on Flegg, as some rumours indicated, he had missed her gentle humour. Fred was relieved to get away from all the girls and offered to work with Win as part of the coppice team. Pip had hired eight men from the Haugh works near Wood Street for the winter season in the Hellesden. They had already felled the alder standards in the section of woodland nearest to Hellesden Hall and were cutting the ash.

In high spirits, Lee rose early the next morning and set out to check the ponies. A man staggered through the yard and sank down on the log pile in the wood store.

"Someone has come under the cover of darkness and taken my tamed mares and put in ones wilder than bears," he complained.

"That was me. Are you hurt?" She asked. The man stopped clutching his leg and immediately stood up and embraced her. Lee pulled away.

"My fair maiden, you're home."

"I wondered who had trained the mares so well. Why are you here?"

"Gragus sent me."

"Did he? Is he still with Frith? Have they gone to Ely?"

"Too many questions for this time of day but, yes, they went to Ely to seek news of Gisla."

"Well, they will not find her there. She was at Dummoc."

"Never!"

"Yes. Right under our noses. Alcuin was there too. He planned to make her watch Gragus hang. And now he spins another web. Gisla is much closer to us than we think. Alcuin has guessed I have the seaxe. He is going to send word to say it is found hoping Gragus will rush in. And then..." Lee drew her hand across her neck but Ædwine did not laugh.

"You've made that up, you wicked maiden."

Lee sensed his intenseness and moved away from him.

"I heard it from the Bard's own lips. And barely a few days have passed since. I came so close to being caught. And I am afraid."

"It's good to be afraid when there's a mad beast loose."

"Do you think Gragus will be drawn in on a rumour?"

"I don't think so. He is cautious, like a lynx, and will keep hidden. He means to contact me as soon as he returns. Alcuin can

178

do nothing unless the seaxe is found. And I trust you have told no-one."

"About what?" She teased.

"But you must tell me," Ædwine insisted.

"I think not." Ædwine stopped unwinding his legging strips and looked at her.

"Are you unhappy?"

"The past month has been a trial worse than Dummoc. If only Gragus had not embraced me."

"You did not object at the time."

"I was too weary, and nothing seemed real. One day I was picking apples and two days later I was swirling about in the mists at Dummoc."

"You did look lost and sad. I would have struck your Will and killed the Thegn, but I feared we would be arrested again."

"You must learn to forgive, dear boy." As she spoke her brother stepped into the courtyard.

"What's happened? Forgive what?" Pip asked.

"The new ponies – they are very wild," Ædwine replied.

"Are you injured?"

"Nothing which will not heal."

"You must go inside. Lee, fetch the rub."

"The one we use for swine?" She asked as she raced away.

"Excuse my sister she is a high-spirited girl. She means well...."

".... but she's always in trouble," Ædwine added.

"Do you know her?"

"My sister was just the same," he concluded.

Ædwine went inside and sat down by the hearth. Lee soon returned with the medicine and handed it to him. She saw his leg below the knee was pitted by a large scar which she helplessly gazed upon.

"It's a battle scar," he said.

"Oh. Not a lynx then? What is your sister called?"

"Sæwara. Slavers got her."

"I hate slavers!" Lee stamped her foot as she spoke. She suddenly felt hemmed in and left to find Fred.

Evening quickly arrived and Lee reflected on what the day had revealed. She was glad Ædwine and Pip had great respect for each other but wondered how Pip would react if he discovered his most dedicated worker was an oarsman – and a very wild one. But was he wicked? Was it not wicked to trade people for money? The man, Wolf, was wicked and knew his Black Dog, very well. They were a pair of slave traders! Lok was master of the *Green Blade* the vessel which transported the captured - so he must be wicked too. And then there was Alcuin… He was more than wicked. She must find out where he held Gisla. Wolf certainly knew. Gisla was not in woodland but in an open place at the bottom of a bishop's garden. She recalled all the halls the bishops owned – it had to be close to the Hellesden, but none came to mind.

Ædwine was in the habit of leaving Linden Pits at dawn to tend to the horses before breakfasting at Hellesden Hall. He appreciated the plentiful dishes Hilde provided and Pip was happy enough to reward his hard work. Lee was not at the breakfast table because Fred was being difficult. His body ached so much he could not move.

"Leave him," said Pip. "He must have over-exerted himself yesterday."

"We have been shut away like caged finches for weeks," Lee complained. "But I will keep him busy in the workshops. Hilde says you need some more soap."

"And ointment – I've used it all and I wouldn't want your swine to suffer for lack of it," said Ædwine.

"Our swine are too intelligent to get kicked by a mare," she teased.

Pip and Win rose to leave for the woods. There was much laughter as the three men made their way through the orchard to the sunken lane.

Fred did not rise until midday which gave Lee the opportunity to look at the documents she had found in the chapel as she had fumbled her way to the locked door. Lee hoped they would give some insight into Alcuin's business. However, they were meaningless: nothing more than lists of names and trees.

Later Fred and Lee, like released birds, flittered about the orchard looking for fallen apples to coax the new mares to trust them. Lee climbed a tree to check the leather bundle which contained the silver buckles, coins and some of her rock collection. It was still there. From her high perch, she looked south-west along the sunken lane to the end of the Long Mead and then to the north right up to the Hellesden.

"Is the seaxe hidden in a hollow too?" Fred asked. He climbed up to the branch where she sat and began to prod a stick into the pruning scars.

"What seaxe?" Lee dropped a key amongst the buckles.

"What was that?" Fred asked.

"A key I found. It may be useful."

"Have you found some treasure."

"Not yet. Remember our treasure is Gisla. A wolf thought she was in the Hellesden, but she is not. But he knows where she is."

Fred was not sure he understood what she meant.

"Are there wolves in Hellesden?" He asked.

"Only when it's a bitterly cold winter."

"Where do the Hellesden wolves come from?"

"The great forests in Mercia and Essex," Lee explained. "And our sea-wolves come from the north and east or maybe Francia."

"Will you tell Pip who Ædwine is? I didn't like it yesterday when I overheard him talking with the other men. I am sure he tells all sorts of lies - and he likes taverns."

"We must not tell Pip until we have found Gisla."

"Why?"

"Because if Ædwine leaves we will have no guard."

"I could sit up here and keep watch," Fred suggested.

"It's too cold."

"But we could build a watch tower with wattle walls."

"What a good idea Fred!" Lee exclaimed. "I know the Chief Thegn will be back - though I do not want to meet him ever again. If his thegns see a watch tower, they might not be so eager to creep up on us."

The yard was searched for suitable building materials, and they soon made a start on their project. Poles were passed up the tree and tied together with cord. It was almost dark when they had put some corner posts and uprights in place. Lee suggested Fred could bring home some birch tops from the coppice and she could weave them between the uprights.

"I can hear voices Lee," Fred whispered. The sun had sunk below the horizon, and they could not see far. The two huddled on the platform hoping to remain unseen. Pip and Win appeared over the bank.

"Come down you two. Fred, if you've got enough energy to pile sticks in a tree where they will blow away in the first breeze, then you should have been with us doing useful work. Lee, have you finished the soap?"

"Sorry Pip." Fred stood up. "We forgot. We've been busy hiding."

"Hiding? We saw you from the woodland edge. It's not very well hidden for a hiding place," observed Win.

"O this? This isn't a refuge, it's a look-out tower," Fred corrected.

"You come down too, Lee. You are too old to be playing all

day. I'm younger and must work," Win complained.

"We are not playing. This is where the Chief Thegn caught us. From up here you can see the lane to the Rookery – it's the way he came." Fred was quite indignant his effort to protect his sworn friend was not taken seriously.

"And what if he appears from behind the holly hedge there?" Pip pointed to the dense blackness a short distance away. Fred was speechless and slowly climbed down to join the two brothers.

"Come on Lee! I know you are up there. You need to think like the enemy. Admit your plan is flawed," Win continued as he stared up towards the platform. Lee stood up and made her way to the branch below, from where she leapt down upon him. Win was knocked flat amongst the tussock grass and saw her knife at his chest.

"Who's flawed now?" She asked. He groaned and rolled himself away. Fred looked amazed and admired her even more as Win was a large youth. Then Ædwine stepped out from the shadows of the holly hedge and deliberately frightened him. The point was proved. They did have a weak line of sight if the Thegn approached from the east.

Lee served supper and settled down to eat at the far side of the hearth. To her surprise Ædwine joined them.

"Ærn meets Lynx? Almost as good as the *Swan Princess*," he said half smiling and serious at the same time.

"Why are you here tonight?"

"I wanted to see you."

Their intimacy did not go unnoticed, and Pip decided to keep watch over his coppice worker.

"You must tell me again what news you have received for I believe Gragus is already on his way here."

"Is he?" Lee asked.

"And not because of the seaxe. He loves you."

Pip saw his sister blush.

"Will you work tomorrow?" Pip asked. Fred looked up wondering why Pip had spoken so loudly. His plate was then snatched away, and Pip made his way to where Lee and Ædwine were huddled together.

"Lee says I have to drag the birch tops home for her tower." Fred replied.

"Do you mean to waste more time on that?" Pip criticized as he leaned ever closer to his sister. "You could be fixing the geese fences."

"I will secure the pen," Ædwine offered. "And I can help with the tower."

"She doesn't need a look out. The Chief Thegn is far away and I'm sure he has better things to do."

"You don't know what he's like," Lee objected.

"He admitted he was wrong. And our Blackheath Thegn has commended him for his repentance."

"Yes, but…"

"But what?"

Lee could not answer. She would seek an opportunity to speak with her kin at Riscmere Hall herself for Pip would fret if he learned about the marriage conspiracy.

"A look-out would be useful," Lee protested. She thought it would be useful to see all the way to Riscmere Hall. "Ædwine doesn't mind helping us."

"He has work to do at Linden Pits. You must finish it yourself."

"And I will." Lee declared. "It was so good to be working under the heavens today."

"Were you confined at Bures?" Ædwine asked.

Lee was annoyed by his untimely question and lied.

"No. It was pleasant enough there."

"Until Uncle Greg came to church," interrupted Fred. "And

we had to face the enemy."

Lee stared at Fred as fiercely as she could, but he had already said too much. Ædwine, who knew the Chief Thegn's name, was troubled.

"If the man has molested you, I will kill him."

Lee trembled as she thought Ædwine had betrayed himself. Indeed, Pip was alarmed.

"Are you talking about Greg our Chief Thegn?"

"How did you know his name, brother, and I did not?" Lee rebounded. "Such knowledge would have saved us a great deal of trouble."

"Have you upset him again?"

"No. But I know he remains humiliated over Dummoc. He holds to his revenge - one way or the other."

"Revenge!" Pip cried. "Does he mean to harm you?"

"Much worse. He has paid money to mother's kin at Riscmere for my hand in marriage. I will not be safe from him unless I find Gisla."

"He has not spoken to me about this," Pip wailed. "He ought to have discussed the matter with me."

"He has no regard for you. I was sent here to keep watch over her."

"Who sent you here Ædwine?" Pip demanded.

"Will, one of the traders at Dummoc."

Fred was ordered to leave.

"Do you know this man?" Pip demanded.

Lee refused to answer.

"I think you ought to tell your brother the truth," Ædwine urged. "If you will not, then I will."

"I thought you were a genuine coppice worker," Pip muttered.

"I was with your sister at Dummoc."

"Is that why you left Bures? Did you know he was here?" Pip

pressed.

"No, I did not! I have never asked for anyone to protect me. Not Os, nor Ædwine. What good has it done? While I was *safe* at Bures the repentant Chief Thegn of yours has pressed so far forwards in this battle I might as well surrender. I will be his wife before Holy Mass."

"Lee, may I say something?" Fred asked. The lad had crept back to listen to the discussion.

"Is it sensible?"

"Yes. The Chief Thegn saw the betrothal letters."

Fred had been impressed by the action Os had taken even if Lee had made a mess of things.

"What letters?" Pip asked.

Ædwine wanted to know more but remained silent. Lee did not answer. Ædwine looked at her as if to urge her to tell the truth. But the truth was too complicated, and Lee felt threatened. The conversation had gone badly from the start. Ædwine ought not to have interfered. She began to resent his presence in her own hall.

"Letters which confirm I am officially betrothed to my Will."

"Him!" Ædwine exclaimed.

"Yes. We believe in forgiveness, not revenge. He's a scholar; a man of peace – unlike you."

She stood up and left the room. She had not liked the way Ædwine had out manoeuvred her. Fred called after her and then followed. Lee was in no mood to discuss the matter and ordered him to go to his mattress.

It was as if Ædwine had been unexpectedly cast into a raging sea. He had been delighted to meet her again but her sudden revelation about a betrothal had thrown him overboard. Pip was also in great turmoil and turned on his coppice worker.

"My sister has made her choice, and it was not you."

"She is not a prize I desire. My motive was to protect her."

"By deceit?"

"Do you want me to leave?"

"Yes," Pip mumbled. "You cannot be trusted."

Ædwine hastened back to Linden Pits where he threw himself down to sleep. His leg ached and his mind was in confusion. He had already sent encouraging words to Gragus about the maiden who now revealed she was betrothed - and officially so. He had been certain the maiden from the Hellesden was smitten by his friend but now she revealed she was betrothed to a cold-hearted cleric.

And he had not tried to seduce her. He had gone to her because he hoped for warmth and laughter but both brother and sister had been as angry as hornets. He would leave at once to warn Gragus.

Like Ædwine, Pip barely slept. He could not afford to lose the best of his workers. He would have to reason with him and keep him away from Lee. Pip rose early to speak to Ædwine out in the mead.

"Where's the young man?" Hilde enquired as she served at the table.

"Ask Lee." Pip's angry reply caused Win to look up.

"Did I miss something? Isn't he with those wild beasts of hers?"

"No. He didn't turn up."

"Has she offended him so soon?" Win gasped.

"Yes."

"I knew he had come back here just to see her. And you thought he wanted to discuss the making of spears!"

"You were right. They had much to catch up on."

"Are you saying she knows him?"

"Yes."

"Don't worry brother, I'll warn him about her when I get to the coppice."

Pip did not smile.

"Did you know our Lee was betrothed to Will?"

"Betrothed? I don't believe it."

"You said she pined for him - though I had not noticed."

"I may have been wrong. I understood Will was offended by her actions at Dummoc and vowed never to see her again. He's at Medeshamstede now, isn't he?"

"I don't know. What can I do?" Pip asked.

"Let the Thegn and Will sort it out for she cannot marry both of them!" Win declared. "It's a pity she did not stay longer at Bures ... " Win stopped midway because Fred and Lee appeared.

"You are late, lad," Pip complained. "Eat your breakfast and come directly to the alders. I have no time to wait. Lee, today you help Hilde."

Later, Lee implored Hilde to let her walk with Fred as far as Black Poplar Mead for she planned to send him to ask Ædwine to meet her there. After a restless night of deliberation Lee thought it would be wise if he knew the true nature of her attachment to Will.

"Lee, are you still here?" Fred called when he returned.

"Yes, up here. Did you tell him?"

"He's not there. They said he left at sunrise."

"Where has he gone?"

"They don't know." Lee jumped down from the tree. There were tears of frustration in her eyes. "I think you've muddled everything up again Lee. Pip is bad-tempered about it, and I must go back before he notices I am not there. He said I shall go back to Spring Farm if I cannot keep up today."

"I'm so sorry Fred. I'll come back later to help you, but I must go and sort out the new mares as Pip didn't prepare their roots."

"And you must put up the goose fences," reminded Fred. "Do you think Ædwine has gone to find Gragus and Frith?"

"Yes. And I am left to find Gisla without their help."

Lee watched him bound towards the coppice and wearily made her way back to help Hilde. Her thoughts turned to the Chief Thegn. Perhaps her brothers would be pleased if he jumped from behind the high holly and carried her away. She paused to look at the platform in the apple tree. It was a folly. A half-built tower!

As she passed through the orchard gate a hand went over her mouth.

"Where's the seaxe?" The man demanded.

This time Lee reacted more quickly. She kicked out and caught him on his shin. He cried out in agony and let go.

"I am not betrothed to Will. Os forged some papers so we would have time to contact my brothers in Wessex. They will not be pleased when they hear what the Thegn has done. But Os did not realize how soon the Thegn intends to marry me. Before Holy Mass." Lee cried out and lent against the gate. "I have upset my brother - I am more burdensome than eight sons," she said thinking of the turmoil Eth's mother endured. "Perhaps I should marry the Thegn so Pip can live in peace."

"You must not marry him. I will not let you."

"And who are you to tell me what I must do? I don't know you or anything about you except you like fighting and the women at Wolven Pit."

"I have never been to Wolven Pit Lee. The men like to chat about pretty maidens. And I have wrestled a few men by agreement – it is a sign of brotherhood, and they like to cast lots to win silver. I have oft wrestled Gragus to the dust. I am his friend, from childhood," Ædwine said. "I know he cares for you. And I have already sent word to him to say you care for him. I think you do."

"I care about Aunt Gisla," Lee protested. "I want her to be free and I want Edmund to come back to his home and see she is well and safe."

"And I want Gragus to be happy. He does care for you. We are tired and weary with losing people we love. You know we are oarsmen - and we thought Frith would die in Francia."

"Was he badly injured then?"

"Yes."

"And the terrible Dark Thegn hit him!"

"Gragus was concerned about his pain, but they looked after him at Dummoc and it's over a year now since his battle wound healed."

"I thought you heathen oarsmen welcomed death on the battlefield?"

"Not yet perhaps."

"Are you here to spy out our ways? Will you bring harm to us?"

"Three will make no difference when the three thousand arrive."

"Three thousand?" She looked at him in disbelief.

"Don't be afraid. There is no certainty in what I have heard. But they have stolen too much and laid waste to the farmlands of northern Francia so there is a famine there. Wise raiders are like children who learn to leave one egg in the nest of a mire hen, for it will come back to lay more. If you take them all at once it will abandon the nest and build one which is more hidden. In Francia they have left their fields and have found places further inland. What will so many raiders do? Where will they go next? Your Edmund must watch his borders. There are wilder raiders than you yet realise, and I hope you never meet them. You will be safe with Gragus. He needs a wife to comfort him - for our Weland is dead." His voice had fallen to a whisper, and he hesitated.

"Who was Weland? I thought he was one of our old gods."

"He was our captain. We served with him a long time, almost ten years. He died several moons ago."

"Did he die in the battle - when Frith was wounded?"

"Gragus will tell you if you ask him. I will say no more. I miss Weland. He would have loved this kingdom; he wanted to settle down amongst you."

"Is that what you want to do? Settle amongst us?"

"Frith does. He says I should too, but I am not the settling kind."

"Do you mean to leave the coppice team then?"

"I have offended your brother. He does not trust me - with you."

"Then tell him you see me as no more than your own sister, and you are here because of Gisla's imprisonment. He will understand. Pip is a lovely person. Don't say anything to Win though."

"Not so lovely?"

"He only considers himself."

"He is young. Treat him kindly and he will love you for it."

"I promised him a wonderful feast at St Clements Day for his friends. I must help Hilde with the preparations – to make it special. Will you join us? It's like the old Weland Day – St Clement is our saint of blacksmiths. Was your Weland a blacksmith?"

"Yes, he was. He taught me all I know."

"Are you really a blacksmith then?"

"You will have to ask Gragus," he teased.

"I do not expect to see him again. You must tell him I am not betrothed - though he will not be pleased either way. He fears deception I think."

"How well you see. He was betrayed by a woman's wicked deception, and he finds it hard to forget."

"Did he think I would betray him?"

"Yes. When I was there within the walls of Dummoc I could not rest either. I sensed betrayal was at hand. I hoped you would not turn; that I had judged you aright, but I had visions of black swans up in the rafters waiting to swoop down and peck at me until I struggled no more."

"Black swans? I overheard Wolf speak about a Black Swan. She was the mistress of the Dark Thegn. It was he who injured Frith. Some say he killed her and then himself, but Wolf did not think so."

"No?" Ædwine murmured.

"No, he thought the Chief Thegn had ordered his death as revenge for his beating. Do you think he did?" She paused but Ædwine made no confession. "I will return your money which fell amongst the chaff, but the buckles belong to Edmund although I did give them to Gragus. I suppose you can keep them as loot."

"I understand you collect seaxes as loot." She did not know if he had said it as a jest or not. Both knew they were talking at a deeper level, but neither would give way for Lee reasoned the Chief Thegn had kept the coins and buckles and Ædwine had taken them from him.

"Was it you who beat the Thegn so cruelly?" Ædwine knew his deeds were exposed. It was his habit to lie but he could not, so he nodded. "And his dog?" She asked in revulsion.

"You are so direct my fair maiden. What can I say?" He paused and acknowledged his deeds. "It is what I do when I face conflict."

He felt ashamed of his violent ways - and it was a long time since he had shown remorse about anything.

"He did not describe a fair fight," she pressed.

"He spoke to you about it?"

"He made his way here and collapsed at my feet. Pip had to take him to his hall. He was in terrible pain."

"Will you tell your brother I was the one who caused it?"

"No. I have already willed myself not to. Some things cannot be spoken of. I already knew in my heart it was you. I saw your seaxe the day you dropped the coins. It is very much like one of those I have in my collection." He saw she smiled faintly as she spoke. There was no malice or revenge in her eyes. She looked solemn like a mother chiding a wayward child. "I understood why the Thegn thought they were one and the same. As you know from the trial, Fred described it perfectly."

"And you discredited the evidence with such wit and cunning he forgot runes do not lie. I helped forge the seaxe; I know what is written upon it."

"What do you mean? What was written on it?"

"His name – Gragus - Grey Goose. The runes said 'Goose'."

"I did not know that."

Ædwine looked at her and understood she had not played a sophisticated game with the Thegn at the trial. Fate alone had demolished the only reliable evidence he had.

"Do you have the seaxe? Gragus sent me here to find it."

"You said he sent you to watch over me."

"I understood what he did not say."

"Has he ever said he cares for me?"

"I know his heart and what is precious to him."

"The seaxe? Then Alcuin knows him well. He said the seaxe was precious. Should I fetch it now before you leave?"

"Do you have it here? I looked in the tree but only found a key, my coins, buckles and a few smooth rocks. I had thought to look below the waters. but this place has so many ponds."

"Why?"

"Because in your tale the sword was lain in water. It was a very northern saga – with wolves and slumbering ships."

"Alcuin said he feared you northern wolves."

"Did he say more? "

"He said Gragus would have to pit his wits against him, in the open - he was playing a game of words with his slaver friend, Wolf, who immediately guessed where Gisla was hidden. I did not understand any of it - I need to find out what Alcuin likes to hunt and where a shed is in the bishop's garden."

"I can ask around. One of the coppice team might know."

"No, it's too dangerous to ask strangers."

"You do not see me as a 'stranger' then? If I stay, can I sit by the hearth with you again?"

"Not if Pip forbids it."

Fred could hardly believe his eyes when he saw Ædwine talking to Pip. He was overjoyed and asked if Lee knew he had returned.

"Yes, she knows. I will watch over her for a while longer."

"Thank you. You have saved my life," the lad declared.

CHAPTER EIGHT
WAYLAND DAY

"I've brought the birch tops," Fred announced as he returned from work. "Pip says we can finish the tower. Ædwine is going to do the roof."

"We must wait until I have time, Fred. I have too much to do for the feast next Thursday. Did you see the new goose run?"

"Yes, Pip and Ædwine are hammering the posts in a bit further."

Fred helped himself to one of the cakes Lee had made.

"Has Ædwine come back here then?"

"Yes, Pip says he is to stay here with us."

Lee was not sure if she wanted Ædwine to be so near, but she would be bold and ask him to go to church. He would see for himself what a fine community they were – one not to be feared. However, when she did invite him to accompany her to mass, he was more hostile than she had reckoned.

Os arrived unexpectedly on Sunday. He wanted to be assured Lee had settled back into everyday life. Pip did not mention Ædwine and was glad he had refused to go to church with Lee. The oarsman very wisely returned to Linden Pits. Os decided to stay to help with the preparations for the feast and, very conveniently, Lee was too busy to find time to converse with him.

When the feast gathered pace, Lee remained in the kitchen

hall organizing the host of servants and helpers. A great number of guests pressed into the main hall where the music and revelry grew louder as the daylight faded.

Lee went to pen in the geese, and on her return, she saw the Chief Thegn approach the hall. He did not go in but lingered in the temporary stable area. Lee sank back into the shadows and made her way to the orchard and climbed the apple tree. To her surprise, the sides of the look-out tower had been completed and she stayed there until the Thegn had gone.

He entered the hall peaceably enough. However, when the wretched man reached Os, he began to make his complaint. He would not let poor Os go, and Pip whispered to Ædwine.

"See how he holds his prey? His hound was the same until some brute slaughtered it. Go and see what he wants. I'll find Lee."

Reluctant as he was, Ædwine made his way towards the Thegn. He overheard him accuse Os of neglect of duty and being ill-advised.

"Who counselled you in this? I insist I see her letter from Will. I could not find her. Is she not here?" The Chief Thegn was determined to prove his case.

"I advise you to keep calm my friend and reflect upon your reckless behaviour at the harvest celebrations. It was not long ago, and people do not forget."

"I must ask her if the letters are false. This is not written by his hand." He once more shook the letter. "Where is she?"

"Lee is not here," Ædwine intervened.

"Not here?"

Ædwine lied for he knew where Lee had hidden herself.

"She was called away by Æthel's friend. The baby is sick. She has taken some of her sweet water."

"Whose baby?"

"The one at Hollins Hall. It's not yet a week old and has a

196

fever."

From the moment he had arrived, the Chief Thegn's attitude had irritated Ædwine. The oarsman was determined to silence him.

"Is the letter addressed to Lee? I will pass it too her when she returns."

"That is my letter." Os interrupted. "And you had no right to enter my private rooms to get it!"

"I did not overstep any boundaries," the Chief Thegn objected. "Your sister was very obliging."

The oarsman began his stirring.

"Wonderfully convenient when this busy ætheling is absent."

"And what do you imply?"

"I imply nothing. I state directly you are a man who worms his way into households to take advantage of young maidens."

"How dare you! I have done what is right."

"Then continue in your good ways and return the ætheling's letter at once. The Blackheath Thegn is nigh and will arrest you before you have effrontery to spoil this feast. Do you want to repeat your folly?"

The Chief Thegn hesitated. The man before him spoke with authority and he wondered if he was one of Edmund's men, so he calmed himself.

"I know it's a forgery. It's not the same hand as this."

The thegn took out another letter which he waved around.

"How old is your note?" Ædwine asked.

"It was written four summers past."

"When Will was but nineteen? Hasn't he practiced copying since? I believe he learns the scripts and characters of those at Medeshamstede?"

Os was impressed by Ædwine's familiarly with the subject. He had been introduced as a coppice worker but there was more to him than he realised. His accent varied but Os reckoned he came from the coastlands near the Yare estuary - though he was not fair like the traders he had met there. His hair was raven black – and wavy.

The Chief Thegn considered what had been said and retreated. Ædwine followed and when the Thegn had passed the outer gates the oarsman called Lee down from the tower.

She did not like Ædwine's prying ways and joined Hilde in the kitchen.

"Did you miss the Thegn?"

"Oh, I saw him well enough Hilde. What did he want?"

"You will have to ask Os. He is looking for you. Here he is."

Os entered the smaller hall and embraced his friend.

"You are cold. Where have you been?"

"Avoiding a terrible man."

"Which one? They are both as dark as each other."

"Whatever do you mean?" Lee asked.

"The man from the coppice team. Does Pip know he can read?"

"What did the Thegn want?" She asked trying to avoid the question.

"Evidence."

They both laughed.

Ædwine stood outside the kitchen hall and observed how at ease the two were. He felt jealous for Gragus and intervened.

"Win is asking for you, Lee." Ædwine lied.

Lee crossed the courtyard with him leaving Os to watch from a distance. He did not like the man.

"Lee, sit with me by the hearth." Os had caught up with her and she knew his request was an order, so she left Ædwine and followed him. "You avoided my question. Is he a learned man?"

"I do not care to know."

"Don't be evasive. He lied without conscience to the

Thegn."

"Did he? Are you sure?"

"He said you had gone to the Hollins. He appears to know about the letters, too. Could it be that you have revealed more to a stranger than to me, your companion from youth?"

"I have told him what he needs to know – my betrothal is a deception."

"You have been unwise."

"Are you displeased with me again?"

"No, of course not." He took her hand. "But neither am I pleased."

"I have told you I will reveal all to Edmund."

"But I am worried. He's not a boy like Fred, nor a kinsman, nor a long-known friend. He's a man you hardly know, and a crafty one. He brazenly bares his gods around his neck. He's a pagan Dane! You cannot stay here. I insist you return to Bures."

"Because of a necklace? They let Christians amongst their kin wear crosses. What has Pip said?"

"Not much. He mumbled something about Dummoc."

"It was he who told me the trader Will was at Dummoc. I passed the information to Eth." Lee felt the admission might end his questions. She was wrong.

"Is he acquainted with Will and Ralph?"

"Yes."

"Do they know he is here?"

"Yes. They asked him to wait here while they seek Gisla."

"Why?"

"Because…." Lee's voice faded as she saw Ædwine rise from the bench where he sat across the hall. Os was very aware he was being watched and was pleased he irritated the oarsman.

"See how he acts like a jealous lover."

"He watches over me because he fears no one else will."

Lee turned and looked at Ædwine and beckoned him to join

them.

"This is Os. I know you have already met," she said.

Ædwine sat down beside her.

"I understand Will and Ralph are your comrades."

"Yes, they are."

"How long have you known them?"

"Long enough."

"What sort of answer is that? You need to convince me you are not here to take advantage of this honest maiden."

"I am here because Ralph is concerned about Lee's safety. When Gisla is released, I will leave."

"You show remarkable loyalty to your companions."

"The maiden saved Ralph from hanging - and he is my brother."

His sudden revelation startled Lee. She understood at last why Ædwine had looked so familiar when they first met in the stable shelter. Then she wondered why he had not told her they were brothers.

"It explains your dedication," Os began. "The Blackheath Thegn was very impressed by Ralph's patient attitude and gentle manners. I understand he's interested in finding a hall here."

"Yes, he feels at ease amongst you."

"And Will? Have you known him a long time?"

"Yes."

"Does he have a wife?" Os asked.

Lee grew uneasy with the manner of his questioning.

"No."

"And has he ever had a wife?"

"No."

Ædwine saw Lee was unsettled and Os observed how well they read each other. He was shaken by the way the oarsman held sway over his spirited maiden.

"Do you have a wife?"

Ædwine faltered. He knew he must not lie - though he wanted to.

"Yes, I do," he murmured for the truth was bitter and he reeled because of it.

Lee was furious but Os had no intention of stopping.

"Doesn't your wife miss you?"

Ædwine shook his head and left before his interrogator could goad him further.

"You had no right to put him on trial. I am ashamed of you."

"You needed to know, didn't you? He's a married man Lee. Keep away from him."

Lee busied herself talking to Win's companions and Ædwine watched her from the far corner of the hall. He was pleased she had disagreed with Os because he did not want her to return to Bures.

Several of Win's friends were keen huntsmen and Lee sat listening to their tales until Pip urged her to help Hilde. When she returned the hunting-party had dispersed except for one very shy lad who now took courage to speak to her. She discovered he knew all the packs of hounds in the kingdom. He knew what they hunted and who kept them.

Alcuin hunted with a young man known as the Hethel Ceorl whose pack of hounds hunted tarda geese. Lee soon learned all about the large birds which roamed the quieter heathlands; how they would run rather than take flight and how they could change colour. She laughed aloud at his description of how it was done. Ædwine smiled but Os wondered why Lee was so merry and went to her side. The young man grew timid again and left to refill his cup.

"You were very ill-mannered earlier," she reminded Os as he sat down. "Ædwine will not think much of our ways if you humiliate him."

"If you love a man Lee, you need to know if he has a wife or not. Do you want to bring disgrace to your kin?"

"I love no man in the way you imply."

"But you did not know he has a wife, did you?"

"No, I didn't," she admitted. "But Ædwine is like a brother."

"I fear you do not know the true nature of these men."

"What do you mean?"

"You know very well they are more than traders of cheese." Lee felt her face grow hot. "I would like to know how Gisla became acquainted with them. Do you know? She has much to answer for. If she is released, I will be the first to rebuke her for leading you astray."

"Do you think I am on the wrong path then?"

"You should have refrained from embracing the trader at Dummoc."

"He embraced me."

"And has he embraced you," he asked as he met Ædwine's stare.

"No."

Since Dummoc their talks always ended in discord and Lee was distressed. She did not want to offend Os.

"What do you want me to do?" She asked. Tears began to fall.

"Go and rest now and think about what I have said. I do not want these men to bring you harm."

Lee left the feast and rested but early the next morning she went out to meet Ædwine at the stables. She knew he would be there though most of the guests who stayed late into the night were not yet awake.

"Os is not unkind or ill-mannered," she whispered and Ædwine looked up. "He watches over me just as you do."

"He made you cry. Have I made you cry?"

"Not yet. Why didn't you tell me Frith was your brother or you had a wife?"

"Frith and I have the same father but were born to different mothers. And my wife is dead."

"Dead? I do not believe you." He looked down and said nothing. "How long have you been married?"

"Long enough. And I'm not looking for another wife. What did he say to make you cry?"

"He rebuked me for allowing Gragus to embrace me at Dummoc. I wish I had been born a boy – they often embrace in friendship, and I could be with Edmund my king and ride and hunt and be free - and go off on adventures. If I were a boy, I would have found Gisla by now."

"If you were a boy, who would I have to gaze upon over breakfast?"

"Hilde?" She said at once.

He laughed and threw the remains of the chaff over her. She did the same and they laughed as they battled.

"I will be careful Lee. You are my fair sister."

"Another brace of brothers will not trouble me," she smiled. "Unless you demand I arrange a feast for you as well."

He looked at her. It had been a long time since he had trusted anyone outside his group of close friends. He had trained himself to be cautious and she now knew more about his past than he wanted her to know.

"It was not a brotherly embrace at Dummoc," he reminded her for he had witnessed it. "Do you love Gragus? Tell me what happened when you met him in the Hellesden."

"Did he not tell you?"

"I would like to hear your version of the story – the truth."

Lee described all that happened, and he realized how innocent she was with regards to their activities in Edmund's kingdom.

"I did not know what Gragus thought." Lee concluded.

"Until Dummoc."

"I can only think he was so overjoyed with being set free he would have kissed Hilde had she been the Swan Princess."

They were still laughing when Pip came to find them.

"Ædwine! Go and fetch your axe. We must make a start, or we will never finish the fell before the week is out. And Lee, Os is waiting to leave. He has been patient with you – though you deserve a thorough rebuke – so I'll have my say in this matter. Ædwine has made work in the Hellesden easier this season and I am not going to criticize him, but you must ensure you are not alone in his company."

"He is not dangerous."

"Unless you promise not to go off with him, I will send him away, or you can go back to Bures."

"Very well, I will go and pack my bag!".

Os was waiting for Lee at the place they had parted company the previous evening. The hall was empty, and they sat in silence.

"I shall have to find a Danish wife," he unexpectedly said. "They must have a surplus of women since all their men are away seeking our maidens."

"Don't be hasty Os."

"I hope you listen to your own advice and reflect upon your behaviour. It is your duty to pray for wisdom. Did you pray when you gave the puppy to the Thegn? Didn't you consider his heart might turn towards you?"

"No, I did not. Why should it?"

"Now I have him prowling around waiting to discredit me because of my letter."

"If he opposes you Os, he will have Edmund to reckon with. Do you know why he has been delayed?"

"His task has not been easy, nor has mine. Please do not oppose my advice; every day you must ask the Lord how to be his humble servant fashioned in his image. Don't demand your own way in matters of the heart. Is this man, Will, honest and noble? If not, then have nothing to do with him."

"I will not seek to meet Will again even if Ædwine may urge me to do so. I will not go to him or leave our Edmund. I promise Os. I do not know where my path will lead. I will keep to the narrow way. I want to find Gisla."

"Did you know your hair if full of chaff?"

"Is it?"

Lee kissed Os and he left for Ældor Hall to meet the Blackheath Thegn and she went to help Hilde. Several of Win's friends were already under the old lady's command. Lee helped the very shy lad pack the baskets of food for the poorer in the community. He continued his tarda tales, beginning with those he had learned from his grandmother. One of his recollections related to his grandmother's companion from youth. Lee discovered the same lady was alive and living on Boten Heath.

"I do not recall ever seeing a hall on the heath."

"It's not very grand, but it is most unusual; it's what is known as a lodge. It's built with flints and bricks."

"Like Dummoc?" Lee sounded anxious.

"I have never seen the old fort, but I understand it's wondrous to look at. It is said they used to hunt for eggs on the cliffs, but I don't believe them for those cliffs crumble at every foothold."

"It is a fearful place where the sea claws at the cliffs and mists swirl until you feel giddy. The house on Boten Heath, is it guarded like Dummoc?"

"No. Why would an old lady want to keep anyone away? My grandmother used to visit her and take all kinds of provisions. I went with her when I was a lad."

"When did you last visit the place?"

"About four winters past. Just before grandmother died. It's fallen down a good deal since then. The place is crumbling away like your cliffs."

Lee's heart missed a beat.

"Perhaps that is why I have never seen it."

"It cannot be seen from any of the highways which cross the heath. It's in one of those hidden dips. Even when the birches drop their leaves you can't see it because of the rise and the roof turves though you might see the smoke drifting through the tufts of grass."

"Really? Could you tell me how to find it?"

"Before you go out onto the common you must follow a narrow track along its western edge. You will come to a birch coppice which has a double bank. Follow it until you find a miry valley and head west. When you find the spring go up and through a pasture where there are ant hillocks. From the top of the rise, you will see the dwelling nestled closely to a bank. Don't go straight down to it though. You must walk around the rise to the south and when it begins to sink into the furze you will see a track."

"I will take her some provisions. I'll take Æthel and Eth with me. We could visit her on Friday. Should I send a message from you?"

"Just say the swine are all well and I will send one of the fattened geese at Christmas. I must be on my way to the Riscmere. We are threshing wheat today while the breeze is brisk."

Lee thanked him for telling her his tales and went with him to the outer gates where she met Æthelric, who was preparing his horses for his return journey. It was not long before she discovered they were going to visit the kilns to the north to purchase some pots. Lee pleaded with him to take her as well for she wanted to buy Hilde some new storage jars; and he did not hesitate in offering her a place in the party for two of his sisters travelled with them. Win agreed she could go.

The sun was almost at full height when Win arrived at his place of work, and he was greeted with loud cheers and whistles. The pony pulling the logs along the ride was startled. Fred struggled to keep hold of its reins so Ædwine quickly dashed over to help guide he pony to the log pile. While he waited Fred climbed up onto the stacked logs to see if Lee was at work on the look-out tower.

"You'll break your neck," warned Ædwine.

"It's the Chief Thegn's horse!" Fred cried.

Ædwine jumped to his feet and joined Fred on the log pile. He caught a glimpse of the horse and rider as it descended into the lane.

"The crafty sorcerer," he whispered. He called out to Pip. "The Chief Thegn is riding down the path. Make haste. He may take your sister."

Pip dropped his saw and started off at once but was intercepted by Win. Ædwine ran to where they stood.

"Don't delay me," Ædwine said. "She's not safe."

"Lee's not at home." Win said very calmly. "She's gone to purchase some pots with Æthelric."

"When did she leave?" Ædwine demanded.

"Mid-morning. She will be leagues away by now. Æthelric has the fastest horses around these parts."

"Is she going back to Bures with the Ætheling?"

"No, they've gone to the kilns. Don't be concerned. They will return her tomorrow, with the pots, unless she breaks them - which is very likely."

"Where are the kilns? Which direction?" Ædwine anxiously asked.

"Wood Street," interrupted Pip. "They will cross the west-east highway at Wolven Pit and continue north. The kilns are along the west ridge near Wood Street. I am sure they will not lose her."

"But she intends to lose them. I fear she has gone to find Gisla."

"Gisla?"

"Yes. Lee thinks Gisla is being held captive near Wolven Pit. Does your Bishop have a hall in Wood Street?"

"What is this to do with bishops?" Pip asked.

"I made careful inquiries about your Bishop who resides at Dummoc. He buys slave girls," Ædwine said bluntly. "He has a new hall near Wolven Pit for entertaining his hunting guests, but I have not been able to locate it."

"Who did she speak to Win?" Pip asked.

Win's face had reddened. He looked guilty and confessed all.

"He was telling her his old hunting tales. You must have seen her talking with him last night."

"She said nothing to me this morning before I left," pondered Ædwine.

"I saw her with him again today; not long before she left," Win revealed. "And I have weighed the same rumours as you. The bishop's new hall is near Edmund's North Wood."

"When did she make the arrangements to travel?" Ædwine asked.

"Just as they were leaving," admitted Win.

"I fear she rides headlong into danger," he warned.

"What danger? The Chief Thegn is at the hall and doesn't know where she has gone," Win protested.

"If she has gone to the place where Gisla is imprisoned, she may be captured by Alcuin's men."

"Alcuin?" Whispered Pip. "Os warned me he was involved. He's a dangerous man. Where is the lad? We must find out what was discussed."

"He is working in the threshing barn at the Riscmere all day," said Win.

"It's not far." Pip said.

Ædwine followed the young brothers through the Black Poplar Mead onto the highway which wound its way towards Riscmere Hall. Several horses grazed in the mead near the oak grove. Pip fetched the bridles from the barn and three horses were prepared for the journey. Win, meanwhile, found his friend at work. He told him about the old hall on Boten Heath.

Pip rode west to alert the Blackheath Thegn and Ædwine rode east with Win as fast as they could towards the main highway which they crossed west of Sedge Green at the place where a large stone marked the meeting of three ancient boundaries. From there they could see the church at Wolven Pit. Between the stone and the church lay a wild area of ancient earthworks, known as the Green Ditches. Most feared to walk that way where sounds were deadened and the earth beneath sounded hollow as if gloomy caverns lay below.

They rode on through an area of small fields and homesteads until the hedges gave way to open heathland. Another huge stone marked the most southerly end of the heath where the furze and brambles thrust into the patchwork of fields with their high banks and pollards. Win kept to the western edge and with great difficulty found the narrow, overgrown track which cut through the perimeter bank. He followed it until they reached the birch wood but could not find any path back onto Boten Heath. They had almost given up hope of finding the place when Ædwine came across the double ditch. The birch had invaded the heathland which lay to the east and obscured its boundaries. They dismounted and led their horses through the overgrown area between the ditches. It was not long before Ædwine found Lee's tracks.

He traced Lee's progress through the miry shallow valley but as it rose towards a low ridge, he lost the way for the ground was very dry and the rushes were now replaced with fine tussock grass. They approached a clearing and decided to tether the horses there, for beyond the hollow was dense bramble thickets interlaced with bracken. They made haste because the light was fading. Win tripped several times.

"Ants," he said in disgust.

They fought their way through the undergrowth as quietly as they could. The dense bracken deadened the details of sound so all they could hear was the delicate murmurs of the wind blowing through the birches and the rustle of furze thorns as they brushed over their clothes. It was Win who smelled smoke, but he could not see where it came from. Ædwine looked up and saw a thin plume against the face of the moon. He traced its source and was first to see the low squat building pressed into the sides of the horseshoe shaped hollow below. He had seen similar buildings in the northern isles but said nothing. They continued west and crawled to the rim of the dell and at once heard voices. The old lady was not alone. Ædwine reckoned there were more than ten men present and backed away.

"I will find a way down," he whispered. Further along the rim he abruptly stopped. "What was that?"

"I heard nothing."

"There she is. Down there, about to break cover. She hasn't seen the guard. Stay here Win. Wait for dawn's light and flee if I do not return."

Win crouched low, sifting the sounds of the night. His sister was stealthily intercepted – though he neither saw nor heard anything. The man was swift and silent, and she had been unable to call out. Not long after, Win caught the muffled sound of horses approaching and watched as they crossed the overgrown courtyard where Lee would have been if Ædwine had not stopped her. Down below, amongst the furze, the hand over her mouth pressed more tightly and she ceased her struggle. He turned her round to face him and gently put his hand to her mouth.

"Are they here yet?" A voice called from the overgrown courtyard a stone's throw away. "I waited long enough at that wretched place!"

It was the unmistakable voice of Alcuin the Bard! Two armed men were with him and held torches which cast light to the foot of the furze where the two intruders had sought shelter. The furze bush was old and draped its spiny evergreen branches to the floor. Inside its cover was a domed space where Ædwine knelt with Lee beside him.

"No sir, he has not arrived. Let me take your horse while you go inside and warm yourself by the hearth," said the guard.

"Light the fire here in the courtyard. And bring me the woman. It will be a touching re-union."

The men lit the fire with their torches and the furze tinder leapt upwards spreading sparks towards the night sky. From his vantage point Win watched the sparks fade and disappear as they met the darkness. A bound figure was brought from the building. Win thought it was his sister, but as the light from the fire grew, he slowly became aware it was not Lee, but Gisla! He cast himself down and lay looking upwards towards the stars. How had his sister known?

The crackling of the blazing furze died away but even so Win could not catch what was said but Ædwine was very close and hung on every word.

"I have waited for this moment Gisla," Alcuin said. "He is on his way. My men saw him south of the fords and I will have him soon enough. A little bird draws him in and will send him here."

Ædwine was confused. Lee had assured him Alcuin would set the Chief Thegn to find the seaxe before he drew Gragus in. His fears swept away reason. Lee had deceived him! She had waited until he had left and then sneaked away. What a fool he had been. He took a band from his jacket and placed his hand over her mouth again before he fastened it there. Lee had no time to protest for she thought he passed the cloth to dry her tears.

"You should not have used the maiden," Gisla protested. "She fears her brother. Wasn't Dummoc enough?" Gisla pleaded.

"Do not mention Dummoc. I relied on others, and they failed. I will not fail this time for I know certain things which you do not."

"I know you have silenced the Bishop's man," Gisla answered.

"And a few others. Where there is discord and deceit I cannot fail. Her brother does not know she has handed the seaxe to me," he declared.

Lee tried to remove the bands from her mouth but Ædwine prevented her. He pulled her jacket, so her arms were disabled and bound her hands. Inside she struggled with her thoughts - Pip did not know about the seaxe. Then she prayed for wisdom and lay still and quiet so Ædwine would have no cause to harm her.

"She is a foolish child, Alcuin, and knows not what she does."

"I am sure she will convince him."

"He does not trust maidens, does he? Why would he this time?"

"She knows the way to a man's heart – more than you Gisla."

"What do you mean?"

"What did you offer him, cheese? She has a very precious seaxe."

Ædwine peered between the mass of branches to look at the older woman who had caused Gragus to stumble. Her gaze was directly on Alcuin who had her firmly under his control. He took great delight in taunting her and reminding her Gragus was about to die.

Lee tried again to communicate with Ædwine but he pushed her head to the floor. Lee closed her eyes. She knew Ædwine was angry. And she knew what he had done to the Thegn.

"Do you mean to release me?" Gisla asked.

"Only if you take a vow of silence."

"About your meeting at Elmham North?"

Lee did not see Alcuin take the document from his bag and throw it to the flames.

"There was no meeting," he declared. Then with great rhythmic melody he recited a list of names - names familiar to Lee but without meaning to Ædwine or Gisla. They were all the names on the document she had taken from the chapel at Bures.

Lee heard sounds of an approaching horse. Her heart leapt for she feared Gragus had been lured to the place to collect his seaxe.

"You!" Alcuin shrieked as he saw who had dismounted on the far side of the fire.

"Where is she? You told me you would not harm her if the seaxe was returned," the Chief Thegn gasped.

"How you have changed!" Alcuin declared. "Wolf said you'd grown soft."

"Do not play games. I know she was on her way to this place."

"Yes, she was. And you have blundered in before she has arrived."

He walked with the Bard towards the open door of the dwelling. Then he turned and saw a woman seated beside the fire. At first glance he thought it was Lee but when she looked up at him, he uttered a pitiful cry.

"You have Gisla here? What is the meaning of this? Have you had Gisla bound all these months?"

There was a desperation in his voice which Lee did not expect. She knew at once Alcuin had deceived the Thegn. Ædwine understood betrayal all too well but did not grasp what it meant. He watched as the guards disarmed the Thegn and forced him to sit next to Gisla.

"You can discuss your Swan Princess with her keeper. I have written another song for her to desecrate - about seaxes."

Alcuin took a weapon from his belt and threw it at the Chief Thegn. He ducked and it found its mark in the post behind him. Alcuin roared with laughter. The Thegn feared Alcuin had killed Lee, but he did not enquire about her coming. He knew her brothers had left their work in great haste because she had run off but no matter how fiercely he threatened the Riscmere lad, he would not talk. Of course, the poor lad could not talk. Even when the steward calmed him, he stuttered so much the Thegn could barely comprehend his directions. The Thegn had spent much time searching at the hunting hall and Ditches before he found the way.

"I demand her release," he said with deadened authority.

"Quiet Greg," Gisla whispered. "He is in no mood to listen."

Alcuin continued to walk from the fire to where he could see down the track. The Chief Thegn waited until Alcuin was beyond their hearing.

"Have you seen Lee yet?" He asked Gisla.

Ædwine caught what was said and his fists tightened. Alcuin was waiting for Lee! A blinding fury filled the oarsman's mind.

"Lee? What is this to do with Lee?" Gisla asked. "She's in Bures."

"Your Bard mentioned the Swan Princess."

"Say no more, Greg for he is sorely grieved by her performance at Dummoc. You were there, what did you think?"

"I do not know what to think. How long have you been here?"

"Since Dummoc," Gisla admitted.

"Has Alcuin been here all this time?"

"He barely arrived before you. He has lured the oarsman here."

"With that wretched seaxe?" The Thegn cried out and turned once more to gaze upon it.

"It is an enchanting weapon, isn't it?" Bellowed the Bard on his return. "Bind him and take him inside. He is no use to me. And the woman – bind her mouth for I will not have her whispering in the dark. I must go and find the out why Gragus has been delayed."

The Thegn was a hardy fighter and put his hand to the fire and drew out a log and hit the Bard so hard he slumped lifeless at Gisla's feet. Both Lee and Ædwine watched as the outnumbered Chief Thegn succumbed to the armed guards. He was dragged away and barred inside a workshop. Ædwine saw his chance to escape and dragged Lee through the furze. She kicked out and sent him to the floor where he lay dazed by anger and surprise. It was some time before he raised himself. He feared discovery. Like a stealthy hunter he went back towards the old hall where he caught Lee as she was about to mount a horse.

"Lee," he hissed. "Would you endanger your own brother? He is up yonder."

"It was not me he referred to," she whispered. "I would not bend to Alcuin's will, not ever, for I love Gragus."

"And Win loves you and has done nothing but speak of your bravery."

"I am so cold."

Ædwine took her in his arms and moved away from the horse. It neighed, and an armed man was soon at its side. He led it to shelter and Ædwine took Lee back to the place where her brother waited. Win kissed her and shed tears and she felt sorrow and joy fighting to overcome her. She did not recall riding away in the moonlight across the heath to the tavern in Wolven Pit. She roused herself enough to help Win with the untying of her bootstraps for she dimly recalled she had something to hide. Voices whispered around her and then she felt the warmth of the covers as they pressed down upon her before she fell asleep.

It was fully light when she opened her eyes and peeped at her muddy boots beside the bed. Horses rode past, and she heard galloping which drew to a sudden halt outside the building.

"They've arrived at last. Win, come with me!" Someone called.

"Are you sure you can manage without me?" Another asked.

"Yes. You stay here. She'll soon be awake. Pip is late but we cannot delay now the thegns are here," Ædwine urged.

"Take care of her," Win instructed as they left.

"I will."

Lee remembered how cold she had been the night before. How it had numbed her sight and hearing. She sat up.

"Gragus," she whispered. Her voice was soft and calm, and he turned to gaze upon the maiden he had embraced in the Dummoc mists. "Alcuin said a girl was about to lure you to your death. Ædwine thought it was me – but it was not."

"Ædwine only saw in part. We received a note which implied you were to meet us at the Ditches. We watched the place and saw the Chief Thegn was waiting for someone there. A maiden with golden hair all tight with curls arrived and threw herself upon him. He cast her off with such disgust Frith could not refrain from laughter, so we withdrew."

"Alcuin has captured our Thegn," Lee said.

"I know and your thegns are riding to rescue him – and Gisla."

"I should be riding with them. Where am I?" She whispered.

"In the tavern at Wolven Pit." He stood up and looked out through the narrow lattice high under the eaves as if to remind himself where he was.

"We must go with them," she said. Lee pulled her boots on.

"Pip will be here soon. Win has sent for him," Gragus said. He turned again to see if her brother drew near. "It's busy today," Gragus murmured. He turned back towards her. And there she stood like a priestess offering a sword to the gods.

"I found this, but it isn't yours." Lee gave him the weapon which Alcuin had thrown in anger. She had retrieved it before Ædwine had found her beside the horse. "And yours is safe enough – I have told no-one where it is. Not even Ædwine."

"I cannot believe what I see." Gragus gazed at the beautiful knife in his hand. "I last saw this in Francia, - it belonged to Weland."

"Your captain?"

"My beloved friend. How I miss him."

Lee put her hand upon his but he turned his back to her so she would not see his tears. She understood and waited for him to turn and as he did, she shivered so he took her cloak from the bench and wrapped it around her. For a long time, he held her close.

"You arrived not long before dawn. Frith heard the horses and, as usual jumped to his feet before I could stir. I did not believe it when he said Ædwine was outside. He saw him there on the horse – like a ghost in the moonshine – he said. I looked at you in your brother's arms and thought you were injured or dead. We ran to help, and the keeper's wife bustled around. She found you some warmed blankets."

"I remember Win couldn't undo my boots."

"They were soaked through. Ædwine was very worried about how he had mistreated you - and what I would say."

"He was very angry I think."

"He was confused by what he overheard."

"So was I," she murmured.

"And he told me you are not betrothed to Will." He kissed

her again. "Tell me what has happened since Dummoc."

They remained in each other's arms and Lee told him about her sojourn at Bures and he told her about his futile journey to find Gisla.

"I expect you think I acted rashly yesterday?"

"Even though you acted without counsel no harm has come of it – he has not caught me, and he has lost something he did not mean to."

"But he still has Gisla."

"The Thegn is with her. Ædwine will return by nightfall and I will send word to you."

"Are you leaving? You can stay here with Ædwine. Pip needs a few more to work in the Hellesden."

"We must wait to hear what is accomplished today. If Gisla is not released, then I will need Ædwine with me. I know he's grown fond of the Hellesden, but we must stay together until our task is done."

"Why did you part company? At first Ædwine said you sent him here to protect me, but I know you sent him for your seaxe - and Frith's. Did you mean to kill me with it?"

"Was your play meant to punish me? The Swan Princess with the seaxe through her heart? I have read it many times."

"It was meant to make you question what you did."

"Do you think our tale will end in sadness?" He gripped her hands, but she would not look up at him.

"I do not know how it will end. I do not know you – I need to hear your thoughts about what happened at Dummoc."

He quietly told her his story. He spoke freely and many times he said he cared for her. He had wept for her when he left the Hellesden in his haste to escape. He felt her arms tighten around him, but he did not falter in his account. Not once did he speak of love.

Then a voice called for her from the courtyard.

"You must go," Gragus said tenderly.

"Its Eth. Pip is not here," she observed as she peered between the shutters. Gragus went to her side and saw the young lad who had surrounded her with his band of thegns at Dummoc.

"May he protect you, my maiden, until we meet again," he whispered.

"I will miss having Ædwine as my guard."

"Did he not frighten you?"

"Not at all," she declared. "He is gentle like his brother."

"Has he told you they are brothers?"

"Yes, and how Frith was injured in Francia. He said he has a wife, but you and Frith have none."

"He must trust you," he whispered.

Gragus kept watch at the shutters until she passed from view. Then he could no longer hold back his passion; for her and for Weland. When Ædwine returned at nightfall Gragus lay asleep with Weland's seaxe grasped tightly in his hand. He took it from his friend and grieved anew for Weland.

Their success at Boten was put behind them for Gisla was not amongst the released. They rode in silence to Theodred's Ford.

CHAPTER NINE
RESTORATION

Eth led his band of Junior Thegns along the broad highway in silence. They rode as far as Cattishall where Eth had been instructed to report to the ældormen everything his father had undertaken. It was a quick report for a storm was nigh and young Eth was anxious to get home. Before they reached the woodlands south of the bleak heath a furious squall fell upon them. It parted the furze and pressed the fine grasses against the earth so they looked like ripples on mudflats. Eth led the gallop and they found shelter in the lee of one of the ancient barrows - a group of four which lay close to the way to the King's Hall. Lee, however, refused to dismount and complained she was cold so young Eth had to leave his place of shelter to continue the journey to Ældor Hall.

Eth dismounted first and took her hand to help her from her horse. At once he began his tale about the skirmish at Boten and beyond. Lee went straight inside and sat in front of the great hearth at Ældor Hall. Eth followed and shooed his brothers away in a vain attempt to encourage her to listen. The youngest of his brothers continued to run in all directions, diving over the high back of the longbench and poking Eth with wooden swords. His mother, Flæ, bustled about trying to restore order and sent Lee to lie down.

"Where is Pip?" She asked her son.

"With father. They did not want Lee to spend a moment longer at the tavern, so I was sent ahead. She must be hungry; she's not herself."

"She is very likely worried Pip will give her a sound beating. He was frightened beyond his wits when he called yesterday. I had to give him a measure of strong wine. What will become of her?"

Lee slept uneasily and woke up to find her brother sitting beside her bed.

"They didn't release Gisla did they?"

"You should have told the thegns where she was before you set out."

"But there was no time - Gragus was in danger."

"You nearly got yourself killed."

"Ædwine saved me," she murmured.

"You are never to see any of them again. Flæ wants you to stay here and I hope the Blackheath Thegn will reprimand you for I am lost for words. Whatever was Win thinking when he left you alone with a strange man? Your reputation is barely restored from Dummoc."

"I've done nothing wrong."

"We have to avoid every appearance of evil and you did not."

"I was tired, and I am still tired. Go away."

"That's exactly what I am about to do – and I must sort out the coppice team. How am I going to replace Ædwine?"

Despite Flæ's gentle encouragement to wait for her husband's return Pip rode back to Hellesden Hall. The Blackheath Thegn entered the gates soon after and hastily dismissed his men.

"Is she here?" The weary thegn asked his wife.

"Yes, she's safe. I don't think she will do the same again."

"I would differ," he returned. "I think she will. She is a bold one. I wish all our young thegns showed such courage."

"Perhaps it would have been best if they'd all been boys like ours," she said as she kissed her husband. "And the Chief Thegn? Does he live?"

"He had a narrow escape, but young Ralph saved him."

"The trader from Dummoc?"

"Yes, he proved to be quite a fighter. Alcuin's men left the Chief Thegn bound and set fire to the lodge. Ralph did not hesitate and went in through the roof. His brother threw a rope down and hauled them both out. I don't know how Ralph dared to face the heat, but he escaped without singeing a hair on his head. When we caught up with the stragglers, he rode straight in."

"Do you think he is a trader? Or more?"

"It was a delight to see Ralph again, trader or not. He told me his name is Frith. He wants me to find him a place to live."

"Does he have any kin apart from his dreadful brother?"

"Lee might know. Has she said anything about Will – the other trader? Ædwine said he had gone to search the bishop's hall. Was she alone when Eth called for her?"

"He did not see any oarsmen he said. But Pip was in a terrible temper with her and has gone home angry."

"I think she and I must talk," he said. He took his wife's hand and kissed it.

"Not today, my love. Let her rest on the Lord's Day. She is tired and blames herself for Gisla's absense."

"All three traders have gone after her. I could not spare any of my thegns, but I have sent word ahead. We must organize our men better. We need to be free to act without having to report to every self-important ældorman who thinks he pays for the thegns. I must speak to Edmund about it at the winter festival."

"You work too hard dear," she said. They embraced again. "Will you make her welcome here until then?"

"I would, but Eth and she are rascals when together. We

must support her brothers and advise them how to guide her."

"I was sad to see Pip looking forlorn and anxious. He has borne too much since his father died and the brothers left."

"But he has a good heart my love, and inner strength. Win was very masterful at Boten. He was so proud of his sister's courage – he would make an excellent thegn."

"You can't leave Pip on his own as steward of the Hellesden."

"Of course, I can't," he agreed. "I will seek someone to help him. Æthelric is very able. He's going back to Hellesden Hall so I expect he will throw some light on how Lee managed to leave their party."

"Æthelric is a wanderer, my love. I can't see him organizing the coppice work or felling trees."

"It would do him good, he's getting fat and lazy and needs more discipline."

His wife laughed at her husband's bluntness.

"I hope he purchased the jars for Hilde. All this trouble with Gisla has made Lee irresponsible," she observed. "When those three find Gisla Lee must make a new start."

"Will she leave them behind? Edmund must ensure they return to their longships before some worse dispute breaks out."

"But you said Frith wants to settle here."

"Then I will have to make it difficult for him to find a hall."

Lee accompanied the family to St Æthelberht's Church at the Holy Cross but as soon as she arrived, she complained about the cold. In fact, the day was exceptionally mild for late November, and many discussed delaying the winter slaughter of swine and cattle as the pastures remained productive.

On Tuesday afternoon Pip received an urgent request to go to her without delay because the mild fever she had endured since Sunday had worsened. Os was already with Lee when Pip arrived. The Ætheling had passed by to discuss Lee's future and

223

found her fighting for her life.

"How is she?" Pip asked.

"Restless and burning up. I can do nothing to help her. I'm not sure if she knows I'm here. I should have insisted she came back to Bures."

"I should have let her return with me," Pip sighed. "She thinks I have abandoned her." He lay his hand on her forehead, and she tossed and turned.

Os dampened her forehead with the cool cloth, but she fought to rid herself of it and called out for Gragus.

"Who is Gragus?" Pip asked.

"The one who called himself Will at Dummoc."

Pip took her hand and told her how he loved her and wanted her to be happy. He had forgiven her. He even promised to find Gragus and Frith and have them tell their tale of Dummoc around the hearth at Hellesden Hall.

For two days, she languished half-out of consciousness and growing weaker. However, on Thursday morning Pip found her quietly speaking to three of the younger children who had placed a litter of kittens on the covers to cheer her up.

Os made enquiries about the Boten Heath skirmish and determined she would never meet the oarsmen again. He considered sending her to Lidgaet. Pip insisted she stay at Ældor Hall.

The furze dell incident left Lee more determined than ever to solve the meaning behind the names and places on her list. Why had Alcuin made such a show of reciting them before burning the mysterious document? How were they connected?

Lee was in no hurry to be parted from the books and manuscripts at Ældor Hall. She hoped she might find an answer there. The task also kept her from facing the emptiness she felt in her heart. She was convinced she would never see Gragus again.

Eth, however, soon prised her from the library. He knew she could not resist working with the horses. He tried to make her smile and laugh but she would not for her thoughts were fixed on Ædwine who had trained the beasts - he had lied and led her astray. Gragus did not love her. It was the seaxe he loved.

Eth persevered for he pitied the lonely maiden and persuaded her to join him in the Shield Hall where the junior thegns trained. He placed her grandfather's sword in her hand and although it was heavy she held it high and some indifferent energy flowed down giving her resilience and determination. Lee felt safe amongst them; closed to emotion and free from passion. It was as if she and Eth were children again. They spurred each other on to explore isolated places and forgotten routes. One day they rode to the Green Ditches by the boundary stone and hid themselves amongst the brambles. Eth soon tired of listening for the voices from the fabled underground caverns and wandered off so Lee stretched herself out as if she were the Swan Princess. She was warm and alive and there was no seaxe. Weland's seaxe came to mind and she wondered how it came to the Kingdom of East Anglia. How had it fallen into the hands of Alcuin?

"Lee," whispered Eth who had returned. "I can hear voices or at least a voice. Come over here."

Lee followed her friend and saw a young maiden sitting on the boundary stone singing festive songs. She was very beautiful, and her golden hair was all curls. Eth thought she was an angel, but Lee reminded him about the girl who had confronted the Chief Thegn the evening before the Battle of Boten. She urged Eth to go and find out who she was, but he refused. When Lee laughed at his blushes, he determined to prove his courage and approached the angelic maiden to ask why she was there. She lied and said she was waiting for her brother. Eth insisted she identified who her brother was, but she would not. He told her to go back home for such an isolated spot was no place for a maiden to linger on her own. Then she threw herself upon Eth and he ran away.

On their return journey Lee, could not stop giggling at the sight of her friend freeing himself from the clutches of an angel. Eth felt humiliated and refused to tell her what the maiden had said. When they reached the Hall, they were no longer on speaking terms. His parents noticed the rift at once and were relieved they had parted company.

Lee was not deterred but set off on her own to explore Lutian Hall which was rumoured to belong to Alcuin though no one had ever seen him there. The surly steward had abandoned the place to assist with the swine slaughter and she walked in as boldly as the Chief Thegn might. Once inside she tried the key from Bures in all the smaller chests hidden behind the wall hangings. Lee was astonished there were so many. Her key did indeed undo a chest which she emptied into her bag without inspection. She uncovered other hidden bundles in a disused larder below the floorboards but did not unwrap them until she reached Buchan Woods.

Early evening Pip visited and urged her to return home, but she would not. However, two days later she was stopped by the Ascefeld Thegn close to the Bishops Lodge at North Wood. He had followed her from Boten Heath and his stern rebuke brought to her senses. Lee returned to Hellesden Hall before Edmund's Blackheath Thegn learnt where she had been.

Pip observed how much she had changed for it was impossible to engage her in conversation although he earnestly tried. Ten days later, at Holy Mass Eve Os joined Pip at church. Lee was not with her brother. Os left early and found Lee at home sitting with papers strewn around her.

"I have good news Lee," he smiled. "Gisla has been released." He had expected some response, but Lee continued to stare at her notes. "I need you to talk to me Lee. I know you are troubled in spirit."

"I do not feel troubled, not in the least." She stood up,

gathered the papers, and left him.

A week later, on the first day of January, Edmund returned to his hall. They were all invited to his feast and Fred urged Lee to leave with him early in the day so they could walk through the frosty lanes to Hollin's Hall to meet Æthel. Once more Lee turned away.

Later Win persuaded her to travel with him. They rode through lanes where the twigs remained white with frost and abandoned pasture sparkled like jewels in the sunshine. Lee appeared to revive but was soon overwhelmed by the mass of people in the banqueting rooms. She escaped to the Shield Hall where a few thegns were occupied honing their skills. They greeted her and then proclaimed her aunt was free because of her bravery. Lee was soon engaged in a mock battle with Eth who had not forgotten his encounter with the angel - and Lee's laughter about his manliness. He was not a child and he fought hard to prove it. She was determined he should not win and, as the blows grew fiercer, she gained confidence. She adeptly fended off his wearied blows unaware Edmund had entered the hall. She fought on and, with her strength almost gone, her partner sensed victory. Lee drew back and cast aside her shield, he hesitated, and she lunged forward and disarmed him with a sweeping upward twist of the sword. Cheers went up from those who watched. Edmund moved forward to greet her.

"I know much about you, Lee, but I did not realise you were a Shield Maiden. Well done Eth. I see you are worthy of the honour I have bestowed upon you as guardian of the juniors."

Edmund took her hand and smiled and ordered one of the juniors to return her sword to its place in the scabbard which hung on the wall.

"Today we will talk about old times and tomorrow I will learn all about your adventures."

Her king spoke kindly but many weeks had passed since Lee

resolved to tell him her tale and she had changed.

He led her back to the feast. Fred and Æthel were sitting behind the wattle panel with the musicians. She joined them happy to escape from the crush within the hall. Her two young friends tried to extract musical notes from some of the instruments left there but they soon grew bored and went off to explore leaving Lee asleep amongst the cushions. Os saw her and sat beside her until Edmund joined him.

"She's not recovered, has she?" Edmund observed. "My Thegn's lady can watch over her tonight, and I shall speak with her tomorrow."

"I don't think she will be persuaded to discuss what she knows."

"Our most worthy fighting men sometimes fall captive to heaviness of heart after a great battle. Think of Elijah, the great prophet who called fire down from heaven on Mount Carmel, he was unsettled and ran off. Lee won the battle but thinks she lost."

Edmund left his hall before daybreak and walked the short distance to Ældor Hall, where his friend and advisor, Eth's father knelt in prayer. He needed wisdom because he did not want the wound in Lee's heart to deepen. Later Edmund found her sitting alone by the fire.

"You look tired and weary Lee, though you slept so soundly in the hall amongst all the merrymaking." He took her hand in his. "I've been told about your efforts to secure Gisla's release. Your faith and courage have been rewarded – but I see you are not happy. What pain is it you bear? Why are you distressed? Those men you met, are they to blame?"

"No. I am weary with the keepers of your kingdom."

"Why? Go back to the beginning and explain. You first met the men in Osier Way?" Edmund paused to see whether she would take up the story from there.

"I didn't meet them. I had climbed to the top of the old fallen willow and when something flashed in the distance - near the boundary apple. I hid myself behind the roots and waited for them to pass. But they stopped and lent against the willow close to my hiding place. They looked like ordinary traders and spoke pleasantly to each other - like long known friends."

"Were they armed?"

"There was a seaxe – no more than the size of an everyday knife. They took turns slicing apples with it while they spoke about Gisla pursuing Alcuin. I revealed their presence to Pip alone because I thought they might have told him more about Gisla, but he never saw them."

"They weren't singing then?" Edmund mused. Lee looked at him and remembered all her untrue words at the trial. "When did you first speak with Frith and Gragus? I believe those are their true names, are they not?"

"Yes."

Lee felt as if Edmund was putting her on trial which was what he was endeavouring to avoid. He did not want to ask questions; he wanted her to freely tell the tale.

"Go on then," he urged.

"I decided to try and find them and pay them for information about Gisla." Once more she paused.

"And how did you find them when all my thegns failed?"

"It was by chance. I went to our hut to collect some of those buckles we hid there – you said we could use them in times of need - and Gisla was in great need. That's where the men were, in our hut."

"Were they alarmed when they saw you? Did they harm you?"

"No, not at all. I asked them about Gisla but before they could answer we heard the pack of hunting dogs and horses thundering towards us. I urged the men to climb the oak and I ran off dragging a blanket to lure the dogs away." Time had covered her innocent action with a sense of shame, and she paused.

"Why did you do run?"

"Because the Chief Thegn had treated me with great contempt the previous day. I thought he would kill the two men without question, and I would never find out about Gisla. I laid out the false trial for Gisla."

"It was a dangerous act, Lee. If you had been caught it would have made you look very guilty indeed."

"But I wasn't caught. I was going home but decided to go back for the buckles and the men were still in the tree. I don't know why they hadn't run off. I gave them the silver buckles and explained the way to Gipeswick. This was in exchange for their information about Gisla. They did know her."

"How?"

"They had worked in a dairy with her."

"Are you sure Lee? Why would two men like those work in a dairy?"

"Didn't you ask Gisla about them?"

"I had no opportunity. You must explain."

"Frith had been unwell, and her ladies in the dairy nursed him back to health. It's all I know."

"And who told you I had seen Gisla?"

"Os hinted you had seen her."

"I told Os to keep quiet about it, but I know he is very close to you. He has defended your every action. He could find no fault in your performance at Dummoc. He said all your actions and compromises had sprung from a noble spirit. I was surprised."

"Why? Do you think I had some other purpose?"

"No. I was going to say I was surprised Os did not rebuke you when you embraced the man."

"Has he told you every detail?"

Her thoughts went back to Dummoc. She wanted to be honest

and had made a huge effort to push Gragus from her thoughts. What more could she do? Gisla was found. Gragus was lost.

"I embraced the man so he would know I had forgiven him. It was an embrace of forgiveness. Are you saying I ought not to forgive?" Lee protested.

"Of course, not. We must forgive for our Lord requires that of us. Tell me what it was you had to forgive."

"He tried to take my life," she said without feeling. Edmund let go of her hand and put his arm about her.

"How?"

"I had to run away from him - in the Hellesden ..." Lee explained how she had avoided the man's wrath. "It was not until Dummoc I saw him again - although I had to pretend I had never seen him. When he left, he embraced and kissed the Swan Princess, not me."

"And the seaxe?"

"I will return it when I can. I will give it to Frith - he wants to settle here."

"My Thegn has told me as much. Frith impressed him a great deal. It is pleasant to know not all strangers are raiders. Give my Thegn the seaxe then it will not worry you. Does Frith have a family?"

"He has not said. He may be betrothed but I do not know for certain. I do know he is tired of wandering and wants a place to settle down."

"And do you think Gragus is of the same mind?"

"I don't know."

"Is he a raider or not?"

"If they had once been such men and now wanted to change, would you object to their remaining amongst us? They speak our language and are good traders and work hard."

"I do not object to honest men settling amongst us. That is required by the Lord, for Moses wrote the command – those who seek refuge may settle wherever they want. I will keep to this principle provided they are peaceable. I will ensure Frith is given favourable terms if he returns to find a hall. However, I will not let you leave with any of them, you know that don't you?"

"Frith is a dreamer and loves the thought of making his home with us, but my heart tells me his companions would never settle here."

"I can see you have thought all these things through. Remember it is not language and place which separate them from us; they worship many gods, and we know the Living Lord. We have put our old ways and gods behind us, and they have not. How can you mix the two?"

"I thought Rædwald did."

Edmund rebuked her reckless comment and insisted she explain the events which led to Dummoc.

"There's much which troubles me," Edmund concluded. "My Chief Thegn pressed you over the matter of the seaxe for he appeared to know what he was searching for but did not find it."

"He wanted the story about the enchanted seaxe to be true because he had so little evidence," she protested.

"I questioned him about the trial after Holy Mass when he was in South Burgh, but he was very evasive about the seaxe, so I concluded it never existed. And now you reveal you do have a seaxe."

"Only a very plain one. He was looking for something quite different."

Lee's thoughts turned once more to the Chief Thegn and all the grief he had caused her. She suddenly buried her head in her arms. Edmund put his arm around her again to comfort her.

"It was never my desire to have anything to do with Dummoc!" Lee exclaimed. "Fred and I were taken there by force. He had us bound. And Gragus was right to be afraid. The wicked Chief Thegn was going to use our words against him and Frith.

232

He sought to prove your kingdom was threatened by oarsman spies who took advantage of women and children. But it was the Chief Thegn who threatened your kingdom when he set out to demolish justice. He is the dangerous one amongst us for he tried to undermine everything you stand for - and you have let him get away with it."

There was great bitterness in her tone and Edmund knew he had missed something. He had listened to Os and his own Thegn and knew about the rift between the Chief Thegn and Lee, but he thought it was to do with their difference over marriage proposals.

"I understand Lee, why you are upset about the Chief Thegn's actions at Dummoc but there is not enough ..."

"Evidence? Is that what you were about to say? I am more than upset Edmund. This is a matter of justice. If the Chief Thegn had been honest then Frith and Gragus would have passed unnoticed through your kingdom, as many others do. I would never have reason to see them again. Instead, the man, who you think is worthy to remain in his post as a senior thegn, coveted silver. It was his love of money which brought me face to face with Gragus. Was I in pursuit of my own desires? I was not!"

Lee's outburst warned Edmund to remain calm and tender.

"Did he accept a bribe?"

"I think so. The day before the trial a man came to see him. I do not know who he was, but I do know Alcuin was at Dummoc at the time and he could have sent one of his men with the payment."

"I have not been told Alcuin was there."

"Well, I overheard him say it himself. And Gisla was there too. Did she tell you? Why should I have to answer all your questions? Other people know more than I do and yet they are not pressed and made to feel guilty. What have I done wrong? Perhaps I should not have helped Gisla? She has not been questioned by you, has she? Why did Alcuin want her to watch Gragus hang? Perhaps they are the ones who are lovers - for I am not. You have no right to be angry with me because of him."

"But I am not angry. It is you with clenched fists and raised voice. Why are you so full of wrath? Why?"

"Because you have asked me too many questions. I wanted to discuss these things with you as an equal." Lee knew she was not his equal and calmed down. "I am sorry Edmund. When we were young, I used to correct you, and advise you with the plays and such, but now you are high above me, and I am not important."

"You will always be important to me. I want you to be direct and honest - even when I do not want to hear it. And I shall be honest and direct with you; it has always been the way between us. I know you are hurting but I do not know why – except it has to do with Dummoc and the man on trial there. I do not want you to entangle yourself with an oarsman, not in any way. I know your lives have crossed, at the Hellesden, at Dummoc and then at the tavern. You must judge your own heart."

"I will not set my heart on him Edmund. Why did Will leave me?"

"I do not know. What makes our hearts grow cold?"

"The Chief Thegn has a very cold heart. Do not let him marry me Edmund, I beg you."

"Os was very rash when he forged those letters."

"I had nothing to do with that."

"I know, he told me. He did it because he loves you and I would have done the same."

His answer surprised Lee. She began to relax again.

"I would not be a suitable wife for the Thegn."

"No, you would not. Os hopes to urge Will to be reconciled with you and I hope you can forgive him."

"Has he forgiven me? He said I had belittled him at

Dummoc."

"He was angry."

"But why? Does he think more of his books than me? Did he care I had been abducted? He showed no compassion. In fact, he treated me with contempt and stood apart from me. If he had stayed by my side, I am sure Gragus would have avoided me. But he did not. Gragus saw me there, abandoned and ... "

"I have not abandoned you, Lee. Pray for our Will. Being a good scholar isn't the most important way for him. He needs to get alongside people more and explain the Scriptures as he did in the past and encourage people in the Way. We must walk as He did with His disciples."

"I still feel abandoned. Will Gisla be returning to Riscmere Hall?"

"She will return, but not until Candlemas."

"Candlemas? That is a long way ahead."

"And Will should be here as well. So, you have plenty of time to catch up with your studies. You must work hard and impress him."

"Then I will practice with my sword in the morning and study your books in the afternoon," she declared.

It was not quite what Edmund had intended but he had noticed how much the junior thegns had improved their swordsmanship and battle skills since she had been amongst them. She had been sword fighting since the day she could run. Her older brothers had once been proud to teach her all they knew. Edmund hoped she would lay her sword down once he had dealt with his Chief Thegn, but the wily fox had gone to ground again.

At Epiphany, the three former friends would disperse, and Edmund was determined to bring them together. He arranged a meeting at his Hall, but Lee did not turn up. He and Os discussed Gragus.

"Why did she call his name if she says she does not care for him? She will not face what has happened. Her wounds are not healed, and we are losing her. We have already lost Will. He has abandoned us – and her."

"But it was never true love between them, was it Os?"

"No, I suppose not. We were all brothers. I liked those days."

"We must try to win back her trust," Edmund urged. "She is full of wrath because of the Chief Thegn's scheming, and I have not been able to question him – he has disappeared."

"Has he?"

"Yes – no one will say where he is. What do you think Os? Is the Chief Thegn determined to have her as his wife. Is it revenge or love?"

"He was angry at her St Clement's Feast. He could neither find her nor prove the letter was a forgery. Lee had already changed though," Os sighed. "She was pleased when I left the feast early because I had chided her over her behaviour with the man Ædwine."

"He is the one whom she has kept from my view. Why Os?"

"Because he is very wicked, and she cannot bring herself to see it. And he is very clever, for it was he who drew her heart away from us. Yes, it was his purpose, to win her for Gragus," concluded Os.

"Was it Ædwine who stirred her heart so she cannot rest?"

"Yes, if he had not encroached on our Hellesden, she would have forgotten Gragus."

"Now she desperately tries to forget and cannot," observed Edmund.

"Yes, because Ædwine's pretence was worse than I saw; he was preparing her to leave. I fear he will return for her."

"Then her rashness at Boten has bought us time. While he is away, we must make her see how precious she is to us."

CHAPTER TEN

BROTHERHOOD

Before they parted at Epiphany, Os and Edmund renewed their vow of brotherhood and sealed their pledge by exchanging sword rings. They remembered their two lost brothers, Will and Lee, and swore to restore them to the one true Way.

Edmund's loving kindness had already begun its work in Lee's heart, and she took up Pip's offer to work in the Hellesden. Two weeks later Edmund visited her there. She was in high spirits working alongside Eth's junior thegns. Edmund took great delight in her smile as she glanced up in wonder at seeing him there.

"Edmund, I thought you had gone to Southwic to see Gisla," she said as she hastened alongside his horse.

"I have been delayed. My Chief Thegn has not returned to his hall, and no one will tell me where he is. Until I speak with him, I shall feel as though I have failed you."

"I'm sorry Edmund to burden you with sorting out my wrongs. Os said I had been foolish when I bought the puppy for him."

"You are young and lack wisdom in certain matters, but it is no burden to protect you. I have warned your mother's kin I will use my authority to nullify their agreement with the Thegn. Gisla will certainly overrule them."

"You did not reveal that my betrothal to Will was false, did you?"

"No. Perhaps all the rumours will hasten our brother's return."

"Your Chief Thegn is competent in spreading unfounded information – which can be very dangerous when we have so many traders settling here," Lee warned. "His methods are mean, no more, they are malicious ..."

"Don't be too harsh," Edmund intervened. "The betrothal letter *is* a forgery. He knows when things are not right."

Lee turned away. Her king dismounted and stood before her.

"I do not even like him Edmund nor his methods."

"I do not understand the man either. But in his eyes, the gift you gave him bound you together. And he will not give way for he thinks too much of himself – although he has reason to, for he is a very fine thegn. I would not like to face him on the battlefield; he is stern and ruthless and stands his ground. His men all fear him."

"If they serve him because they are in terror of him and he is killed in battle, they might all flee. The juniors serve you because we all love you."

"I see your training as a Shield Maiden has made you wise in these matters Lee. I will be shrewd in my dealings with him for I would not like him to become my enemy."

"I would marry him to save you Edmund," she declared.

Edmund was deeply moved by her devotion. He embraced her and kissed her cheek. The coppice team, who were resting at their midday break, watched their king. Pip said nothing. Win grinned and looked down at the dead leaves and twigs. Eth was pleased the king looked upon Lee with favour and wished he was reconciled with her over the matter of the angel.

"That was very wicked of you Edmund," Lee blushed.

"I am following the ways of your wild oarsman." Her king looked up and laughed. He took hold of the horse's bridle and began to walk down the ride. "Will you accompany me to your hall?"

Edmund moved ahead to speak to Pip while she finished her task tying the birch tops. When they were out of hearing Edmund asked her again what troubled her. He was direct and waited a long time for her reply. A wren flittered amongst the piles of birch tops. Lee watched it awhile until it passed from her view.

"When the Thegn took us from the orchard and led us to this lane, I prayed we would be kept safe and return. I hoped justice would be done, as you would wish. We did rely on the Lord's strength, and he brought us through the trial. We thought we had won; our spirits were lifted at the outcome of the Dummoc hearing. It was so exciting; I expect Os told you about our performance."

"Yes. Perhaps you erred when you came to the choice of play though, your ones from the Scriptures were always excellent."

"I did not have long enough to refine what I had written. We wanted it to be solemn because of the injustice they were about to commit. All I wanted to do was to move cold hearts. Will hated it. He was wholly offended, and I tried to apologise but he would not listen. He left me standing alone in a bitterly cold courtyard. I was crying because it felt as if I was the guilty one. I should have thought upon our Lord who also stood in the courtyard alone. He heard Peter deny him three times and yet he did not give in to self-pity, he did not lose heart, but I did. I did not rest in his strength. I was caught unawares and taken into the arms of the man."

"Gragus?"

"Yes. I wish I had never met him."

"Lee do not let fear rule your heart. You cannot move forward because you have besieged yourself. Os said you were not like this at Bures. He blames Ædwine."

Lee looked up at the watch tower and remembered her friend.

"He made me laugh and I felt safe when he was here. He always knew when danger was close, and he was a blessing for Pip - we miss him."

"Did he ask you to go with him to find Gragus?"

"No. Did Os tell you that? I said I thought he might ask me to meet Gragus again - but I said I would refuse. I did not expect him to be there when I woke up after Boten."

Lee turned to Edmund, they were at the gate, and she paused to unlatch it. He put his hand on hers.

"And your love for him surprised you?"

"Yes, but he did not mention love. And he has not returned even though I invited him to meet Pip. I called for him, didn't I?" Edmund nodded. "And Pip overheard?"

"Yes, and Os."

"I called for him because he was the only one who understood how alone I felt at Dummoc. For it was there, where the mists swirled, a chill wind came upon my heart. There is something wrong in your kingdom Edmund if strangers can be betrayed; no, worse, sold to settle some dispute between bishops and men like Alcuin. You need to find out what was discussed at the meeting in Elmham. What has been Alcuin's purpose in all this?"

"I know there are great issues to be resolved but you are more important. Face your fears, Lee. If your heart is pure, and I truly believe it is, then let our Lord know how you feel. It is he who protects and guards our hearts. Follow his ways, wholeheartedly as you used to."

"I will try but I do feel abandoned since Gisla left."

"I know. Even so, you were at peace last winter and spring. It was the summer excitement and the strong bond we all shared which left you feeling alone - long before you met Frith and

Gragus. You need to press ahead now for there is much to look forward to. You did not join Os at my hall at Epiphany and we missed you. We renewed our vows of brotherhood - and we need you with us. We must stand together in such times. Do you know what has happened in Francia?"

"Ædwine said northern Francia is ravaged beyond recovery, and all is burnt and we must expect the same."

"I know Charles is fighting back but his kin do not stand united with him. It is why my Æthelings must work as one with me – no divisions Lee. I am going to invite Æthelric to take Will's place."

"He knows the kingdom well, particularly our trading centres."

"He warned me our ports are vulnerable but if the oarsmen strike those communities, then they hurt their own traders – and they have a lot of silver. Why would they steal from their own brothers?" Edmund asked.

"They do strike each other. Each lith has its own jarls and loyalties."

"Many will be thinking about their farms. They need to return to plough and sow."

"But there are many in this generation who have no farms to return to," Lee pointed out.

"I will not prevent those who want to settle here from doing so. If they love our meads and woodlands as you do, then they will forget about raids and plunder." Edmund knew his dreams of peace might not be as simple and so did Lee.

Edmund took her hand. They renewed their words of brotherhood and prayed. Lee urged him to take some refreshment at the hall before he left but he would not be delayed.

She entered her hall singing but ended abruptly when she saw Will standing like a bleak hunched heron watching the cold grey ashes of their hearth. Her sudden joy flowed away, and he raised his cloaked head.

"I thought Edmund was riding this way."

"He did, Will, but he has gone."

"Do you know why I am here?" Will stepped closer to where she stood in the doorway and threw back his hood to reveal his Mercian tonsure.

"Yes, I have a fair idea. I have overheard the rumours too."

"Have you?" He made a swift move and slapped her across her face.

"How dare you pretend you had nothing to do with them!"

Edmund stood upon the threshold of the outer door and Will stepped back from Lee. The king had seen Will's entourage and was eager to speak with him.

"Leave her Will. Let me explain. Go and find those refreshments for us Lee." Lee left and crossed the courtyard to the kitchen and did not hear what passed between the two former friends. When she returned with the platter of food Will looked sullen. Edmund had obviously won the argument.

"I will right this confusion," Edmund said. "But why should Os suffer for it when the Chief Thegn is to blame? And why take such offence? There are many of noble blood who would be pleased to be betrothed to one as faithful and full of grace as Lee."

"I was going to explain everything around the hearth at Holy Mass," Lee interrupted. "But you did not return to us."

"I had better company to keep than spending time with a foolish girl."

"I am learning to walk in wisdom. I have one of the letters here. It was my protection for a short while in much the same way as my Swan Princess was at Dummoc."

"Is that what Dummoc was? Lies?"

"Say no more about Dummoc," ordered Edmund. "I will

make no judgement about the trial until all the evidence has been gathered."

"What further evidence do you need? Those two men are the very same who have robbed God's property across Francia where their kin burn and pillage and rape and murder to this day." Will objected.

"There was no proof they had committed any crime here. For now, they are free to wander in this kingdom and if any man should harm them, he will be held to account. We are not at war and if we are raided then we ought to be thankful for all the years they have overlooked us. You grew up in those times and I expect you to rejoice in them."

"Rejoice in them?" Will echoed. "It was no accident which caused my father's death. It was them – and they beguiled mother too."

"Those were rumours. There were no oarsmen involved."

"I do not believe you."

"No oarsman gained from your loss."

"They usurped our trade which belonged to the Church."

"Those lands belonged to me, not the bishops. Elmham has plentiful estates, but they are always greedy for more. You must ask why. The Church ought to follow the example of our Lord and own nothing more than the simple necessities of life. It is the gold on corrupted altars which will bring the oarsmen down upon us."

"That is not true. They burn our books and despise our liturgy. They do not keep their word and cannot be trusted."

"But the God I serve is faithful. I trust him and will keep to his ways; the ways I find in the Holy Scriptures. They are my guide. We are urged to love our enemies and do good to them. And he warned the religious rulers about their greed and cold-heartedness."

"Having mercy on them will not hold back their swords ..."

"And what are you doing to stop them attacking us?" Lee

demanded.

"I am studying and making arrangements."

"The same sort of arrangements as Alcuin perhaps?" Lee pressed on because she had not liked the way Will had opposed Edmund.

"What do you mean? You, foolish girl."

"I know what he said to you at midsummer. Have you had further contact with him?" Edmund asked as Will turned to leave. "You will answer me my friend or I shall delay your return to Medeshamstede."

"Yes, I have. He was at Elmham North when I was preparing papers for Medeshamstede. I did not arrange to see him. He just appeared one day and freely admitted he does know Gisla. His former denial was innocent enough – he does not want to be known as an acquaintance of one who keeps company with oarsmen. And neither do I. Alcuin is as embarrassed by Gisla as I was by Lee's performance at Dummoc. Even so, he promised to diligently look for her."

Lee glanced knowingly at Edmund.

"Have you not received the news about Gisla's release?" His king asked.

Will looked at Lee and then at Edmund.

"No. Where had Gisla been?" Will realised Edmund knew more than he did but did not rein in his hostility.

"She was at Ely when we looked for her last summer, and then she was moved to quarters in Dummoc." Edmund paused and watched to see how his old friend responded. "When the trial failed to procure its victims, she was moved on."

"Procure?" Will echoed.

"The charges made against the two traders were dubious and their arrest prearranged. That is not the kind of justice I hold to. Lee's playacting was more honest than the man behind the trial. He never revealed his hand, and he deceived my Chief

244

Thegn."

"Who did?"

"Can you not make a guess?" Edmund urged. "Alcuin is a liar, Will."

"I did not believe him last summer," Lee added. "He has deceived two good men, you and Greg."

"How could I have known he lied?" Will objected. "Gisla is headstrong. and prefers markets to abbeys and foreign traders to her kin. I do not know what trouble she has caused, do I? Alcuin had reason to ... "

"To do what Will? To undermine the law of this realm? To take a hostage and let us believe she is dead?"

Edmund sought repentance but his words fell on hardened ground. Will's heart already appeared to be thoroughly trampled by the meaningless traditions of men.

"If Alcuin had taken her captive all those months ago, why didn't he demand payment or terms?" Will argued. "Are you certain she is free? The Chief Thegn did not mention anything about her."

"Have you seen him?" Lee rebounded.

"Well?" Edmund pressed.

"He came to Medeshamstede four days after Holy Mass. He boldly congratulated me and hoped my forthcoming wedding would be a happy union. I was not alone and had to leave important guests. It was terrible to be humiliated at my place of study. I told him he could have her."

Will turned his back to them to read the letter she had passed him.

"Whatever must the Thegn think of me?"

"Let me read it," Edmund insisted.

Will handed it to his king who read it with interest before casting it to the heightening flames.

"A few months ago, you would have been proud to have

created such a masterpiece. If only you had remained that passionate youth, Will. All those dreams we shared, where have they gone? I was away for a short time and returned to find two of my closest friends changed into ice giants."

The former friends turned to their king. Lee discerned his meaning, but Will was offended by the reference to Scandinavian lore.

"Where is the Thegn?" Lee asked.

"When he left, he was going to Salham."

"Who does he know there?" Edmund asked.

Will said he did not know and left the hall with Edmund. Lee was immediately annoyed with herself. She had not asked the right questions. She turned once more to her box of letters and before she locked it, she took out the Bures papers which puzzled her. What did they mean? Will might have known - and indeed he did.

Frustrated with losing such an opportunity she went outside earlier than usual to prepare the food for her mares. The sky was clear, and the frost had already crept up the blades of grass causing them to sparkle like the frozen tears of the Swan Princess. Her heart may have been frozen for a while, but it was warmer since Edmund had returned. She was no ice giant.

As she approached the stable, she felt her loss of Ædwine and thought about their plans to train the new ponies. They had just begun and what excitement they had as they tried to put bridles on them. Ædwine had no sooner approached them than they would spin round like water skaters on a summer pond and escape. How they had laughed. She wondered if he missed the Hellesden and Hilde's feasts.

Ædwine, however, had already cast aside the calm interlude in his restless life. He was not at peace and increasingly sought ways to forget all which troubled him. He did not want to remember his time at the Hellesden or the maiden. Though

Gragus urged him to return to watch over Lee he bluntly refused. Frith thought it was the recent wielding of his sword at Boten which had unsettled his brother and shared his concerns with Gragus. They thought a time of merrymaking at the winter festival would improve his state of mind.

It did not.

"You must go back. That's an order!" Gragus insisted.

"It will serve no purpose. You understood what Gutti's man said, didn't you? They need us to join them. You enjoyed the isle before. If Frith wants to stay here, then let him - send him back to watch over the girl for you."

"I need Frith with me. We must discover why Alcuin has targeted us."

"He wants to separate us from our kin, and so does she. I insist we stay as one for now," Ædwine argued. "The girl does not need any of us. Let her defend herself."

"Why are you so changed brother?" Frith demanded. "You once said how much you liked the maiden."

Frith was dismayed Ædwine remained angry and took him to one side so Gragus would not hear their exchange of words.

"I do not like the way Gragus is either. But I do not blame the maiden. You were the one who arranged for him to be alone with her. I wanted him to ride with us to rescue Gisla. You should not have interfered, brother."

"I thought the girl would come with us. She gave me every indication she would. His spirit is low because of her deceit."

"She did not come with us because we did not ask her."

"Well go back and ask her yourself! It would have been easy for me to follow the Chief Thegn's example and take her by force. You try it!"

"And have her king at our heals?" Frith returned.

"If she was with us, our brother's spirit would revive."

"If only Gisla had sent word to us. We made great sacrifices to guarantee her freedom."

"Your sacrifice was without reward. We could have been active in Francia - and getting rich."

"Who has made any fortune there since we left? All the silver has been moved to the heartlands - out of reach. And there is famine in the north - which is why I think they will come here."

"Gragus fears they are already lurking in the Tamysemouthe marshes."

"And he has sent word to find out which lith leaders are there." Frith cried in frustration.

"If it is the Brothers, they will not welcome us. We need to return to the liths in Francia. Ragnor's sons despise the name of Weland – and you know why! When I saw his seaxe it all flooded back."

"Which of the liths can you trust brother? None! I am determined to start again here in this kingdom. The fields are fruitful, the woodlands well-managed, the rivers are plenteous, and the rules are kind and generous. You loved being with Lee's kin."

"Did I? I do not remember."

"You said it was peaceful, and there was laughter every day and wonderful breakfasts. And music ..."

Frith's words faded on his lips. It had always been impossible to restore his brother's senses.

"You are right Frith it is a fine kingdom. So why don't you go back then? Marry the girl – follow her gods."

"I would not marry without love. You said her heart is with Gragus."

"She lied!"

Ædwine had punched a nearby tree and stood clasping his hand.

"Is your ill-temper to do with Weland or Lee? Perhaps you grew too fond of her and that is why you are so angry."

"It was a difficult command and pointless."

"You failed because it was too difficult for a heartless man like you."

"I have never failed in battle."

"Until now."

The two brothers were about to strike each other.

"Ædwine can come with me to Dyflinn," Gragus gloomily announced as he wandered their way. "We must find out where Halfdan is. Gutti may be with him. He will know what is happening in Francia and the north. Will you find Gisla for me Frith and make sure all is well with her?"

Frith lowered his clenched fists and nodded. The news ought to have satisfied Ædwine too, but he dwelt upon what his brother had said about failing on a mission. He was sorely offended for he never failed. His thoughts tossed about all night. He saw the black swans laughing at him. Their taunts bruised his pride and reproach tore open old wounds. In his visions Gragus appeared amongst the pillows all pale and anxious. Ædwine was gripped with fear. He was not clothed for war. His boar's cover had been tossed away and he could not reach it. He saw himself in the Hellesden working with his axe but without a shirt. His heart was all uncovered. He woke from his night dreads and lay awake until dawn. He feared Frith would be lost forever if he was left there alone. Edmund's kingdom had softened him. He and not Frith would go back for the maiden. This time he would not remove his ruthless hide. He was not what she had seen. He was one who came to conquer!

"Frith. Where has he gone?"

Frith raised his head from his covers and blinked. It was dark and very cold; he wondered why Gragus was already dressed for the journey.

"Who?"

"That mad brother of yours."

"He was wandering beyond the campfire long into the night. Are you sure he's not over there?"

"He's taken his horse as well as his pack – he's gone to capture Lee."

"What!" Frith sat up and wrapped his cloak around his shoulders. "I thought you told him we would wait and return in the summer?"

"It was what he agreed."

"He thinks you grieve for her which is why he has gone to find her."

"I do Frith, but it is a pleasant pain, and I can bear it. If he seizes Lee by force, then I have lost her forever."

"Do you think he will try to steal her away?"

"He has equipped himself for battle."

"Then we must make haste." Frith feared his brother would ruin his plans to settle in the realm he had grown to love.

They left without eating and were soon chasing their quarry back to the heart of the kingdom.

The ponies were hungry and crossed the mead to where Lee stood at the rail. She had set the bucket down at her feet and stood there watching the bright blue sky. The sun was not yet low enough to cast its magical long shadows, but she lingered there watching to the crows returning to the rookery. When they had passed by Lee gave each pony a root from her bucket and fussed over them for a while. They obediently went to the open front of the stable while she walked towards the side entrance. The bolt was cold and groaned as she wriggled it loose. Ædwine had fixed it there – he had argued it was superior to wood because metal did not swell with the damp. Iron was very cold though. Once it was drawn back, she picked up her buckets and kicked the door open. The ponies were already in full flight back to the frosty mead. Then all turned black. She fell to her knees. A hood had been thrown over her head and a binding pulled tight across her mouth so she could hardly breath. Before she had time to struggle her arms were pulled back as they had been at Boten. Someone roughly bound her wrists. This time she struggled as fiercely as a frightened doe, but she was already caught fast in the snare and the bonds tightened so her hands grew numb. Then her legs were bound, and she was lifted onto her captor's shoulder.

Lee was thrown upon a horse and covered over like a piece of baggage. She struggled and received a blow from her captor. He did not mount the horse but walked alongside and Lee vainly tried to take note of the direction she travelled in. The woollen hood was suffocating, and she had great difficulty in breathing. Blood rushed to her head so she thought she would faint. The cords around her wrists bit hard. Her captor was cruel, and she feared the worst; that one of Alcuin's men had returned and she would be sold as a slave.

When the shadows lengthened, the woodsmen returned to their hearths. As weary as they were, Pip, Win and Fred made their way home in a joyful mood for they expected Edmund and his thegns to be there with Lee. Fred looked forward to serving his king with the best food Hilde provided so when he saw her hastily crossing the courtyard with a jug of wine, he immediately offered to take it to Edmund.

"He left long ago!" Hilde snapped. "I've had every lord from leagues around visit me today and now the man who brought so much trouble to Lee is back."

"Has Edmund gone?"

"Yes. Gone before mid-afternoon. Go and wash and then hasten over to the kitchen."

Fred washed himself with great speed because there was already ice on the bucket of water and the kitchen would be warm. He was afraid to go to the hall in case the Chief Thegn was there for him.

"Be careful," he warned as Pip entered the lesser hall. "You have a visitor – I think it's the Chief Thegn."

Pip hoped Lee had hidden herself and went to confront his uninvited visitor. He stood warming himself in front of their fire.

"I have come for your sister. She knew I would."

"Is she not here?"

"I do not see her. Do not delay me! She has told enough lies."

"Did you see Edmund?" Asked Fred. He had followed Pip to the hall.

"Edmund? Do you think Edmund will stop me? I will not leave empty-handed this time."

Fred began to revive and thought of a plan. He ran from the hall. Pip offered a cup of wine and tried to calm the man.

"Don't you think my sister has suffered enough because of you?"

"How has she suffered?" The man demanded.

"You have to respect her opinion ... "

"Respect? She agreed to my proposal."

"Then you have deceived yourself as much as you did us. This is *my* household, and I will protect her from you, and any other who think they can take what does not belong to them. You have cast such a long shadow across my sister's heart. Do you intend make it all black?"

"Perhaps it was black before we met. A merry game she has played. How well she performed at Dummoc." His voice had fallen to a low menacing whisper.

"I do not know what you mean." Pip was trying to be as honest as possible, but he was unable to restore any sense of calmness. "If Fred discovers where she is, then you must listen and do what she desires."

"I will choose for her. She will come with me tonight."

"Then you must fight me for her," Pip declared. The man before him did not hesitate and drew his sword and Pip stood before him unarmed.

"Sit down!" The man commanded. Pip obeyed and sat down in front of the fire. He stared into the flames. He wished he had followed his sister to Dummoc where he could have protected her from – everything ...

"If you harm her, I'll make sure Edmund removes you and all you have from this kingdom." Pip declared. Win burst into the hall.

"What's this?" Win demanded as he saw the man wielding his sword.

"I've come for payment. I suggest you make haste to find her, Win. I am not in a patient mood. My sword is unsheathed, and you have witnessed how I use it in battle. I will not rest until she is brought to me."

"Go up to the stable Win, she's usually there until dusk. I thought it was where Fred rushed off to. Tell him not to run for aid or I'm a dead man." Pip humbly turned to face the one who threatened him. "If you take her, then take me as well – as your servant or slave if that is what you desire. I will not be parted from her."

The aggressor turned away for he could not face such love. As he did Fred burst into the hall. He was in tears and could barely speak.

"The horses were out in the mead - but the food and water buckets were all tipped over inside the stable. I found her knife," young Fred sobbed. "And I found this in the lane." He held out Lee's bundle of keys.

"I don't believe you!" The man yelled. "You've tricked me out of my wages and now you do the same with the girl."

"Here, she said you could have these silver buckles and coins back." Fred thrust the bag towards the man, and he took it willingly enough. The lad turned to Pip. "Lee has been taken by the Chief Thegn – I know it! And I thought I would find her safe with Edmund when I got home. Why didn't you return before it was too late?" Fred asked the one with the sword.

The man faltered and Pip saw his hand tremble.

"Put your sword away," Fred requested. "What would Lee say if she saw you? She counts you as her friend and brother."

Ædwine slowly lowered his sword. His anger ebbed as he began to take in what had happened.

"I will go to the stable," he whispered. "And see how long she has been gone. Win, prepare a horse to ride with me. Do you know where the Thegn lives?" Win nodded. "Then make haste."

Win left the hall and Ædwine placed his hand on Pip's shoulder.

"Your offer was noble; I have never met your kind before."

"My sister is precious to me," Pip said. "I will stay here with Fred in case she escapes and returns. Take care of Win and release her if you can."

Win rode beside an old companion in a new guise. He did not feel safe, but he was not afraid for they had one purpose – to find the maiden.

Lee kept moving and stretching so she did not succumb to the cold as she had done the evening under the furze. She began to wonder if it was Ædwine who was taking her captive but surely Gragus would not have allowed it.

It was dark when Lee was taken from the horse. She feigned choking and the band was loosened from her mouth and the hood pulled up though it remained over her eyes. The band was refastened but not before she saw where she was. When she heard her captor knock on the door of a nearby dwelling and enter, she smiled at the irony of it. Her captor had taken her to the threshold of the processional way which led to the amphitheatre where she had learned to act. It was a place of performance and Lee began to stir. She moved towards the dovecot where she removed her ring and placed it in between the boards. Perhaps Pip would find it and ask the shepherd where she had been taken.

She overheard their conversation as their voices travelled far in the frosty stillness. Her captor was identified. Her spirit lifted. It was not Alcuin – it was the Chief Thegn who had abducted her.

The Thegn drew close and mounted his horse and she was passed up to him. Her head now rested against his shoulder, and he wrapped his cloak around her. She was not pleased to be so close to him.

All the escape plans she devised required her to run – which was impossible.

"What do you think you are doing, Greg?" Her voice was soft and fearless. "Take me back home at once."

He pressed her head closer to his shoulder and tightened the cloak around her. But she strained to keep her head away from him.

"You will lose your post and never be an Ælrorman because of this."

"I do not care," he said quietly.

"Of course, you care." She argued. "I don't want you banished from your command. Edmund needs you. Don't you care about him?"

"I cannot go back now."

"Yes, you can. Untie me and I will run back and blame Alcuin. I can say I escaped. Or you can take me back and claim you released me. And then you can discuss our future sensibly."

He drew his horse to a halt and removed the bands from her eyes and then the hood. She blinked and saw him in the moonlight as he looked down on her. Moonbeams shone upon his damp eyes and Lee was greatly alarmed. She threw herself backwards and landed heavily on the frosted earth. He responded to her pained cry and hastily sprang from his horse. However, she had already moved into the shadows.

"Come back!" He ordered. "I'm not going to harm you."

Lee, in her disorientated state, tripped and he recaptured her.

"Take me back to Pip."

"It is too late," he insisted.

"No, it is not. Don't you remember the story from the Scriptures about Amnon and Tamar? How did it end? He was dead and she forlorn for the rest of her life. Why? He did not love her. In fact, it turned out he hated her more fiercely than he had ever thought he loved her. I want you to be happy and you will never find contentment with me. We are not suited. I will always struggle against you, and you will grow tired of me."

"If this is the only way you will listen to me, then it has to be done."

"I don't want to be near you." The cold echo of her voice distressed her - how heartless she sounded. "Take me home. I am cold, so cold."

He was alarmed for he knew how close to death she had been after Boten Heath. He was cold too and his senses returned.

"It is closer to my home from here, I will take you there. Mother will care for you. I cannot set you free here in the dark."

"I will not run. Unbind my legs and I will ride behind you."

Lee mounted the horse, and they rode west under clear starry skies. His thoughts steadied. He knew his mother would understand what he had done. She could nurture the maiden and gently instruct her in household duties. Was it so wicked to snatch her away from her unruly household where her brothers had thrown her into the path of the dark-haired villain?

They crossed the highway and the track fell into the steep entrance of a more ancient way. Sounds of the night deadened so Lee could hear her own heart beating. The horse was also nervous and paused where the two ivy-covered layered hedges had collapsed hindering its way. Several times Lee raised her hands to guard her head and was not sure what happened as they left the lane. At the ascent, she caught sight of a shooting star. But as she straightened, she realised it was below the horizon. The dreamlike hush of the lane was left behind. Her pounding heart sounded like a horse in full gallop. Before them a swirl of approaching light held her gaze. It was like the curving patterns on the enchanted seaxe. It was a sword!

The Thegn's horse reared. She jumped clear but her captor was stunned. Lee took his sword from the saddle and struck with all her strength. Both horse and rider were startled. A sword flew upwards and the one who had wielded it lay with a blade pressed against his chest.

"Lee," he said weakly. He gazed up towards the moonlit hair rippling over her shoulders. "It's me. Win is not far behind."

"The Thegn has not harmed me. He has repented. Now get up and put your sword away."

Lee withdrew her weapon and Ædwine rose to his feet but not before Win had seen him laying sprawled before his sister. The dazed Thegn moaned and struggled to stand. Lee stood firmly between the two men and Win jumped off his horse to join her.

"That's one lucky thegn," Win whispered. "For your man had moved in for the kill. I was left back there."

"He was doing what he thought was right." Lee spoke in Ædwine's defence. "No good can come from going around forcing people to go where they do not want to go." Lee turned to the Chief Thegn. "You should be thankful no one was harmed. Now go home and meditate on the story. And you Ædwine, let him go on his way in peace for I am cold and damp. Take me home Win, Pip will be worried."

When she was seated on the horse behind her brother, the weary Thegn took his cloak and wrapped it around her. He shivered and hastened to his home where his mother greeted him and wondered why he had returned from Medeshamstede without his cloak. He was weary and stricken with remorse – he had lost her, and to an oarsman!

Pip was surprised at the speed of their return and seated Lee in front of the fire. Frith offered her some warmed rosehip cordial. Gragus put his arm around her.

"I should have taken up your offer to meet Pip sooner. He has forgiven you Ædwine." Gragus looked at his friend who sat the other side of Lee. "And you must forgive him Lee for when he puts on his battle garments and straps on his sword he is as mad as a boxing hare."

"I hardly believed it. He gave me such a fright."

"You didn't look frightened," Ædwine mused.

"And the Thegn was so shocked he barely said a word," she added.

"How did the man live to see another sunrise? Men rarely escape Ædwine's sword."

"I will explain," Ædwine insisted. "I was terrified Gragus; look at my blade." He showed Gragus the deep notch. "His sword must be very fine."

"Did he strike you first?" Gragus asked.

Lee wondered what Ædwine would say.

"The Thegn was helplessly pinned down by his horse and would never have risen to fight another day, for the ærn swooped swiftly enough. But there was a mad she-lynx in the shadows who turned and defended her helpless cub."

"You should not have laughed so readily when she felled me," Win said. "And she has trained in Edmund's Hall with Grandfather's mighty sword since then. I would not like to face her."

Gragus turned to his friend and grinned.

"I am lost for words."

Ædwine laughed.

Pip was relieved. Gragus and Frith had already impressed him. Frith had done most of the talking although it had been Gragus who explained more about Dummoc and how they eventually outwitted Alcuin at Elmham, where Gisla was set free.

Unfortunately, Alcuin had slipped from their grasp, and they had not met up with Gisla. She went straight to her kin at Southwic while they had joined with their own kin on Horsye Isle for the winter festivals. Pip was pleased to learn they already had some family in the kingdom, even if they did live in the wild margins beyond the fens of Flegg.

"Why didn't you scream and run? That's what you told me to do."

"He bound me, Fred, so thoroughly I thought it was Alcuin."

"How did you get free then?" Asked Win.

"We stopped at the dovecot near Sutton church, and he took the band from my mouth,"

"That was very rash," laughed Win. "I expect you made a moving speech and promised him you wouldn't run if he untied you."

"I tried to run, then he agreed to take me to his mother. I saw him differently tonight – not a stealthy hunting dog but a poor lost puppy."

"He is a ravenous cub still," warned Ædwine. "Remember it was the cub who betrayed the Swan Princess."

"Whatever do you mean?" Pip asked.

"The cub caused her to have pity and she looked into its eyes, and she broke her vow, 'Do not look into the eyes of the wolf or you will be lost.'" Frith added. He knew exactly what his brother meant.

"I wish I'd never written the tale," Lee sighed.

When supper was over Fred, Win, Frith and Ædwine left for the bower hall but Lee remained with Gragus and Pip who was stretched out on the longbench dozing amongst the cushions.

"Pip told me how ill you were after we parted. If I had known, I would have come to your side."

"Did he tell you I called your name?"

"No, he did not say."

"I was in a terrible dream and saw you hanging at Dummoc - Gisla was looking on, just as Alcuin desired. I was sitting on the courtyard wall and when I looked down at myself, I was not the pure white Swan Princess I was one of those wicked black ones which haunt Ædwine. I had betrayed you and I did not know it. I kept calling for you, but I could not reach you." He kissed her hair and she lay her head on his shoulder. When at last she looked into his eyes she saw they were misted with tears. "I have hurt you without meaning to, Gragus. We are not the same. You are from the far side of the great grey sea which I have scarcely glanced at. Ædwine was wrong when he said I was a lynx for I am not even a wildcat, only one who loves to lay in front of the fire in a safe hall. You are the lynx – happy to wander free in wild places and I cannot tame you."

"Dearest Lee, I am no lynx either. There is nothing I desire more than to warm myself in front of a fire in a hall such as this - but what you feared is upon you. Their *micel here* is gathering on Thanet, the isle south of Essex, and the Kentish thegns have not harried them. I do not know which of our kings leads them or what jarls have gathered their men under his banner. It could be one of Ragnor's sons, or worse, two of them. They are wild ones and to be feared. But there are other kings closer in spirit to the noble content in this realm. They may persuade them not to strike - and I must give them aid."

"Please stay with us."

"What would your king say?"

"He would not be offended. You could work with Pip and Win. Ædwine knows our ways."

"Ædwine was not himself when he was here. He warned me it is very bewitching to dwell in this realm."

"Like lying in a swathe of sweetmead?" Gragus looked confused. "It's a tall plant, which has a sweet sickly smell - very overpowering. It grows in our meads in the summer and makes you just want to lie there watching the clouds go by."

"I know it." Gragus smiled and kissed her cheek.

"We have much to learn about each other's lands."

"Let's make a pledge then," he said taking her hand. "I will learn more about your woodlands and you can learn about the seas."

"You can learn stories from my Scriptures, and I will find out about the heroes in your tales." Lee pondered the differences between their ways.

"We are not so unlike you Lee, but it may be many moons before I can rest. Will you wait for me?"

"Yes," she whispered. "But I am afraid. Edmund says I must face the fears I feel in my heart and choose my path wisely."

"I was afraid at the tavern," the oarsman confessed. "The seaxe you found made us face what we had evaded by resting in your kingdom. I do not want to leave it, but I must."

Before Lee could reply he kissed her again. Pip woke up and coughed. Lee left for her sleeping quarters and Gragus stood up.

"Edmund will demand a high price for my sister," Pip declared.

"And I cannot pay," replied Gragus. "Is that what you think? I would no more betray my own than you would, so do not go there."

"It's an impossible situation then?"

"I fear it is, and the battle may be closer than we think."

"What do you mean?" Pip asked.

"You must tell Edmund that many oarsmen have gathered at Tamysemouthe. I will go and find out who they are and how they intend to act - for Lee's sake but say nothing to anyone except Edmund or his jarl, Os. Your king should have built those bridges."

Pip thought he referred to allegiances between the Saxon kingdoms for that was why Edmund had spent so long in Essex during the autumn. However, the Mercians had ended his hopes of building an alliance against the oarsmen.

THE OARSMEN DEPART

Gragus slept peacefully amongst those who, given time, he hoped would be his kinsmen. Before breakfast he joined Lee out in the frosty mead where she was urging Ædwine to steady a wildly bucking horse.

"He does well," Gragus said. He went and stood beside her at the rail.

"The ground is very hard; it strengthens resolve," she whispered.

"If he breaks his leg, I will leave him with you."

"Then tell him to dismount for he was a poor enough patient when he had a bruise," she laughed.

Gragus signalled to Ædwine who jumped off the beast and removed the bridle. The mare ran off to the shelter of the holly hedge.

"You must train them yourself for I cannot spare Ædwine - but he told me you are the finest horse-maiden in the kingdom. Though I would urge you to wait for the thaw for I do not want you to break any bones either."

"It might snow. That would soften any fall. When I was a young girl, I remember jumping from the ponies backs into the drifts. My older brothers taught me the importance of knowing the lie of the land - I jumped into a drift over the pond. It gave them a fright because the ice was thin and I went straight through it."

"Ædwine told me you have three older brothers. Will they return?"

"They are married to Wessex maidens," she revealed. "My father had land far from here. When he died my brothers had to take possession of it to avoid being challenged by other kin. Pip and Win will take control of mother's estates here when they are old enough – Edmund has other tenants in place until then."

"Is Edmund your guardian?"

"My older brothers made Gisla my chief guardian - but her husband made her task difficult," Lee hesitated. "You did know she was married?"

"What kind of man is he?" Gragus asked avoiding the question.

"He was jealous of Gisla's high status in Edmund's household when he himself was kept at a distance – and for good reason. He separated her from her son and daughter. He's ill-tempered and vain. His daughter grew to be like him. She married one of his retainers."

"And the son?"

"He went away without telling Gisla. Did she ask you to look for him?"

"No. She mentioned him once in a tale - and he was very young. Where does her husband live?"

"Far from here." Lee answered vaguely because she remained troubled by her entwinement with Gragus.

Gisla's husband ruled Edmund's vill at Sudbourne. The position had been bestowed on him against the young king's advice. His former counsel never lived to see the outcome of their folly. The death of his brother, Will's father, had never been accounted for. Edmund suspected Sudbourne was the guilty party but lacked proof. Lee was tempted to tell more of the tale. But she did not because a young trader like Frith had been accused of the murder. Lee had never ventured to uncover the mystery which was forbidden ground because Will's mother disappeared about the same time. No one spoke about her for fear of hurting Will.

"He's not your guardian, is he?" Gragus asked. He wondered why Lee had hesitated.

"No, and you must not go near him," she said. "Did he know you were looking for Gisla?"

"Perhaps he did."

"Was she worth it?" Ædwine cut in, coldly confirming he was listening to their conversation. Lee was thankful she had been cautious.

"Don't you like my kinswoman?"

"I haven't met her," he declared.

"You never said."

"There is much I have not said."

"Ædwine joined us after we had left Gisla's dairy. He sensed something was amiss when we failed to reach Theodred's Ford and only caught up with us after we were arrested in Gipeswick."

"How did news of the arrest reach you so quickly?" Lee asked.

"I sent word abroad that Gragus had not kept our rendezvous. I knew he was being pursued and was anxious to know if he had been captured."

"So, you *were* expecting trouble? Did the Thegn have reason to pursue you?" Gragus did not reply. "Will you overthrow my king?"

"I will never betray you, or those you love," Gragus declared. "I have told Pip I intend to find out why the liths are gathering."

"And you?" Lee asked Ædwine.

"Last night you saw what I was. How can I deny it?"

"Why don't you go and find your wife?" Lee suggested. "Then you can settle here – in Flegg perhaps."

Ædwine looked down and laughed scornfully. Lee did not know what to say but Gragus put his hand on her shoulder.

"It has not gone well between them Lee. And I do not want him to go near her again. She is not worthy."

"I am sorry Ædwine, I thought … "

"And I don't want her back. I can take another wife at any time."

"You can?" Lee asked.

"It's why your men fear us. Os was thoroughly offended – did you not understand why he asked so many questions about wives? It's because we have so many."

Gragus was offended by his companion's indiscretion and Lee noticed how well the two men read each other. Ædwine turned and left.

"Ædwine is unsettled, my love. It is true some take more than one wife, but I have taken none."

"He told me he had a different mother to Frith - but I thought she had died. Did his father have more than one wife?"

"Yes, and they were always arguing. In the end, he settled for one."

"But not Ædwine's mother?"

"No, nor Frith's"

"How many wives did he have?"

"I only intend to have one." Gragus took her hand.

"Then don't go to Thanet for I have overheard all who dwell there have many women."

"Most is rumour to shame us, though some are very wild - your abbots and their retainers are no better."

"I know. Alcuin provides their concubines, doesn't he?"

"It is as I said, we are not so different." Lee did not laugh, and he knew he had not spoken wisely. "I do not approve of their deeds Lee. A man cannot be faithful when alliances multiply – and all sorts of falseness and betrayal rush in where pleasure rules. When young, I followed that path. I left those ways when Ædwine's brothers died. Can you forgive me?"

"Yes. Our God forgives and commands we do the same." He kissed her. "Please stay with us," she urged. "Do you have to go back to them?"

"I wish I could stay. I will return to you and more quickly if I leave now."

"Will you leave today?"

"Yes. It is too soon I know, but I must find out what is happening."

"Do you mean to see Gisla? You must love her very much."

"She befriended us and helped when we needed a surgeon to aid Frith. She was our valued adviser in a kingdom we did not know well." He feared he had not been direct enough and added. "I have never embraced her. We are friends just as you and Ædwine are. No, not even that close, for she does not know my thoughts and you read Ædwine well. Gisla may have guessed we are more than traders - but you know what we are."

"Oarsmen?"

"Is that what you thought Ædwine was when you saw him in his battle gear?"

"He looked like an Ætheling."

"A jarl?"

"It makes no difference to me what you were," Lee said bluntly. "In Edmund's kingdom, the lowliest of servants can become high-ranking stewards, and our king is servant to all. He follows the Way of our Lord Jesus who in greatest humility stepped down from his noble position in heaven and lived for thirty years among his kin - so they could be set free. We who believe are counted as his kin, but proud men, whether high born or low, cannot understand such ways although it is only way to redeem us."

"It makes no difference to you if I am not 'high born'?"

"No. Outside our Lord's heavenly kingdom all are slaves to their own ways whether they were born as jarls or not and inside his kingdom we are all of his kingly line - by faith."

"There are things I do not comprehend. When it comes to gods, I know little for they are far away. Ædwine fears them and makes his sacrifices but what do they care about me? I once thought I would like to go to the Great Hall to eat and drink with my brothers but when Weland died, I changed my mind. His fellow warriors did not honour him. Their duplicity has lately returned, and in Dyflinn Danes and Norwegian are murdering each other."

"Did fellow Scandinavians assassinate Weland? Is it what troubles Ædwine?"

"No, much worse. They scorned him."

"But why?"

"Can you not guess?" He asked bitterly. "Do not mention this to Ædwine, for he has been stretched in mind since he saw the seaxe you recovered at Boten."

"Because I have not returned yours?" Lee asked. "I can go and find it and be back before noon."

"Leave it for now, I have Ædwine's." Gragus threw it at the gate post. She saw how similar it was to the one she had hidden. And it was not unlike the one she had retrieved at Boten. Then, in jest, she dashed away with it through the orchard, over the bank and into the lane. He followed. Lee proclaimed it was part of her collection and after a lot of running, feigning, and avoiding, she eventually returned it to him, and they made their way back to the hall.

It was a pleasant breakfast. It was agreed Lee and Win could accompany the three guests as far as the great east-west highway where they would direct them to Thorney. Lee was anxious to retrieve her ring so a detour through the Hellesden was arranged. The horses were made ready, and they parted company beyond the sunken lane.

Fred and Pip walked towards Alder Fell and Win led the way to Elm Green.

The journey began merrily enough. Frith swiped his brother with a willow twig and a great game began.

"I don't have my herbs with me today if they fall off." Lee commented. The two brothers continued to taunt each other. Gragus smiled but a sudden seriousness fell upon Lee. "I hope to learn more about herbs and healing. I will be more useful caring for our wounded than sitting at home despairing when we are invaded."

"If I am wounded far from you, then I will think of you running amongst the frosted orchard trees; it will lift the pain from my heart."

"There is pain in my heart too for I do not want you to go."

"I feel very sorrowful my love. Poor Frith is trying to make me laugh but I cannot. There is too much I have not said, and I do not know where to begin. Say no more about me to Gisla ... "

Ædwine then raced past and Lee warned him to slow down.

"There's a mire ahead!"

Ædwine pulled up his horse.

"I know these woods, Lee. Win told me the hunting is good up the old road towards Carr meads. It was fair hunting on Flegg at the winter feasts. Gragus brought down some geese. He can call to his own kind."

"Is your name Gragus?" Lee asked.

"It was the first name I remember being called."

"He is named after a longship. It was a beautiful vessel – have you seen one?"

"I have heard them described in tales. I didn't know they had names. Why were you named after one?"

"I was born on it." Gragus admitted.

"Your poor mother."

"She lived to tell the tale and my father was very proud of her – he had one wife," he whispered. "Father said it made me as much at home on the sea as on land."

"I have travelled some of our rivers but have never gone further than where the fresh water mingles with the sea's saltiness. Have you rowed where the sea is sapphire blue?"

"I have rowed on all sorts of seas," Ædwine interrupted. "Wild, raging tempests and calm millponds, grey, brown, blue and one red with blood. And cliffs of all shapes and heights."

"You must have seen some very beautiful sights – not the blood of course," Lee noted.

"There is nothing more worthy or beautiful than to die in the bloody throes of battle," Ædwine argued.

"It will be my tears which wash away your blood for am I not a swan princess – or maiden as you call them."

Ædwine was caught off guard and ceased his game.

"We are not eager for battle yet," Gragus concluded. "And I will see Frith settled first. Did you see his scars?"

"No." They continued their way in silence.

When the ring was recovered Lee quietly urged Gragus to keep it. He kissed it and threaded it between the beads on his leather neckband. In return he secretly removed his ring but kept it safe in his hand as his attachment to it held him back. He wondered at his own foolishness. It was the ring which Weland had made and given to him. They had sworn eternal fealty on it - and it was precious. Much later, when they drew close to the Holy Cross Gragus held out his hand towards her.

"Keep this until we meet again."

Ædwine did not observe how Gragus parted with their great leader's gift which Ædwine had hoped would forge a new alliance amongst the liths.

At the east-west highway they dismounted beside a small bourn which murmured its way between icy banks. Gragus kissed Lee but her heart was heavy. Ædwine mistook her sorrow for coldness and held back from embracing her. It was a miserable parting.

The highway to the east was all mud so Ædwine suggested they travel through the yellow-flowered furze along the northern edge of Blackheath. He was travelling away from the route suggested by Pip for he feared pursuit. They made camp along the ancient route north which cut through an area of circular ponds. Ædwine complained the place was haunted but Gragus would travel no further.

"I am weary my friend. Lay down between us and forget about the pools. I am sure Lee has some explanation for their shape. How I wish she were here – have I really passed her by again?"

"Do you want to return to her hall?" Asked Frith.

"Yes, I do but they will not release her. What do I have to offer? There is much I cannot reveal. What do you advise my friend?" He asked Ædwine.

"I hope to see Stein tomorrow. He may have discovered more about the man who had Weland's seaxe. I need to know."

"Do you think he was in Francia when it was taken?"

"No, I remain convinced Weland's Christian wife stole his hoard along with his seaxe."

"That is your opinion Ædwine," Frith protested. "I don't agree."

"My judgement was made after you had been taken from the battlefield, brother. I was the one who stayed behind and saw what they did to Weland. If he had not followed her to his doom, we would have a mighty lith and many would now be fighting under our banners. I should have pressed him to come with me to repair the ships, but I left him with her. What did she do but lead him like a dumb animal straight to the king's hall?"

"He went because certain men grumbled against him; they were jarls and he was not," Gragus corrected. "He was trying to buy their loyalty."

"He should not have left his liths."

"Weland did not abandon his men. He went to buy supplies and the king delayed him," Frith intervened.

There were many tales about the purpose of Weland's sojourn in the Frankish court, but no one knew with any certainty how Weland's victory became his defeat.

"Our ships were in a terrible state," Frith continued. "And he needed good timber to repair them and there was none available for our coastal coppice had been plundered and burnt."

Ædwine remained silent for he knew Frith rebuked him. Months before Weland's death, shortly after his liths had razed Melun, Ædwine had begun to suspect the king's men were playing a game of cat and mouse with them. Weland continued to deny it until the king refused to sell him timber from the Brie Forest which lay adjacent to the old quarries where they were camped. Ædwine had stolen away from the old monastery one eve and set fire to the tinder dry coppice making it look like an accident. But the king's men were waiting for a reason to burn the coppice at Seinemouthe which belonged to the Norsemen. Their revenge had been swift and thorough.

"I acted in haste," Ædwine admitted. "Weland should have sent Gragus to the court; he would not have been deceived."

"I was already in Seinemouthe by then," Gragus protested. "Frith would have died if I had turned back. We have discussed this many times; Weland sent me here to watch over Frith. I was determined not to fail as I did before. I was the one at fault then."

Gragus turned away and Frith told his brother to keep at peace. Ædwine lay down but his troubled past began to cloud his thoughts. Lee had called herself a Swan Princess and he could no longer separate black from white for all swans brought disaster. He wrestled with his gloomy thoughts. He wanted to leave the kingdom and never return. Gragus must do the same and forget the maiden.

On Tuesday, stormy weather made it impossible to work in the Hellesden and the coppice team stayed inside repairing ropes and sharpening saws. Several trees were uprooted. Lee was worried about her absent trader friends; were they already sailing across the wind-tossed seas, she wondered.

Lee had fastened Weland's ring to a cord woven from green dyed linden and the silver threads the Swan Princess had worn in her hair at Dummoc. The precious token pressed close to her heart. She was at peace about her pledge - at least until Edmund returned and discovered what she had done.

During the storms her king was far away at Hunestanestede where the raging tempest threw giant waves at the foot of the cliffs causing great sections of the brown rock to shift. At morning prayers Edmund assured his household thegns good would come from bad, and the loosened rocks could be used later in spring to build the base of a new watch tower.

The storms quietened during the evening and by the morning a thick sea mist extended far inland. Edmund began his search of the hall where Will had been charmed by Alcuin's words. The King's thegns discovered a labyrinth of transactions and toll evasions and secret deals; some of which appeared to barter services for goods. However, Edmund could not uncover what secrets the wicked Bard hid there.

The King decided to draw up an inventory of everything in the hall and premises. Manuscripts and documents were inspected, and copies made. However, the port had not kept adequate records for many moons. They lied and said the records had been stolen but Edmund knew better. And his fears proved to be well founded. A large trading vessel closed in on the port but veered away as if warned by some secret signal. Edmund knew it was done to avoid inspection. The port thegns blamed the weather. However, Edmund's men were thorough and uncovered a large quantity of timber in a warehouse. It was the cargo the vessel had refused to collect – very valuable and extorted from bookland to the south. Edmund pledged to send some of his own administrators to re-establish control and justice.

Edmund set up his court at Gisla's Hall which lay inland from the coastal settlement. The homestead included a group of medium sized halls used as accommodation for travellers though they had once been places of healing. Two tradesmen, who intended to board the vessel which abandoned its landing, had arranged with the steward to stay at the halls. Edmund was curious to find out if they were involved with the illicit timber shipments. He invited them to dine with him and his thegns.

At dusk the weary traders crossed the home pightle to meet with the king in his hall. They had been travelling for weeks and were anxious to leave the kingdom. The king entered and greeted his guests with a friendly embrace. His suspicions about the pair were confirmed by the arrival of a third man who had harried his thegns at the port. He knew the interview would not be easy. Fortunately, Eth was on duty elsewhere and did not witness the deception.

"Where have you travelled from?" Edmund asked.

"We came up from Theodred's Ford," Gragus began. "We had been in North Burgh before then," he added. He tried to be as truthful as possible.

"My port thegns said you were waiting to board the vessel which did not stage here. Were they expecting you?"

"No." Gragus answered with great reluctance which the king misinterpreted as guilt.

"What is your trade?" Edmund demanded. The king's

persistence sparked Ædwine's restless spirit. Without hesitation he jumped in. He was concerned Gragus might decide to reveal who they were.

"I'm a smith and Helmstan is a carpenter."

Edmund remained calm and smiled.

"It's a fine trade. My Lord was a carpenter. Come, eat and you can tell me how trade is in these parts."

Edmund discerned they were reluctant guests, particularly the dark-haired smith who had harangued his thegns. Edmund began the conversation again and talked about the recent storms and shipwrecks. He told them about the old folklore which said if the weather was wild and stormy on St Paul's day, which was the following day, then winds and rain would wreck the coming harvest. It was the opportunity Frith sought and he carefully steered the conversation towards farming. Edmund was delighted. Gragus and Ædwine listened intently and wondered when Frith would betray himself.

"Do you have land in your own kingdom?" Edmund asked.

"No, it was my cousin who inherited the farms. I was cut off."

"And why was that?" Edmund enquired.

"It happens."

"And you?" Edmund asked Ædwine. "Have you been dispossessed?"

"Yes," he replied abruptly.

"It is why we wander as tradesmen," Gragus intervened.

"What sort of carpenter are you?" Edmund asked the man who he perceived was their leader.

"I build barns and halls and sometimes ships."

"Have you been ordering supplies from our woodlands? I have been examining the passage of goods through this port and find many shipments of timber exchanged for no payment. Do you know why?"

"I have not ventured here before so I cannot answer. It grieved us to see the despoiled coppice here."

"I am trying to discover who is responsible for its ruin. Coppice needs to be well managed if it is to yield high quality products. My own coppice in The Hellesden is said to be the finest in the realm." Edmund raised his cup. "Here's to our woodlands and those who tend them."

Edmund directed the men to the benches placed around the hearth and as Gragus sat down he saw Lee's ring amongst the beads. It confirmed what he has suspected. The man before him was the one who had captured his maiden's heart. Edmund was disappointed. He had trusted Lee's judgement, but the man was not worthy. They stared at each other, a king who would guard his precious flock with all the strength he had, and one who was cloaked in deception; a wolf wandering amongst his sheep to steal his precious lamb.

"So, you are Gragus," Edmund said at last. Ædwine moved swiftly and made ready to take up his seaxe but Frith was vigilant and stayed his brother's hand, hoping Edmund did not see.

"Yes. We have come from Hellesden Hall. I left a message for you with Lee and Pip. Many oarsmen have set up their camps on Thanet. The Kentish jarl has restrained his hand and keeps his thegns penned, so more gather there each week. We are going to Eoforwic to find out who has beckoned them."

"Why Eoforwic?"

"The traders there have connections with camps in Francia and the ships on Thanet come from there. I will send any news to Lee."

Gragus was as honest as he had ever been but Ædwine was as troubled as skies which herald storms from Thor himself.

"Lee has told me about Francia and advised me to make further defence works but I refuse to lay the burden of heavy taxation on my people. We raise our children to be free and merry not weighed down by divisions and taxation."

"You will be neither free nor merry if they overrun your kingdom," Gragus warned.

"We will rejoice in our freedom while we can. If I took all the money from all my subjects and built the best defence works I could, it would not be enough. We are a small kingdom and have not fared well at the hands of Mercia. It is there you will find gold, for they emptied our chests and stripped our religious houses in my grandfather's days. I have no desire to seek what I cannot hold. We bring nothing into this world and can take nothing when we depart. I am thankful I have enough food to eat and share, and I rejoice with my people. We sing and dance and dispense justice – as you have experienced." Edmund hesitated to see if Gragus would show some gratitude. The oarsman, however, was lost in his thoughts about Lee. What would she think when Edmund presented his report? "My Chief Thegn was misguided at Dummoc, and I have dealt with him." Edmund added.

"He is more than misguided," Ædwine scorned. Frith kicked him.

"He spoke well of you and your efforts at Boten."

"You should not listen to vanities," Ædwine continued. His hand made ready to fight. "He was not thankful when we met a few days past."

"Where did you find him? I have men searching wide and far," Edmund revealed. He turned back to Gragus. "He went to Medeshamstede to discover the truth about Lee's betrothal to our Will. Did she tell you what she had done?"

"She has been left without protection in these matters."

"I know and I regret she has had to suffer."

"Why didn't you act then?" Ædwine interrupted. "That is your weakness – you knew ill would happen and yet you did not prepare! It is the same with your defences."

Edmund was astonished at his directness.

"You agreed Ædwine," Gragus intervened. "The Thegn will not return to Lee's Hall. He knows how deeply she was offended. He crept away like a hound which had killed its master's best hawk."

"What has he done?" Edmund asked.

"He stole her away," continued Ædwine. "The same day you and your stony-hearted crow called on her. He must have watched for you to leave and waited in the stable. He captured her easily enough."

"And you released her?"

"No, she rescued herself, but we took her back to her hall."

"Her older brothers will not be pleased when they hear this. You know about them, don't you Gragus? They are not like our gentle Pip and young Win," Edmund warned.

"Do you think Gragus is afraid?" Ædwine angrily retorted. "If he had desired the maiden, he would have taken her - but he does not want her."

"Then why does your friend wear her ring?" Edmund asked.

Ædwine lent forward to look and was unable to conceal the tremor of offence at what he saw. His jarl openly wore the maiden's ring, and the king knew it. He looked at Frith who did no more than shrug his shoulders.

"We have exchanged rings." Gragus admitted. "However, we do not know when our paths will cross again. What can I do to persuade her kin?"

"I fear her brothers will not be won over by your conduct so far. You must hope they do not hear any rumours. The eldest two have harried the Welsh Lords and are more battle hardened than we are. If they think she is in peril they will take her back to their lands. If she is summoned, you will see her no more."

"You must keep her here," Gragus protested. "She would try to return, and I do not want her to endanger herself. Would you consider petitioning her brothers on my behalf though I am but a stranger?"

"I would urge you to abandon your attachment. You have nothing but sorrow to offer her. She is young and inexperienced and thinks she can change you."

"We are tired, my Lord," Frith intervened.

"I am tired as well. You two may leave but there is more I have to say to you Gragus - it will not take long."

Ædwine and Frith stood up and Frith raised his cup before he left. His cheerful smile concealed the turmoil inside for he knew he would need much wisdom to steady the hand of his brother who was trembling with fury.

When they left, Edmund sat down again and looked at the stranger now separated from his dark guard. He hoped they could speak more freely.

"I am here in this place to establish what role Alcuin has played in the imprisonment of Gisla. You must disclose all you know and freely, for I do not understand why you did not say who you were. I can only assume you have much to hide."

"I do not know as much about Alcuin as you think. I have more reason than you to solve the riddle about him for I do not understand why he is determined to put me to death. I have seen him but once, and that was years past when I came to Dummoc with a friend to trade our silver."

"He has many guises," Edmund warned. "He is known as Albion in Wessex. It is one of his lyrical gestures as the great scholar Alcuin was also known as Albion amongst those who are familiar with Latin."

"The code of your religious halls? Alcuin treads lightly in your sacred houses and perhaps those in Francia too – I hope to find out more."

"If you discover he has been at work in Francia I would like to know. Send word to Lee."

"Do you permit me to write to her?"

"I will read everything you write," Edmund warned. "Alcuin is not welcome in my halls nor places where my bishop Hunberht has influence but I have another bishop here who is not of the same mind."

"Æthelwold?"

Edmund nodded.

"He conceals much," the king revealed. "He is a Mercian, and it was he who arranged the Elmham meeting which offended Gisla. I fear he has silenced her, for her son-in law at Southwic is much in his debt."

"Will he order her death?"

"Blood continues to be shed amongst her line. If she is wise, she will not pursue the matter. Leave her Gragus, for she has suffered enough and is content to find happiness with her grandson."

"So Gisla will not return to care for Lee?"

"Lee is wise enough to find her own way. She has Pip and of course she has Os and me."

"How will you guide her in matters of the heart? Are you willing to give me a second chance?"

"She knows my opinion and I have left her to examine her ways. I am sure she will forget you in time. I urge you not to trouble her."

"If I discover no more about Alcuin, I will not write to her," the oarsman offered. "I will not stir up what cannot be settled. However, you must keep the Chief Thegn away from her. I do not trust him and there is something she knows about him which she has not revealed to any of us."

"I will watch over her," Edmund said. He raised his cup to signal their parting. Gragus took up his cup and blessed the king. Edmund wondered if there was anything wholehearted about the man before him.

"Frith was serious when he asked permission to occupy a

hall in your kingdom. He is trustworthy and I will send back Lee's ring with him when he returns. I cannot throw it back to her now as if it meant nothing to me."

Edmund reflected upon his first meeting with Gragus and decided to send for the three men the next day to aid him with his investigations. He sent Gragus to Alcuin's Hall to read the runic script there, and Frith to Eth to advise him with the beacons for he trusted Frith more than any of them. Eth embraced him and together they set about their task with great enthusiasm.

Edmund was determined to keep Ædwine near to his side for he recognised him as the dangerous spark amongst them. But Ædwine could not be found. Had Edmund witnessed the discord between the three traders the previous evening he would have understood, instead he concluded Ædwine was an enemy agent. He could not allow such a man to roam abroad in his kingdom.

On the day of their departure Edmund called Frith and Gragus to dine with him. The king gave Frith the lease of Chadsacre Hall which lay on the borders of the Hellesden not far from the Holy Cross. Frith was delighted. Gragus remained closed and Edmund could not read what was on his heart. He knew he had wounded the oarsman when he persuaded him to give up Lee and waited for him to plead to keep her. But he did not.

Late in the afternoon, the two oarsmen took their place amongst the rowers to head north to Eoforwic. Ædwine made a last call appearance and avoided Edmund. None had observed the proud warrior pass a bundle to Eth. It was for Lee and the lad discretely hid the package in the folds of his garments.

Ædwine threw his pack down beside his companion and took up his oar. They were soon midway in the Great Bay. Many old tales sought to explain the nature of the rocks in the cliffs at Hunestanestede which Gragus fixed his eyes upon as he departed from Edmund's kingdom. Some said the white was ice and the red, fire and the wrestling between the two had produced the fertile soil of the kingdom which was represented by the nethermost brown rocks. Ædwine also pondered the beauty of the cliffs and at last broke the silence.

"Nothing but dunes and reed beds to the north and south. However, these cliffs have all a man can desire; the red blood of the battles won, the brown stallion you rode against the Frankish king, and a pure white swan." Ædwine's words were light for a purpose. "Is she worthy of Weland's ring?"

"Yes."

Gragus looked at his friend and then back to the remarkable cliffs. His maiden was fair and purest white, and the red was his blood which would have been spilled had not his Swan Princess intervened. The brown was the waters of the bay - a great gulf which separated their two hearts.

"I found Stein at last," Ædwine revealed. "I told him things had changed."

"You did?"

"Yes, Gragus. You are not the same."

"I know I have changed. Are you offended?"

"It has unsettled me, but who am I to oppose the gods? Weland's ring was a love gift and I hope she realises what it has cost you." Ædwine hesitated. He was searching for the right words to say. "I have sent her Erik's talisman until we return."

Gragus raised his tear-misted eyes in astonishment and caught a moment of great beauty for he sensed something had been restored. His lith brother had given away what he held precious, and for her protection.

"It was a fine thought," Gragus said.

"I removed Mjöllnir," Ædwine added. "I did not want to insult her god. I sent it with young Eth. And a note."

"You did well. My deceit and presumption sorely offended Edmund. I agreed to return her ring."

"Then what is that amongst your beads?" Ædwine observed.

"I will cherish it for a while longer – though my heart is heavy."

The youngest one overheard and looked up.

"This is no time to be down-hearted my friend," Frith replied merrily. "I am back at the oar. When you arrived in the realm I was as good as dead. And here I am. Love may have every appearance of being dead, but it is like fire hidden amongst the ashes. Would you like a song to cheer you?"

They nodded and Frith began his merrymaking so the whole vessel was lifted in spirit. Gragus quietly considered his sojourn in East Anglia and began to plan what he would do next. His future did not lie in the hands of Hastein, nor Halfdan nor any of Ragnor's offspring, but with Alcuin. He needed to discover what had happened in Francia in the weeks before Weland's death. Where had Weland gone before his arrival in Charles' court? How was it Alcuin had his seaxe? Did he have the rest of Weland's vast hoard? Or did he think he or Frith knew where it was? Perhaps it was why he pursued them.

CHAPTER TWELVE
UNMASKING THE THEGN

"Can't we go to the feast now?" Whined Fred. "Candlemass was yesterday."

"No," Lee patiently replied for the third time. "We must finish our studies, or we will lose what we have gained."

"But I studied the psalms on Tuesday and the prophets on Wednesday - I thought you wanted to meet the brothers at the Minster today to ask them to help me with my Latin?"

"I did Fred, but the Chief Thegn is in Beodrickworth. I cannot face him."

"You're right Lee. It's barely two weeks since he frightened you, isn't it? I wonder where Ædwine is. Pip misses him, and so does Win. He says your Gragus will be back before the new moon."

"If Gisla has come to the feast, then please do not mention him."

"Why not?"

"Because she must remain on good terms with her kin so she can stay with her grandchild."

"Oh," the lad replied. He had not understood her answer.

Lee had given her guardian's absence much thought. Both she and Edmund wanted to discover what Gisla had learned during her captivity.

"Is Os coming over to Edmund's Hall?" Fred asked.

"Yes, and his dearest mother," Lee warned.

"I will finish this then. The later we arrive the better."

Os had brought his entire household with him to the Candlemas services at Beodrickworth Minster. His kin from Meleforde were there as well. When Æthelric arrived at the King's Hall for the feast he immediately asked for Lee.

"I haven't seen her yet," Pip replied. "I expect she and Fred are avoiding the Chief Thegn."

"I have learned some of the tale – if a man loves a woman, then why doesn't he ask her plainly to be his wife?" Æthelric observed.

"Does he love her? I doubt he does," Edmund whispered.

"She will be a challenge for any man, I fear. She lost me easily enough." Æthelric smiled as he recalled how Lee had slipped from his gaze on the way to the kilns.

"She has resolutely refused him," Edmund continued. "His persistence irritates me. I am about to have him moved to the Borders."

"Not our borders at South Burgh I hope, for I cannot abide the man," said Æthelric. "His lineage is of no consequence and yet he imagines he is my superior."

"Do not rest your hopes on your ancestors. We are old rootstock which is perhaps best dug up and burned."

"What do you mean, my lord?"

"What loss will it be if we are the last generation of the Wuffingas to rule this fair realm? We must put our trust in God to bless the good we have sown and to help us keep to his ways."

"Do you fear the oarsmen?" Æthelric asked.

"Of course, but we have an enemy older than those northern pirates."

"Mercia?"

Edmund sighed and Æthelric understood.

"Who told you about the Thegn's latest blunder?" Edmund

asked.

"It was young Eth. Lee practices her skills of escape to great effect, but the Thegn will not forever be outwitted by her."

"I am her protector and I have decided to send him to keep order in the Mercian Borders. His time will be fully occupied there - and he will not be grieved for it is a higher post."

"He may not see it as you do."

"Maybe, but had he acted more wisely Lee would not have been thrown to the wolves."

"Do you refer to her oarsman?" Æthelric asked.

"They have gone. I watched all three rows out from Hunestanestede and strongly advised them not to return."

"Does Lee know?"

"It depends if Eth has found time to tell her. I doubt he has because his father is determined to keep the two apart."

"It will not please Lee."

"I have done much which will grieve her. I was not gentle with Gragus and told him not to pursue his hope of betrothal. I do not want her to take on the yoke of marriage too soon for oxen have to walk together and, as you know, she runs in all directions."

Æthelric looked at his king and laughed at the image. He also wanted the maiden to run free for as long as she could. His own fair sisters were very independent, and he would not release them from his household lightly.

Lee arrived late at the celebrations at the King's Hall because Eth's mother insisted she took care over her appearance in honour of their king. Her arrival at the feast was, therefore, noticed by all for she looked enchanting. Her gown was the richest she had ever worn and beautifully embroidered by Flæ's maids.

"Where have you been?" Os asked.

"At Ældor Hall studying – what was it, Lee?" Intervened

Fred.

"Logic," replied Lee. "Is your mother trying to call you?"

"Yes, she wants to speak to you so take care. She remains convinced you need her guidance."

The Ætheling's mother made a great fuss of the lad but said little to Lee who turned to speak to Branda. They discussed ideas for studies and garden improvements as Lee maintained it would be important to grow more food if the oarsmen came ashore. And more herbs would be needed for the healers to treat battle wounds. It was a significant exchange of ideas as it spurred Branda to make enquiries about spending time as a novice at a healing hall.

Early in the evening an exceptionally graceful lady joined Branda's mother and asked the girls many questions. She was about to address Lee when Edmund drew close and urged her to join him.

"The one who has your ring travels to Northumbria," Edmund whispered. She was taken off guard and blushed. "He was with me in Hunestanestede and left for Eoforwic on Saturday."

"You spoke with him?" Lee hoped all was well. "I thought they were to leave from Gipeswick and go to Thanet Isle."

"And Pip thought their destination was Dyflinn. They appear to change direction on every whim."

Lee began to feel uneasy.

"What do you mean?"

"They are not to be trusted, Lee. You have friends here to protect you."

"Do I?"

"I am about to deal with my Chief Thegn."

"I don't want to talk about him. I wish he would go away."

"Then your prayers will be answered. I have made certain arrangements in the Borders so your paths will rarely meet. I do not want his persistence to deflect you towards another."

"Did you speak to Frith?" Lee asked. She wanted to avoid mentioning Gragus and their pledge.

"He came with me to explore our farms. He loved the north-western corner of the realm. It is like you, very beautiful but vulnerable to oarsmen."

Edmund smiled and then kissed her cheek. He wanted to tell her Gragus had annulled his pledge, but he could not find the right words.

"You did not like Gragus?" Lee whispered. Branda joined them and he gave no answer.

Os wondered what his two friends discussed. He had seen Lee's cheeks burn red and noted how tenderly Edmund had kissed her. His mother had made a comment and sent the unwitting Branda with a message.

"Mother has agreed I can visit you at Hellesden Hall – but my sisters must accompany me."

"Your brother looks cross," Lee observed. "Did he object?"

"Mother is being overbearing," she whispered. "Os must greet all her acquaintances, or she will brood for weeks."

"Who is the noble lady who questions him so thoroughly?"

"She's the mother of the thegn you bought the puppy for."

Lee rushed away and Branda realised she had upset her new friend without meaning to. The younger maiden looked at her king, felt awkward and returned to her mother's footstool wishing she had the same courage as Lee.

In the Shield Hall, the junior thegns cheered at Lee's sudden appearance in her battle gear. She exhorted them to seek perfection for their king and lost herself in battle.

Fred found her there. He watched with delight as she overcame the youngest thegns. They were not much more than his age and persuaded him to join in. Lee taught him the skip side-step of battle. He protested at first because he felt more like a silly girl than a thegn, but Lee assured him good footwork was the key to success in battle.

Later, Lee sat down exhausted on a bare longbench near the great hearth in the lesser hall. Fred kindly bundled up her new dress to make a pillow for her head before he left his sister shield maiden to rest by the fire. As he crossed the yards, he saw Eth and sent him to watch over her.

Eth was disappointed he had arrived too late to watch her sparring. He had been on duty at Beodrickworth all day and looked for an opportunity to give her the package from Ædwine. However, she was already asleep.

When she woke up it was Os who sat next to her. She sat up stiffly and groaned from the heaviness of her limbs. He put his arm about her and told her she was rash to prefer battle garments.

"I would rather wear these than a wedding gown. Your mother and his are determined to measure me for one, and I will not yield."

"I know, and I am on your side Lee. Did Edmund tell you he sent your pursuer on his way?"

"He mentioned the Borders."

"I didn't mean Greg," he corrected. "Our king has ordered your coppice worker and his companions to leave."

"He *ordered* them to leave?" Lee cried.

"They behaved shamelessly in Hunestanestede."

"What did they do?"

"Ædwine was the worst – he nearly drew his seaxe on our king and would have done if Frith had not intervened."

"And Gragus?"

"He pretended to be a carpenter and used the name Helmstan. How many names do they have to use Lee before you realise, they are men without conscience? You must forget them!"

"How can I?"

"You must. Ædwine is a liar. He lied about Gragus. The man does not love you. All he wants is influence and power. Pip should have shown more wisdom when he hired Ædwine. It was plain to see he was a wicked man. What sort of influence has he had on young Win? You need to show better judgement Lee; daydreams are dangerous. Scripture says that leopards cannot change their spots. Those men are heathens! Edmund was wise to exile them."

Lee jumped to her feet.

"It was Ædwine who saved me from the wicked Chief Thegn. He is the one who needs to be exiled!"

"What do you mean?"

"Hasn't Edmund told you what he did?"

"I know he proved your betrothal to our Will was unfounded ..."

"His wrath over the letter was merely a distraction. He has not repented at all."

"What has he done?"

"Ask him!"

Lee dashed out of the side door into the cold night air. Eth stood nearby and escorted her to the bower hall where she was to stay with Branda and her sisters. They stood in the porch a long time discussing what had happened between Gragus and Edmund in Hunestanestede.

"I will stand by you, Lee." Lee wiped away her tears. "I am sorry I have been distant and mean recently. I never told you about the girl – the one who sang so sweetly while she sat upon the stone. She is the old Hethel Ceorl's daughter – her brother has a hunting pack trained to seek tarda geese. She travels with him for it is said she worships her brother, and his friends adore her for her singing."

"She did look like an angel."

"As does he."

"Really?"

"I must go Lee. Father is sending me into Beodrickworth again tomorrow morning – very early. Will you be attending prayers there?"

"No, I'm staying here. Can you join us later?"

"I must stay as I'm on duty at the gathering of Ældormen. Don't ask any questions about the Hethel Ceorl – I will tell you more later. Father is calling – I am sure he is keeping us apart Lee. I am tired and I promised to take my brothers up to Cattishall Way to see if there are any lambs yet. I should have asked Ric."

"I will take them tomorrow, with Ric and his sisters - and Branda - she's quite different when she's away from her mother."

Lee smiled at the thought of calling Æthelric, Ric - but thegns had all sorts of names for each other, and she was a young thegn.

Eth was surprised when he was invited to accompany Edmund, Os and all the Ældorman to their meeting where they discussed matters of security and mustering. He felt honoured his opinions were sought and spoke passionately about ways of improving the beacon warnings around the northern coast. His thoroughness impressed his father.

After a simple mass, Lee rode towards Cattishall with Ric and his sisters. When they arrived at the lambing shelter there were four new-born lambs, and more were born as they watched in silence from behind woven hazel hurdles. Their journey back was not as quiet, the girls marvelled at the lambs' efforts to stand and the ewe's devotion to them, especially to the twins. Ric laughed at their sentiment but noticed Lee's tears.

"I am sorry Lee. I had forgotten your mother was taken leaving twins to fend for themselves."

"I am not offended Ric," she said softly. "We have Hilde. She makes a good sheep hound."

Ric laughed loudly. All eyes turned their way.

"I understand the hound you bought for the Thegn is

proving very difficult to guide and train," he whispered.

"Just like me then," she said with a smile.

Ric laughed again and tossed his thick brown hair back and his sisters giggled. Lee caught their gaze and turned the conversation to the more serious matter of rivalries within the bishoprics of Elmham and Dummoc. Ric's concerns were far away at Salham where the powerful monastery, founded by St Felix, had authorised the ascendancy of a little known but ruthless Mercian ældorman.

"Is he the one who has tested Edmund's patience?"

"I imagine he is, for he has attended gatherings at Hauochestone recently to discuss regulating traders and the passage of slaves."

"Slaves?" Lee echoed.

"We cannot impose our ideas on other kingdoms and as you know, Salham Abbey has close ties to the foremost See in Mercia. We cannot regulate them, but we can seek to remove certain links which have been forged in the Borders which means holding down this ældorman's power. I think his wealth is from slaves. Our Chief Thegn will have to deal with him."

Lee felt the weight of what she knew about the Chief Thegn.

"Perhaps Edmund should send you, not Greg."

"You can't possibly mourn his departure."

"I won't, but he ..." Lee was going to say he was already trading slaves and may welcome the opportunity to extend his influence, but she held back. She must confront the Thegn soon to discuss what Wolf had said.

"Forget him, Lee. Let's have a game with the lads. Find the furze?"

Lee smiled and agreed. They organised Eth's brothers and played amongst the furze bushes until the sun began to sink. Later, Branda's mother was not pleased to discover her daughters were as dishevelled as the lads – and on the Lord's

Day. She changed her mind about Branda's stay at Hellesden Hall.

Lee, however, was determined Branda should visit her hall. The following day she dressed herself in her new gown to persuade Branda's mother it was a straightforward walk to her hall without mud and thorns.

When they set out the ground was still hardened by the frost which lay white like snow. At Carr Meads they turned east to enter the woods by the Birchin. The young thegns, however had raced ahead to skate and slide over the Gean Mire. Lee paused at the place the seaxe had flown through the skies towards her and wondered how Gragus would fare in Eoforwic. The lads thought she hesitated because she feared to tread upon the ice. To prove them wrong she played there until they were thoroughly exhausted.

Later Fred looked up at the graceful standards of the Birchin and said they looked like pure white swan maidens against the bright blue February skies. The junior thegns laughed, and Fred tried to explain what he meant. Lee had heard his Dummoc tales many times and lingered amongst the aged, broken bracken. When she had fled from Gragus the fronds had been shoulder high, but winter had withered their cover exposing a greater beauty – a golden carpet of fragmented bracken. Even if her love was crushed there was a steady golden glow in her heart.

At the crossroads, she met the Chief Thegn. He was travelling to Edmund's meeting in Beodrickworth. Lee was alone. She had not noticed how she had drifted from the party.

"Lee, I scarcely recognised you," he said. His horse drew to a halt alongside her. "You look very lovely. Have you come from the Candlemas celebrations at Edmund's Hall?"

"Yes – I must catch up with my young wards,"

"You were not at Beodrickworth?"

"No. I ..."

"Did you meet my mother?" His voice had a bewildered

urgency and Lee felt obliged to answer him though she longed to spring away.

"Yes."

"She is very noble and would have cared for you the night I erred. You have forgiven me, haven't you?"

"Yes," she replied. She did not dare look at him.

"I had to explain my actions to Edmund," he paused. "The truth is I was wearied from a long journey - and I was angry about your trickery. But I have forgiven you." He paused. "Have you forgiven me?"

"Yes," Lee whispered. "And I am sure Edmund has forgiven you as well. Whatever he says, you must resolve to do your best to serve him, - he is more important than our quarrel."

"I am not opposed to you. Is that what you think?" He dismounted and Lee drew back.

"We hardly agree on any matter, sir."

"We must lay our past differences aside."

"It is not just the past ..."

"I meant you no harm," he whispered. Before she could step away, he gripped her hand. "Come and visit mother next week. We will know by then what Edmund intends to do with me and we can discuss what happened at Dummoc."

"It is not just Dummoc," Lee continued. "There are other things I have not told Edmund."

"I know."

She tried to remove her hand from his.

"Then tell him yourself before you are completely adrift."

"Adrift? My dearest maiden it is you who has gone after heathens."

"Please let me continue," she pleaded. However, he remained standing in her way. "I must catch up."

"Not yet."

"But I am afraid, sir."

"Why?"

"I am just afraid. I cannot walk to places I have always walked. I will always fear you lie in wait for me for I will not be your wife – ever!"

"I cannot undo what happened - can't we be friends again?"

"But we have never been friends. I hardly know anything about you; except you made my brother's life very difficult. He might have stayed but you made sure he did not."

"Is that why you find me so disagreeable because of a mistake I made when I was no more than a junior thegn?"

"But you have not changed. You twisted judgements at Dummoc by accepting money."

"I was misled there. I did not intend to cast aside our laws."

"Are you saying no one paid you?"

"Yes," he lied.

He desperately wanted to be reconciled with the maiden before he faced Edmund. How could he explain what he had done? He unwisely attempted to draw her closer to him.

"People ought not to be traded like mares!" Lee passionately cried. She leapt away like a young doe.

"What is wrong Lee?" Asked Fred as she overtook him in her haste. "I thought I heard a horse. Was it the Thegn?"

"Yes."

"Did you look into his eyes?" Fred asked. His distress did not escape the ears of the young thegns.

"The sun was behind him. He was all black like a marsh dog."

They all laughed and ran to catch her. The Thegn overheard their merriment and knew the maiden was laughing at him and immediately regretted he had been so tender.

Os, Pip and Win arrived at the Hall at sunset where they found the thoroughly exhausted maidens lying upon the longbench in front of the fire.

"They are quiet," observed Os. "What have you been doing, Branda?"

"We skated and chased and planned the new garden and then chased the horses and climbed some trees ..." Branda murmured.

"It's as well your mother did not see us," Lee interrupted. "Branda was as black and slimy as a boar hunted across mudflats."

"You are very wicked Lee," he smiled.

"It's the Chief Thegn who is wicked," Fred objected. "Lee should be allowed to bring her sword home."

"I don't think so," Win added. "She is annoying enough with her new stave."

"Branda's mother made her leave it at the King's Hall," Fred pressed. "Just when she needed it to prod his horse."

"Greg was riding through the Hellesden," Branda tried to explain.

"Did he speak to you Lee?" Os asked.

"He did, but the sun was in her eyes," Fred interrupted. Os did not understand what the young lad meant.

"I spoke very politely to him - but he never listens," Lee complained.

"Well Edmund caught his attention. He's transferred him to the Mercian Borders and heaped countless duties upon him. He won't have time to trouble you anymore."

Lee looked up at Os and he knew he must discover what had been said. When he left the next morning, he spoke to her at the stables.

"Lee, say goodbye to Branda for me when she wakes. I'll be back in ten days and remember Gisla intends to call early next week. Be wise and cautious when she is here. Her husband is a churlish rebellious man and Edmund suspects he is up to no good. At least Greg can be trusted."

"Can he? His arrogance dismays me. I thought I was direct enough – but he would not confess."

"Confess?" Os asked.

"About his dealings with Alcuin."

"You are mistaken Lee; he swore under oath he did not know Alcuin was at Dummoc. Gisla confirmed it."

"There is something he conceals," she sighed.

"You must keep away from him," Os commanded. "I will question him again when I return - though I think you are mistaken."

Lee let the matter rest and began the task of digging the new garden for a warm wind had driven the frost away. By the end of the week Home Pightle had been transformed from grass to a mosaic of well tilled beds. The young thegns dug and raked while the girls stacked the turves to make a wind break along one side. When the area close to the existing bank was dug, the girls uncovered a colony of semi hibernating slowworms. Their discovery brought great delight and they built them a new place to shelter by adding birch tops to the base of their new turf bank. The twig tunnels were carefully covered, and the sleepy slow worms tucked inside.

Rain on Saturday drove Lee and Branda to the wood store to make hazel wind breaks and supports for the herbs. Not far into the afternoon the young thegns returned with Eth. They joined him and sat warming themselves in front of the hearth. They told tales about their training sessions and when Eth learned Branda was interested in treating wounds, he described the worst he had seen. She was sick and Hilde was not pleased.

Lee tucked a blanket round her friend and began some longer tales about her adventures with Will and Os the previous summer. Without warning Gisla arrived. She urged Lee to continue her tale. Gisla was moved by memories of her days at Sutton where the young Lee first learned the art of storytelling.

She kept up her delightful performance until she came to the part of the story which concerned Fred.

"It's easier if I go straight to the trial because everything was explained there. Fred, can you find our play-script?"

Gisla listened with interest as Lee went over the details of the trial. She was careful to treat the Thegn's role with great respect which surprised Gisla who thought the young maiden despised the man. She and Fred once more performed the play about the Swan Princess.

"Here, I must apologise for not singing the *Willow Song*. We have had complaints from the author of it. We do not have permission to destroy it again." There was much laughter. "And as you know, Branda, I came straight from the trial to your house at Bures and there we met a dragon – er Drega - who had a remarkable uncle. Your brother was not amused and sent them both away and then your dearest mother sent us home to our beautiful hall where we discovered Pip had found a strong man to work with the coppice team. He could tame the wildest horses Ric could find. He could make nails and hinges at the forge. He could carve the finest of flutes and chop up logs for Hilde and sometimes the other way round for we could not tame him, and he bolted."

Fred laughed so much Lee had to stop but she was glad her ordeal was over. Eth saw the relief on her face and turned his thoughts to the package Ædwine had given him. He had hidden it for now and wished he had not. Then Pip and Win arrived home and Lee left to help Hilde serve the meal. Gisla joined her in the kitchen.

"Thank you, Lee, for your dedication to finding me," Gisla said.

"I am glad you are free again," Lee said kindly. "We prayed for you, and more earnestly after I saw you at Boten."

"I was surprised you were there."

"I almost walked straight into a trap."

"Alcuin would not have spared you. It was Greg who saved you."

The comment startled Lee.

"I had not thought of it like that."

"I am going to visit him, and you must accompany me."

"Why?"

"To apologise."

"For what?"

"For having him sent as far west as is possible. Poor Lady Flæd is very upset. She does not want to uproot herself."

"She doesn't have to go with him," rebounded Lee.

"But he has no wife, and she feels responsible for his care."

"I am sure he will find a maiden to marry soon enough."

"You can be so unfeeling Lee. You have broken the poor man's heart, and you are not a bit ashamed."

Lee froze.

"I thought he despised me."

"He has never despised you. He is too important in this realm to have a maiden spreading lies about him. You should have known what sort of man he is. Duty comes first, before matters of the heart. Is that so bad?"

"It would have been bad for Frith. He would have died!"

"Don't let your version of events obscure the truth. There was no need to shame poor Greg. He knew what he was doing and would not have let Gragus and Frith be condemned without reason."

Lee did not like what Gisla said and began to feel troubled.

"Did you find out what was discussed in Elmham?" Lee asked.

"No," Gisla answered very abruptly.

"Edmund is determined to find out." Lee would not be stopped.

"Is he? The only evidence was the document and Alcuin burned it in the fire at Boten."

"Can you describe it? What sort of parchment was it written on? And the ink – what colour was it?"

"Don't trouble yourself Lee. It is not a matter for you to fret over. Edmund knows as much as I do and does not need you to interfere."

"I am concerned because Edmund is over-stretched. Our kingdom is under threat. What do you know about Alcuin?"

"Not much. When I first met him, I thought he was a worthy man - very witty and clever - but our meeting was many years ago. He appeared to be man who knew what duty was."

"Duty? Why do you speak so much of duty? It is not like you. You taught me to question everything. And I will question those who have something to hide."

"And do you have anything to hide Lee?"

"No."

"Greg has told me more about the trial than you did."

Lee said nothing but anger suddenly flooded her heart.

"He has concealed much more."

"Such as?"

"Ask him about his friend called Wolf."

"Wolf?"

"Yes, Wolf from Ramsey. If he could explain why Wolf sells beer to the *Green Blade's* master Lok, then I may be satisfied he is an honest man. You see I saw Wolf being paid in gold by Lok who kept the tiny coins in his legging strips. He paid Wolf in great secrecy for two grades of beer, fair and dark. He seeks more supplies of the fair. Ask him why. Tell him I know."

"Perhaps Greg's kinsman brews ale."

"Perhaps he does. I only know the *Green Blade* exports it."

"Greg is a very diligent man; he works tirelessly training all those thegns – what does it matter if he trades beer? Don't try to remove a speck from his eye when you have a plank in your own."

"A speck!" Lee shouted. Win overheard her from the wood-store. He moved towards the open door of the kitchen. "It is not a speck of dust I refer to. Ask him!"

"You have grown ill-tempered Lee. You would not dare call out like that if your other brothers were here. Perhaps you need to go to them."

"I called out in anguish because you are not listening to what I am saying. I cannot bring myself to trust our Thegn unless he explains about Wolf. I have given him a chance to account for what I overheard - and he refused to tell me. I thought you of all people might understand deceit."

"You are behaving like an over-indulged child who is used to getting its own way. Perhaps Will was wise to abandon you."

"I offended Will because I stood up for Frith at Dummoc and I stood up for Frith because I thought he was your friend. It was Will who persuaded us to return from Hunestanestede last summer when we had very nearly found you. Os thought it was the memories of his loss which unsettled him, but he was in too much haste to begin his studies at Medeshamstede. Do his studies enlighten him in any way? He has cut himself off from the ordinary to pursue some intellectual higher knowledge. He grows cold at heart, but I am zealous for the truth."

"You are so self-righteous Lee. Perhaps you need to humble yourself before someone else must."

Lee let Gisla have the final word as it seemed pointless to say more. Win moved away from the doorway and returned to his task of fetching new logs for the fire.

Lee was pleased Gisla decided not to stay. Win took her to Riscmere Hall and returned later.

"She asked a lot of questions about you," Win warned.

"Such as?"

"The nature of your attachment to Frith."

"She thinks I am attached to Frith?"

"Yes, and I did not say otherwise. Frith will understand."

Win had foolishly exaggerated Lee's love for Frith because he knew he was the most respected of the three oarsmen. He wanted the Chief Thegn to realise it was pointless to pursue his sister.

The Chief Thegn was a man who liked perfection; there were right ways of holding and bending a bow – and wrong ways. Too slack and the arrow would not meet its mark, too tight and the arrow would fly away and never be found. When it came to love, he was not well trained for when he had been too determined she had flown from his grasp and then he had been too hesitant. She had not immediately sprung away as he expected, in fact her faltering had surprised him. He thought if he had been bold enough sooner and taken the girl into his arms she would have yielded. But he had lost her. Edmund dealt him a severe blow. He was being sent to the Borders.

He had tried to resist Edmund by arguing he would not find another to replace him, but the king would not give way. Perhaps the girl did know more than he suspected but if a man had evidence he would use it - and the maiden was a champion in the art of bluff. He went over the methods she had used to discredit him at Dummoc and reached his hall late. He scarcely slept and arrived early for breakfast looking very downcast.

"You must not give up, son, for now I have met her I can see why you are so fond of her. She is a lovely maiden and very practical; I was impressed with her plans to grow more food and herbs in our gardens. And she is very keen to train as a healer - so you must find a way for her. She will never be one to stand around content to be admired. She is shy and bold at the same time, don't you think?"

"How can I help her now I have been sent to the Borders?

Edmund will not let her train at Dernforde, will he? He wants me out of her way."

"Don't grumble against the king," his mother warned.

"I won't. Lee said I must stay loyal to Edmund – it is my chief duty in life."

"You see Greg, she does understand you - and you must be patient."

"I had to be harsh with her at Dummoc and she said she had forgiven me - but not for the night I returned from Medeshamstede. I frightened her and she is determined to put distance between us. What can I do?"

"Did you ask Edmund?"

"No."

"Then ask. He may agree if you are willing to wait – what is a year or two? The Brandune Ætheling has relinquished his claim. He was offended by the men you took to Dummoc - and you know why. His mother was led astray by a Scandinavian trader, wasn't she? It's why she exiled herself."

"I do not know mother. It was a long time ago."

"And don't worry about those Dummoc men - Edmund has sent them on their way."

"Has he? Do not listen to rumours, dear mother. They will be back unless she returned the seaxe when they ..." He did not finish as he bitterly recalled his humiliation when the Dane had borne down on him all clothed as an oarsman raider. There was more to be uncovered concerning the men and the girl would not stand in his way! If he had some proof of their intent she might be humbled and turn to him.

For days, he nursed his ill-feelings towards the oarsmen and his simple passion for the maiden was over overshadowed by his desire to subdue and bring to heel all those around him.

Gisla, having chided her wilful former ward, went to Sutton Hall to dispatch her remaining possessions to Southwic. A few days later she visited Lady Flæd to apologise for Lee's behaviour.

"How is Greg? Has he recovered? I feel so responsible for his wounds at Boten."

"He is thankful he was not burned. He does not hold you accountable Gisla. You were in an impossible situation and could do nothing to help. He is strong again and is back to zealously training his thegns. Why Edmund is about to undo what he has accomplished is beyond understanding. He's sending Greg to Kentforde."

"Edmund told me he was happy with his promotion."

"Greg is not happy at all Gisla. It is not the posting; he's in love and she will not yield. I have asked him to seek your help, but men are often too proud in such matters."

"Lee is being impossible. He needs to speak with her again and be firm with her. I understand she has certain concerns which I am sure he can explain." Gisla did not want to mention the beer to his mother so remained rather vague.

"He will be back soon," Lady Flæd said. "He is out walking the young dog Lee bought him."

"She bought him a dog? When?"

"When she was in Bures. She knew he sorely missed Arrow and sent young Fred to find a replacement. It was done to lift his spirits."

"So, they have been close?"

"I think so."

"Then it is no more than a falling out which can be overcome. Is Greg pleased with the dog?"

"It is not as finely bred as Arrow, but he is fond of it though he oft weeps for the poor hound which was so cruelly taken from him."

"What happened to it?" Gisla enquired.

"It was struck down by a seaxe when Greg was in the stables at the Beleham Ferry."

Lady Flæd left to find the servant girl. She could not bring herself to mention her son's terrible wounds following his beating and sent her servant to call him.

"You look well Gisla," the Thegn greeted. He wrestled with the leash and hauled in his unruly hound. "Your family have restored you to health."

"They have been very kind. You must have made a quick recovery after Boten if you were able to travel to Medeshamstede for Holy Mass."

"Did Lee tell you? I went to see young Will. I suspected her secret betrothal was rather convenient, so I went to find out for myself."

"And he knew nothing?"

"He was extremely vexed and has told her so. It was Lee who insisted she was betrothed but he does not love her at all."

"How deep is your love for her Greg?"

"Her brothers have let her run wild. We did not realise how needy she was until Dummoc. Mother spoke at length to Os about the sad consequences of being deprived of guidance at such a tender age."

"Os blames me for Lee's lack of refinement. I would have stayed on at Sutton, but I felt I needed to look for my son while I had opportunity. I thought Edmund had appointed other guardians."

"I do not blame you Gisla. Mother requested guardianship but Edmund insisted he would watch over Lee himself. When does he have time? I know she remains in contact with those men ..." The Thegn paused because he could not give away recent events. "The man who worked with Pip's coppice team has kept the lines of communication open - and he was the one who hardened her heart against me."

"She spoke at length about a strong man who had helped Pip, but I do not know him."

"He is an oarsman of the worse kind – he flaunts his pagan images, and no one challenged him."

"He has gone Greg, and she will forget Frith soon enough."

"Frith?"

"The untimely embrace at Dummoc was one of his merry gestures. It was nothing Greg. You must take every opportunity to win her heart; draw it back to you. It can be done, and quickly if you tell her about your partnership with a man called Wolf – from Ramsey."

"Wolf?" He thought back to his time at Bures. "Ah, it was Wolf who sold this pup – dog - to her at Bures. What did she say about him?"

"She told me he bought and sold beer, not puppies."

"Beer? Whatever gave her that idea?"

"She was very convincing. She described your sales of light and dark, but light was to be preferred. The fairer, the more valuable," Gisla tried to repeat the exact words Lee had used. She noticed the Thegn looked perplexed and continued. "I did not understand either. You need to speak with her about it."

"Did she say more?"

"She knows the *Green Blade* exports beer - and your involvement. But don't worry Greg, I have mentioned none of this to your mother for I know she feels strongly about the over consumption of beer."

The colour drained from his flushed cheeks. The girl was an expert in her use of words – he had learned that much at Dummoc. How had she found out? He would kill Wolf.

"Did she say more?" He was ruthless and spoke so fiercely Gisla jumped. "Did she mention any other names?"

"She said she saw Lok take gold coins from his legging strips to pay Wolf. I expect she assumed it was a dishonest transaction. If you explain …"

"And if I cannot explain?"

Gisla looked at him and did not know what to say. She wondered what all the fuss was about.

"Tell her it is the way beer is traded these days. There is no need to cause yourself such agony Greg, you look quite unwell. Do not let her do this to you. I would not have repeated what she said if I had known it would cause you such agony."

"She knew well enough. It is why Edmund has sent me abroad. It is her revenge!"

"Calm yourself Greg. Speak to her - but gently."

"How can I get near enough to speak with her!" He shouted and leapt to his feet. His mother overheard and rushed in to join them.

"Greg," she said. The lady put her arm around her son and sat him down. "You must not upset yourself like this. It is too high a price to pay. There will be another; do not let her ruin your happiness."

The Thegn struggled to restore his self-control. He was successful but left their company. His mother was very anxious about his state of mind and turned to Gisla.

"Say nothing of this, please. The girl has unsettled him. He has been like this for months and he has done all he can to win her over; he has even begun to diligently study the Scriptures to impress her."

"I am so sorry. I had no idea she had caused such heartache. I knew he was concerned about her at Boten, but this is more than I had expected. She needs to understand it is impossible for her to marry Frith and then she will yield. I will speak to Edmund and if he will not listen then I will speak with the Bishop."

Æthel was introduced to Branda in the usual meeting place by the vines which were but small pruned stumps and gave no shelter from the chill winds. Æthel complained about the cold and Lee hastily arranged to meet her at the Carr Barrows on

Wednesday afternoon. Lee also arranged for her sword to be taken there so she could show it to Branda.

Wednesday was a warmer day and Æthel hardly complained. Branda took great delight in watching the thegns demonstrate their battle skills. Lee was encouraged to engage in the entertainment and Fred also had a turn with one of the thegn's swords. Later, Lee took her knife and sharpened some of the ash poles stored there and challenged them to spear throwing.

The sun was low in the sky when they made their way home but Lee had planned a late return so they could watch the wood hen's circular display in the open areas of the Birchin. She had them all hide behind some heaps of cord wood and when they were quiet three birds appeared. Their flight was undulating like a slow woodpecker. They veered round in wide circles. Lee said it was done to impress the maiden birds. Branda giggled. They watched the display until the sun had sunk below the coppice line unaware another was also watching from the other side of the glade.

In her haste to leave Lee forgot her sword which she had leaned against the far log pile. When she retrieved it, she turned to catch up but thought she saw a horse and rider come between where she stood and her friends who she had told to keep walking for darkness was rapidly falling.

Lee hesitated where an impenetrable blackthorn obscured her view. Her hand was already on her sword, but everything happened too fast. A horse charged, and if she had not acted with the instinct drilled into her then she would have been cut down. The rider had drawn his sword as Ædwine had done and at the last moment she raised hers. But it was too late to twist and turn, instead she stumbled back disarmed. He stood over her with his sword at her throat. The young thegns heard the faint clash of swords and called out.

"I should have killed you at Dummoc, and those two. Alcuin

would have paid me a fortune had I have done so," he said with great bitterness. "But I did not. I played fair and you have played foul! So, tell me, my little Swan Princess, tell me what you know about the Wolf."

It was no time to play with words for the Thegn was at his darkest.

"I know he is a slave trader, and he pays you a share. Which means you are one as well, doesn't it? He's the man between you and Alcuin."

"How long have you known?" He demanded.

"Since Bures," she said quietly. Her calmness would have impressed many an adversary. But not the Thegn.

"Go on. Perhaps you lie and know nothing at all, but what choice do I have? This is how you die isn't it? With a sword in your heart?"

"I saw Wolf with Lok, the master of the *Green Blade*, and Alcuin. They were at the Chapel meeting room. It was the night I ran away when Os was furious because I gave you the puppy - but I gave you the dog to keep you away from me. I do not want you near me. I ..."

"And you have reported what you think you saw to Edmund?"

"No, he doesn't know. Nor does Os."

"Then why have I been relieved of my command?"

"Edmund is moving you away so you will not trouble me again."

"Trouble you!" He roared. Lee felt the blade press against her chest. She began to fear for her life. "You are the one who troubles me so I cannot still my own heart." Lee knew she had tested him beyond his limit and had not been wise to put those words into Gisla's mouth. "Shed as many tears as you can little Swan Princess; I will not be moved by them." His voice turned cold as ice. "What you know will die with you."

"But I have told Gragus and Ædwine," she revealed.

The Thegn was wounded. and great bitterness overwhelmed him.

"So, you would rather confide in those who buy slaves?"

"You need to repent. It is a wicked thing to sell your own countrymen into slavery and you should not let those heathens tempt you into such vice."

"Who are you to instruct me? You, unworthy maiden. It's a pity I did not sell you at Dummoc, for you've proved to be a fine concubine."

She removed her knife and he yelped with pain. Lee rolled away and caught up her sword and stood there with a bloody knife in one hand and a sword in the other. She had never drawn blood before and was shocked to see how he winced in pain. Slowly she backed away while he stemmed the flow of blood. His hand remained on his sword, and she dare not run.

"It is not right to ensnare the innocent, not me, nor anyone," she protested. "Wicked people like you pierce themselves with many griefs in eagerness to make money."

"Do not quote Scriptures at me," he commanded. "You are the one who has pierced me, I have not done it." She looked at the blood-soaked strips as, with enormous effort, he climbed upon his horse.

"I am sorry Greg," she said as she moved towards him. "I will call the juniors to take you to Ældor Hall." Her sudden tenderness made no impact on his icy heart and being afraid she began to back away.

"Do not try to creep into the shadows tonight you wicked whore! If you move, I will run you through."

"I tried to discuss this with you," she protested. "But you would not listen. You are always angry with me. I am trying to do what is right."

"You have wounded me! What is right about piecing your

own thegn? A wretch like you needs to learn obedience. Now stand still." He turned the beast around and she backed towards the pile of logs. "I have told, nay commanded you to stay where you were, - do not move," he said brokenly. "Gisla thinks your stubbornness is beyond reform."

"It is you who has stubbornly clung to your sin. I have neither bought nor sold anyone. Yet you are happy to see them go to their ruin."

"At least I have not sold myself. Why should I let you go to him? Why should he have you?" He prepared his sword for a second assault.

"Kill me then if you must, for I would rather die than belong to you," she cried in defiance. "Gragus will tell Edmund why, and Gisla will see I have judged you fairly when I said you were dishonest."

"Gisla sees nothing. And neither do you."

"What do you mean?"

"Have you not the wits to see what she was to Gragus? You always wanted to walk in her ways, didn't you? And you have!"

"I hate you!" She yelled.

The dumb beast saw the shadowy figure rise from the blackness and reared in fright. The Thegn struggled to regain control of the horse but not before its heavy hoof had come down upon her. A junior thegn cried out and the Thegn turned his horse and galloped away.

Two young thegns carried Lee across the courtyard to her hall where they laid her upon the longbench. Win feared the worst. Fred ceremoniously carried her sword and her brother assumed one of the lads had wounded her.

"When Edmund hears of this you will be in trouble. Who has taken the sword from its place?" Pip demanded.

"Someone on a horse attacked her from the shadows. She defended herself with the sword so you see, if these two had not have fetched it for her then she would be dead. Please help her Hilde," Fred pleaded.

Hilde sat the lads around the table to eat while she and Branda looked at the wound. Once Lee's cloak was removed, Hilde unclipped the broaches which fastened her over-tunic and saw Lee's light vest of mail. Hilde was full of praise for the maiden. It had prevented the sharp hoof from tearing the flesh. Lee was bruised and winded but would recover.

"He ran me down with his horse," she whispered.

"Who did?" Win asked.

Lee began to cry, and he could not comfort her. She lay back down and closed her eyes. When Pip returned, he knelt beside the bench and took his sister's hand in his and sat with her all evening.

"I could not escape Pip," she said when they were alone. "But it was my fault this time and you must not let Win pursue him."

"Who?"

"The Chief Thegn - I thrust my knife into him. He was bleeding terribly!" She cried. "Edmund will never trust me again – or anything I say."

PART 3

TEARS OF
THE WOLF

CHAPTER THIRTEEN

BREAKING NEW GROUND

It was a fine morning when Os returned on Saturday. Æthel and Branda were already out planting seeds in the freshly raked garden.

"How is Lee?" He asked, for word had been sent about the incident.

"She is better," Branda replied. "But Hilde says she must rest for another week. Do not trouble her if you are angry."

"Edmund has already gone to her side, and he is far angrier than I am. Now show me around this fine plot."

Os walked over to the far side of the pightle, and Win joined him.

"Branda says Lee has recovered. Has she?"

"She tries to be cheerful but is in terrible pain," Win admitted. "It might be some time before she can go back to her sword practice."

"I think Edmund is about to forbid that. Greg is badly injured."

"Then he should have dealt with him earlier."

"Edmund has been very quiet since he learned what happened and his silence does not bode well for either of them."

Lee sat in the side room with the shutters wide open so she could watch the mares in the Long Mead as she sewed. She looked up when she heard Edmund approach and immediately knew he was going to be severe.

"What can I say?" He began gently enough. "I fear I have made yet another enemy when I need allies."

Lee looked back down at her work. A sudden pain pierced her side but she neither cried out nor let him see her agony. He waited for her to speak but she could find no words.

"Win overheard you arguing with Gisla," he continued. He paused again to wait for a response. "What was your contention?" He suddenly demanded. "I told you to be wise in what you said."

"I have packed my things to leave for Wessex. I will go now if you wish. Tell Greg you have had me banished. That should satisfy him!" She tried to stand up, but a sudden surge of pain forced her to sit down again. She bent over and lay on her side.

"Lee, you are in pain - but he is too. I have tried to console him. He has a deep wound in his leg. I am ashamed that one, who I thought was so gentle, could do such a thing. I blame myself for I should not have let you continue in the Shield Hall. Though my household Thegn blames your contact with those men. I will take the sword with me, and you are not to handle it again. And do not use your knife in such a way. A domestic blade is a friend and must not be used as a weapon, or have your oarsmen taught you other ways? I told you to examine your heart."

"I did, but your Chief Thegn would not. He lied!"

"About what?"

"About Frith and Gragus and Ædwine. And me."

"Those men have gone Lee, and you are not to dwell upon them. I sent them away."

"I know you did, but why?"

"I am your king, and I don't want to see you hurt."

"It wasn't Gragus who hurt me. He loves me!"

"You are mistaken Lee. He is returning your ring, and you must return his. Give it to me now so I can settle the matter."

"Never."

"Do not force my hand, Lee." She tried to stand up again but fell forward onto the open panelling. Edmund went to help her.

"Greg is demanding justice Lee, and you will not oppose me."

"He is the one who opposes you and your ways!"

Edmund was standing over her when Win hastily entered the room. He had overheard the king's reprimands and had come to defend his sister. He saw tears upon Edmund's cheek and faltered. It had grieved him to rebuke the maiden.

"Come and sit by the fire, sir. I will bring some refreshments," Win said anxiously.

He left and Edmund helped Lee to the great wooden bench.

"I am sorry Edmund," she said. Each breath caught the pain. "I do not mean to offend you, but Greg must tell you himself what it is he has done."

"I will speak to him again Lee. Gisla muttered something about brewing, but this is more than a matter of drinking beer, isn't it?"

"He is a deceitful, wicked man," she whimpered.

Win returned with a cup of ale and some bread and cheese.

"You must send for one of the healers from Ryscebourn, Win, for she is in great pain. I misjudged the man. It was not his feigned love for her we had to fear, there is something darker at work and I have not made time to examine what it is. I thought he had been manipulated by Alcuin, but I erred. He is caught up in some evil and she will not tell me."

"I fail to understand him, sir. How could he try to press our gentle Lee into marriage when he is so cruel?"

"She struck him."

"He provoked her – his words were cruel I tell you," Win insisted.

"I do not know what he said but Lee has never injured anyone before and will grieve over it. Self-reproach will lead her into more danger than her sword," Edmund sighed.

Win left them alone and the king sat quietly with the maiden in his arms and reflected upon his rebuke. He wished she and Gragus had never met - but they had.

"Let me see his ring," he asked.

Lee obeyed. He knew at once it was of rare workmanship and costly - more than he could grasp, so the king placed the ring in the maiden's hand. She looked up at him and said she bitterly regretted all the trouble she had caused. He asked her what the Thegn had said to provoke her attack and she told him. He understood the gentle maiden was determined to walk wisely and told her to keep the ring safe.

Branda watched over Lee for the few days remaining until she returned to Bures with her mother. Lee straightway hastened to her studies. She had all her papers strewn about when, mid-afternoon, two letters arrived, one tucked inside the other.

"The Thegn and Lady are settled in Kentforde. He has confessed what you would not reveal and is determined to right his offensive ways. He was bold enough to reprove me because I was harsh with you. So, given time, I will restore your grandfather's sword. He has sworn to be loyal and will serve all in this kingdom including those who have chosen to settle amongst us. I have appointed Wigstan over the Horna's Heath thegns. His age and generous nature will command respect. He will have two extra men of senior rank to aid him with the new training plans. The wound you inflicted is healing well and will leave him with no more than a scar. He suffered great remorse over the injury he caused you and I have given him permission to write to you and enclose the letter. We are all bruised, my child, and you must forgive. It is more difficult to forgive ourselves than others don't you think? You must

not grow proud or cold Lee - continue to walk humbly with your God. Look into your heart and deal with all the Lord shows you. I have spoken to Gisla, but she was unwilling to listen. I do not know what the Thegn has written – and his letter is very lengthy - I advise you not to reply. You know why.

Lee   Edmund had given me this one chance to convey my thoughts to you and I regret I cannot speak with you face to face. I do not know if he will ever allow me to see you again so I will try to say now what I should have said many weeks ago. I could not say it then because I was held captive by pride. As you may remember, when I was young my father was defrauded by his half-brother -who was possibly responsible for his death – I do not know. I resolved to restore all to my dearest mother – the lovely lady you met - but my determination and zeal for family honour led me into many temptations. You know how I hated to be made fun of by your brothers and when I misconstrued Aesc's governance over the household at Meleforde and the stewardship of all the mills I failed to give him opportunity to be reconciled. Much bitterness sprang up and I turned from the true measuring line and corruption crept upon me. It was not by deliberate intent I began to trade 'beer' rather than grain along our waterways; one deal led to another, and I was drawn in. I make no excuses for myself because I could have chosen to look at what I was doing but preferred to ignore my conscience. Had I have known you had discovered my darkest depths weeks ago then I would have faced all this. Perhaps I would not have lost you or hurt what I truly cherished. I do not know how you raised your sword against the wild oarsman and in my defence! If you had let him pierce me, I would have been no more trouble to you. But you saved me and waited for me to confess. The day I chanced to meet you in the Hellesden - when you looked so beautiful in your new gown - I was so sure you cared for me. You encouraged me to admit my faults, but my eyes were closed and then - I hardly

319

remember what happened. I was very angry. I had hardly slept - not only had you rejected me for a Dane – you were about to ruin me. After Gisla had unwittingly passed on your message about beer I became like a warrior in the thick of battle striking out in all directions. When I think how close my sword came to taking you to your grave, I can only beg you to forgive me. I knew you had not defended yourself so boldly as you had defended me. When you laid upon the grass at my feet you did remind me of the Swan Princess and pity stayed my hand long enough to spare you – but despair flooded over me, and I senselessly repeated my accusation. Then you struck me, and I will never be able to think upon the day without shedding tears - dearest maiden please forgive me and wait for me. When you see the fruit of my repentance perhaps you will reconsider my offer. Edmund has told me about your exchange of rings, but I sensed he was troubled to think you had chosen to be unequally yoked with a heathen. Do not go that way – even if you choose another to be your husband, may he be a Christian. How can you serve a man who is not? I have vowed to serve Edmund wholeheartedly and I will do my utmost to right the wrong I have done to you and to those innocent ones. You must also vow to serve Edmund wholeheartedly and keep yourself safe at home – do not go wandering down unknown ways or into hidden dells for I fear those you call beloved and friends will show themselves to be our enemies.

Take care my dearest maiden, Greg

Lee put the two letters in her wooden box and locked it. It was time to sow the peas and beans and a few early herbs would be safe enough if she kept watch for frost.

Following Lee's example at Hellesden Hall, Fred and Æthel decided to restore with the garden at Chadsacre. It was close to Spring Farm where his uncle lived. He said it was his contribution to growing more food if the oarsman demanded payment from

Anglian crops. Neither he nor Lee knew Edmund had recently leased it to a new occupier.

Lee resumed her weekly studies at Ældor Hall where she and Fred stayed overnight and returned early the following day. Towards the end of February, the pair were in the garden at Chadsacre Hall when the farm steward called by.

"I hope the new thegn will appreciate your work," he said cheerfully.

"A new thegn? Do you know him?" Lee asked.

"No. I understood he was one of Edmund's Northumbrian kin."

"The wounds in their kingdom deepen," Lee sighed. "I expect he has taken refuge with us. When will he arrive?"

"Edmund did not know. He has been delayed in Eoforwic."

"Eoforwic?"

Lee kept her thoughts to herself. When they arrived home the hearth at Hellesden Hall was ablaze and Lee heard singing. Ric was there. Although he said he had called with his sisters to see how well she had recovered he had something else to discuss. Lee had lately been leaving messages with young Æthelred at Ældor Hall for him to pass to his brother Eth - to bypass their father's prying eyes. However, Æthelred had been passing them to Ric and he discretely passed them back to Lee.

Lee immediately took the notes to lock them away in her box. When she returned Ric was alone. She slumped amongst the cushions on the far longbench.

"You look exhausted. Os said you would not rest for long, so I have brought you three new mares."

"We didn't see them in the mead." Lee wearily replied.

"They are across the highway, on the wood pasture by Hilde's Hall. They need to be quiet."

"Are they wilder than usual?"

"No, they are tame enough, but they are heavily in foal," he said.

"And you have constrained them to journey here?"

"They were found abandoned south of the Sygelsmer. Edmund's steward at the mills has not been able to trace where they came from. I suggested you watch over them. They are beautiful beasts and prized stock – so someone will claim them in time. They must be stolen, don't you think?"

"It is dangerous enough to steal one horse. He's a dead man."

"Unless he is an oarsman under the protection of a Swan Princess," Ric merrily replied. Lee was unmoved. "Fred gave me your Dummoc script, but you can have it back because it's in my heart now."

"Don't you have better words to meditate on?" She angrily replied. "You are Edmund's Ætheling while Will is away and must turn your thoughts to higher matters."

"I have been assigned to uncover the mystery of Dummoc," he declared. "And who can understand what happened there if the Swan Princess is ignored?"

"If Os had arrived sooner, we wouldn't have needed to perform it."

"Those who saw it can never forget it, so I understand. Have I ruffled your feathers?" He teased.

"I don't want to be reminded about it, Ric," she sighed. "I made more errors of judgement there than I care to remember."

"Edmund does not think so. He would not tell me what Greg confessed, but Dummoc is still unfolding. There are depths even Os cannot reach which is why he has employed me. I know certain parts of the kingdom better than he does and it appears the pursuit of your two men began in North Burgh."

"It's the Elmham North bishop's fault. You must go there."

"Ah, that door has been firmly closed but Greg has agreed to report back to me what he uncovers in the Borders. Elmham has been strengthening its ties with the monasteries there since the time Gisla's husband left Creic."

"Do not blame Edmund. I am beginning to think Sudbourne did murder his brother," she revealed. "He's wicked - whereas Greg is stubbornly blind. Why send a blind man to ponder the subtle pigments the Mercians wear?" She asked scornfully. "He cannot tell black from white."

"Dummoc has changed him Lee, and you must pray he walks wisely for Edmund's sake."

"I will." She promised.

"And you must be wise in what you do. Why are you and Eth collecting hunting tales?"

"Because we like them."

"Lee!" Ric exclaimed. "I know you two are up to something. But take my advice. Write nothing down. Sometimes it is the smallest detail which gives you away, so take care. I have discovered the Hethel Ceorl is very cunning. Would you like to know more?" Lee nodded and listened carefully.

It was amongst the thorns, briers, and spikes of furze the Hethel Ceorl's son had won a name for himself. He was a hunter of high repute and much celebrated for his aptitude in hunting tarda geese in those spacious sandy droves north of the River. The prized fowl were as wary as cranes and as testing as wild boar to stalk because of the way they lay hidden. It took great skill and cunning to flush them out from between furze and hawthorn. Hunting dogs had to be expertly trained to drive them up into the sky where spears and arrows could target them - for rarely did those large birds fly.

From childhood, the young Ceorl had trained his hounds on the heathland his father tended as a béoceorl. His family had a long history of supplying candles and honey to the Minster at Elmham. By fourteen he was already familiar with ecclesiastical halls and the crooked ways of the clergy elite. The old ceorl and his gentle wife helplessly watched their beautiful son clothing himself with layer upon layer of corruption. He had all the outward beauty anyone could ever desire, but, like a rich man's grave, there was dreadful corruption below purest marble. His lust for the thrill of the chase spilled into other areas of his life and he craved wealth for himself through chance and speculation. He utterly spoiled his beautiful, self-assured sister who was four years younger than Lee. Her confidence masked her youth, and her brother knew she would make some wealthy thegn a very attractive wife, so he guarded her more closely than her family ever did. Confinement irritated the young maiden, who was as familiar with the open heaths as her brother, but she was equally determined to live a life free from the constraints of her God-fearing parents.

Edmund instructed Ric to continue what Will had begun by seeking office to study within the church. Will had found the keys to re-occupy Elmham North but had locked them all out. Ric knew he would have to harness his thoughts with greater diligence than he had ever shown and asked Lee for guidance on theological advancement. Lee tried her best but eventually grew tired of all his out of place comments and turned the conversation back to the mares. Ric thought they might have been stolen in the Essex marshes because they were on their way to Theodred's Ford where stolen stock was frequently resold.

A few days later Lee sat alone amongst the brambles on the wood bank keeping watch over the three mares. Eth silently made his way towards where she sat, then startled her by throwing the Hunestanestede bundle at her feet. She immediately stood up and backed away into cover for she recognised the leather package. Fred had given it to Ædwine weeks past. It contained all the beautiful gems she had stolen from Lutian Hall. She was about to run when Eth called her name.

"You've startled the mares," she complained.

He picked up the bundle. "Did you recognise it?"

"Yes, it's what I stole – from Alcuin. I thought I was rid of it."

"No wonder you jumped. It's from Ædwine – open it."

Lee sat down beside her friend and carefully untied the package. The gems had gone but there was a note. As she eased it out, a smooth black circle skilfully inlaid with silver slid from the folded parchment and fell amongst the dead leaves. Eth caught hold of the chain and drew it out of the leaf litter to examine it.

"It's his charm - but without the charm," Lee mused.

"What does the note say?" Eth asked.

Wear it. Whoever does not recognise the ring will know this and you will be protected. When you are safely secured I will claim it again. Until then I will not leave him. Keep away from the thegn even if he sheds tears – remember.

"He does lack charm," Eth laughed. "He commands you to wear it."

He helped Lee fasten the silver chain and she looked down upon the black disc in her hand.

"I wonder what these patterns mean," she whispered. "I hope Edmund does not see it."

"Tuck it out of sight Lee so the Chief Thegn never sees it."

"I had a letter from him as well," Lee confessed.

They discussed everything that had happened while they had been kept apart. So it was, the two young thegns became close again. They gathered and connected information which was passed over by those of more senior rank and none but Ric knew.

Eth occasionally kept watch over the bishop's new hunting hall by Boten Heath. The latest steward had moved south from near Sydsterne and his son had been made overseer of a new stud farm east of the Lily Mere. Eth appointed others to keep watch there.

Towards the end of March, the weather grew cold again and it snowed more than it had for years. Win constructed wattle panels for the open sided shelter in the mead where the three mares roamed but they were hardy and appeared not to heed the cold. On the third day of snow Lee and Fred set off for Ældor Hall and called in at Chadsacre on the way but there was nothing they could do in the garden. The steward was concerned about the lambs which had been born on the heath and they promised to check all the ewes were safe enough under the shelter of the furze bushes.

They had not left the heath long before it began to snow heavily and by the time they arrived at Ældor Hall they were white. Fred said they looked like two prowling wolves, and they decided to make a dramatic entrance at the Hall. Eth's youngest brothers were keeping watch for their arrival and giggled each time Fred pretended to freeze to death. Lee and Fred then circled like wolves and charged at the children right up to the hearth where they landed like two snow covered fur rugs.

"Lee, there's someone to see you," said the Blackheath Thegn. Lee sat up and found herself looking into the soft blue eyes of her friend Frith.

"You are a pair! Is this a new play? Do you have a song to go with it?" He held back his mirth just to watch her gaze at him in wonder. Then she leapt upon him, and Fred upon the children. Snow flew everywhere and all the children squealed as they were chased with cold hands. When they grew tired of the game Fred and Lee helped themselves to some warm drink which was stood inside the hearth.

"Can you see Frith, what chaos these two bring to my hall?" Edmund's Thegn observed dryly.

"I can indeed," Frith replied lightly. "But they are fine

performers and must bring laughter to your hearth."

"They do - the boys adore them. And they work as hard as they play."

"We must get started on our studies Fred. We are very late. We stopped on the heath to check the lambs."

"Are they all well?"

"Yes. Twenty-eight we saw today," Fred said as he followed Lee to her books. She had not been seated long when Frith came and stood behind her and dropped a cloth bag on the table. He kissed her hair and said, 'from Gragus,' and left.

The storms delayed our departure from Hunestanestede but we had an easy journey to this place, though the youngest suffered terribly from blisters and we had to wrap strips of cloth around his hands. The ærn would have wrapped them around his mouth to silence the loud singing but he dare not. We thought about the rocks in the headland as we left - you must know them well. We discussed the fire and ice from our own tales.

It proved too difficult to access what you might know as the Scriptorium here which was just as well because a certain snake visited, but the undergrowth is thick and I remain hidden. We discovered much about division and betrayal on all sides which made our ærn restless. He wants to fly south but will not leave without me. Do not withhold your love from your aunt – I will try to visit her. Remember, neither her family nor your king cared for her when she was alone. He saw your ring and demanded I return it. Watch over Frith.

Lee read the letter five times. Frith returned to find her with her head in her arms.

"Are they useful?" He asked.

"I have only read his letter," she confessed. Lee stood up to make room on the table for the papers to be unrolled.

"You are a slow reader then – it was barely a letter. More like a note. Though he rarely writes a note -so you must be highly favoured."

"Why isn't he with you?" She asked.

"Don't worry my gentle Lee, he hasn't forsaken you."

"Eth told me how Edmund ordered Gragus to break our pledge."

"And he promised Edmund he would not communicate with you again unless he uncovered information about Alcuin - and that was why he risked finding someone to pass him those parchments. He is determined not to lose you. He made Ædwine read through many of them which did not suit him."

"I had a note from Ædwine," she admitted. "It made Eth laugh."

Frith noted how solemn she was and sat down with her to study the parchments himself. They appeared to be of no consequence, and he wondered what Gragus had seen in them. Eventually Lee rolled them up and re-tied them. The pair began to talk more freely about everyday matters.

Later Lee took Ædwine's note from her purse.

Frith was astonished his brother had parted with his amulet.

"Don't lose that disc," he warned.

"He has put it on a long chain so no one will see it. How did Ædwine know I would have pity on the Thegn?"

"You're a compassionate maiden. Do you have the Thegn's letter?"

"I have it locked away here, so I am not tempted to re-read it."

Lee returned with the letter and gave it to her friend. There was something very beautiful about it and beauty was dangerous.

"How did you injure him?"

Lee confessed what she had done, and Frith saw the snare laid out before her.

"May I keep it?" He asked when he had read it again.

"And Edmund wrote this," she quickly added.

Frith read the King's letter.

"He is very wise. I will keep the two together."

"Tell Gragus to burn them for I have never given the Thegn any reason to think I care for him in the way he thinks – he has misread me."

"Don't worry, he will forget you soon enough - he has to learn about his new settlements and perhaps a beautiful lady will fall in love with his hearth-dog and marry him."

"There is one thing the letter did not set straight. When the Thegn opposed me, he implied Gisla and Gragus loved each other. I do not doubt Gragus, but his letter never mentioned love – not once. And he says he is going to visit Gisla. Why?"

"He thinks she might know how Weland's seaxe passed into this kingdom and is anxious to discover more."

"How much do they love each other?" Lee asked more directly.

"They had certain things in common which drew them together." Frith had spoken very awkwardly, and Lee grew more anxious.

"What things?"

"Betrayal. Her husband has not treated her well," Frith said without detail and then added, "I thought you knew all about him – if one of my kin wants a second wife at least he does so openly." Lee was shocked at his directness and blushed.

"I thought ... I was too young to discuss such things when Gisla was my guardian ... I am ... I do not understand all which happened to her. Did she tell Gragus everything?"

"She did tell him some of her tale – I was there so do not be alarmed. Gragus and Gisla were never alone, and you understand why, don't you? Ædwine said you did."

"But I have been alone with Gragus."

"Yes, you have. Trust is everything. If he trusts you, then he loves you."

"And Gisla – will she hate me when she discovers this?"

"Perhaps, perhaps not. Gisla's husband has not loved her for a long time and maybe she is looking for a means of escape with another man – but not Gragus. We both thought she was a very noble person."

"I thought so too but she tried to have charges brought against me because I injured Greg - and Gragus has written I must always love her."

"Has she abandoned her complaint against you?"

"Yes, Edmund made her, but she parted company brooding about it. Greg very kindly intervened or she would have written to my brothers."

"Then write to them first and tell them how well Pip and Win are, or I will ask the Blackheath Thegn to write to them, so they understand what good work you do."

When Lee left, Frith carefully re-read the letters, and rejoiced he had them for the Thegn was more dangerous than he or Gragus had reckoned. Ædwine had seen it - and more.

As soon as they had eaten their meal, the Thegn's children went outside to play in the snow leaving their parents with Lee and Frith at the table. Later they all burst in shouting, "Raiders, the raiders are here!" Their father rose to his feet and feigned surprise – for he had noticed how his children fought back their smiles. He stood in the doorway and there in the home pightle stood a whole army of warriors. Each one had a stick for a spear and beet boss on their shields. He called Lee and Frith, and they were quickly at his side observing the ice men. Then they all laughed. The children urged one another to build a longship but they did not know what one looked like, so their father sent Frith out to play with them. Soon a mighty longship was built and a river with a range of defence works. Then everyone joined in a long laughter-filled battle. When the children were all thoroughly exhausted, the proud parents took the little ones inside to warm by the hearth. Lee and Frith remained sitting in the longship.

"Ædwine will be very jealous when I tell him you reached the battle before him," Lee teased.

"Ædwine would have demolished the vessel, all who rowed in it and the entire defence works before he retreated," Frith laughed.

"My older brothers are much the same; they train with great eagerness to do battle. They always did. I am glad Pip and Win are not the same."

Lee got up to leave but he caught her hand, and she sat down again.

"Give them time to settle in front of the fire. Let me tell you all I know about Gisla," he said gently. "For I do not want you to be anxious."

"Everything?"

"Even the difficult parts. Gisla told us she had chosen to live apart from her husband because of his temper ..." Frith paused.

"Edmund said most people did not know the depth of his wrath towards her because she was so loyal and hid it well."

"He took advantage of her commitment. She was bound to him with strong laws. We allow for easier settlement."

"A few do divorce here but Gisla did not want to," Lee corrected.

"She said she would feel ashamed if she gave up trying to please him and was convinced her god would give her the strength to face all situations. It was what she believed all those years when her children were young. She sheltered them from her husband's quick temper, often by letting the blows fall on herself. She thought it was the right thing to do but they did not thank her for it. There was much conflict, and she often stood her ground and opposed him when it might have been wiser to have taken shelter. I have seen many disputes between men and their wives, - but our wives can live peaceably on their farms - at least for part of the year. And they divorce us if we are too disagreeable."

"You sound like an old married man Frith." Lee laughed and he hugged her.

"Never have I been married. I am trying to be serious, and you are laughing. Your god is too harsh if he expects women to be happy under such circumstances," he objected.

"When I was a child Gisla gave every appearance of being happy. She was our inspiration, our teacher and encourager. If there was a feast to be arranged or some entertainment, you could always rely on Gisla to help. We did not know she was so unhappy."

"She was happy when she was free from him. You were her shelter and when you all grew older, she moved on to her dairy work which became her refuge."

"She did have a dairy here. My mother was alive then and we used to help her when she was busy. You know where you found the craft when you made your way to Gipeswick - under the willow trees?" Frith nodded. "It was where the dairy had stood. It burned down."

"Do you think her husband was responsible?"

"I overheard people whisper all sorts of things. I was too young to make a judgement then. He was probably jealous of her success as a trader. Edmund thinks it is too costly to have women neglect the raising of children and their gardens to be traders. But women who have no household duties can become traders if they want to. And ceorls can become thegns and slaves, ceorls. Though we do not have as many slaves as you do." They looked at each other with great tenderness. It would take a long time to discuss all their differences. "If Gisla had been valued at home then she would not have sought to work in the dairy."

"I agree. A woman needs to be busy."

"It was why my mother never let me have many servants. She said I had to find satisfaction in everyday things and work with a joyful heart."

"She was a wise mother and you have proved it. You are all joy and merriment. But poor Gisla's life was bitter. Nothing she did pleased her husband and he found fault with all her ideas and constantly complained she neglected her household duties. I think it's why she is unsure and restless. And the same fate fell on her children. They were given little approval or encouragement to make them feel secure and all her efforts could not make up for his uneasy temperament. A man who is always bad-tempered can be avoided but one who can show great kindness one day and great wrath the next is unsettling, don't you think?"

"Yes. It is good to be even tempered. He made Gisla feel unloved and alone, but what can I do? I do love her, and I want to share my own happiness and joy with her but now I cannot because she wants to be loved by Gragus. Besides she desires I marry the Chief Thegn and I have refused." His arm tightened around her once more.

"She has shown great bravery and loyalty and I hope she will continue in those ways, but her husband has a new hold over her."

"I know. Her son-in-law is indebted to him, as well as to Æthelwold."

"She has found new joy, I think, in her grandchild but he has control over her visitation. I might be wrong, for I have not seen her since the child was born. We think her husband has threatened to have her cut off from the grandson if she does not conform to his will."

"Does she mean to return to him?"

"I do not think she will – he has another woman with him." Frith hesitated because he thought Lee would not know and her silence confirmed it. "And a child." Lee took a deep breath and sighed. Frith looked at her sadly. "There is much unhappiness for some," he continued. "Which is why you must keep on loving her – even if it seems impossible."

"I will try," Lee sighed.

"I once thought it was impossible to go on loving someone. I was very young, and circumstances separated us – and she married another. But I have always loved her and now her husband is very ill and is not expected to recover. I want to be near her. She loves him very much but when she has mourned for him, I will ask her to marry me. I think I am old enough now. Has that surprised you?"

"It is more than surprise. It's wonderful news Frith. Neither Gragus nor Ædwine mentioned it. Is it why you wanted a farm? To settle here with her? Is she far away? Is she very beautiful?"

"I will answer all your questions, but we must return to the hall or Edmund's Thegn will be thinking it's you I intend to marry. Please say nothing yet, not even to my brother or Gragus."

"Would Ædwine not approve?" Lee looked at Frith and made a guess. "Is she a Christian?"

"Yes, she is," he said awkwardly. "And the woman who betrayed our brothers was a Christian too."

"But she could not have been," Lee murmured. "Not a true follower of the Way by faith. She would not have ... gone to Gragus." Lee looked up at the snow army. It was little wonder the heathens despised their ways if such impostors carried out treacherous acts in the name of their faith. "And he knows I am a Christian."

"And so was Weland's wife," Frith sighed. "Gragus is troubled by the manner of his death. He will never understand your ways if it was her hand which betrayed Weland. The girl I love is from Halland though she was born much further north in the cold forests where lynx live."

"I don't know where Halland is."

"It's part of my old kingdom. When I was a boy, I lived in Halland although I was born in Jylland. We travelled a lot, even then." He said smiling as they began to walk back to the hall.

"Did you travel with her?"

"Our families travelled together all the time. Our fathers served together. When I was nine, we travelled down from Orkney to Frisia - and she was with me sitting on some baskets watching our older kin row when an unexpected wave hit our vessel. We were washed overboard. My brothers pulled me out with an oar, but she was lost. It was almost dark, and we could not see her anywhere though the sea was calm. There was much mourning for her. I felt such pain at her loss – it's how I know I love her."

"But she did not drown?"

"No, she was washed ashore north of Edmund's Yare on the isle we call Flegg, though we did not know until many moons passed that she survived. A family who were Christians found her and she lived happily with them. It took them years to discover where her family were. I was twelve when my older brother Erik brought her back to Halland. She was very beautiful - and still is." They were back at the Hall, and he said no more.

"Come in and have some broth to warm you." Eth's mother called as they crossed the courtyard. They were soon in the great hall where all the younger boys sat around the fire. Lee took her place amongst them but was lost in her thoughts about Frith and the girl from his past.

The following day Frith read the letter Lee had written and liked her way of explaining about the trial and then handed his letter to Lee. He apologised for being vague in places but said he might have to pass it to someone else to deliver.

My farm is under a thick blanket of snow so I am unable to work - much is to be explored. There are wonderful woodlands and well hedged meads. It has a spring which flows all year, so I am told and a stream. The next settlement has dug some fishponds but we do get deliveries of fresh herrings as well. The buildings are all in good order but I shall probably ask my brother to help me build a field barn towards the heath because it is a long way to take fodder. I hope your household can help you in your time of distress – please let me know if there is anything I can do. My friends have been very kind to me and have spent some time digging and planting early seeds in the home pightle. I have told L how you were lost at sea – I expect she will write a saga about it. She has so many questions. And he has answered none - his letter was as brief as an order for brooms. Hopefully it said what was needed but probably not knowing him. G.*

"Why have you signed it with a 'G'?" Lee asked. He looked at her and laughed. "Does she know you by some other name?"

"Yes."

"Were you named after a longship?"

Frith laughed again and folded the letter.

"No. I will tell you it another day."

"I know so little about you all," Lee complained. "If I have brought harm upon Edmund, I will never forgive myself," she said sadly.

"Lee," he said tenderly, "I wish some things were different, but they cannot be changed. Gragus is very cautious, and you must give him time. Don't turn from him even if I let you down."

"I do not intend turning away from him, which is why I would like you to tell me about what brought you to my kingdom."

"I was injured Lee and he brought me here to recover."

"You were well enough last September to run about in the Hellesden. Why hadn't you gone home?"

At that moment, the Thegn's wife entered the room with

Fred and said Eth was about to prepare to leave and they should travel with him back to Hellesden Hall because the skies had cleared. Lee was annoyed she missed the opportunity to find out more, but it was not Frith's fault. She would have to remain patient and not succumb to dark thoughts.

Lee and Fred began their journey accompanied by a sullen Eth. Two junior thegns rode with him in total silence. No one looked at each other. It was only Fred who enjoyed his journey through the snow-laden furze. He was busy looking for new lambs and peered inside the bushes where the weight of the snow had forced the evergreen boughs to part. There were old undiscovered bird's nests which he inspected but left because there were too many other things to collect; an old boot, a good furze hook, a sheep's skull, complete with horns and, finally, a length of thin cord wound round a spindle.

Unable to carry them he begged Lee for her over tunic to wrap them in.

"Don't you find your ward annoying?" Asked Eth.

"Let him enjoy himself. We don't have snow very often. Are you in such a hurry? You don't have to wait for us – we know our way home." Lee was not sure why Eth was being so awkward.

"Do you think I would risk losing you?" He said abruptly.

"When have I been lost?" She asked.

"They lost you when the Chief Thegn attacked. No one dared tell me until yesterday. I would have run to your side as soon as I heard his horse."

"Don't be harsh with the lads, they have much to learn."

"And Red is being difficult and keeps reminding me I am the one who must carry the blame for your absence at the Shield Hall." Eth pulled his horse round sharply.

"It was my fault, Eth. I injured a good man."

"Good? Do you know he is back in these parts – to investigate those mares? He is right at your door again. He has discovered they were taken by oarsmen – those who roam free in the Essex margins. He is going to use you Lee – I know it! You are going to catch the oarsmen for him."

"How? Who has told you this?" She asked as she turned and shouted for Fred. "Let him ride on your horse, then you will know where he is," Lee suggested. Eth dismounted and helped the younger boy into the saddle. Lee then walked with the Thegn's son some distance behind the riders.

"Wiggi knows more – I don't know how he has learned this."

"You are trembling brother, what does he know?" Lee took his arm.

"Have you told Frith about the mares?"

"Of course, not."

"You don't think the rumours about him are true?"

"What rumours?"

"The Chief Thegn suspects that Frith has arrived to seek those mares and deliver them to his master – I think he meant Gragus. Is it what were you talking about when you sat in the longship?"

"He was telling me about his childhood," Lee replied.

"Mother thought he had asked you to marry him, and father was pleased for he does not like Gragus."

"No one seems to like Gragus – except Gisla. I think Gragus and Ædwine have gone to see her. Frith is here to make a home at Chadsacre – he is thinking ahead. He is in love - but not with me. I promised to say no more. He would never risk stealing horses, would he?"

"I don't know Lee. These oarsmen are all indebted to each other, and their code of honour is beyond our understanding. I mean, how much do you know about Gragus?"

"Very little – but the more I learn, the more I love him."

"I know you do, and so do I. Father has misjudged him, and

Edmund was too harsh at Hunestanestede."

"The Chief Thegn is longing to discredit them all to prove he was right. Next week I will ask Frith about the mares."

"Meanwhile, we must move them," Eth suggested. "There is a place up at Water Green where Win's friend lives; it's not far if we take a short cut through Hornbeam Wood."

"Don't lose them Eth."

"Have I ever lost anything?" He demanded in jest.

"Only your way," she teased as she ran amongst the snow laden brambles in the meads.

"It's you who always gets lost," he shouted.

"I was told you got lost in the creeks," she called loudly.

"By whom?" He asked as he caught up with her.

"Your brother. He said you were too embarrassed to tell me."

"At Brancaster Fort?"

"Yes – he said the walls were so high you couldn't see over them."

"I am not short!" He replied as Lee took off again. "There are so many reed-infested margins and narrow lanes between high banks. And in the salt marshes I was completely disoriented."

"You always are!" She called.

Eventually he ambushed her, and they both rolled about in the snow trying to bury each other. The rest of the party did not know if they were arguing or playing for it was how they had always been, so they called to them. Eth remembered his command and shook the snow off his cloak, and they ran to catch up.

"Edmund is about to station more of our thegns near the old fort," he continued. They hastened towards the Hellesden. "It's much like Dummoc but without the buildings."

"Or cliffs."

"Or a bishop."

"Or a wicked thegn." Lee spoke with feigned gloom. "Not much like Dummoc at all then?"

Their high-spirited silliness continued for the rest of the journey and Lee did not observe Fred make a detour to the stable shelter before he went inside the hall. He hid his furze treasures there and his behaviour took a sudden turn for the worse.

CHAPTER FOURTEEN
DARK SECRETS

The following day Lee met Eth by the frosted hawthorn, and they set out with the mares. Lee led the way, and they soon came to the old habitation where the seaxes lay hidden. The snow had caused the roof and walls to collapse. Lee was tempted to tell Eth about her plunder hidden there but said nothing. The mares were left with the young man who had given Lee the directions to Boten Hall. He had since become one of Eth's trusted informers. They warned him not to resist any persons who might come for the mares but make careful note of what they were like and where they journeyed.

Lee and Eth did not retrace their steps but turned north-west to Sutton Hall where Lee quickly prepared one of her horses which grazed there. Once in the saddle she challenged Eth to a race her across the common. The Chief Thegn saw the two riders approach Sutton Church, but he did not call out as he had nothing to say to the virtuous maiden who had so obviously rejected him. He was wounded because she had not replied to his letter and frowned upon her playful revelry in the snow.

The Thegn's patience rapidly dwindled and he resolved to use the mares as a weapon to separate her from her oarsmen for good. He intended to call on her the next day to collect the evidence and he would not be hindered.

An unexpected overnight thaw and heavy rain caused

floods which obliterated all the marks Eth and Lee had left when they made off with the mares. Many bourns overflowed and halls were undermined and collapsed so the Chief Thegn was called to give aid to those in need. Reports reached him concerning the mares and he was frustrated he had not been able to visit Hellesden Hall before they were stolen from their mead. He assumed they had been taken when Lee was out roaming with Eth, so he wrote a damning report to Edmund's Thegn who, once more, resolved to keep the two apart.

On the last day of March Frith called at Hellesden Hall to help with the additional work the deluge had caused. Win was glad to have Ædwine's brother for company and invited him to the hall to share the evening feast. Fred behaved badly. For some unknown reason, he refused to eat at the table with Frith and called Lee away again and again until she gave up trying to communicate with her brother's guest. The boy then went outside and lit the outhouse fire and insisted Lee should sit with him.

Fred sulked when Frith was invited to stay overnight and would not go to his mattress in the hall with Pip and Win but preferred to lay upon the longbench in front of the fading fire. Pip asked his sister what was wrong, but Lee did not know. The next day Frith joined Win at the church services and later they left for Chadsacre to check the livestock on the heath. It was very late when her brother returned. Fred had already begun to cast doubt on the wisdom of allowing Win to go off with an oarsman. He hinted Pip might find him murdered out on the heath and his body hidden in a furze bush. Lee wondered if Fred was about to be ill with a fever and blamed herself for allowing him to get wet in the floods. The situation grew worse. On Tuesday, the day of their studies, his whining delayed Lee until midday when she forced him to trample through mud and water to find Pip.

"I have a problem dear brother. Fred here insists he will not go to his studies. We missed last week because of the floods, and I must go today because unlike him I keep my word." Lee glared at Fred.

"Go and sharpen the saw blades Fred or I'll send you back to Spring Farm," Pip said impatiently.

"I don't care if you do. I would rather die there than be fed to eagles next year."

"I don't know what he is talking about Pip. Should I send for Sig's wife?" Lee asked.

"I told you not to tell him your tales."

"I haven't frightened him - but I will if he does not behave himself. I'll send you to my brothers," Lee threatened.

"Good, then I'll tell them about the person you love. They will soon be here to kill him and his friends."

Lee was shocked at Fred's answer and sat down on the log pile. She wanted to be at Ældor Hall because Eth had returned at last.

"Take him back home Lee, I'm too busy to sort you out."

"Can I go on my own?" Lee pleaded.

"I've got to take the spear shafts to the workshops at Edmund's Hall Pip, I'll go now, shall I?" Asked Win. "Lee can take some as well as it's too muddy for the wagon."

Lee thanked her younger brother for rescuing her.

The ash poles were already bundled so it did not take long to strap them across the flanks of the horses. Win and Lee crossed the causeway through the Black Poplar Meads and joined the highway at Riscmere Hall. From there they headed north to Holy Cross. Their route avoided the mires around the Carr out-meads and took them past Chadsacre Hall where they tried to find Frith. He was not at home.

Lee left her horse at Edmund's stables where many thegns had gathered to ride to Kentforde. It was the Chief Thegn who ordered their ranks. Lee called but he ignored her. Three times she tried to gain access to him and three times he avoided her. She stomped across the rutted heath to Ældor Hall where she discovered Frith had been waiting for her but had since departed with Eth. Therefore, Lee went to her studies very late and in an unsettled state of mind.

Edmund's Thegn was equally sullen and as soon as Eth returned, he sent him to the Shield Hall. He then complained about the sea of papers in his private quarters which Lee had not put away and pretended not to hear when she asked him about the stolen mares. Lee slept uneasily and left early to call on Frith. She was determined to ask him about the purpose of his return if only to grasp why young Fred was behaving so badly.

"You're about early today," Frith greeted.

"Everyone has been cross since the thaw," Lee observed. "Fred has gone back to childhood, the Thegn's wife is worried about pleasing her bad-tempered husband and I annoy everyone."

"Is that why you have called to see me?" Frith smiled. "Come and have some breakfast. It's not quite as good as Hilde's." He laughed merrily as they went inside. "How is Win? We had a good time on Sunday. Did he tell you about it?"

"I forgot to ask. Fred has distracted me with his pathetic whimpering. Have you said something to him or threatened him?"

"I've not said anything to frighten the lad," Frith replied. He was as mystified as Lee about Fred's temperamental manners. "He was all right when we built the longship but since then ... Perhaps it unsettled him to learn I knew all about them. Has Eth's father made a complaint?"

"Only about me," Lee sighed. "He is pleased with all the reports about you from your time at Hunestanestede. Eth told me Edmund had such confidence in you he did not make you swear fealty."

344

"That is true. Did Eth tell you Gragus refused to swear on anything but your ring?"

"Yes," Lee whispered.

"It was difficult for Gragus to concede his independence, but he did, and it was done for you. I know it cost him a great deal."

"I know it has Frith. But there is so much I do not understand. Did he send you back to watch over me in place of your brother or are you looking for something you lost?" Frith jolted violently as if caught without a shield in the direct path of a spear flying towards him. Lee did not see and continued. "Tell me plainly Frith, for Eth and I have risked Edmund's wrath for you, do they belong to Gragus? The Chief Thegn believes he and Ædwine were taking them to Thanet." Frith was certain he had been found out and turned to confess but she stood up and cried out. "I know he's lying! He's furious because the floods delayed him - and I uncovered matters before he did."

The colour drained from Frith's face for he was caught in a snare.

"What have you uncovered?"

"They came from Essex."

"What did?"

"The mares; the ones stolen from Hilde's Mead."

"Win told me they were missing but I could not help," he said.

"I still have them," Lee confessed. "I hid them away because I thought you had stolen them."

"No, my dearest maiden I did not." He gently kissed her hair. "You truly thought I had, didn't you? My lovely Lee, I will not have you take such risks for me for I know you love your king; you are faithful and true."

"Fortunately, no one has asked me anything," she whispered. "The floods have delayed Edmund's return and I have time to right my wrong."

"Take care, Lee. I will ask Ædwine if he knows who owns the horses. But some lith's are easier to consult than others."

Lee wondered why but decided not to annoy Frith by asking too many questions. They left to feed his new livestock and then parted company at the corner of the heath near Chadswell Wood. However, she had not gone far when she decided to turn and send a message to Gragus. She swung her horse round and, over the hedge, caught sight of Frith in the distance parting the furze bushes and peering into them, then Eth came into view, and she turned back again.

"Father was troubled because mother let you wander off on your own and sent me to see you safely home."

"Sent you to me?"

"Yes. And I have important news." Eth pointed upwards.

"More floods?" She asked as she thought he indicated the clouds would burst forth again.

"Her name is Raen," he laughed.

"The angel from Hethel?"

"She has fallen," he continued very solemnly.

"Off the stone?"

"Her parents are distressed." Eth replied seriously.

"Then why haven't they demanded she return?" Lee asked.

"They seem to be in dread of the son's acquaintances – mainly Alcuin. He has employed the young ceorl for at least five years, but Raen has only joined them recently."

"I thought as much. At Boten Alcuin said a maiden had the seaxe. He must have meant her - I wonder how it fell into her hands?"

"Is there another seaxe?"

"Yes, Ædwine took it. He gave his to Gragus – who lost his own. I must find it."

"Please don't Lee. No more seaxes or mares," he implored.

"Stay at home. I have been warned about terrible tales of raids across Kent. It's those oarsmen who camp on Thanet. Londun is flooded with the silver they've extorted, and they wander at ease in some parts of Essex. I fear those mares may tempt them to venture here."

"What mares?" Lee merrily asked but Eth continued in his gloom.

"This is serious Lee."

"I know and I pray every day for their return to Francia."

"Are they from Francia?"

"Yes – Frith told me. At least they are not quite as ferocious as those in the far north who mercilessly kill everyone they can - which is almost everyone, for who can flee when the sea is all around?"

They continued their journey in silence until Eth suddenly pulled his horse round.

"You have assumed Raen owned the seaxe."

"No, I haven't. She took it from her brother. I don't know where he got it, but Gragus said it belonged to his friend Weland."

"And I have discovered he was the leader of the largest raiding fleet on the Seine. Not with a few men like Gragus and Frith - but hordes."

"You sound like your father," she commented.

"What would you do if you discover Gragus was one of Weland's commanders? A high-ranking oarsman?"

"Don't say that Eth."

"Weland's seaxe hides many secrets and I am glad it has been returned. Did Gragus know when it was stolen?"

"I could not ask because Gragus was overcome with grief and Ædwine had already hinted Weland's downfall was by subversion."

"Subversion? That is a malignancy which wreaks havoc on both sides!" Eth declared. "Edmund suspects the Dummoc

347

trial was subversion against him - and not your two traders," he revealed.

"Then he must act for I understand those raiders on Thanet are very skilled in exploiting divisions. We must do all we can to aid our king in uniting this kingdom. We must uncover what plot is being brooded at Elmham North. Ric has gone to investigate the young Hethel Ceorl's connections there - which will be dangerous for him."

Eth went on his way and Lee discovered Fred sulking in the kitchen where Hilde had left him in charge of the butter churn. It was endless work and Lee was not kind. When Pip discovered what she had said he reminded her she was not without fault as Edmund's Thegn had forbidden her to wander the countryside with young Eth and she had taken no notice.

By Friday the butter was completed, and Lee fled further punishment leaving poor Hilde with stacks of chores in preparation for the approaching festivals which marked the end of the fasting season.

Lee found solace at the far end of the Long Mead where she laid out obstacles for the young mares to jump as they circled on the lunge leash. Before the sun was at full height a fair-haired maiden applauded her skill. Lee immediately looked towards the holly hedge where three strangers stood. The maiden approached leaving the men by the hollin grove.

"Are you looking for mares?" Lee boldly asked as she greeted her.

"Yes."

"These are all I have at my hall."

"Forgive me, for I was certain you had been sent three mares in foal."

One of the men swiftly moved forward to block Lee's way of escape but the girl signalled to him, and he withdrew.

"My brothers are uneasy," she said. "We have spent our

father's silver on new stock, and they were stolen."

"Do you have the purchase tokens?" Lee asked.

"Yes, but they were stolen beyond your borders - in Essex."

"Then you have done well to trace them this far for our thegns are watching the highways for intruders," Lee warned. "Are they worth so much you risk coming to the heart of our kingdom?"

"You do not know my father," she said calmly. "He does not let anything slip from his memory."

"Do you mean he does not forgive?"

"Never!" She declared.

"Not even his own children?"

"Of course, he overlooks our errors but not those of horse thieves."

"I am a guardian of mares, not a thief. They were found abandoned and brought here weeks ago," Lee paused. "No-one claimed them."

"They are mine," growled one of the men. "Hand them over or I will burn your hall down."

"I am very sorry," Lee smiled. "I lost them."

"What do you mean?" He demanded.

"I mean, if I had not been so careless this hall would be carefully watched, and you would have been intercepted. The thegns are looking for enemy thieves from Thanet - and you have every appearance of an oarsman. Whose lith are you from?"

"My own!"

The angry man leapt forward and as she turned to run Lee tripped over an obstacle laid out for the mares. He caught her by the arm and took her to her knees. His sister was full of wrath and scolded him in their native tongue and once more he retreated. The fall caused Ædwine's disc to fall from the folds in Lee's garment and it swung in full view on its fine silver chain. Before she could conceal it, the girl helped her to her feet.

"I'm Lindi," she said. "These are my brothers, Valr – he's the quiet one on the bank, and Gutti – the angry one who speaks before he thinks."

At once they called to her in their own tongue and Lee guessed they were incensed she had exposed their true identities.

"I am Lee. My two brothers, Pip and Win, are at work in the coppice over there. They can be just as ill-mannered."

Lindi smiled and took hold of the black disc.

"Where did you find this?" She asked and her brothers drew closer to see what had caught their sister's attention.

"A friend gave it to me."

"A friend?" Gutti scoffed. "What was his name?"

"Ædwine," Lee replied. "Do you know him? His brother is called Frith."

"Gudfrith?" Valr asked breaking his silence.

The two men conversed in their language, and she overheard them mention Gragus.

"Are you named after a longship as well?" Lee asked Valr for she knew his name meant falcon. "I understand they have bird names such as Falcon and Grey Goose."

Gutti knew what she implied and removed his seaxe from its holder. It was narrow bladed and looked more deadly than any sword. He warned his brother to stand aside.

"Ædwine gave me this." Lee held out the disc. "To guard me against hasty oarsmen who think all is won by wielding a sword, or a seaxe. My brothers do not know where the mares are – they think you have already stolen them away." Lee explained. "It is too close to foaling to have them journey back to Essex. I will restore them to the mead which runs down to the woodland over there and you can return for them after harvest."

"All the mares in the land will be ours after harvest," Gutti growled.

"Really? Then why the haste to take them now?" Lee asked

defiantly.

Gutti grasped his seaxe so tightly his knuckles whitened.

"Brother," Lindi called gently. She was concerned Lee had unwittingly angered her brother and searched for a way to hold him back with words. However, he was beyond the reach of her command. "Hold him, Valr! We have come this far without bloodshed. Remember what father said."

"He does not understand maidens from these isles. I do not trust them neither does Gragus or our brother Ærnbjörn."

"Ærnbjörn?" Lee repeated.

"See Lindi!" He bellowed. "If he had given her the talisman, she would know his name."

Lee then realised why Ædwine had laughed so much about eagles – ærns which swooped down.

"Ædwine told me it belonged to Erik – his brother. And I know you are not his brother for they are dead and at the hand of a woman who called herself a Christian. Is that why you are angry? Return for your stock in the autumn or use your seaxe now for I have chores to attend to."

Lee turned to leave. Gutti pounced. But she was ready for him, and he felt the lash of the leather cord as it wrapped round his wrist. The seaxe fell from his grasp. Valr retrieved it and returned it to his brother and stood firmly between them.

"Are you his wife?" Valr asked. He laid the disc on his palm.

"He already has a wife. You must know her?"

"I am familiar with her," interrupted Lindi.

"Has she travelled to Thanet to find him?" Lee asked. Both men laughed. "Surely she loves him?"

"He's not the sort of man a woman keeps for long. Perhaps it is why he did not tell you his name. How long was he with you?" Lindi asked.

"He worked here last autumn when I was away. Gragus sent him to watch over me after Dummoc. Are you familiar with the trial?"

"We have received reports," she said.

"Do you know Alcuin? He is a bard, a poet, more of a changeling. He has many names."

"And how many names do you have?" She asked. "The tales from Dummoc involve one called the Swan Princess." Lee blushed.

"Ædwine knows me as Lee."

"And he has not taken you for his wife?" Valr persisted.

"No, why should he?"

"You have his talisman – something his woman desired but he would not part with."

"Well, I am neither his wife nor concubine," she said plainly. "Does he have more than one wife? Are you his wife?" Lee asked the maiden thinking she may have offended her.

"Father would kill him if he as much looked at my sister," Gutti stated. "And she knows him too well to succumb to his flattery, but you obviously do not. He will kill you for taking this." He took hold of the necklace and inspected it. "Where is Mjöllnir?"

Lee did not want the wild heathen to stand so close and the chain pulled tight against the back of her neck as she set her will against his.

"He must have removed it before he sent it to me." Lee suddenly snatched at the disc and almost fell backwards as he let go. "He would have seen you under the hollin long before I did. But as you see I learnt nothing." Lee laughed and silent fury gripped the oarsman's mind. Women usually understood his wrath and fled. "Will you kill me or join me for lunch?" Lee held his gaze. He immediately looked away and Lindi laughed.

"She must be the one. Leave the mares in her care."

"We may never see them again," Gutti complained.

"You have my word. I can send them as far as the Essex

border at Belindune or to Gipeswick but not until the foals are strong."

Lee turned and they followed her. She was surprised such wild kin entered the confines of her hall so readily, but they seemed at ease and much friendlier after they had eaten the best of Hilde's pies.

Lee learned the younger brother was Frith's age and Lindi was not much younger than she was. Gutti was the same age as Gragus. Valr did not look much like a fighting man for he was thin and pale but although Gutti was dressed like a trader he bristled with warrior pride.

The younger oarsman seemed content enough with the arrangement and Lee gave them three gold coins she had salvaged from Boten as a pledge. Lindi embraced her and urged Lee not to trust Ærnbjörn for he was a cruel, ruthless man. Valr embraced her and told her what the mares were called and requested she choose names for the foals.

Gutti remained aloof.

"When he returns for this." Gutti grasped the chain and pulled the talisman to view. "He will show you no mercy."

"I have not asked for his mercy – nor yours. My God knows everything and if I must suffer, my God will be with me."

"I know all about your god," he mocked. "He will not save you. And his priests are easily bought."

"You mean the priests in Essex – not ours."

"They stole my mares and rode for safety amongst Edmund's halls."

"I am sure my king did not know. Which halls?"

Gutti laughed scornfully and Lindi urged him to leave. Neither she nor Valr could have foreseen what Gutti was about to do. Once mounted he swung his horse round and galloped towards Lee who lent against the rail by the hollies. She knew she must avoid him and darted into the dark dell. His stallion jumped the barrier and descended towards her. Lee threw herself into the holly thicket where he thought there was no escape.

"The talisman is not going to save you today," he scorned.

"I did not ask for it!" Lee exclaimed. "If you dare touch me, I will set our Black Dog on you."

"You have sent him beyond your aid," he laughed. "You see how well informed I am?"

"You know nothing. I am going straight to him," Lee threatened before she climbed the bank on the far side of the hollies.

"My brother is wild and hasty," Lindi apologised as Lee scrambled through the hedge.

"And I am tame and predictable," Lee smiled.

Gutti suddenly leapt the rails.

"Valr will hold him back but stay close to me. Gutti is fond of hunting so it's wise to play dead."

The oarsman strode up to Lee, but she did not move. Valr pleaded with him in their native tongue and Gutti turned in fury to confront him. He thrust his hand into his jacket to draw out his seaxe, but it had gone! He swung round and froze in utter disbelief - the maiden held a knife by the blade inspecting the detail upon the handle.

"Next time we meet, keep your distance," she warned. Lee threw his seaxe, and it landed deep in the turf between his feet.

Poor Lindi was horrified. She knew what her brother would do. However, there was no-one amongst the oarsmen as unpredictable as Gutti. He snatched up his knife and disappeared into the dell. Valr followed and called for his sister. All three galloped away towards the east.

Her encounter with the Thanet kin troubled Lee. She had spoken without wisdom and acted rashly. As she prayed at church on Sunday morning, she made up her mind to take Fred to retrieve the mares. If Gutti returned he would be satisfied, perhaps, and overlook her opposition.

The journey lifted Fred's spirits and Lee encouraged him to sing as they rode through the woods to the hidden mead. The mares caught her scent and ran towards her. Fred took some shrivelled apples from his bag and offered them to the hungry beasts. By nightfall the mares were safely back in Hilde's Mead and the following day the old lady was full of joy at their return and forgot about the missing pies. Fred laughed to see Hilde so full of life and Lee was relieved to see him back to his usual self.

When he travelled with her to Ældor Hall he was full of enthusiasm again. Later in the day Lee ventured towards the Shield Hall but was prevented from entering by old Wiggi.

"I understand your mares have returned," he said.

"Hilde is delighted," Lee smiled.

"Were you surprised?"

"No."

"Then I will not tell him how quickly they reappeared once he reached the Borders."

"I tried to confess – you know I did. But he rode right past declaring he had more important matters to attend to."

"Do not trouble yourself my child, you did what you could."

"But I so wanted to tell him - I should have insisted he listened. He promised me he would change his ways."

"I am sure you will see him soon enough."

"But Edmund's Thegn said he will not be here at the Easter Courts for he has urgent negotiations in Mercia - and I do not want him to learn about my wicked deeds from anyone but myself. If I write a note, can you send it over to him at Kentforde?"

"Of course, I can. Go and write it and it will be sent today."

Lee went to the writing table and wrote to the man because she did not want to give him opportunity to accuse Frith of acting against their king.

Greg,   I tried to tell you what I had done - it was foolish of me, and I feel I have let you down. I know you were watching my hall for oarsman again - and without telling me. I was angry and moved the mares myself. I tried to tell you but you would not even look at me. I thought you wanted us to be friends? Two days after you left the oarsman owners arrived and I tried to negotiate with them, but they were real oarsman this time and I felt their treachery. Gragus and Frith were honest men, but these were harsh and conceited. I have told no-one, and they did not harm me. However, you must expect many such incursions before they attack. They are proud and despise us, so they should be easy to identify. Those I met had evidence their livestock was purchased openly by them in Essex and I will urge Edmund to restore the mares to them when the foals can travel – they are not even born but it is likely they will be delivered soon. They are beautiful and strong – perhaps you could go over to see them in Hilde's Mead when you are here for the Easter Courts. Please tell me then if you have forgiven me or do you mean never to speak to me again? Thank you for your letter – I so wanted it to be true. Lee.

She plainly marked the note 'urgent' but when it was delivered to his rooms in Kentforde it remained unopened for he had gone straight to the Ditches. Wigstan was careless in such matters.

On Palm Sunday Win and Pip took Frith to the services at Beodrickworth minster and stayed all day with the Blackheath Thegn. Fred and Lee met Æthel and took her to see the mares in Hilde's Mead. They sat for a long time under the hawthorn listening to Fred playing his flute. When Æthel took her turn, Lee whispered to Fred she had written to the Chief Thegn to admit her dark secret about hiding the mares and he laughed.

Early on Monday morning she was in the stable with Fred feeding the ponies when he unexpectedly confessed he had a dark secret too. It was something he had found amongst the snow-laden furze. He had hidden it in the hay in the corner of the stable. Lee watched as he retrieved a chestnut-coloured leather bag.

"There are a lot of papers inside," he muttered. "I have been too afraid to look at them."

"Why?"

"I've seen it before," he said weakly.

"Where?" Demanded Lee.

"At Holy Cross - the day I gave chase after my goose. Frith had it across his shoulder but under his coat."

"Why have you never mentioned it?"

"I had forgotten it."

Lee hastily unrolled one of the bundles and was shocked to see all kinds of charts and maps marked with familiar handwriting. Both had been recording information. They were not even coded! It was their boldness which broke her heart. If they had used runic script, she might have forgiven them, but all was plain to see.

"What do you think Lee?"

"They are directions to various woodlands and coppice, and some are river crossings and pack ways."

"Were they spying?" Fred asked anxiously.

"I will have unroll the other bundles before I can judge."

"Are you angry with me? I really did not remember the bag until I saw it. Perhaps it's not theirs."

Lee looked at the bag and held it up so the light fell across it. She caught sight of the emblem which she knew had terrified the people of Francia; a raven stamped inside an outline of a wind vane.

"I can't see much Fred. The buckle is plain enough. We'll put the papers back and I will take it to my table to unroll the others."

"Do you think they belong to Frith and Gragus?" He asked

anxiously.

"It seems very likely."

"I have been too afraid to tell you, but you said yesterday we must be honest and open. Will we have to tell Edmund? Perhaps we should have told the truth at the trial. Perhaps the Thegn was right all the time."

"We were right to stand up for Frith and Gragus because Alcuin wanted to kill them. Had it not been for the stolen coins they would have left the land – and without these." Lee held up the bundle of maps. "If we had never met Frith and Gragus Edmund would not have realised what a dangerous man Alcuin is. Gisla may have died. You just don't know Fred."

"What do we do now?"

"I will look through the documents and make up my mind - and I will take the blame for any harm done. It was not your fault you had so completely forgotten the bag until you saw it again."

They finished the work in the stables and returned to the Hall. Fred left with Win and Pip his spirit renewed for a great weight had fallen from his young shoulders. It was Lee who had to bear the burden of unmasking her betrothed and his companions.

No matter how the papers were sorted and re-sorted, it was impossible to avoid the glaring truth – Gragus had been gathering information about highways and crossing points, and garrisons and earthworks.

When Fred returned from work Lee told him she would go to Ældor Hall alone the following day. She planned to leave the bag with the Blackheath Thegn with instructions to pass it to Edmund when he returned.

Lee hardly slept through heaviness of heart. Nothing lifted her spirit. She set out early and none of the beauty which stirred in the Hellesden comforted her. When she came to the place where the willow leaned over the track she stopped and lent against the deeply fissured trunk as Gragus had done. At her feet, the flag irises were pushing up new growth. They looked like a field of seaxes emerging from a long-forgotten battle site. She wished she had told Edmund about the decorated seaxe as well as the plain one. She did love Gragus, but she must walk the narrow way and bring to light what had been done.

Many skeps had been placed amongst the furze on the heath and everywhere there were clouds of bees. Lee realised, at last, what Frith had been looking for and hoped she would not meet him. She wondered if he had come to Chadsacre Hall only to search for the bag. Perhaps he was working for Gutti who had claimed to be a lith commander; one who was set on raiding her land.

Very reluctantly she left the package on the Blackheath Thegn's table at Ældor Hall. She wrote a note and made her way to the kitchen.

"Are you on your own again?" Flæ asked.

"Yes, Pip needs Fred to help catch up with his orders before the Easter rest days. Will the Thegn be here today? I have left something on his table for Edmund."

"He went out early to call on Frith. We learned he has received news of a death amongst his close kin and must leave." Lee must have looked worried for the gentle-hearted lady added, "It's not his brother or Gragus."

"I will wait by the fire and dry my shoes," she murmured.

The Thegn's wife brought Lee some warmed cordial and put her arm about her waist for she had noticed the maiden looked forlorn and wondered if it was the oarsman's ring she had left for Edmund.

"What is it dear? Matters of the heart are never easy. Wigstan said you had written a lengthy note to the Thegn at Kentforde."

"I needed to speak to him when he was here but now

everything is worse than ever," she sobbed.

"Why?"

"I should have told him where I had the mares. I was wrong to oppose him before, and now – oh how can I explain to him?"

"Wigstan said the man deliberately chose to turn away from you, my love. What has happened? Is another wave of conflict about to break forth?"

"I don't know," whispered Lee. "We agreed to work together to support Edmund but how can I when he will not tell what he is doing, or listen to me?"

"He's a brash and thoughtless man. Don't let him trouble you, my child. If he would not listen to you concerning the mares then it rests upon his shoulders, not yours. They are safe and Edmund will know what to do."

"But it might be too late." Lee thought about the oarsmen and the bag.

The Thegn's wife left. Lee lay down with her head upon the cushion and closed her eyes. Later someone drew near and sat down with her. A kiss was lain upon her braids, but she did not open her eyes.

"How is Fred?"

"Very frightened," she whispered.

"Will you tell me why?"

"He has remembered more about the attack at Holy Cross ..." Lee faltered and could not go on.

"Is that what ails him? I did not lay my hand upon the lad there. I pushed Gragus away from him - and he has confessed he acted hastily. I thought you had forgiven him."

"We have. We acted in good faith at the trial. We did not deceive either of you in any way. As far as we knew you were being ruthlessly pursued for no good reason and were not given a fair hearing. Perhaps you should have stood trial though – and before the king. He would have questioned you more thoroughly than I ever did."

He caught her meaning and remained quiet. Lee sat up.

"Ask me what you need to know Lee. I will be honest."

"Did the Chief Thegn have good reason to charge you with spying?"

"Yes." They kept each other fixed in a daring gaze until the young warrior was overcome with remorse. "That madness is behind us, Lee."

"Is it? I have recently met two more oarsman and I am wiser. Were you working for them? Were you paid?"

"Who have you met?"

"It is not your concern. I need to know about you and Gragus. Why didn't you tell me?"

"I have told you some things but not others - and the reason I did not tell you is because I have lied to Gragus. This is how I have repaid his kindness to me." He paused and turned away.

It was not the answer she expected. She put her arms around him.

"No matter how we have willed ourselves to be truthful Frith, we have been deceitful," she sighed. "But I do love Gragus. And I always will - though it is impossible for us to ever meet again. You see, Fred found the bag. Is it what you came here for; to retrieve it and then run away?"

"I will confess everything Lee and you will see what a liar I am. We left Fred lying on the path to the Holy Cross – his wound was no more than a scratch. We were pursued so I ran off across the heath to draw them away from Gragus. He did not want me to, but he is my commander whom I love just as you love your king. I forgot I was carrying the bag! I knew it was likely I might be captured so I buried it in the dark depths of a furze. Then they were upon me. I don't know how I outran them. I plunged into the alder carr, and they did not follow. I rested there and eventually met up with Gragus at the old barrows. I was ashamed for I had made no note of where I threw the bag. I did not want him to go back and seek it, so I lied and told him I had burned the evidence. The maps were not coded or in our script so could have been written by one of your own, so I left them. In Eoforwic Ædwine pressed me to return for the seaxes. I remained weary from the rowing and missed your fair land. There came a day when I was so angry with his constant harrying, I said it would take but a moment to find the seaxes for unlike me, you would remember where you had hidden them. I don't know why I said it, and he would not spare me until I had brought to light my dark secret."

"O Frith," she cried. "How can your brother be so cruel?"

"How can any of us turn back what has been done? Gragus came here to restore me to health. Ædwine joined us much later - it was he who urged us to take full advantage of our stay here to make those charts for our gain. But our task was not commissioned, it was for the highest bidder. The Holy Cross incident and meeting you has changed us – I think forever. But the truth is we did traverse your kingdom to arm ourselves with knowledge before we returned to our ships."

"So, you do have ships," Lee murmured. "Valr hinted you did."

"Was it Valr you met? What did he say to you?"

"Very little. Lindi said more. They came for their mares."

"Oh, Lee I should have told you more before now!" Frith cried.

"Gragus hardly mentioned your past; it was Ædwine who warned me thousands of oarsmen were on their way. I did not really believe him until Eth told me about the size of Weland's fleet on the Seine."

"Gragus wanted to tell you about Weland, but I advised against it – at least until you had left your kingdom. It is true we were with Weland in Francia and on the Seine. Ædwine and Gutti

362

..." His voice faded.

"Do you know Gutti?"

"Was he with Lindi as well as Valr? You did not mention him."

"I did not like him. I knew he was a lith commander before he said."

"And so is my brother. They worked as one until Ædwine's woman..." Frith hesitated for the truth might be too much for her ears.

"Ædwine told me he has a wife – Lindi knows her well. They argue and fight she said, and they are not loyal at all."

"I fear is true. He met her when he was in Hastein's camp."

"Hastein? I overheard Valr and Gutti mention his name when they spoke in their native tongue."

"He is their father," Frith admitted.

"Do you know him?"

"He is the mightiest leader in Francia now Weland is no more. Ædwine joined his raiding party – the one which dared to sail past the Saracens into the Mediterranean. My brother returned to Loiremouthe early because his battle partner had been killed. He then tried to reach us on the Seine at Melun. He was surprised Weland had sailed beyond Paris, but it was wide open at the time. Ædwine remained with us for a few months until we went on our fruitless raid to Meaux. He refused to go. We were outwitted by the king's thegns and were cut off from our ships. Yes Lee, they were our ships. We were hard-pressed and I was cut down. Gragus would not leave me. I do not remember much. It was Ædwine who found us. In his fury, he cut a way through. He helped Weland win a great victory, so he stayed with him while we found help here. Gragus then received news that Ædwine was not happy, neither with Weland nor Hastein, and looked to create his own lith. Gragus did not want Ædwine to press ahead without his aid. You see, Gragus remains burdened

363

by the slaughter of our kin and has vowed to be with us to the end. He asked Ædwine to wait until I had either recovered or died. Then Weland was beguiled and breathed his last in what Ædwine considered an unworthy manner. His liths were without leadership and other jarls began to oppose Ædwine. They wanted the pick of Weland's mighty warriors. After much harrying the wisest of Weland's lith leaders intervened and many followed him. He sent Ædwine to Gragus and in his simmering disillusioned state he pressed the mapping task upon us and then went away again. We did not see him until our after our arrest in Gipeswick."

"So, Edmund was right about Ædwine? He is our enemy."

"I wish it were a different story but is the truth. I do not want to go raiding any more, Ædwine does and Gragus is torn between the two of us. He knows Ædwine will not rest until he is in some company abroad and Ædwine knows Gragus will not rest unless you are with him. For the last few months Gragus has delayed making any decisions. It is why he was willing to help with Gisla's release and why he is now trying to discover what Alcuin is doing. Our future is finely balanced. You must give me the bag. I promise I will destroy it – everything. I was never going to hand it over to Ædwine. Never Lee! I want you and Gragus to be together."

"I cannot give you the bag," she sobbed. "I cannot."

"Has Fred told another?"

"No. I promised Edmund not to go against my heart and my heart says I must surrender the papers to him, not you or Gragus."

"You must not do this Lee, Ædwine will see it as treachery," Frith warned. "And you do not know my brother – he kills without remorse."

"Lindi told me I was mistaken about him though he has never hidden his old ways from me. I know about the Thegn's hound." Frith tightened his arms about her.

"I feel so weighed down by it all. You do not deserve this. He will look upon this as betrayal – I know he will."

"As will Gragus," she said sadly. "I wish Fred had never seen it; If only it had not snowed. It was the weight of the heavy snow blanket which forced the branches apart, so it was revealed. I know what I have done will cause Gragus to doubt my love, but I cannot throw away what I am. Edmund is my king and I desire to be his loyal servant."

"I understand your loyalty to your king. I was loyal to Weland. If he had not been struck down I would have gone back into the battle for him. I know what loyalty is, so does Gragus. Weland was our king and we loved him. You love Edmund and we have come between you and him. I understand Lee. Everything."

Frith was shaken by the fateful twist of events and sat for a long time in silence with his arms around the maiden they had bruised.

By then the Blackheath Thegn had returned and gazed upon the package on his table. He read the young maiden's note.

Fred found this on the heath. He was shaken by what was inside and I have carefully read them. I am so sorry Edmund - we thought we had done what was right at Dummoc when we poured scorn on the Thegn. Do not blame little Fred he only did as I asked. Eth does not know about this so please do not punish him further. His friends at the Shield Hall miss him – perhaps you should send me away to Wessex. Lee

He had authority to take matters into his own hands and find out what the letter referred to but when he saw her with Frith his heart was moved.

She was calm and resolute, and he was in tears.

"I have read your note my love and locked it away. Is Frith so grieved at his loss? I will send Eth to accompany him."

Lee remembered what the Thegn's wife had told her about the death of his friend's husband and she clung to him more tightly. Frith's future at Chadsacre had been ruined by her honesty.

"Please let me stay in front of the fire for a while longer, sir. I am in terrible agony from my shoulder. Lee is not to blame for any of this. I have hurt her and brought trouble to your hall."

The Thegn was suddenly alerted to the graveness of the situation and left to find his wife. When they returned, by the warmth of the roaring fire, Flæ removed the young warrior's shirt and gently rubbed some herbal lotion onto his shoulder. Lee looked at his scars; the wound was extensive, and she cried at the sight of it. It was a miracle he had been so carefully restored, the blow had missed his spine and arm. A blade's width higher and his head would have been severed. Yet it had not been a sword which had struck him for the wound was too massive. Lee pitied him for the pain he must have suffered and for Gragus who had been there with him. Why did men delight in warfare? Why couldn't they all be farmers and battle with the land?

Eth returned to share the midday meal and was surprised to find all his brothers sitting silently round the table while his mother and father were absent. He soon discovered they had lain Frith down on his bed away from the main hall. Lee was there sitting beside his mother.

"Shall we begin?" Eth asked politely. "Are you joining us Lee? My brothers can't wait a moment longer."

Lee kissed Frith and stood up.

"I'll see how you are before I go home," she said with great tenderness.

"What is wrong with Frith? I thought he was leaving today. You look so pale Lee."

"Let me find my place. I need some stew and bread."

But no matter how she tried she could not eat her supper.

She said she had a headache and left the table to take some further helpings to Frith.

"What is wrong with Lee?" Eth asked his father. "Do you think it wise to let her sit alone with Frith? Should I join them?"

"Yes. Tell her you are leaving, and she must go with you."

Eth looked forward to his discussion with Lee but was disappointed because she hardly spoke a word on her return journey.

"Is she home and safe?"

"Yes Father. But what is wrong with her? It's not like Lee to remain so closed. Did you tell her not to speak to me? I cannot bear all this father. Let us be friends – that is all I ask."

"I am surprised she did not tell you; perhaps she has at last questioned some of her actions. What did she say to Pip?"

"She complained her head hurt, and Hilde made her lay down to rest. What did she say to you Father?"

"Very little - but she's left a package for Edmund. Papers I assume because her note said she had read them. The explanation lies there."

"She promised she would not search Lutian Hall without me. Has she has found evidence against Alcuin?"

"She had found evidence of sorts, son, but I fear it is against another."

"Not Frith?"

"If he flees then his guilt will be proved."

"His guilt? Has Lee found out something about his past? Is that why Fred was threatening him? What is it Father? Is he truly an oarsman?"

Lee felt numbed by the action she had taken, and desperately prayed Frith would forgive her and put his trust in Edmund's protection rather than flee to Ædwine and Gragus. She wondered when news would reach them about her betrayal. She was neither afraid of Ædwine nor death, but it was the dread of doing wrong when she desired to do what was true and noble which disturbed her. And she felt terribly guilty because Greg had been right all the time.

Lee toiled in her pightle gardens and tried to forget. She did not go to the Holy Week celebrations. Pip and Win took Fred with them to the Easter Courts at Edmund's Hall. Lee waited patiently. Edmund was deliberating on the best way to punish her.

On Good Friday, she went to Hornbeam Row and with great difficulty retrieved the seaxes from their hiding place below the collapsed building. She put them both under her mattress where silly girls would be expected to hide such items. During the long hours of the night, she held the seaxe to her heart as if she were the Swan Princess. Then she laughed as a sudden thought had come to mind - if only Fred had found the skeleton of his goose inside the bag and not the charts!

On Saturday, the Blackheath Thegn found her in the stables brushing one of her mares which was beginning to shed its winter coat.

"How are you, Lee?" He said as he put his arm around her shoulder.

"I've been busy. I didn't think Pip wanted me to go to the gatherings, so I stayed away. I am waiting to see Edmund. I sent him a note, but he has not replied. He must be very grieved by what I left with him."

"He hasn't opened the package yet. Frith is waiting patiently too – I think it's Edmund's way of testing you both."

"I know sir," she said humbly. "Tell Eth I understand why he has not been to see me."

"Edmund may rule your friendship with Eth must end," he warned. "Our young thegns must learn to discern what is right without bias."

"Oh," she muttered.

The Thegn left to find her brother.

Lee had borne her isolation with great resolve up until then but on hearing she was to lose Eth's friendship she went to the hay loft where her low spirits spiralled downwards. She made plans to go to Kentforde to confess to Greg.

"Did you speak to Lee yesterday?" Edmund asked his Thegn late on Sunday eve.

"Yes. She was very tearful. You must open the package and see what it contains."

The Blackheath Thegn unlocked the chest and handed the package to the king. He looked at the bag and took out the rolls of charts. They inspected each one and put them away.

"They were very thorough," his Thegn commented.

They sat down to eat their supper.

"Poor Lee. I did not think it was important. I have made her suffer all week. And Frith – where is he?"

"At his hall," added the Thegn.

"He is a brave man. He could have fled and re-joined his war band."

"He has been very seriously injured Edmund. I was sickened by it - about two years ago, he said. Without his companions, he may have settled here peacefully."

"I will hear his account tomorrow. And then I will go to see our Lee. We will keep this to ourselves."

They ate and drank and discussed the cases they were due to pass judgement on during the following week when the open trials took place. Edmund retired to his bed but could not sleep, Lee had been calling for him and he had not responded.

The king found the one he had humbled amongst the hurdles and hoops in the sheltered pightle where she was sowing more seeds. She was surprised to see him and more so when he gave her the sword.

"When I wrote to you, I said you were to have the sword. It

is yours and your sons after you. Keep it safe."

"I do not think I can take it," she faltered.

"You must. This has nothing to do with those maps my child. I was too hasty when I took the sword from you. My Thegn tells me the juniors are becoming slack again. We have agreed you must return to the Shield Hall."

"I do not deserve such favour, Edmund." Lee took the sword and scabbard. The king was moved by her graveness.

"Yes, you do. But don't go to Kentforde and strike my other Thegn with it." He laughed but she showed no joy.

"He was right all the time Edmund. Yesterday I almost saddled a horse to go and find him in Kentforde."

"To apologise?"

"To say I will marry him if it would persuade you to set Frith free."

"I would not allow such a sacrifice. I hope you did not offer to be his wife in the letter you sent with Wigstan. Did he reply?"

"I did not know about the maps then - and he hasn't replied. I expect he is busy rebuking the Mercians."

"He has gone to discuss trade in the Borders. I saw him briefly at Lidgaet before he took up the matter of the mares."

"I wrote to confess it was I who stole the mares - and when he hears about these maps, he will despise me forever."

"The contents of the bag are never to be mentioned to him. But that does not make it a light matter. My heart is heavy, very heavy because of it."

"My heart is like stone. I have tried so hard to do what is right."

"I have been too harsh; I know you willingly did what I asked. You held fast to our Lord God - and it is no easy task."

"Please don't have Frith killed," she wailed.

"I will not harm him, Lee. When he began his mission, he was unaware of our ways. Our Lord declares he will overlook the times when we have acted in ignorance, so I shall do the same. I see in Frith someone who is weary with having to raise his sword. If he wants to stay here as steward of Chadsacre then he is free to do so. He trusted me enough not to flee."

"Have you spoken to Frith?"

"He sent a letter requesting my company, to discuss matters of great importance. It was not until yester eve I had time to look at the bag. I went early this morning to apologise to Frith for my lateness. He was very honest. We talked at length about his coming to my kingdom and his future here. He said Gragus thought he had already burnt the papers, so I threw them to the flames. All their hard work was destroyed. If ill comes of it then the fault will be mine, not yours Lee."

"No Edmund, all this has been my doing. Even now I am... am struggling. No, I am deceiving you. Deliberately so!" Lee cried out for she had kept back certain papers. Her confession did not surprise Edmund for all he knew about the maiden lifted his heart.

"I understand how your constant love shelters him." He took her hand, and she raised her sad eyes to meet his tender gaze. "You do not have to say more," he added.

"I could not betray Gragus," she wept. "Though he is an oarsman."

"I am sure they will strike one way or another and Gragus and Ædwine may be among them. That is what we must face."

"I will not leave this kingdom for him; not to live in tents or skulk in deserted places. I will make them explain why they did this."

"Lee, how many others have been here and taken away their charts to ponder and plan attacks? We must trust our Lord and if we lose, let us lose without bitterness."

"I loved him, Edmund. But how will he know that since I have betrayed him?"

"He will know it was not deliberate. Pray for Frith. Your brothers took him to some of the Easter celebrations. Do you know who has died?"

"The man whose household helped him during his recovery."

"Where is this household?"

"Somewhere called Horsye, north of Flegg, I think. His widow is from a Scandinavian family. Frith and Gragus have known her for many years."

"Are they all here again?"

"Yes. Gragus sent me some papers from Eoforwic. I have his letter with me. He tried to uncover more about Alcuin, but the papers are but lists which I must check more thoroughly."

She took the letter from her bag, and he read it.

Edmund handed it back to her and she gave him Frith's seaxe. The king took it, commented it was plain enough and then returned it to Lee for her to pass on to Frith because he had already left.

Frith arrived too late for the funeral feast. His excuses about the weather and floods were not very convincing and he was worried Kadlin would think he did not care about her.

"Gragus sent you an urgent message," Ædwine reprimanded.

"I know and I have apologised. I will speak to Kadlin again when her guests have gone."

"Did you find what you lost?" He asked bluntly.

"No."

"Did you look for it?"

"Yes, of course I did." Frith felt downcast and wanted to avoid any arguments with his troubled brother.

"Then you must go back. Was there any point in coming all this way when you had missed his day? We will be delayed for another month. And they are ready to leave. Did you know they met our Hellesden maiden? She has hidden Gutti's mares – she's good at hiding things, isn't she?" Ædwine had a firm grip of his brother's arm and twisted it. "That fool Gutti left without them - and I don't expect she gave you the seaxes either."

"I did not ask her for them. She was generous to Gutti – though he did not deserve it. He knocked her to the ground and intimidated her."

"I know, he told me. It was a pity his interfering sister stayed his hand! I will give you two weeks Frith. If you don't find what you lost before then – and the seaxes – I will tell Gragus."

"There's no point in threatening me brother, I'm going to confess everything. Then you will have no advantage over me."

"Have it your way," Ædwine said menacingly. Kadlin returned with Gragus. "There's your captain - tell him now!"

Gragus had observed how tired and drawn Frith looked and was not pleased with Ædwine. Frith slumped down and put his head in his hands.

"I was delayed Gragus because I had to wait to see Edmund. Things did not go well for me. I have lost my hall and everything. Please don't tell Kadlin because she knows how much it meant to me and I do not want to add to her grief."

"We will talk about it later," Gragus gently replied. He turned towards the angry brother. "We still have guests. Do you want us to be disgraced? Let Frith rest. He looks ill. Go and walk through the dunes - it will calm you."

"You have no idea what he has done, nor what the girl is about to do." Ædwine looked back at his brother and left the hall with Gragus. "I want to be back on the seas, not here. If you want her, then send me back for I know where she is, and she will not outwit me like she did her Thegn."

"She is not going to have any bands tighten round her ever again. If she wants to leave it will be freely done. She must choose."

"Did she send word to you?"

"No," he admitted.

"And I know why!" Ædwine shouted as he headed for the sea.

Kadlin heard the shout and returned to Frith's side.

"Your brother is worse than ever. You must take him with you when you return to your hall and leave him with Lee. She tamed him for a while."

Kadlin took his hand.

"I said I would be here for you, and I wasn't."

"What has happened to you Frith? You look so sad. What does Ædwine know?"

"He is angry because I did not find what he sent me to look for."

"Do you mean Lee?"

"No. I went to find his bag. When Gragus and I were cornered at Holy Cross we fled over the great heath, and I discarded it - and all the charts. Charts my brother pressed us to make so he could aid Gutti. Gragus fretted enough because his seaxe was missing, how would he have felt if I told him I had not destroyed the evidence in the bag? I cannot excuse what I said or did. It was done in haste for he was being hunted down and I needed to be a decoy – and without the maps. Then young Fred found them!"

"The lad at the trial?"

"Yes, he recognised the bag and gave it to Lee – and she passed it to Edmund."

"Why?"

"I don't know - and I was too late to stop her."

"So, she had deserted Gragus?" Kadlin cried out louder than she meant to. "Do you think he overheard?"

She left quickly to speak with Gragus who remained outside

in the courtyard.

"He is not well, is he?" Gragus said as she drew near. "Has he learned something I would not like to hear?"

"He is worn out with anxiety. Did you know Ædwine commanded him to return to Holy Cross? He needed to rest. You nearly killed him when you took him all the way to Eoforwic. What were you thinking about?"

"He was cheerful enough when we began. He should have told me he was in pain."

"He was as great a warrior as his brother. Can he forget so soon? Of course, he would not admit to being in pain. His brother has treated him cruelly. See he has returned." Ædwine strode into the courtyard. "Make him tell you why he is being so unkind to Frith."

Kadlin turned her back on the one who had offended her and left.

"You have upset her at such a time." Gragus lamented. "What do you know? I overheard Kadlin say something about Lee deserting me. Is it true?"

"Much worse Gragus," he said bitterly. "I should have killed her when you commanded it, but she bewitched me."

"What have you found out? And how? Since you have been far from the Hellesden."

"Gutti found me – he said she's gone to their Chief Thegn, to Mercia. Your other woman, who caused this trouble, she is in Mercia to celebrate."

"Do you mean Gisla?"

"Yes. You sent me to Elmham, but she had already left to attend a wedding in Mercia. Their wedding!"

Gragus reeled at the revelation.

"Lee is married?"

"Yes, and to the thegn she saved from my sword." Gragus fell against the low fence. Ædwine put his arm about him. "This is not what I wanted you to hear Unnulfr, my king. My brother is feigning exhaustion. He has lied to you before."

"Why should Frith lie to me?"

"To ease his own guilt, why else?"

"You must have some doubts for you volunteered to go back for her."

"It would please me to steal her from him. But I could not guarantee she would live!"

"When did the Thegn marry?"

"A week ago."

"Then ask Frith where she was. When did she leave her hall? Now, come and let us all sit down together. We have not treated Frith well. His fall at Meaux has harmed him more than can be healed."

Frith's exhaustion cast him into a deep sleep, and it was not until the next day they sat down to discuss their dilemma. Gragus had lain awake thinking through what had happened, and tears had fallen. Surely Ædwine was mistaken?

"Did you deliver my letter to Lee?" He asked Frith.

"Yes. On the day of my arrival."

"Did she reply?" Asked Kadlin.

"No, but she gave me these for you to read. One is from Edmund and one from the Chief Thegn."

"That man! You see they were writing to each other all the time." Ædwine took the letters before Frith could pass them to Gragus.

"Edmund shows some sense at last." Ædwine bitterly commented. "But he was too late. Her heart had already turned to the wolf-cub!"

"She told me she had only read the letter once but wanted Gragus to see it and then throw it in the fire," Frith explained. "The Thegn has been to the west with his fyrd for weeks."

"You are lying brother. She told Gutti she was going straight to the Thegn. He married her in Mercia without you knowing."

"In Mercia?" Frith repeated.

"Edmund sent him there to seek help against those on Thanet. And I have proof."

"When did he marry her?" Frith gasped.

"Between their two sacred festivals."

"But I was with her brothers on Easter Sunday - and she was at her hall. And I spoke to Edmund on Monday, four days ago, and he was about to go to speak to her about the ..."

"So, she cannot have married the Thegn," interrupted Kadlin. She looked up from the letter she was reading.

"Unless it was done secretly," Ædwine accused.

"Lee would not marry without Edmund's approval. You have no idea, brother, how strong the bond of loyalty is between them. I witnessed it and I am still wrestling its depth. To you it would appear she has betrayed us. I know it will."

There was a long silence as Ædwine tried to grasp what his brother had said. Kadlin passed the letters back to Gragus and put her arm around Frith; they all knew something was very wrong.

"How has she betrayed us? Are you trying to tell me she is betrothed to Edmund?" Gragus asked bluntly.

"Never! Every time I saw her, Gragus, she told me how much she loved you. It quite broke her heart to hand Edmund the bag – the one I said was destroyed. It was my fault. I will take the blame. I have ruined everything for you, my friend. You should have left me to die in Francia."

"She found my bag!" Ædwine exclaimed.

"Do you think she recognised the writing? Did she say Frith?" Gragus asked with increased urgency.

"She knew." Frith whispered. "If only you had said you loved her Gragus. Did the letter declare what you felt?"

"Not directly."

"It said nothing at all."

"It offered good advice," he objected.

"I am sure it did, but she needed to feel secure. She has no mother or father, and she would have left everything for you if you had made her feel confident you were committed to her. Why did you mention Gisla? She has let Lee down very badly and yet you advised her to be kind to her - as if she hadn't been kind enough! Gisla showed her no affection Gragus. She is as cold as you."

Ædwine was offended by Frith's defence of the maiden.

"You did not witness how Gragus despaired when he learned she had turned to another," Ædwine said coldly.

"She has not turned away - but she needed to know the depth of your heart Gragus. When you saw her at Wolven Pit you should have explained more about our past. She is not offended by it – she adores him though I will never understand why." Frith pointed to Ædwine. "If you had gone to her brothers and declared your commitment, they would have let her leave with you. And now times have changed. There are many rumours about the purpose of those on Thanet Isle and she is as loyal to Edmund as we were to Weland. She cannot sever those bonds as easily now as she could have those few months back."

"You defend her with such eloquence, brother, but she has betrayed us. You cannot deny it."

"It depends how you define betrayal." Frith argued.

Ædwine was not softened by his brother's words.

"Betrayal is to do with enemies. Someone from the opposing side pretends to take you into their confidence and then gives you away - which is what she has done. She has pretended to care for you like those Frankish fiends pretended to care for Weland when he said he was a Christian - but they are all liars. The girl cared more about her repute than you Gragus. Would it have been so terrible if she has destroyed the bag without telling anyone? There are shadows here, my lord. The girl has betrayed you – for she cannot both love you and condemn you, can she?"

Ædwine left the hall and went to sit by the sea. He had enjoyed his time with the fair maid and her brothers and now his memories of her were ruined. He must leave the kingdom. He would follow Gutti and return to Hastein for he did not like Ivar or his companions in Dyflinn. Halfdan needed men but he was at sea. Where to turn troubled him as much as the maiden because Weland was dead. And why was the noble warrior dead before his time? Because he had followed his Christian wife! He hated her and he hated Lee! He must persuade Gragus to leave without delay.

"We have been trying to find you all afternoon. Where have you been?" Kadlin asked Ædwine.

"Walking. Where is Gragus?"

"He had to leave to catch the crossing."

"Has he left without me?"

"He has gone to ask Lee to join us. He wants you to wait here until he returns. Be patient and let Frith rest for a week or so."

"She will not leave, I know it."

"Then Gragus will need your comfort when he returns. You know he loves her."

"As do I," he murmured. "Forgive me Kadlin for my thunderous temper today. I loved the maiden very much - not for myself though. Every day she made me laugh – I have not known such simple happiness since our brothers died. I trusted her. Is there nothing in this life we can hold on to? Does nothing last except pain? I am weary with thinking."

Tears came to her eyes as Ædwine slumped onto the bench and rested. How little they understood him. He had revealed more feeling in those few words than he had done since he arrived, and she wished Gragus had been there to hear what was said.

Gragus took great care to travel as quietly as possible through the anxious kingdom. He took passage on a vessel and rowed to Gipeswick. It was the quickest way even though he had to pass under the shadow of Dummoc. The cliffs of the promontory had slumped further into the sea and the freshness of wood made the new flight of steps visible. He had not seen them when he had rowed north after the trial as mists had concealed the way Alcuin had fled with Gisla. Her sudden change in affections troubled him and he was determined to discover if her ward was as fickle. Ædwine's outbursts had swayed his confidence in Lee and he felt cold and miserable.

He missed his merry companion Frith. It had been easier to forgive him than he expected. Frith deserved good not bad. Why should the gods have a fourth brother so soon? Who would remember Frith's brothers if Frith or Ædwine were no more? As a community they had become fragmented and without a camp all their collective memories were scattered like leaves thrown upon the oceans. What was the purpose in dying so young if no one remembered their heroic deeds? They had no children to continue their clans and no lands to make them feel secure.

He passed the outer ditches of Gipeswick and found a vessel travelling to Thorney. Again, he rowed to pay for his passage. His thoughts were stilled by the spring beauty. The willows were bursting with colour, twigs glowed yellow and brown, and buds swelled with the press of leaves.

Upstream from Thorney the bourn meandered through meads where early lilies bloomed and where banks were strewn with pale yellow primroses. Then he passed through coppice where clouds of white wind flowers grew. How wondrous the Hellesden must be in Spring he thought – as pure and beautiful as his maiden.

The second craft came to a sudden halt at the far osier

meadows where he was invited to stay with the owners for the night. On Sunday, most ceased from trading and he was left to walk the few leagues to the old mill pond. When he reached the pool, he sat down and re-read the letter the Chief Thegn had sent to Lee. The man had some hope she would turn to him he pondered.

Gragus hesitated as he passed through the outer gates. The old man on guard called for his wife who took him to the Hall. Lee was not there.

CHAPTER FIFTEEN

GUARDIANS OF THE MARSH

"Did you see the dragons?" Fred asked.

He was kneeling in prayer alongside Lee.

"Dragons?" Lee whispered. "Did you see longships in the reed-beds from the lookout?".

"Of course, not. I mean the dragons outside on the corner posts."

"They are wolves, Fred. To remind us of the Wuffingas."

"They look like dragons to me," Fred insisted.

"If you don't believe me then ask Edmund. Now be quiet the bishop has arrived."

Bishop Æthelwold of Dummoc entered the sacred building. Edmund and his party stood up and Lee pulled her hood forward. She did not want any of the bishop's men to recognise her from the trial at Dummoc. Fellowship between this bishop and Edmund has always been cordial so she determined to stay in the background.

Twenty years earlier the clergy under Æthelwold's leadership had made certain canonical resolutions which had undermined the permanence of the Kingdom of East Anglia. Æthelwold supported the growing powers at the Holy See rather than the local clergy Edmund favoured. The bishoprics had chosen that path generations ago leaving Celtic church traditions to dwindle. The rise of Charlemagne's forceful kingdom had since boosted the power and influence of the Latin popes whose grip on Mercia and Wessex grew tighter with each generation.

It was, in all truth, a struggle for power and wealth rather than faith.

The Scandinavians plundered the northern coastlands of Francia and the Saracens the southern borders threatening the economic security of the new papal empire. It vied with any small kingdom to consolidate its power base and, therefore, usurped Edmund's authority. He preferred to follow the old ways of Patrick, Felix and Fursey which were more in line with the path Christ had walked.

Early in his reign Edmund had strengthened the declining network of healing halls scattered throughout the kingdom; communities where small groups of brothers and sisters both cared for the sick and injured and trained herbalists. Bishop Hunberht was humble in spirit and shared Edmund's vision of a return to simple discipleship. Christ had said the kingdom of heaven was within and among his followers. It was not like any other kingdom for it could not be seen visibly but depended on faith. To be a true disciple required a new heart and a new spirit but 'men loved darkness instead of light because their deeds were evil.' The early church fathers had written at length about the many evil deeds which had seeped into simple fellowships, spurring on church hierarchies which slowly poisoned hearts and minds. Most loved riches more than Christ and many continued to cling to deeds of darkness and 'no longer knew how to blush' - as the great prophet Jeremiah had said.

Lee was lost in such thoughts when Edmund took her hand. She looked at him and smiled. Perhaps his example would stir cold hearts and make people realise true discipleship produced noble fruit which could not be replicated by the controlling powers of the Holy See. Their fruit was rotten. But lives built up by faith through the Spirit would produce love and joy, goodness, and gentleness. It was Edmund's goal and treasure. Bishop Æthelwold's treasure and desires were not those of heaven. His treasure was at Dummoc; in the land he held, and in the authority he had usurped. Hunberht's evicted officials had since worked from the temporary halls at Elmham South. There were no gem-encrusted tombs there to lure in the greedy pirates and no relics to encourage superstition. Instead, there were gardens and sheds for drying herbs and for craftsmen to graft and make hurdles and potions. All the things she would like to do better.

When the long service ended, Lee took Fred to investigate Icanho's gardens along with Eth and his junior thegns. Edmund and his retinue greeted the flocks of abbots and officials some of whom accompanied him on the journey to the royal vill at Sudbourne. It was about an hour's journey on foot across the causeway. Lee and the juniors remained at Icanho to await the king's return. Fred sat down to draw the wolves.

Eth, however, grew bored and persuaded Lee to explore the margins of the marsh. A track wound its way down towards the bay into the reed-beds. They were soon lost. Each way led to a dead end. Eth began to fear they would have to shout for help which would be very embarrassing.

"I'm such a fool Lee," he sighed. "I'm hopelessly lost."

"We must test each way and follow landmarks on the horizon."

"You're not angry?"

"No. It's a challenge," Lee said as she smiled and looked down at the water seeping up through the root mass. The path grew more fragile, and she moved back towards the junction. It was a long time before they finally found their way to dry land and when they did the minster at Icanho was a long way off.

Nearby they saw a craft tied up in the inlet. Lee dived for cover. Eth followed.

"Keep down. It's Lok's craft, the *Green Blade*. And look there's Wolf." They crouched behind the reeds. "Slavers Eth. Alcuin may be here with them. And I don't have my sword."

Eth sensed she was very afraid and confidently said.

"I will not let you get caught."

"You are just a boy. If you are in danger Eth, you pray first and put your trust in the Lord - not in what you think you can do, for sometimes we can do nothing."

They silently prayed. The men moved away from them. Lee and Eth made a dash across the open space and up the low cliff. It was a long way back through the furze and broom and they were quite out of breath when they came to the minster's neglected banks. Fred was still there making notes and the juniors were down by the water's edge catching newts and frogs. They paid no attention to the return of Eth and Lee. Their games were shortly interrupted by the arrival of their escort to Sudbourne.

The two friends walked with the rear-guard and turned to cast a last glance towards the towers of St Botolph's.

"Please, don't tell our king I took you into the marshes. I promised Father I would not, would not find myself alone with you. He said not to."

"And you did?"

Eth was overcome with embarrassment.

"I just did not think. I forgot my age."

Lee laughed.

"And so did they," she said. "Did you hear them naming those newts and yelping with excitement when they found a frog? We are brothers, remember? We must tell Edmund what we saw."

Unfortunately, Eth did not tell Edmund in private and one of Sudbourne's household thegns sent a runner to warn Alcuin's men. The *Green Blade* moved on and was not found by Edmund's senior guard.

Pip was alone when Gragus arrived at Hellesden Hall. He overheard Hilde greet the visitor and sighed because he did not want to be disturbed. He hardly knew what to think when he saw Gragus. He wondered if Edmund had known he would return – perhaps it was why he had taken Lee and Fred with him to Sudbourne. The king had muttered something about Lee being at risk and Pip wished he had listened more carefully.

"I need to speak to Lee."

"She's not here," Pip said. He crossed the room to greet the oarsman.

"Where can I find her?"

"Have you travelled all this way from Eoforwic?"

"I've walked up from the Osier Meads today."

"Walked? Are you alone? Sit down."

Hilde came in with some refreshments and Gragus thanked her. He began to grow anxious and wondered what reason Pip had to avoid answering his questions. Perhaps Ædwine's words were true and Lee had married the Chief Thegn.

"Is Lee away for long?"

"For a few weeks," Pip replied. "It has been very peaceful so far."

"You rejoice she has gone?"

"It has been but a few days. I expect I will miss her soon enough."

"Has he taken her far from you? I would have been content here."

Pip was not sure he understood what Gragus meant.

"She will probably cause some drama and he will send her back," Pip laughed. "I pity poor Eth – she will probably kill him."

"Kill him? Why?"

"Edmund has returned the sword to her. But I don't expect you knew our king ordered her to leave it with him. He thought she might use it in anger but the dispute with the Chief Thegn is resolved - and he is healed."

"Yes, I understand that much."

"He had a good healer." Pip went on.

Gragus was overcome and stood up. He thought Lee was the one who would heal him and wash away his pain.

"I must go," he whispered.

"Go? But you have only just arrived. What would Lee say if she thought I had neglected to offer you shelter for the night?"

"What does it matter now? Tell her I ... I called and ... "

"Sit down my friend. She will want to know what troubles you. Is Ædwine still galloping around the kingdom in his battle gear?"

Pip tried to lighten the heaviness which had fallen upon Gragus, but he looked worse and did not sit down.

"Ædwine desires to leave this kingdom but I could not. Tell me plainly why your sister left your household so suddenly."

"Yes, it was hastily arranged," Pip agreed. "Edmund feared you and Ædwine would be angry. It was Fred's fault. His behaviour dismayed us all - so we sent him with her."

"To the wedding?"

"Whose wedding? Edmund did not mention a wedding."

"His Chief Thegn's wedding."

Gragus waited for Pip's response, for he was not sure if the young man was being honest.

"No one was invited to that! Edmund was furious and said he would tell Lee about it himself."

"It was not Lee who married him then?"

Pip slowly lowered his cup and looked at Gragus.

"Marry him? And not you? How little you know my sister. When she makes up her mind to follow a difficult path nothing will persuade her otherwise. Which is why I have not argued against you. Did you think she would turn from you so soon? She knows you are a Dane – what could be worse than that?"

Pip realised at once what he had said but Gragus smiled.

"Will you tell me where I can find her?"

"Edmund is at Sudbourne for the Rendlesham Court hearings. Lee and Fred have gone with Eth as part of his band of junior thegns. They are travelling with him as far as North Burgh. Did you really believe Lee had married the Chief Thegn?"

"Ædwine was convinced she had."

"He's not lurking outside with his sword, is he?"

"I left him to care for Frith. He's not well."

"I heard Edmund was stern with him – he can be fierce when he's resisted or displeased - as Lee knows. But I understood Edmund had forgiven whatever Frith had done. Do you know what it was? Lee would not say."

"I do know but I cannot say either. Did Edmund demand payment from Frith?"

"Whatever for? Has he married one of our maidens without permission?"

"No."

"Then he is wise for Edmund does not look upon illicit marriages lightly – and our Chief Thegn has married a Mercian! It has maddened our gentle king – when Lee hears she will probably be just as furious – she doesn't trust Mercians."

"May I write to her?"

"It's no good asking her to marry you Gragus – Edmund will not allow it," Pip declared in a sudden outburst of honesty.

"I know, but there are other matters of some importance – I will try and find her in North Burgh, but I will leave a note here."

Lee.   I called at your hall to reassure you I love you. I understand why you had to give your king what you found. I have never used any knowledge I gained against you or your kin and never intend to do so. It is so difficult to write, my love, because so much can be turned against us. Sometimes opportunities are lost forever; please do not let it happen to us. I love you Lee and I should not have left after Boten Heath. I should have been there when you called for me. Even when I returned I left you again without telling you how much I love you. And now I have found your brother alone and you gone. I would have waited here for you and worked with Pip but he says you are away for many days. I must return to Ædwine because he is persuaded you married the Thegn. I have never seen him so turned against everything. I must tell him you are loyal and true – how I love you. I will protect your freedom as you protected mine. Unnulfr.

Take care if you see your aunt for I am not sure if we can trust her. Something has changed. I fear an unknown hand works against Edmund. You must discover what woman your Thegn married for your brother told me she is from Mercia and it is from there Edmund will be opposed.

Gragus travelled back as far as Gurlastuna where he discovered Ædwine had taken Frith and Kadlin south to seek Gisla. Ædwine had persuaded Kadlin it was a friendly call for information but deep within he feared they were all about to be caught supporting the wrong side. His intent was murder for he had determined in his heart to sever bonds he did not approve of. Fortunately, Gisla was not with her daughter at their hall and Kadlin was able to convince the girl they were friends of her mother from the dairy. She was told Gisla would return in a few days.

"Your plan was hasty," Kadlin complained. "You should have been content to wait for Gragus on Flegg. Did you see those men staring at us from the store? I didn't like the look of them. Was it so important to see her?"

"I wasn't just going to see her," he mumbled.

"Did you intend to kill her?" Kadlin cried. "She is Frith's friend!"

"She has cast a spell over Gragus, and he cannot break free. You know how women have a habit of bringing death upon us."

"Lee did not - she saved Gragus and Frith."

"And then led them to a cliff face to watch them jump."

"How can you believe such a lie? A few days ago, you said you loved her. Frith told me she misses you."

Ædwine was silenced. Eventually they came to the place where a hawthorn marked the parting of ways. Ædwine could not be persuaded to go Ryedone Hall where Frith was resting with Kadlin's friends.

"I'll watch you from here. It's safe enough," he insisted.

"I want you back there with us!" Kadlin demanded.

"I am not going your way."

"Then tell me where you are going."

"I am sure you do not wish to know. I will see you tomorrow."

"Can't you wait until Gragus is back? He will be here today or tomorrow. I am sure she will be with him."

"And I know she will not! Even if what Frith thinks is true, I shall never trust her again. If Gragus has found her then I shall go my own way. I want to forget. I need to forget."

He turned and left her there. He did not even look back to see if she arrived safely at the hall. He was not a man to keep his word. Kadlin, however, was determined not to lose him. She turned and ran.

"I will come with you then. Your brother left me, didn't he? But if I had followed him, I might have prevented Gragus from walking straight into the snake pit. There have been times Ædwine, when I have been overcome with remorse, but I have faced it. I loved Erik. I truly did. Don't you ever deny it!"

"I know you did Kadlin and so did I. He was a better man than me."

"Was he? He didn't take me with you because he was tired of me, isn't it what he said? But I loved him."

Ædwine turned to face her. He knew she mourned for her Anglian husband; his death had stirred up memories of her previous loss. He did not like to see her so upset but he was tired, tired of thinking about what Lee had done. She had despised Erik's talisman. Why had he parted with it? It was precious and she was not worthy to wear it!

"Walk with me to the staithe. We can wait to see if Gragus is on the ferry and then I will take you back to Frith. We are almost there now."

She took his arm and walked with him. The path drew close enough to the river to watch the vessels passing as they went to and from the landing place. Ædwine sat down with Kadlin and waited.

He was soon asleep. Kadlin watched each boat as it came into view. The sun was about halfway in its descent when she saw Gragus on board a vessel crowded with passengers. She strained her eyes to see if Lee was with him but there was no sign of any maiden. Gragus looked very dejected, so Kadlin decided not to wake Ædwine. She hoped Lee was sitting amongst the cargo and she had not seen her.

At the staithe Kadlin rushed ahead and threw her arms around Gragus. In his despair, he clung to her. He whispered Lee had not married the Thegn and Kadlin could not stop kissing him. Then she remembered Ædwine and they ran to the place she had left him. He had gone! She had failed to watch him - and other eyes were watching over the marshes.

Edmund completed the court hearings at Rendlesham and prepared to make an early departure for Dunnwic on

Tuesday. The king was intrigued by reports about the tiny fishing settlement which had burgeoned into a lawless trading post. It was five leagues journey and they arrived early afternoon. Edmund learned the *Green Blade* had left the harbour earlier the same morning bound for Blythburgh where it was scheduled to pick up beer.

"Do you think there are two vessels of the same name?" Lee asked.

"The master of the vessel fitted your description." Edmund was eager to understand how the slavers operated with such ease.

"But it's a long journey from Icanho to here."

"If the *Green Blade* is a small vessel and they could have hauled it over the banks at Old Burgh. They have hired two more ships from this wretched place."

"The *Green Blade* was working with other vessels when the Chief Thegn took us to Dummoc."

"And it is like the Scandinavian ships. I know they are easier to haul than ours. There are no short cuts to Blythburgh though. If we make an early start tomorrow, we should be able to intercept them. But say nothing to anyone Lee. I will leave my senior thegns here."

"Why?"

"It's a feign. There are enough thegns at Bythburgh and the men I leave here can watch this foul settlement."

Lee knew Edmund was angry. The evening feast arranged by the chief man was devised to impress the king. Edmund, however, was not swayed by the lavish offering. He drank a cup of wine but refused the beer. Neither Lee nor any of the juniors attended.

The journey to Bythburgh was also subdued. When they arrived, Edmund strode into the shield hall and called the leading thegn to prepare for action. Fred and Lee were dispatched to the

Minster while Eth was sent with the juniors to keep watch at the bridge.

The great wooden bridge had been built the same year as Lee was born. The Mercians had made several incursions there in previous generations and since their expulsion the East Anglians had improved the defences there. The bridge was covered like a warehouse to provide protection for thegns while engaging enemy ships; a forerunner of those Charles had recently built over the Seine in Francia.

Lee felt humiliated she had been separated from the juniors. She did not sleep well at the Minster. Doors kept opening and closing during the watches of the night. The following morning, as soon as Fred was settled in the Scriptorium, Lee went to find Eth.

Eth, however, was not pleased to see her and sent her to help with the sorting of arrows. Lee worked alongside the two youngest juniors. All were bound to silence. At midday they were given their rations and the strict rule appeared to slacken. Lee saw an opportunity to look out over the marshlands and crossed over the bridge.

It was through the slits where archers could let loose their arrows Lee watched Gragus fall into the arms of another woman. She shrank back and looked again. The girl was still kissing him. Then the maiden took his hand and led him away into the reedbeds.

Eth was peering further out towards the estuary and did not see Gragus, but he did catch sight of the *Green Blade* making its way upstream. A watchman went south to alert Edmund. Eth took up his position by the north gatehouse. Everything was well rehearsed. However, Lee did not want to go in the same direction which Gragus had taken. Therefore, she left the bridge to the south. Her horse was tethered in the meads and without thinking, she led it down a sunken way to the east along the southern margins of the broad inlet. Every now and again, through gaps between the furze, she caught sight of the slaver's vessel.

Lee wondered what business Gragus had in Blythburgh. Was it by chance he was there at the same time as the rebels? And the woman? Perhaps she was just another maiden who had been captivated by his silent beauty. Lee shivered. The wind blew in from the northeast over the cold grey sea where he had been born. He was a lynx from a far forest. She must hide!

Ahead was a gap between the hawthorns and she left the trackway. Further on was a shallow dell partly overgrown with ferns and Lee decided to tether her horse there. She felt dazed as if she had stayed too long in the sun during the hay harvest. Her battle gear felt heavy but his ring around her neck was heavier. She must return it.

The knot in the linden band had pulled so tight she took her knife and cut it away. The ring fell into the grains of sand. It was beautiful. Weland, the ferocious leader whose liths had destroyed many communities along the banks of the Seine, had made it for Gragus. Had the man she loved led that sort of life? She knew he had. How could she love such a man? But she did! Her heart ached, for she had lost him.

Eth and the junior thegns found her asleep amongst the ferns. He scolded himself for not telling her the battle tactics and feared she had been captured. However, he had taken her advice and prayed he would find her. In the silence, he had heard the swish of her horse's tail.

"Lee! Whatever happened to you? There was such confusion. Men ran from all directions and spread out over the heath. There were slaves crying and moaning. Edmund was furious because I did not know where you were. He has gone ahead to Gisla's kin, and we must join him there. If we follow this path, we should arrive at the ferry where we can cross over to

Southwic."

"My head hurts," she moaned.

"It's because you've been lying down asleep with your helm on."

"I'm not taking it off now. I'm as good as you even though you sent me away. Or do you mean to lose me in the marshes?"

"You can lead then." Eth's reply was sullen and distant.

Lee knew she had spoken too hastily to Eth but did not bridge the gap between them. Her thoughts were fixed entirely on what she had witnessed at the bridge.

Eth was disappointed with her behaviour. Much later as the light faded he had his revenge.

"Who has got us lost now?"

She was angrier than ever because she had watched every turn.

"I'm going to wait here and listen," Eth suggested. "We might catch sound of the ferry."

Eth climbed a bank and listened. Lee continued down the track. He saw her move ahead but raised his hand to prevent his juniors from following. The rising mists obscured his view, but he did not lower his hand. Ahead Lee saw smoke rising above a small hut and she thought she had found the ferry yards. Then curling mists drifted in from the bay and she lost sight of the building. She urged her horse forwards. The mists were torn apart. She saw a man with a woman sitting close to a fire. Lee's horse breathed heavily and the man moved to reach for his seaxe which lay between them and the hut. Lee drew her sword. He could not see against the light of the fire and the rising mists, but she saw him standing before her. She could have turned her horse around but she did not. The man was a swarthy warrior, his tense arm muscles held her gaze. Would he throw the seaxe?

He thought he saw a phantom warrior with a sword which flashed a ghostly green and silver. He blinked but could not focus.

He cursed the mists.

"It is nothing." The woman said. She swished her raven hair like a wave crashing upon the shore. As she turned the light from the fire fell upon the heavy silver woven torc which hung low around her neck. Lee stared in despair at the wicked shrine priestess. She did not want the pagan oarsman to see her! In her despair she swung her horse round and disappeared into the wavering mist.

Eth was waiting for her to admit she had made a wrong turn. Lee muttered the path ahead was a dead end, so they turned back. A chill wind blew in from the sea and the mists receded. The lights on the ferry wharf beckoned them on. They broke into a gallop and raced towards it. The junior thegns boarded in great merriment, but Lee stood quietly by her horse and removed her helm. She looked back across the river and reeled. Eth caught her in his arms and laughed. She closed her eyes and trembled. It was as if the naked truth had suddenly crept upon her, the light was fading, and she wanted to sleep.

Gisla's kin garrisoned the thegns in a lesser hall while Eth took Lee to Edmund in the spacious grand hall.

"You found her then," Edmund observed. He was not pleased Lee had let him down.

"She had hidden herself just beyond where the horses grazed. She feels safe amongst them." Eth explained. "Be gentle with her my lord, I think the river crossing has made her feel sick. I must get back to the lads."

"You did well Eth," the king replied. "I did not expect so many to be there. We got some of them. Don't blame yourself, you did not have enough support. Even the senior thegns were outwitted. When I shouted at you it was because I was worried about Lee. I thought she might be planning some over-heroic act." Edmund fixed his eyes upon her, but she did not reply. "It was not as safe as I assumed at the Minster. She was wise to hide herself."

The king smiled at Lee and Lee looked at Eth. Edmund saw how well they understood each other as battle brothers did.

Later Lee sat with Gisla's grandson in her arms. The baby was a few months old, and Lee pondered his gentle innocence. He slept so peacefully even though noisy guests bellowed within, and the wind howled in the darkness without.

The gale kept Lee from sleep. At first light she went to the beach to watch the sunrise. Many years before, her father had taken her to the shore beyond Gipeswick and they had stood and watched the great burning red disc appear above the far horizon. She missed her father. He would have understood how alone she felt. She closed her eyes and remembered how he used to whisper words from Jeremiah's Lamentations. Words which he loved so well, "Because of the Lord's great love we are not consumed, for his compassions never fail. They are new every morning; great is your faithfulness."

A hand was laid gently on her shoulder. It was Edmund.

"Tell me your thoughts. I was unkind again, wasn't I?"

"And I failed you again. I was thinking about Father and what he used to say whenever I got myself in a muddle." She repeated the words to her king, and he put his arm about her. "I saw Gragus in Blythburgh. He was on the vessel which drew in before the *Green Blade*. I was on the bridge. He went down the path on the north side but was lost from view before the commotion broke forth. I didn't listen very well and went back to wait by my horse. And later I was cross with Eth and got him lost in the margins and we nearly missed the ferry."

"Did you tell him you had seen Gragus?"

"No."

"Was Gragus alone?"

"Yes. Until the girl on the quay threw her arms around him."

"A maiden was waiting for Gragus?"

"Yes, and she was very beautiful and kissed him," she sighed as her voice faded to a whisper.

"Do not cry Lee," he comforted. "The Lord will restore your heart."

"I know Edmund, but I am sorry I failed you and Eth. I did not expect to see him there. I gave way to fear; I am neither fit nor worthy to be with you. I'll go home and if you see Gragus you can give him his ring back."

Lee felt for the linden band around her neck.

"You must keep it for now and stay at the hall. Gisla returns today and she might know where he is. She brings news about another which will shock you. Let us move away from this desolation Lee, the wind chills my heart."

They moved to the shelter of the low cliff face and sat down amongst the mounds where the cliffs had slumped to the beach many seasons ago.

"What news Edmund? Has she caught Alcuin?"

"I think Gisla is tired of trying to solve mysteries. Though she has been to Mercia to a grand wedding at Salham Abbey."

"Has Godgyfu been married so young?"

"It was my new Kentforde Thegn," he murmured.

"Greg is married?" Lee recoiled. "It is too soon Edmund!"

It did not escape his attention she called the thegn by his name. He had dismissed the idea she loved him but there was a good deal of tenderness there.

"It was very hasty. I do not want you to follow his way, Lee You must never marry in secret or outside our borders. Promise me you won't."

"O Edmund, I will not. I want you to be there and all my friends. Not that I will get married now I have lost Gragus."

"You will," he whispered.

"I loved him Edmund and I cannot understand how quickly he has turned to another. And Ædwine ..." She said faintly as she recalled the lurid vision she had witnessed at dusk.

"Is Ædwine here as well?"

"Yes, but not with Gragus." He observed her tears and held her hand.

"He wasn't with the slavers, was he?"

"No, he was with a woman ..."

Lee turned to her king and laid her head on his shoulder.

"They are wild oarsmen Lee. Don't allow them to command your heart like this. You have a more noble path to walk. You said you wanted to learn about healing, and in a few days I will take those slaves we released to Hunberht's Hall near Elmham South. I will make enquiries to see if he has a place for you there. I am sure he will welcome you. It is where Gisla would have found contentment rather than in the marketplace. When she returns, you must listen with interest – no more. If she is not content with Greg's wife, then do not let her make you feel guilty. There's nothing you can do now – he has made his choice. And say nothing about your oarsmen, not even Frith. Nor about what happened yesterday. It is likely Alcuin is in these parts – I saw one of those who has been befriended by him. He wears a long leather chestnut cloak, trimmed with paler fur. Avoid him for he is loyal to no-one but himself. Even his father the Hethel Ceorl cannot control him."

"He is here? Have you told Eth?"

"Not yet, why do you ask?"

"He has met his sister, her name is Raen,"

"Does Eth know Raen? You must warn him to keep away from her. She seeks nothing but their own pleasure."

"Is he really like her? Does he have golden hair which is tightly curled and cold green eyes?"

"Yes?"

"Can he sing as sweetly?"

"No, his voice is as cold as icicles when they fall from the eves. His tones never warm - like Greg's did."

"Don't say that Edmund. I wanted him to be happy."

"As did I. How can a man be so foolish?"

"He could have waited for me," Lee said as she climbed the cliff.

"He should have waited for my consent," Edmund laboured.

It was a steep climb up the cliff, but Lee had insisted they take the short-cut back to the Hall. It was a sudden return to their childhood, and they were joyous and happy when they arrived at the breakfast table.

"Have you recovered?" Asked Eth.

"She has just taken me on one of her short cuts," Edmund smiled. "You have much to teach her Eth so I will leave her with you while I return to Blythburgh. But don't worry I have persuaded her to look after Fred in a worthier manner this time."

"Was Fred in danger?" Lee asked her king.

"He was in a workshop making ink when the slavers swept through. The novices though he had grown bored and gone off to follow you."

"So, if I had obeyed you, I would have been taken?"

Edmund embraced the maiden and laughed.

"You have never obeyed anyone, my dearest horse maiden."

Eth smiled. He was pleased the king was willing to share his merriment and resolved to do better.

However, Eth's determination to please his king was more difficult than he anticipated. One of the juniors had lost his sword as they raced for the ferry and Eth agreed to go and look for it. Lee insisted Eth took her sword while the lad borrowed his, for she was worried Alcuin's men remained abroad. She had Frith's seaxe amongst her battle garments and her own knife and thought she would have no work for a sword.

The baby cried most of the morning and Lee decided to go

out and explore the quiet lanes and difficult cliffs of Southwic. She took Fred with her. The settlement was cut off to the south by the river and marshes, and to the north by countless lagoons and more marshes. It was linked to the great heath by a broad open bridge and walkway which crossed the tidal creeks. Of course, there might be secret ways through the salt marsh meads and Lee was keen to discover them.

A network of massive banks crowned with stunted thorns of various kinds protected the meads from the tides. Fred and Lee found a particularly luxuriant stooping hawthorn to sit under while they ate their loaves for lunch. From their vantage point they watched a party of subdued passengers leave the ferry and make their way towards the settlement. Eth's thegns had not returned, but a body wrapped in a blanket was carried from the vessel.

"Someone's dead," Fred commented.

The colour drained from Lee's face.

"Ædwine?" She whispered and the boy saw her pain.

"He went off with the oarsmen months ago. It could be Eth."

"If it were Eth the juniors would be with him. Ædwine came back and I saw him at dusk, yesterday."

"Where?"

"At a hut in the margins beyond the river. We must go and find out if it was him on the bier."

"Wait for Eth to return first." Lee was not listening.

"They will take the body to the Market Hall," she said as she shook the crumbs from her tunic. "We can hide amongst the boats and get a closer look."

"I don't want to look at a dead body," Fred whined but Lee could not be stopped. She had to know if it was her friend. If only she had called out to him! He would have joined her, and Eth. But she had melted away in fear.

In due course, they traced the bier to the port thegn's rooms. A stream of on-lookers went to identify the body and Lee joined them. Fred hid himself in a dark corner near the foot of the steps which led to the upper storey and the watch tower beyond. Only a year had passed since poor Fred had seen his mother all laid out in her shroud and he wanted to flee.

Lee gave no sign she recognised the body. She had trained herself well for the Dummoc trial and walked calmly to the place beyond the bier where Fred should have been. She looked around, and when all eyes were turned away, she made her way up the steps. Fred was at the tower chatting to the port thegns. He looked down and saw Lee on the platform below. She was windswept and looked annoyed, so he made his descent.

"Was it him?"

"No, worse."

"Not one of the thegns? Not Eth?"

"It's the woman," Lee whispered.

"What woman?"

"I saw her at the hut with Ædwine. Her neck has been broken."

Lee bit her lip and tears filled her eyes. She hoped he had been caught this time. And Eth was out there in the margins with a wild murderer.

"Who is she?"

"No one knows. She has not been seen here before. I'm cold. Let's go and sit inside at the top of the steps. I'll dry my tears and wait a while for people must not think we know her."

"Do you really think Ædwine killed her?"

"I hope not," she said as she sat down behind some baskets with Fred. They listened to the comments from the people below and Lee overheard many stories, but they were all fanciful. No one described a man like Ædwine and she thought he must have escaped. Then a sudden wail echoed from below and woke Fred.

Lee froze. She knew the playact!

"It's my poor girl," Alcuin howled. "He's murdered her! Where are those dawdling thegns?"

Someone ran up the steps to the tower. Fortunately, Lee and Fred were hidden from their view. They listened to the wealth of sobs Alcuin created. His companion made a great pretence in comforting him.

"Everyone away!" The clear cold command made Lee shiver. "Will you add to my uncle's grief? You should be out on the marshes looking for the oarsman who did this - before he does the same to your daughters."

Lee knew at once he was the man Edmund warned her about.

"It's the Hethel Ceorl's wicked son," she whispered.

Fred trembled and they waited silently as the hall below was cleared.

Alcuin ordered his men to lift the bier. The girl's identity had been confirmed, so they thought, and the port thegns allowed his men to take the body.

"Very convenient, Fred. He pretends she is his daughter murdered by an oarsman and takes the evidence. Something is not right. Ædwine did not kill her Fred; it was Alcuin. I know it. We must find Edmund."

"What? Why can't we wait for Eth?"

"Do you think Alcuin is here alone? They have their own men. Eth would not have taken so long to look for a sword. He has been intercepted, or driven away, by Alcuin's men. We must fetch our weapons and flee."

The maiden's sudden calmness amazed the lad; she had worked out what had happened and what they must do. He was quite overcome by Lee's daring and followed quietly in her footsteps. They approached Gisla's Hall from the salt marsh creeks and took shelter in the far wood store. They had scarcely settled there when it began to rain. Two men ran to shelter in the adjoining section.

"Let's wait here while he delivers the message for Helm."

"Where is he?"

"Waiting for his mother-in-law at Blythburgh, poor man. But our Bard is charmed indeed to find her away as she has much to settle with him. Mind you, she is charmed too – I have never known any of his women to escape if they cross him," the older man said.

"This one didn't. Wasn't she the one who stole his jewels?"

"Yes, and she never revealed where they were hidden. He feigned forgiveness and restored her, but he never found them - unwanted concubines have their uses, hey?"

"Did he know she would be found like that?"

"I'm not sure. She was meant to deliver the Breton to Alcuin. He promised to overlook the missing stones if she was successful. It was arranged for her to take him to the hut by the oak in Ryedone coppice. Our huntsman was waiting there for her to deliver the Breton, but she had other ideas."

"Did he escape then?"

"She told Longcoat the Breton had thwarted her plan. He saw a spectre rising from the marshes and ran off before she could give him enough of the wine she drugged. He was almost back to Blythburgh before her potion overcame him. The heath was swarming with thegns, so they had to throw him on the wagon returning to the Merholt. Thorney will be surprised!"

"Did Alcuin kill her even though he got his man?"

"She was dead long before they found the Breton. Longcoat was full of malice because she took the man to the margins and not the woods – he loves his details. They will blame the Breton of course; who can prove otherwise? Dead men don't talk, do they?"

"Why did Alcuin want him so urgently? Did he threaten to

uncover the mustering at North Burgh?"

"The Breton was at Dummoc though none knew it - and Weland's man has come south again. Alcuin hopes to use the Breton to draw him close."

"Is Alcuin still festering over the trial, after all these weeks? Longcoat is not happy he has made this diversion."

"Longcoat is never happy! He may well kill the Breton if he doesn't find the seaxe. He didn't have it when they found him."

"What seaxe?"

"One he found in Wessex. His sister lent it to Al who lost it at Boten."

"Where is she....." Their voices faded as they walked away.

When they were out of sight Lee rushed into action. She and Fred boldly walked into the Hall and quickly dressed themselves in their travelling clothes. Fred was hungry so they went to the kitchen where they packed some food for the journey.

"Do they mean to kill us, Lee?"

"No, worse, they will keep us here until Ædwine is dead and Gragus captured. We must go, hurry Fred we must not get trapped here."

The maid approached but stopped when the baby cried again so no one saw them at the hall or observed their flight across the meads. They followed the line of the thorn hedge and were thankful there were no guards on the bridge. They hurried across and dropped back down to the ditch.

"How did we escape Lee? There was a man down the highway watching and another beyond the lane."

Lee smiled. They were already amongst the thick furze and thorns.

"How are we going to get to Thorney without our horses?"

"We are not going to Thorney," she corrected. "Ædwine has been taken to North Burgh, Merholt is their beautiful coppice."

"I thought he said Thorney."

"He said 'Thorney's'. He was put on a wagon and there was a wagon unloading yokes in Blythburgh yesterday. Thorney's must be a workshop. The Merholt supplies hornbeam to the riverside workshops where they make yokes and parts for rigging."

The furze gave way to birch scrub and they hurried onwards to a despoiled hornbeam coppice which was overgrown with brambles. It was little wonder the supplies of hornbeam timber had to be shipped from North Burgh when the local coppice lay ruined by reckless felling. The abandoned woodcutters hut near a huge oak tree was half hidden amongst brambles but had a good mattress and fresh blankets. They slept soundly and at daybreak set out in earnest for North Burgh.

CHAPTER SIXTEEN
A PLOT QUELLED

Lee and Fred were blessed to fall in with good company and steadfastly approached North Burgh by the Yare River. The wind was favourable, and they reached the settlement beyond the Merholt without difficulty. One of their journeymen whose family firmly supported Edmund gave them shelter. After supper, when Fred was asleep, Lee told them Edmund was investigating supplies of equipment to ship repairers and builders and asked if they would help. She quickly discovered the exact location of Thorney's workshop.

The following day, after Sunday prayers, Fred and Lee bade farewell to their hosts and set off down the highway towards the crossing. However, once out of sight Lee cut across the fields back towards the Merholt and then took a sunken lane to the river margins. It was not long before Fred caught sight of a small coracle type craft concealed amongst the arching roots of an alder tree. Lee paddled it downstream as far as the tannery. The putrid wharf was deserted. Fred held his nose until they left the stench behind. At the sharp bend in the river, they caught hold of overhanging willow branches and saw a broad walkway ahead leading down to the wharf. They secured the coracle and scrambled up the bank. The narrow-fronted warehouses were angled away from the river; Thorney's was beyond a large rope store.

Lee and Fred were carefully crossing the walkway when the afternoon bells sounded. Fred immediately darted into the rope store and Lee followed. They heard a nearby door unlatch and a man left Thorney's workshop.

Further down the road he met his colleague.

"Has he come to his senses yet?"

Fred froze. It was as if he had been blown upon by an icy breeze.

"He has – Alcuin woke him at daybreak, and he feels pain at last."

"Good. Whatever was put in the wine has delayed us too long. Now let me get to work on him before Al returns – I want my seaxe back."

"What are your orders for Merholt?"

"Keep those at the hall away from the ale, or I will flay them. We must be ready to strike tomorrow - early."

Lee realised insurrection was nigh and told Fred to find a way to the port thegns - and warn them to approach Merholt Hall with caution.

"Remember Fred, this is for justice and for Ædwine."

He left and took the coracle upstream to find a safe way through the tannery yards to the main settlement.

Lee entered the far section of the building and, once inside, waited for her eyes to adjust to the gloom. There were lines hanging from beams and stacks of coiled ropes of all twists towered above her head. She made her way through them and came to the dividing wall. It was damaged where rope piles had fallen against the brittle wattle panels. She squeezed through a place where the joints had snapped. On the other side was a spacious high hall used for stacking tanned hides which were draped over suspended beams. They creaked and moved as the brisk breeze ventilated the building. Down the middle of the hall was a walkway where yokes, mallets and spindles of all sizes were piled haphazardly. At the far end discarded strips of hides draped a doorway concealing foul deeds being carried out in the pit.

Lee heard a whip lash through flesh and fled back amongst the suspended beams taking care she did not disturb them or cause them to change the pace of their rhythmic moaning. She waited in the darkness then armed herself with two mallet heads and moved towards the leather curtain.

"We need more weights to stretch him."

Lee moved back into the darkness. A monster was about to climb out of the pit. As soon as she saw the devil, she threw the smaller weapon high into the roof space. It clattered down amongst the suspended beams and the man looked up to see what had caused the noise. She hit him very hard, and he fell to the floor. Lee dragged him to the far side and bound him with ropes as if he were a wild heifer which needed to be quietened. Before he regained his senses, she took his silken scarf which protected his angel curls from bloody splashes and gagged him with it.

Through a gap in the drapes Lee saw Ædwine. He was turned away from her, tied between the beams and suspended above the floor. His guard moved towards the fire with his arms loaded with logs. He stooped down to add them to the roaring flames. Lee clomped down the steps and he did not turn for he thought it was the bold young Ceorl returning with his instruments of torture. Ædwine heard the thud but he could not see what was done.

Lee quickly cut the ankle cords so the prisoner could bear his own weight. He was very weak and slumped over, so Lee had to lean across his bloody scourged back to reach his wrists. When he saw whose seaxe it was which severed his bonds he muttered his brother's name. Lee continued her task in silence when he suddenly called out another name. She immediately turned and

Frith's seaxe spun through the air as accurately as it had done the day in the Hellesden when Gragus had aimed at her heart. This time it hit its mark.

At the foot of the steps a man fell to his knees and toppled down the steps. His companion thought he had tripped and fallen down the steps and rushed to his aid. He knelt beside the Bard and was immediately felled by the released oarsman who wrenched Frith's knife from Alcuin's wrist. Ædwine staggered from his effort and Lee wrapped his discarded cloak around him and led him away from his place of torment.

It took Alcuin some time to gather his senses. Blood gushed from his wrist, and he tore at his shirt to make bands to tie round it. When it was done, he bellowed very loudly which alerted the men who guarded the building. Without exception, they rushed to his aid. Lee saw her chance and took the path down to the river. However, there was a significant gathering of armed men in the tannery yards, so she turned back and boarded one of the vessels. Very carefully they pushed though the bales of hides and dropped into the murky darkness below the decking.

Hidden between the ribs of the vessel Ædwine lay flat on his furrowed back. He gasped for breath; exhausted and confused he raised his hand. Lee took a small leather flask from her belt and encouraged him to sit up and drink the cordial. It was just rose hips with herbs and mead, but he opened his eyes to see who it was who offered such an unusual draft. It was not his brother. It was the fair maiden from the Hellesden!

Lee held the flask to his lips a second time. He choked, but the vessel stirred so the men searching along the bank did not hear. When they jumped onto the deck Lee lowered herself against the profile of the ribs. Ædwine did the same and she enveloped them with the cloak. She hoped those who sought them would be satisfied the hides were undisturbed - but they were thorough. Boards were removed from the deck to examine the space below. Lee silently prayed the words from King David's psalm, "Let the wicked fall into their own nets, while I pass by in safety."

Her head pressed against Ædwine's chest. In the tense silence she could hear his heart beating. She closed her eyes. When she opened them again all the planks had been replaced. The men had moved to the next vessel. Ædwine sighed and drew his right arm around her. She was not Frith, and his thoughts would not clear enough for him to know where he began or where he was going. He remembered the maiden was from the Hellesden. He had worked with her brother under the canopy where the branches swayed in the wind, singing their gentle songs. He was drifting with them back to his childhood; he and his brothers were asleep amongst the bony ribs in the hold. Gragus was keeping watch as the wind blew them to the isles - or was he looking upon them all dead and laid out on biers? A girl betrayed them, and they were all dead. He moaned and Lee put her hand to his mouth.

"Stay as quiet as you can," she whispered. "They are not far away. We must wait here until the port thegns arrive."

She raised herself and gently brushed his brow and kissed him as a mother would as she watched over a sick child. He struggled with images of black swans and pillows and his friend at rest amongst them. He must not sleep. But she was not the one who betrayed them. And yet she was! Gragus was being drawn in – he was walking into a snare.

"Lee," he struggled. "You must pray Gragus will not be lured to this place. They have sent word to him that I am here, and every way is watched."

"I pray each day for his safety. I love him."

"I love him too. I have failed. Those swans are here," he muttered.

"You are very brave my love, and very lost. They gave

you a strong draught which made you sleep for days, and your thoughts remain drowsy. You can rest while I keep watch."

"Everything is swaying. I could go no further. My head rested on silver threads like moonlight on ripples. It was so beautiful. I thought I was being taken to the heavens, but my swan maiden turned black and charged straight for me. I threw my seaxe at it and then darkness overcame me. When I woke it was Alcuin's face I saw. I have lost Weland's seaxe," he wailed.

"Lie still." Lee urged. "I overheard them say they do not have it."

"Then I must go back and look for it ..."

Lee feared he was about to stagger to his feet and give them away.

"Take Eric's disc," Lee offered. "You sent it to me for my protection, remember? And it worked well. Take it."

"Did Unnulfr give you Weland's ring?"

"Yes," she whispered and laid the ring in his hand.

"He received this ring from Weland as a token, an eternal blood bond so all would know Unnulfr was loved by him and innocent regarding the loss of his sons, my brothers."

"Was Weland your father?" Lee gasped.

"Yes - and I loved him. He would have loved you too, Lee, as I do. I know Gragus must love you deeply to part with it. You must never give it up."

Ædwine closed his eyes and slept.

Lee's thoughts turned to Fred and the armed men at the tannery. She feared the lad had been captured. As the night passed no thegns arrived. Her thoughts wavered and she decided to warn Gragus herself. When the first blackbird sang its pre-dawn song, she woke Ædwine and they left their place of refuge. Two of Alcuin's men remained on watch at Thorney's, but they failed to see the fugitives silently slip over the side of the vessel.

Not far away Lee took possession of a small fishing craft.

Ædwine curled up beneath the cross plank and Lee covered him and her helm with the nets. However, her exertion caused the vessel to cast off leaving the oars on the bank. She struggled to hold on to the overhanging grasses when someone approached.

The maiden smiled like an angel and passed the oars to Lee.

"Thank you, Raen," Lee boldly whispered.

"Do you know me?" She asked as she kept a firm grip on the oars. "Why are you on the river before daylight?"

"Do you see these nets?" Lee whispered. "I must work at dawn to catch fish. Let me have my oars or the sun will disperse the shoal."

"Have you seen my brother?"

"No. Is he nearby?"

"Yes. He and my husband are looking for two fearsome oarsmen – those the Swan Princess rescued at Dummoc. I thought you were her."

"I am," Lee confessed. "Don't let your brother ruin you. Trust me Raen, you are innocent thus far, but Alcuin is a wicked man. He ordered your brother to kill his concubine – the one with the black hair. Women are expendable in their eyes - but I say you are more valuable than anything they have. Free yourself from them and Edmund will see you are protected."

Raen released her grip and Lee thanked her.

The young girl watched the Swan Princess row into the gloom and unhappily waited for her lover to return. She wanted him to take her back to Burnham. She hated Alcuin. He had lost her brother's seaxe and his love for her was no longer the same. And now she learned he was a murderer.

The herring market was deserted, and Lee raised the oars and helped Ædwine ashore. He quickly made his way to the hall he knew well. He lent against the door and knocked upon the latch, but no one came for it was very early. He knocked again and in the half light Lee saw how swollen his hands were. He staggered and she put her arms around him.

"I've fallen a long way, Lee. My nest was high up on the crags."

Lee went to the shutters and thumped upon them. Someone stirred within and soon bolts were being drawn back from the door. Ædwine stumbled inside and fell into the arms of his brother. Lee quickly bolted the door and lent against it clutching her helm in both hands. Gragus saw her and immediately embraced her.

"O Gragus, he feared you were about to be captured. They have torn his back with whips, everywhere," Lee wailed.

"Kadlin, has gone to fetch some water and herbs to calm his pain."

He kissed her again and sat her in front of the hearth before leaving to help the woman. Then Lee remembered who she was.

"He is making himself still and steady, Lee," Frith whispered. "It is how you recover from the distress of battle. You did well to give him Weland's ring - it is all he thinks of now just a circle of silver."

"Should I stay quiet then?" She asked as if in deep distress herself. "I sob as loudly as I can when I am in pain."

Ædwine opened his eyes and almost smiled as he fixed his gaze upon her. Gragus returned with a drink and helped steady the cup.

"Take the ring Gragus," he said when his thirst was quenched. "Put it back around her neck close to her heart."

Kadlin returned with the warmed lotion and she and Gragus began to gently bathe his wounds. Ædwine closed his eyes to meet the pain and Lee turned to Frith and sobbed loudly so she could not hear the moans.

When she awoke Ædwine was lying face down on a low bed not far from the fire and she was on the bench covered with warm blankets. At first, she wondered where she was but slowly recalled what had happened. She turned and saw Gragus sitting close by. He smiled as she sat up.

"Was I very bad-tempered when we arrived? I hardly remember."

"When you began your sobbing, we didn't know whether to laugh or cry. I had so much to say. I went to your hall to find you, but Pip said you were with Edmund."

"I saw you in Blythburgh," Lee whispered. "I was on the bridge. You must give Weland's ring to her. I understand why - but Gragus I did not mean to betray you. And you are still in danger for we met one of the rebels and they must know by now I was on the river."

"We are safe enough. Today they are hunted not us. And Kadlin does not want the ring," he whispered. "Kadlin is my sister."

"Your sister?"

"Yes, my love. She was expecting you to be with me on the vessel which arrived at Blythburgh during the confusion. Then we lost Ædwine."

"He is found," Lee smiled. "He looks so peaceful ...."

"It's because I can hardly move," Ædwine complained.

"I thought you were asleep." Lee went to his side. "I have much to discuss with you when you are well again," she chided.

"Are you angry with me?" He asked. "For I am more than angry with you!"

"This is not a time to be angry Ædwine," Kadlin intervened, not knowing their ways.

Lee looked up at the maiden and embraced her.

"Forgive me Kadlin," she said. "I did not know Gragus had a sister, or he would risk travelling alone to my hall. I wish I had been there."

"I knew you would not turn from him and marry the Thegn," she whispered. "My Frith did not believe it either. Please forgive us. Frith regrets not telling you what he sought."

Kadlin's words reminded Lee what she had brought with her.

"Where is my mail shirt?" She asked, her mind all astir.

"Over there," Ædwine said. "You are not going to put it back on, are you? Don't leave Lee. I will try to understand why you gave my bag to Edmund – you did know it was mine, didn't you?"

Lee pulled two bundles from the shoulder pockets.

"These belong to you," she said and Gragus took them.

"Frith was convinced you handed everything to Edmund," he murmured as he unrolled the papers and looked upon his charts.

"My king knows I kept back some. But I would like to report I saw you burn them, for he burned all the river charts and woodlands which Frith had recorded. He did not look upon your notes and details of our defences."

Gragus acknowledged her rebuke and threw each map into the fire.

"It all seems long ago. Poor Frith must have worried beyond measure about the missing bag and never said anything. Am I such a tyrant?"

"I hope you have forgiven Frith. Where is he?"

"He's gone to report to Edmund you are safe," Kadlin answered.

"Is Edmund here?"

"Yes," Gragus replied. "Frith saw young Eth three days ago. He passed on a message from Edmund to warn me to keep myself hidden. I think he has men posted about the place – but not on the river."

"I thought Edmund had gone to Elmham."

"He had not gone far when Eth and his thegns caught up with him. When he weighed their report, he made enquiries which led him here. Eth has proved himself to be a fine leader. He knew Ædwine was in trouble because he found his seaxe. Then he mustered the young thegns and captured one of Alcuin's men. They learned about a prisoner called the Breton but not where he had been taken. He sought you and Fred ..."

"Has Fred been found? I sent him into great danger," she interrupted.

"We will hear soon enough. Frith has been gone since breakfast."

"I hope Fred did not fall into the hands of the one they call Longcoat."

"He will never recover if he has, even I was afraid of his ways," admitted Ædwine. "Do you know who he is?"

"He is Alcuin's pupil. He comes from Hethel and runs a pack of hounds for the clergymen – those connected with Elmham North. He has corrupted his poor little sister."

"Not the one ..." Ædwine stopped before he said more but Lee would not let go.

"No, not the one you were with."

"You were with a woman when they captured you?" Gragus called out in despair. "How many times have I warned you?"

"I stepped right into his trap. How foolish do you think I feel? And how did you know?"

Lee was reluctant to say and turned from him. He sat up and groaned with the effort and Kadlin urged her to reveal what she knew. Lee then took his hand and solemnly told her tale.

"The girl you were with was Alcuin's concubine. He had grown tired of her and was willing enough to cast her away to catch you. They took her body to Southwic where Alcuin, with a great deal of wailing, told everyone an oarsman had murdered his daughter. He claimed she had been robbed," Lee paused. "I knew at once you were in danger."

"What was missing? What did you take Ædwine?" Gragus

asked.

Lee described the necklace.

"How was it Ædwine did not see you?"

"It was late, and the mists were already rising in the marshes ..."

"I thought I had seen an apparition," Ædwine intervened. "Some ghostly rider of old, whose sword flashed ghastly green. As I leapt to my feet, I felt dizzy and realised I had been drugged so I made haste to leave the place. The woman followed and struck me down."

"It was not the woman," Lee corrected. "She was already dead. It was Longcoat. He wanted his seaxe back – your father's seaxe. I saw it beside your fire, and I should have called for you ..."

There was a loud knock at the door. Kadlin left to see who it was and escorted two people into the hall.

"Is that brother of mine still sleeping?" Frith asked in his merry way.

Lee looked up and saw Pip was with him.

"What are you doing here?" Lee cried.

"I'm taking you back home."

"But I have only just arrived," she protested.

"And so has Æsc," Pip said very gravely. "If you don't come with me today you may soon be in Wessex and your friends hurled from this realm."

"What have you told him?" Lee demanded.

"Nothing. He has been travelling through Mercia and thought he would call on us. When he discovered you were not at home, he prised me from the Hellesden to escort him here to wait for your arrival with Edmund. I did not mention your visit nor your request," he said addressing Gragus. "Edmund advised me not to mention attachments of the heart at present. He wants to speak with Lee before Æsc has a chance to question her."

"You must follow Edmund's counsel my love. These are troubled days, and he may advise us to wait until the future is more certain."

"Is it what you desire?" She asked.

"I do not want you taken from this realm into Wessex," he sighed.

"I mean to go with you now, Gragus," she insisted.

"You will not," Pip intervened. "Gragus must wait. If his love is true, he will be like Jacob when he waited for Rachel. Besides how far will you get? Edmund has the whole trading settlement surrounded."

"He has us surrounded?" Ædwine cried in alarm.

"Not because of you. Lee knows why, for it was she who sent Fred to report the uprising. Edmund discovered a great band of oarsmen were waiting to join the rebels. Their ships were seen upstream in the margins beyond Merholt, but no one can find them. Most of our thegns have returned but some pursue the scattered rebels."

"Has Alcuin been captured?" Lee asked her brother.

"He has been found. His injury is serious - it is said he nearly bled to death," Pip revealed. "Unfortunately, the Bishop will not part with him."

"And Longcoat?" Asked Lee.

"Longcoat?" Pip repeated.

"The Hethel Ceorl's son."

"Edmund thinks he is injured too," Frith reported.

"I know he is because I hit him Frith," she confessed.

"No, it was more. At dawn, in his fury at the loss his prisoner, he set fire to all the vessels moored near the tannery, and as he watched them burn a mast fell towards him. It is thought he was severely scorched and may need help. Edmund sent a search party to the healing halls but has not found him. Without him and Alcuin the mustering fell apart."

Ædwine listened to his brother's report and turned to face them again.

"The wretch would have burned us alive! If Edmund does not find him, then I will," he threatened.

"You are not going anywhere," Kadlin interrupted. "I took my eyes off you at Blythburgh and look what happened. When you have rested for a few days, you are joining us, not charging off on your own again!"

Frith smiled and Ædwine turned away.

"Be gentle with him Kadlin," Frith said softly before he turned to his brother. "They found your bag in the hut along with the jar of whatever was used to drug you. Edmund still has those, but Eth gave me your seaxe." Frith took the seaxe and handed it to Lee. "For your collection," he laughed. Lee immediately handed it to Gragus who remained solemn for it had belonged to Weland.

"I am sorry I have not returned yours," she said. "But I have Frith's." Lee reached for her cloak and the seaxe fell to the ground.

"I will return for mine - and you," Gragus whispered.

"I will make sure he does Lee," Kadlin assured her. "For we have not had time to get to know one another and it was what I wished to do. I am more sorrowful than ever," she sighed.

"We must go," Pip said tenderly for he knew it would be a painful parting for his sister.

Frith and Kadlin took Pip to collect Lee's helm from the far room. Ædwine moaned and once more forced himself to sit up. Lee sat beside him with Gragus at her side.

"I don't want to go," she murmured. "Where can I find you if they send me to Wessex?" She took hold of Weland's ring and closed her eyes.

"I will come back for you," promised Gragus.

"We need assurance from your king about our safety here,"

said Ædwine thoughtfully. "If we are not careful, we will make enemies on all sides. Find out whose fleet came to aid Alcuin's men. Our presence here may be seen as treachery by our kin. My heart is sad for you Lee - and angry. Sometimes your ways are beyond my understanding."

"Are you pleased I am leaving?" She whimpered.

Ædwine did not reply and turned away.

"Go to Edmund, my love," Gragus comforted. "If he cannot help us then I will seek another way. Tell him it is the weak and separated who fall prey to the wolves first. He must keep your realm strong, united, and determined. Tell him to cover up what happened here. Many liths are depleted now but will regroup at the end of harvest. I will return by then."

"Where are you going?" Lee asked.

"Kadlin wishes to visit our kin in our homeland. We will not be gone for long. Frith is going to Gipeswick and perhaps back to his farm."

"Take me with you Gragus," Lee pleaded. "Wait here and I will ask Edmund - but my brother's untimely arrival will make it impossible, I know it will."

Frith returned and she and Gragus went with him as far as the courtyard. Ædwine called her name and Gragus urged her to go to him.

"Find my cloak," he asked.

"You are not strong enough to leave," Lee pleaded.

"I know. If I had strength, I would take you away today. Gragus is mistaken to throw himself upon another's mercy."

"I would never forgive myself if the port thegns arrested you for kidnap – and it is what it would come to."

"Or theft," he said tenderly as he took her hand. "Look in my cloak, I think the silver torc is hidden there. Check where it is sewn together." The twist of silver had been concealed within it and she prised it from the cloth. "Keep it Lee for I stole your gemstones."

He threw himself back upon his mattress and stared at the beams. The gentle maiden had unwittingly thrown light into his darkness, and he was deeply perplexed.

"I will give it to my king. I have no desire for adornments."

"You are not like any other woman I have met," he sighed. "They lowed for trinkets like calves taken from their mothers."

"I am sure Lindi did not."

"Lindi? Did she speak of me?"

"She warned me about you. She said you fought with your wife and despised all women."

"I do not despise you," he whispered. "Before we part, I must tell you what I have kept from Gragus." He turned his head away.

"What is it? Please don't say you murdered your wife."

"She has divorced me and has another man. Hastein is furious."

"Why?"

"She is a daughter of his slave and as such is bound to his household. Her children, my sons, were counted as his and she has fled with them."

"Your sons? How old are they?"

"The oldest is nearly nine, the next five and the youngest was not even born when she left me. He's not yet two."

"How is it Gragus does not know?"

"Hastein's camp at Loiremouthe is far from the Seine where Weland settled. I was happy for them to be raised amongst Hastein's offspring, but she stole them away and has followed her man to Thanet. Gutti has promised to look for them when he arrives there."

"And what will a man like Gutti do? Kill their mother? At least she has not abandoned them as you have done."

"Do not scold me, Lee. She did abandon Bjórstein my

firstborn and Lindi cared for him when he was a bairn."

"I liked Lindi."

"Well, she does not like me," he confessed and then surprised Lee by adding. "Pray to your god to watch over them for me. I fear they are in danger. I have been a poor father Lee, but I do not want to be forever separated from them."

Pip called for her and she stood up.

"You must tell Gragus," she said as she left.

Pip was restlessly looking at the sun's descent as he waited for her return. She took Gragus to one side and showed him the silver necklace.

"It's worth a fortune and the Hethel Ceorl will miss it. I will pass it to Edmund but take care for Longcoat is a dangerous man. They seek you because of the seaxe. And Longcoat was trying to get Ædwine to confess something before Alcuin arrived. What could it be? Why do they call Ædwine the 'Breton' for Gutti said his name was Ærnbjörn?"

"His mother was from that kingdom, and it was his old battle name."

He kissed her and watched her leave. Back inside he threw himself down upon the longbench where he groaned at the agony of his loss.

"I am sorry," Ædwine said very quietly. "My foolishness drove her headlong into danger. We must separate and you and she will be spared. It is me they want – not you."

"I promised your father I would watch over you. Do you know why they want Weland's seaxe?"

"No - I don't even know how many moons Longcoat possessed it. He laid the trap to get it back – it's a fine weapon."

"It wasn't him who wanted it - it was Alcuin. His uprising has failed because he was distracted in his efforts to lay hands on it. Was its workmanship worth it? Does the seaxe bear some secret mark which Weland may have confessed to someone? I am sure Alcuin understands what it is, but we do not. If only you had spent more time at ease with your father - I will never understand why you forsook him to fight for that old rogue Hastein."

"I wanted to be with my sons. Lee said I must tell you."

Gragus thought he was dreaming. It was news indeed.

"How many sons do you have?"

"Three."

"And Frith does not know, nor your father?"

"No – and I regret not telling Weland. My desire was for the battlefield and death - not fatherhood. Since I have sojourned here, I have lost sight of those things. I want to see my sons again Unnulfr and put my arms about them. If only Weland was here with us. This kingdom may not have Francia's fabulous courts and renown, but it has life and love."

Gragus was stirred. His friend's words echoed what was in his own heart. Though Weland, his most loyal friend, was lost, his son was not. The two men embraced and Gragus asked many questions about the young boys. They talked long into the night about their childhood and youth and all which bound them together.

As soon as Lee arrived at the hall where Edmund stayed, she began to feel tired but there was no time to rest. She put the silver necklace in her folded mail shirt but then decided to wear it. Outside in the courtyard garden a cool breeze blew between the buildings. She sat down to wait for her king. It was not long before he found her there and warmly greeted her.

"What can I say Lee? Your adventures have become too dangerous my child. I thought you were lost forever. His captors fiercely opposed us at Southwic - and in the margins where Eth had taken the juniors. My men had a hard battle here - and you dared to enter the bloodied chamber!"

"I could not leave him there. They were about to torment him again. He is precious to Gragus, for both he and Frith are pledged to his care; it is more than words; more than kinship. I have urged them to leave North Burgh."

"It was very wise for the Hethel Ceorl has not been found. He is a vengeful man and thoroughly cruel."

"I know Edmund. I think he is looking for this." Lee showed him the necklace. "He hid it in Ædwine's cloak. They were going to accuse him of murdering the girl – the one found drowned near Southwic. Though I do not think she drowned at all. The Hethel Ceorl broke her neck! She was used to ensnare Ædwine - and on Alcuin's orders."

"Did Frith tell you Alcuin has been captured?"

"Yes – although I know you do not have jurisdiction over him."

"I do have Gisla under my care. I intend to bring them together if I can – perhaps we will discover what was discussed at Elmham."

"Did Gisla agree to meet him?"

"I was not gentle with her Lee. Her son-in-law was part of this rebellion, but I prevented him from being with them when my thegns arrived."

"He did not deserve to be rescued."

"Did Ædwine?" Lee made no reply. "Was he badly injured? There was much blood spilled in the room."

"Kadlin has tended to his wounds – the lash furrows were very deep. She was very kind - I did not want to leave them Edmund."

Tears fell as she looked at the flowers in the garden, but Edmund made her look up again. There was great tenderness in his eyes.

"Æsc is here. Had things been different Gragus and his kin could have joined me but if your brother misreads our circumstances and takes news back to Wessex it will undermine us all."

"Does he know where I have been?"

"He knows you were with the junior thegns at Blythburgh, and you and Fred fled from Southwic. Do not say more than is necessary. He will not grasp the nature of your relationship with those wild friends you have. It appears he has renewed his acquaintance with Greg, though I do not know what brought it about." Edmund sighed and took his friend into his arms. "And at such a time dear Lee. When things are calm again, I will arrange a fitting betrothal for you, but they might demand he is baptised for it is the way of Wessex. Find out if Gragus will agree to it. There will be many days of separation for you I fear before you can be his wife."

"I know Edmund. Gragus will be content though. He did burn all those maps and charts. He advises you to cover up the skirmish here."

"Why?"

"Because if Ivar hears word of insurrection and division in our realm he will attack. When they see a weakened lamb, they swoop."

"Then I will advise the port thegns to spread word it was a rift in trade transactions and no more. The Scandinavians who settle here favour riches from trade and dislike disruption. It was those on Flegg who called off the mysterious fleet which twice passed the North Burgh thegns without being seen."

"Perhaps they have realised there is more silver and gold in Mercia and have gone there."

"There was certainly a great display of wealth at Greg's wedding," he sighed. Before he could say more Pip and Æsc came into the garden.

Lee was surprised at the likeness between the two brothers. Æsc barely recognised his sister.

"I can hardly believe you have grown so beautiful," he said. "No wonder Greg was so anxious to keep those heathens from you."

Lee shrank away from him, but he did not detect it because he had swept her into arms. It was a short embrace because his young son was waiting to meet his aunt. Lee greeted the child with gentle eagerness for she often wished her nephews and nieces lived closer. She wanted to take the child to the pond to look for froglets but Æsc demanded her attention.

"You must tell me all about yourself, my little sister. How often does Edmund allow you to go abroad with his thegns? Cenhelm was assured your wanderings would cease. Do I have reason to take you to Wessex?"

"Pip's agreement with Cenhelm concerned 'aimless wanderings' and I am helping the women to order their gardens, so they are more productive."

"In Southwic?"

"Yes, gardens are very poor there. The soil is thin, and they need shelter from the sea breezes. I had hoped to discuss some improvements with Gisla, but she was not at home. Have you seen her?"

"Edmund has had me confined to this hall, so I have not been able to see anyone. There is much he keeps from me."

"It is the duty of the king to keep trading agreements in our favour. Are there shortages in Wessex? I know how Wessex loves to command the best agreements but surely you have enough of your own cheese. Or is it our herrings you want?"

Edmund smiled.

"I am not here to trade," Æsc said. "I was in Medeshamstede and met Will and then learned Greg was about to marry so I made a diversion. Gisla asked me to visit her, and I thought you might accompany me. But when I reached Hellesden Hall you were not there."

Lee wondered what Will had said.

"I hope you took pity on Will. He needs to broaden his

studies and go to Wessex. His behaviour has been very strange since he went to Mercia."

"I judged yours has been worse."

Edmund laughed and Lee was given leave to take her young nephew with her until it was time for the evening feast.

When she arrived at the feast she sat amongst the junior thegns. Eth was full of joy and their spirits lifted. Recent bruises and wounds were forgotten. Pip wished he had sat with them. He found his brother's company awkward. Later Pip turned to speak with the port thegn. He was a very intense man whose concerns were with ship building and the scarcity of materials and the protection of Merholt and other coppiced woodlands. They discovered each had a great affection for timber and its production, so they did not grow weary or run out of things to say.

Later Æsc left his place and beckoned his sister to join him. Lee rose and went to the hearth where Æsc waited for her.

"You have much to confess sister. Gisla told me you made Greg's life exceedingly miserable because you are betrothed to an oarsman – Frith she said. One of those from Dummoc. I have learnt much about the trial."

"From Gisla?"

"Yes."

"What does Gisla know? Alcuin hid her away for many weeks and she never understood how events unfurled. It is true Frith was one of the traders on trial, but I was never pledged to him. He waits for his own betrothed and then he will settle here. I have met his future wife. She is a Christian and very kind and gentle. You would like her. Did you like Greg's wife?"

"No," he said abruptly. "Greg was always so careful and weighed everything - but not this time. Gisla blames you for his haste. She said it was you who had him sent to the Borders."

"Edmund needs a strong leader in the Borders. Greg was

the right person to send. He should have written to Edmund if he was grieved. But he did not because he was content. At least I thought he was – he said he would let time heal our friendship – such as it was."

"Did Greg ask you to be his wife?"

"Yes. Did you not hear about his negotiations with mother's kin? He said he had written to you."

"What negotiations?"

"He tried to buy me like men buy slaves! He paid them money and then asked me. When I refused his offer, he demanded I marry him. He thought I would not dare oppose him. But Edmund rescued me."

"And I thought he had changed his ways. Why didn't you write to us?"

"We feared you would agree with him. It was left to those who knew us to decide the matter and they agreed we are not suited."

"You were better suited than the one he threw himself at."

"Edmund told me it was done in haste. Is she with child?"

"You are too blunt sister. Edmund has let you tarry too long in the company of thegns."

"They are young lads. Younger than Win. It was you, my older kin, who put a sword in my hand and taught me to fight. Eth has always been my friend. Is it my fault I had no sisters?"

"It is a husband you need not sisters! I have never understood why Will did not ask you to be his wife years ago."

"We were brothers."

"Well, your days of brotherhood must end."

Edmund looked up and saw the maiden looked exhausted and went to her side. He thought how beautiful she was.

"Your sister needs to rest," he said. "She joined my feast because I said we could not celebrate without her. She is a shining light in this realm, and I will not have her hidden."

"She has confessed Greg asked her to be his wife."

"He did, but he was not wise in his dealings with her. They could have grown together as friends, but he was unwilling to listen or make time to get to know her gentle nature and loyal heart. It is wiser to coax than to whip."

"I see there is much Greg has not disclosed. I am sorry Edmund. I understood she was in danger of being abducted by these oarsmen raiders."

"Would I risk the loss of such a precious treasure?" Edmund asked as he kissed Lee's hand. "I will see you tomorrow, my love."

Lee left the feast thoroughly exhausted, and the next day missed breakfast with Edmund. A sealed note lay beside her pillow.

"Fairest maiden. We begin our journey at dawn and already my heart feels sorrowful. A is very pitiful. He told me about his sons. G is delighted he is an uncle and K has offered to care for them if they can be returned to us. I understand G has already shared his hopes with you concerning my sister. I am delighted they have come to such an agreement. Promise me, my love, if Edmund cannot help us, you will find me. If a year passes since the day we met then leave all you have and I will give you shelter. Burn this letter and the other one I left in your tower. Don't let them discover what we must do – not even the one you love and serve. U

CHAPTER SEVENTEEN

PASSION

Lee burned the letters. She was confident no one would uncover her prearranged flight with Gragus and certain she could keep herself busy and out of trouble for five moons. After a few days of hard work in the home pightle Æsc called to see her.

"You've been busy," he greeted.

"I was eager to get back from North Burgh in case the weeds had taken over," she said. "Did you meet Alcuin?"

"I saw him at Elmham, and I had met him before. It was at the Bishop's Hall in Winchester. He calls himself Albion there."

"Did you tell Edmund?"

"Of course," he said as he looked over his shoulder. "I will speak to you later because Gisla is here."

"Is she?"

"Yes - and be gentle with her. That scoundrel has weakened her mind. She trembled exceedingly when Edmund said she must face him. I had to persuade your king to relent. And do not mention her Southwic family either. Edmund has arrested them."

"Gisla, how are you?" Lee asked as the lady came into view.

"Exhausted," she apologised. "There has been a great deal of misunderstanding. I am sorry you had to flee from my Southwic Hall. I did not know Alcuin had posted armed men there."

"Fred and I loved the sunken fields. And from the high banks we saw a fox stalking a heron and more hawks than I can name. The channels are full of frogs and minnows."

"You wanted to take the lad to find some frogs," her brother interrupted. "Shall we go to the pond?"

Lee was pleasantly surprised at his change of attitude for he seemed to have allied himself with her. They enjoyed each other's company at the pond and later, in the orchard, they found both froglets and orange bellied newts amongst the cool clumps of grass. The younger pair pretended the newts were dragons and Lee began one of her fanciful tales.

"What is Greg's wife like?" Lee asked when Gisla had gone to rest.

"She is very refined. You would not find her in a garden or lounging in an orchard. When I met her at the wedding, I was surprised Greg chose someone so opposite to you, for Will truly thought he loved you."

"Will wanted to get rid of me," Lee sighed. "Does Greg love her?"

"He gave every appearance of being satisfied with his alliance. The marriage feast was very grand. Her uncle owns large estates in the chalklands and fens - and so does she."

"So, he married her for her wealth!" Lee exclaimed.

"I think he did."

"Then he has acted very foolishly because Edmund was about to give him Brandune – the richest place in the realm."

"He is a good thegn Lee and will harry those oarsmen who seek a foothold in the Borders. It is as well Gragus and Frith did not go there."

"They have returned to their homeland," Lee confirmed.

"Edmund insists Frith must settle here because he is pledged to marry an East Anglian widow. I hope he did not mean you."

"Of course, not. I told you I had met her. She is very gracious, and her embroideries are the best I have ever seen."

Her brother smiled and they left the orchard to join Gisla at the hall.

"I understand you have met Frith's betrothed," she began. "How is it I never met her when he was at the healing halls?"

"Her husband was alive then."

"What caused his death?"

"I'm not sure. He was not a young man and had been ill for some time."

"Does she have any children?"

"No."

Frith had revealed to Lee that Kadlin felt great shame because no child had been born to her since Erik's son - and he had died at birth. Lee did not like Gisla's interrogation and moved away but Gisla would not let go.

"We cannot always have what we desire, can we? It was as well the husband died before you ran off with Frith, for he never loved you."

"I am glad he has found happiness."

"But Greg hasn't," Gisla chided.

"He chose to marry her," Lee replied. "But, if Edmund thinks he will suffer too much because of it, he will allow him to divorce."

"He has given me permission to divorce," Gisla revealed. "Why should I stay with my husband when he has replaced me with another. He used his influence against me for years. However, my son-in-law has sworn a new allegiance to Edmund. Now I have free access to my grandchild. He had no choice; it was that or exile. In many ways your reckless departure from Southwic worked in my favour. Gragus advised me to free myself long ago."

"Did you discover what assets were discussed at the Elmham meeting. Was it eels?" Lee asked. She was determined to steer Gisla away from discussing Gragus.

"I do not want to think about it. It could have been eels. They have fisheries in West …"

Win and Fred suddenly burst in carrying the ugliest fledglings Lee had ever seen. She would not learn where the fisheries were for many moons.

"You said they would never fall out of the ælder, but they have." Win laughed. Fred could not keep hold of his struggling bird. It squeezed itself under his elbow. Lee caught it in her apron.

"It's as well I wove a new nest," Lee said. "If we wedge it amongst the branches and put the chicks in then the mother will return."

Lee took her nephew to the wood store to fetch the nest while Win fought to keep the fledgling jays contained in his discarded shirt.

Later in the day her older brother caught up with her in the stable.

"You always knew how to slip away before father rebuked you. I understand a person from a noble line has asked to marry you and is about to begin betrothal negotiations. I had hoped you would tell me while we sat in the orchard together. Why are you so secretive?"

"It is no more than rumour," she muttered.

"I am sure Edmund is not in the habit of spreading rumours. He made me swear not to tell Gisla."

Lee was astonished.

"It's early days Æsc," she mumbled. "Edmund says I am to train at Elmham before we marry."

Æsc immediately thought she referred to Edmund.

"Then I am delighted you have resolved to change your ways," he smiled. "It will please Edmund if the ladies at Elmham can make a noblewoman of you. I hope you will listen to their advice – Gisla told me how you thoroughly thwarted Branda's mother when she tried to direct you. She is your example to

434

follow."

"What!" Lee cried. She began to laugh. "Edmund certainly doesn't want me to become over pious like her. He says I must stay as I am."

The weather remained fine and on Thursday evening Lee lay upon a heap of hay which she had used to protect her tender plants from late frosts. She was absorbed in watching the martins catch flies as they swooped and dived overhead. She loved to hear their cries for they brought joy to her heart. Carefree days were about to return because Æsc had completed his round of visiting and would soon return to Wessex. She closed her eyes and considered Edmund's wisdom. Then someone showered her with May blossom. Lee was startled for it was not like Pip to be so light-hearted.

"More snow," the newcomer whispered.

"I thought you had left!" Lee exclaimed with sheer delight.

"I decided to return. My garden needs weeding and I must plant my late beans. Pip says you have some spare seed. I saw him in the orchard as I climbed the bank – just like poor Greg."

"Did you know his mother has moved to Stane Hall? It's barely a stone's throw from Linden Pits! Hilde said the Mercian woman ordered her to leave Kentforde because they couldn't live peaceably together – though there was enough accommodation there for a whole fyrd."

"Why hasn't she returned to her hall on the hill?" Frith asked.

"She didn't want to be lonely!" Lee exclaimed. "Her cousin lives down the road to Water Green and they are close friends. I expect Greg will visit her – and frequently. So much for sending him to the other side of the kingdom – he will almost be in the Long Mead."

"Then you must arm yourself with the fine seaxe you have," he teased. "Where is it?"

"Under my mattress."

Lee stood up and shook the blossom from her tunic.

"You jest!" He said and then chased her with more handfuls of May blossom.

Pip sighed as he saw them wildly pursuing each other through the courtyards and buildings. He was pleased it was the mildest amongst them who had returned and hoped the other two were far away.

When their game was over Lee took Frith to see the mares. It was very close to the time they would foal. Fred was there feeding them some grass from the orchard. The two friends lent against the gate to watch.

"Gisla came to visit me. I had only been back a few days and it was as if she had never been lost. She was kind and gentle and ..."

"Did she ask you about Gragus?"

"Not really - she asked if I missed you."

"I hope you said yes." Frith laughed.

"Of course, I did - Gragus warned me to say as little as possible, but she already knew about your betrothal. I did not mention Kadlin's name, but I said she was the widow I lodged with when I was in North Burgh."

"I miss her," Frith sighed.

"And I miss Gragus," she paused. "As does Gisla."

"There is nothing to fear. He loves you," Frith comforted.

"Something she said warned my heart. She is going to divorce her husband because Gragus advised it."

"I was there when he urged her to free herself from those who despised her. Don't fret Lee I will warn Gragus. He was quite lost without you. I would like to teach you and Eth our language. It will keep you busy and you will need to know it if you are live amongst us."

"You are very thoughtful Frith. Fred is to start work at

Spring Hall next week – his bravery at North Burgh has impressed his kin there and they want him to help at the workshops. I could travel up with him and help you in the home pightle and then travel back with Fred in the evening."

"I will ride over for you both and take you back. It will be good to see Pip and Win, I have so much to discuss about woodlands. Will you and Fred continue at Ældor Hall?"

"No. Edmund's Thegn is not a person I wish to see at present."

"Why ever not?"

"He was not pleased about the incident at North Burgh. He blames me for splitting the kingdom asunder."

"There you go again Lee. I never know if I ought to laugh or cry when you embroider events so."

"Embroider! That is so funny."

"Why?"

"All the Hethel Ceorl's garments were embroidered."

They laughed loudly and Fred complained because the mares moved to the peaceful mire at the far end of the mead. They left the lad and returned to the garden where Pip stood looking up at the sky.

"It's a beautiful evening – we might as well enjoy it before the frosts return," he said gloomily. Lee could not help but laugh. Her brother cast her a bewildered look and turned to Frith. "How long will Gragus be gone?"

"About two moons."

"And Kadlin? Will she return with him?"

"I hope so. Hasn't Lee told you we are to marry?"

"She did - but I did not know how long your people mourn."

"Life is short my friend. We hope to marry after harvest or before. Gragus is happy with the arrangement."

"Will Ædwine be at your wedding?" Lee asked.

"I hope so," Frith said quietly. Lee had not mentioned his

brother at all until then which had surprised him.

"How is he?" Pip asked.

"The sea water helped to heal his stripes," Frith explained. "We went back to the dunes near Kadlin's Hall. At first the water caused him great pain, but he endured. He is anxious to leave this kingdom."

"He will not be returning to work in the Hellesden then?"

"I don't think so Pip, my brother never settles for long ... " Frith paused. "I must be getting back. Will you help me with my horse, Lee?"

She went with Frith to call his horse.

"Ædwine has left us, my love. And it was too soon, long before Kadlin thought he would be well enough. Gutti turned up and persuaded him to go to Loiremouthe. Hastein has forged new ties with Salamon of Brittany."

"Why would a Christian king like him make an alliance with such a terrible lord?" Lee asked.

"Because Francia's ruler has threatened his kingdom – it's not the first time. Salamon needs Hastein's men to guard his borders against one known as Robert the Strong. Gragus fears my brother will never return."

"What terrible news Frith!" Lee exclaimed. "Will Gragus follow him?"

"Ædwine has left us many times. We wish we could hold him to our side, but Gutti has come between us."

"I wish Gutti had never set foot in my kingdom," Lee sighed. "There was nothing about him I liked."

Two days later Gisla briefly returned to Hellesden Hall. She had Æsc's son and Eth's younger brothers with her and was travelling back from Stane Hall. Although it was a long walk, she wanted to see the bluebells which grew in the Hellesden. Fred joined them in the coppice. He had young Æthel with him and all the younger girls from Hollin's Hall.

Lee sat amongst the carpet of flowers helping the young girls fix them into their hair. When Lee's nephew pushed some bluebells amongst Lee's braids Fred proclaimed the Swan Princess had been crowned anew. Gisla did not smile, and Lee wished Fred had not mentioned Dummoc. Gisla retreated and watched from a distance until it grew late.

Someone else had been watching from a distance; someone who now regretted his retreat. He sat at the top of a bank where the wattle fence was thickly covered with honeysuckle, and he looked upon the one he had so inexplicably abandoned. Lee's rejection had chilled his lonely heart and he had fled to another. However, after those first few days in his wife's company, he felt desolate. He returned to Kentforde less than two weeks after the wedding, seeking the comfort of his work with his thegns and defence strategies. Amongst his papers, he found her letter 'I thought you wanted us to be friends?' He bitterly regretted his haste. The Maiden of the Hellesden desired his friendship.

His wife's love was like the shallow heath-land soil; it could only sustain thorns. She was prickly like the furze and already he did not want to be close to her. He wanted depth, and the girl who sat in the sea of blue stirred the depths of his heart. Shallow soils held no water, but she caused springs of joy to break forth wherever she went. He felt drawn to the beautiful maiden crowned with heavenly blue.

Gisla called the youngsters to collect their posies for it was time to leave. Lee accompanied the children to Edmund's Hall where she hoped to find Eth. She had not long arrived when a lone horseman approached from the south. Æsc ran to greet him. But when Lee saw the newcomer's dark curls and pleasant smile, she was suddenly afraid and ran across the practise fields into the Shield Hall. As soon as she arrived the junior thegns cheered. They had not seen her since North Burgh and there she was all out of breath and flushed with beauty.

They urged her to retell the tale of Merholt and she plunged straight in and forgot the Chief Thegn and the flowers in her hair. They pressed her to take her sword from its place and when she held it above her head all cheered and pleaded with her to put on her battle gear. When she returned, Eth was with them. He was in high spirits too and began to feign an attack upon her. She responded in a likewise manner. Very soon they had swords and shields in their grasp, and she was back to her old ways. She played without her helm for it was a hot day and the battle was slow. Eth laughed as the flowers gradually fell from her hair. He had never fought a Bluebell Princess before. The junior thegns were delighted to witness the scene. Their merriment in the Shield Hall was overheard. Æsc took Greg to investigate.

"There is your true sister – the one you have not been allowed to see," Greg whispered. "She is as wild as a foal on the chalklands don't you think?"

"She remembers all we taught her," Æsc replied.

Lee began well but Eth had improved threefold, and she was out of practice. However, when he fought more intensely, she eagerly responded.

"She fights harder now," her brother observed.

"Then stop her Æsc. For she will not."

"What harm can she do?"

"She has taken a warrior from his saddle," the Thegn warned.

"You were dreaming. She could not do that."

"I witnessed it with my own eyes."

Æsc looked at his friend in amazement.

"Was it you then? I know you took her on horseback to Dummoc. Did she gain victory over you?"

"Only with words," he said as he laughed. "It was one of those ... "

All merriment abruptly ceased as Lee fell to the floor in

a swoon. Eth realised his mistake, threw away his shield and weapon and was on his knees at her side.

"You've taken her down with your shield you foolish lad!" The Chief Thegn bellowed. Æsc drew close to his sister who began to revive.

"Greg, carry her back to the hall. I'll put the sword away."

"Don't you touch her!" Eth cried out. "Stand away from her or I shall order my men to arrest you."

"What did you say?" Demanded Æsc as he swung round to see the lad attempt to help Lee to her feet.

"I have hurt her, and I will take her to mother at the hall," Eth insisted.

"You dare override my orders? I am her brother and a thegn."

"My orders came from the king - to protect her. The Chief Thegn no longer has authority here. Ask my father."

"Let the lad take her over to Ældor Hall," Greg said softly. "His mother will check her head. She is hurt and needs attention. Take my horse."

"I can walk!" Lee exclaimed. "Keep your horse away from me."

Lee was angry because her brother had brought her adversary to witness the first time she had fallen at the Shield Hall. She had done well until then in her efforts to stay at home doing domestic tasks - but the Thegn could ruin everything!

She and Eth walked the short distance to Ældor Hall. Æsc watched them leave and turned to his friend.

"She was more than angry with you Greg. And the lad, though wearied, stood his ground against us. What have you done to upset her?"

"I challenged her heart," he haughtily declared. "And she could not face the truth. She sent me to the Borders so I cannot rebuke her oarsman."

"Who is this oarsman?

The Thegn craftily implied Ædwine was there to woo Lee away from Edmund's ways. He was careful not to say too much for fear he might lose her to Wessex. He ended humbly.

"I am not without fault. But when I confronted her with the truth about her oarsman, she struck me."

"I am sure Lee will not abandon Edmund for a heathen."

At Edmund's Hall, the two parted company but vowed to keep each other informed about Lee and Edmund.

The gloomy cold hearth was Lee's refuge while her headache eased. She had refused to lie down to rest and dismissed Eth.

She did not look up when her brother Æsc arrived.

"Greg has explained all to me, I even saw his scar. How could you doubt he loved you?"

"I have never doubted that he thinks he loves me."

"If only I had arrived a month earlier. I would have dealt with you as you deserved. Who are these oarsmen he mentioned?"

"I did not know what he was about to do, did I? I should have taken my letter to him – and not entrusted it to the blithest thegn in the kingdom!"

"What letter?"

"It was mainly about horses - but I said I wanted us to be friends. Then he would have discussed his marriage plans with me and I could have advised against it. There are many fine maidens here who love him."

"But not you?"

"I love another," she declared.

"I know you think you do, but it is not a suitable match Lee! If Greg's wife had not been from Mercia he could have quietly divorced her. There may still be a way to settle the affair and then he could marry you."

"Don't you understand Æsc? I have never wanted to be with

him!" Lee shouted. "Would you prevent me from marrying the one I love?"

"How can Edmund entertain such madness? He needs to make an alliance with Mercia or Wessex before your oarsmen take his kingdom. He has encouraged them to settle amongst you and now he will be fully occupied keeping them in order."

"Do you mean our Scandinavians? Without them we would be without trade and then how would you make your money? What has Greg said?"

"Not much. Except you and the king conspired to have him sent to the Borders because of the trial involving oarsmen – yes, he said oarsmen not traders. I know all about them," he declared though he did not.

"And so does Edmund," Lee added.

"Did Greg advise you not to marry him?"

"Yes, he did. He wants him exiled!"

"What?" He rebounded. He did not understand her answer.

"Have you ever considered what motives Greg may have?" Lee earnestly asked. "And why? The man I love has a better heart and he is of a kingly line. He is worthy."

"I do not doubt it, but times are uncertain Lee."

"Then I will wait." Lee said.

"It would be wiser not to marry him. Let Greg divorce the Mercian and marry you. If he and Edmund come to blows it will split this kingdom and you all will be lost. Now go home and I will speak to Edmund."

Lee rode in silence with Eth until they reached the bluebells. They both dismounted and walked through them.

"You still have one in your braids," he said. Eth stopped to remove it. "It was a good match, wasn't it? They will not forget for a while. I know I got carried away and I am sorry you are hurt. Do you think Ædwine will pursue me with his sword?"

"Don't be silly Eth. It's me he will track down. I was meant to stay quiet and calm while my brother was here. And I did until *he* returned! I hate him Eth. He has told my brother all about Gragus. He has ruined everything. He is like your brother when he didn't win the fishing rod Fred made – he broke it into pieces, so it was no use to anyone."

"Don't despair Lee. I love your ways. You're my best friend and I would like to get to know Frith."

"Then meet me at Frith's on Monday. He is going to teach me the oarsmen language. You must learn it as well."

"Why?"

"If I have to run to Gragus for shelter I will take you with me."

"Yes, you must – you cannot go alone."

"Don't tell your father."

"Then promise me you will take your place amongst us at the Shield Hall. We can spend the morning at Frith's and the afternoon with the lads."

"I do feel at home in the Shield Hall."

"Good and promise you will not leave without me."

"I promise Eth. We will be able to battle using the oarsman's commands soon. You must learn the words for drop, bend, and stoop then you won't hit me again."

Eth laughed and they made their way to her hall.

CHAPTER EIGHTEEN
FAITH OR FATE?

Eth lingered at Hellesden Hall because Lee's headache grew worse, and he felt responsible. She complained bitterly about the Chief Thegn and exaggerated his persecution of oarsmen. It was late when the lad left. The return journey was, therefore, very treacherous and his temper frayed. When he got back the Chief Thegn was in the stables quietly preparing for his early morning departure. Eth fell upon him like a sudden storm.

"I hope you feel shame forever," he began. "What you did today was unworthy. Lee is hurt and I cannot console her. Æsc did not need to know about her betrothal. I hope Edmund exiles you, Kentforde is not far enough!"

Greg was alarmed. The lad blocked his way of escape, and the Thegn did not want to become embroiled in a fight.

"She was felled by your blow not mine. You could have killed her with a strike on the temple."

Eth did not want to be reminded of his folly and swept in.

"She knows I meant her no harm – unlike you! What poison have you whispered in Æsc's ear tonight?"

"If she will not tell the truth, then I will."

"The truth is she loves Gragus, not you. Are you so callous? Do you think you will gain repute by blighting her name?"

"Isn't that what she did to me?" He replied bitterly.

"So, it is revenge you seek!"

Before the Thegn could reply Eth struck.

"It was not revenge," he muttered. The Thegn wiped the blood from his broken lip. "She deserves someone better than an oarsman."

"She deserves to have a chance to be happy with Gragus and you are not going to stand in her way." He fell upon the older man as a wild beast would fall upon an injured deer. Greg had no choice but to put up a fight and the less experienced fell first.

Edmund was incensed by Eth's behaviour and his father was too angry to speak. The Chief Thegn was overcome with remorse and genuinely regretted what had happened. He had landed a heavy blow on Eth's chest and his ribs cracked. His father would not go to him, not even when the pain worsened. Finally, Flæ defied her husband and went to Eth and rubbed the wound with her herb lotion.

Edmund also slept little. His conscience troubled him for he had let Æsc depart thinking it was he who was to marry Lee. And he had to tell the poor maiden Alcuin was missing. But worse, perhaps, she had offended his household thegn.

Before sunrise Edmund wrote a note to Lee. She was dismissed from the thegn band and from the practise halls. She was not to see Eth until further notice. Lee was distressed at the completeness of her ban. It was Pip who consoled her and encouraged her to visit Frith as arranged. He insisted she must obey her king and stay away from the Shield Hall and Eth.

However, on Monday when she arrived at Chadsacre Hall Eth and Frith were eating breakfast together.

"Eth, what has happened? Why is Edmund so angry?"

"The Bard has flown," he replied and then winced in pain.

"Are you injured?" Lee asked.

"Yes," Eth revealed looking at Frith.

"Has Frith hit you?"

Frith explained and Lee sat in silence. She felt guilty and left.

On her return to Hellesden Hall she lay down and complained her head hurt. After three days Hilde sent word to Edmund, and he came to the hall.

"You stirred the lad up and he is suffering for it. Your words have worked their poison, Lee. If you want to be wife to a heathen, I suggest you go and live in one of their camps for a few weeks. If you saw some of their vile ways perhaps you would think again. I hope you will have regained your senses by the time I return."

"You are just like Will!" She called after him.

He left the room without saying any more but did not get further than pightle garden when he turned back.

"Very well Lee, you have a week's ban this time. If you do not abide by the rules, it will be a month. Make sure Eth does not exert himself before he is well enough. You take charge of the juniors for now – they mourn for you as if you were dead. Keep them busy and insist they wear their helms."

"Thank you, Edmund."

"But it was wrong to deceive Æsc."

"How have I deceived him?"

"Didn't you confirm you are to marry me?"

"Marry you?" Her voice trembled. "Is that what he thought?"

"Yes. You have a way with words which is dangerous. And Eth is suffering because of it."

"Please forgive me Edmund. I did not deliberately cause confusion. Greg implied he had told Æsc all about Gragus."

"Well, he did not, but I should have done. Remember I know about those maps and so does Eth's father. Consider what I have said Lee and forget him."

Eth gave every appearance of having recovered and it was not long before he was assigned to take charge of a delivery of some semi-forged blades for the Sygelsmer Forge, a large workshop alongside the main Beodrickworth to Meleforde highway. The settlement lay in a vale adjacent to a large mere. It was guarded by a watch tower on a prominent escarpment which also overlooked Edmund's vill to the north and east.

The Hellesden was visible from the top of the tower. The three juniors with Eth were pleased the Maiden from the Hellesden had been allowed to accompany them to Ramsey.

The five travellers rested at Meleforde where Ric and his sisters joined them for the journey to Bures. A warm welcome awaited them at the Ætheling's Hall although Os was away with Edmund at Lidgaet. Branda had fond memories of her stay with Lee in February and took the junior thegns to see her new garden. Eth did not join them. He complained his head hurt but recovered overnight.

Eth remained solemn and told Lee he did not like Ric's three sisters who had been teasing and flattering him since Meleforde. Lee blamed the weather for his fatigue because it was hot, and the highways were dry and dusty. The sheep's parsley grew tall and sickly sweet.

Eth urged Lee to sit with him in the shade while they watched the goods being unloaded from the warehouse beside the Stour.

"I've had enough of their gossip," he groaned.

"But you learn a lot just by listening to them," Lee said cheerfully. She picked a tell-time to blow away its seeds. They fell upon Eth.

"Do you have to?" He said sharply.

"It's not the girls at all. You are annoyed with everything!"

"Most of what they say is old wives tales – not worth listening to ..."

"It was interesting to learn more about the Thegn's wife."

"Don't mention him. I'm beginning to think I will never be the same."

He winced as he spoke.

"So, you are in pain? It wasn't a headache?"

"I feel terrible Lee – it's like glowing embers at the base of my ribs," he complained. Eth closed his eyes and lay flat against the bank.

"Did your mother send any of the herbal rub?"

"It was so much better. I didn't think I'd need it."

"I have something for bruises and cuts – point to where it hurts."

"I'll be alright. I feel better when I'm on my horse - but it's so hot."

"It will be cooler in the alder coppice. We could go for a short walk while the loading is done."

It was not long into their walk when Eth stopped. Lee insisted he should rest and found a shady place on an alder which leaned over a clear pool. They talked at length about their adventures in Icanho and Southwic.

"You will make a good healer Lee. Your voice is calm and gentle; the way you describe everything in your tales takes away pain. It's so peaceful being with you away from all those squeals. I look forward to being back at Frith's – it's peaceful there as well. I wish I could go and live there to get away from my brothers. They jumped on me to wake me up – and the pain started again."

"I'm sorry Eth. Edmund was right to be cross. I did stir you up."

She turned away but he put his hand on her shoulder and assured her she was not to blame.

"Edmund had other things on his mind when he rebuked you. I overheard Father say it was Bishop Æthelwold who aided Alcuin's escape. No wonder Ædwine hates our ways and beliefs if our clergymen are so rotten. And Edmund can do nothing about it because the Mercians rule Elmham North."

"And Dummoc," Lee added. "Gragus once said Weland

449

should have slit Alcuin's throat while he had a chance. What good did I do by merely spiking his wrist?"

"It was you? We all thought it was Ædwine! Why didn't you tell me?"

"Edmund doesn't know. He was not pleased when I pierced the Thegn. I had just released Ædwine when Alcuin entered the torture room."

"Then you had no choice. You were brave. I will follow your example."

"There is a difference between bravery and foolhardiness - and it is difficult to judge when you are hard-pressed by temper."

"I know Lee, please forgive me."

"Edmund is grieved because you struck a fellow thegn."

"I forgot he was a thegn."

"And I had quite forgotten how unpleasant he is."

"Let's not think about him Lee, shall we practice those words and make our way back to the horses?"

Ric looked very dismayed when they returned. His men were waiting to depart.

"Where have you been? People have disappeared from here!"

"It was my idea," Eth apologised. "I feel so hot, and it was cooler in the alder coppice."

"You would have been hotter if you had been rounded up and crammed into a hold with a dozen others. You're the thegn here, and you could have done something useful."

"You get on your horse, Eth," Lee said very gently. She was not so gentle with Ric who felt the full force of her fury. "How dare you speak to him like that! Your sisters have been nothing but a nuisance to him. He is not well. The wound the Chief Thegn gave him has flared up again."

"I knew there was a scuffle, but I didn't realise Eth was injured. I spoke sharply because I was worried. Those slavers lurk on the border and what would Os do to me if you were taken to Thanet?"

"I am sorry Ric. It is hot, and I do not want Eth to suffer more. I blame myself for his pain. The Thegn was intent on shaming the oarsmen to try to turn Æsc against ... "

"... Gragus?"

"Yes, but he was not named."

"Edmund has written a long letter to Æsc," Ric laughed. "I told him he was as bad as you for muddying the waters. I could not stop laughing."

"Why?"

"It was his fault Æsc thought the betrothal was between you and he."

Ric's boisterous merriment annoyed Eth and he called to be on their way. Ric apologised and followed at the rear with his sisters.

"Did Lee send us back here with you? She's jealous because Eth loves us," the oldest sister complained.

"Eth likes peace and quiet. He has too many noisy brothers."

"Eth is so handsome," the middle sister sighed.

"And brave," said the third. "He wrestled with the ghastly Chief Thegn."

"His wresting was stupidity, not bravery."

"We liked Win's coppice worker from Boten Heath. He had lovely hair, all dark and wavy."

"Oarsmen are like hedge roses. They look handsome enough from a distance in wild places but if you try to reach them you will pierce yourself with many sorrows," he warned. Ric was thinking about Lee.

It was slow progress to Meleforde where part of the shipment was left in the care of Æthelric's household thegns to be taken to three forges in the area. Os took more to Lidgaet and Eth continued towards Beodrickworth with what remained.

Eth insisted they travel on to Street Hall where the river crossed the highway. However, Ric soon re-joined their company having left his sisters with their guardians. He was firm but gentle with Eth and made him lie down to rest early in the evening. After Ric had organised a guard, he took Lee to the watch tower which overlooked the surrounding hills. It was a steep climb. Lee ran most of the way as she wanted to arrive before the sun set. Halfway up the ascent Ric was quite out of breath.

"You spend too long sitting in your saddle," she teased.

"I spend too long sitting looking at strange words," he complained as he threw himself down to rest.

"You have not told me about your Elmham North investigation."

"When have I had time to pursue that?" Ric complained. "Their halls were guarded, and now they have aided Alcuin's escape they will be sealed against all of us Wuffingas. But we have another enemy to test us."

"The oarsmen from Thanet?"

"Reports vary. Some say they are returning to Francia; others indicate they are going to the far north, and others insist they are going to strike us.

Os thinks many are already on Flegg Isle. I suspect they are the ones who know your oarsman."

"He is not in a lith."

"But his comrade is," he said quietly. "The one the girls so admire."

"Really?"

"Have your traders mentioned Guthrum?"

"No," she replied honestly. She did not realise Gutti was Guthrum and did not want to talk about Ædwine. "Have you learnt any psalms?"

"No. Have you done any embroidery?"

"Of course, not!"

"Then we understand each other perfectly, don't we?"

"But you can win battles with words, Ric."

"I prefer a sword."

"You need to keep fit," she said as she took off again. He rose to his feet and followed her.

It was a spectacular sunset and Lee wished Eth had been able to join them. The thegns at the tower were pleased to meet her. Tales were exchanged but not the one Lee wanted to hear. They could not stay long for darkness was falling.

"Ædwine was seen boarding one of Guthrum's longships," Ric said before they had gone far. "Are you certain he did not mention him? It was his fleet on the Yare."

"Perhaps he is the man I know as Gutti," Lee reasoned.

"He has at least thirty vessels, all the same sort. They lie low in the water and are easily missed."

"It was his longships on the river when we travelled up from the ferry at Sutherlingaham. Fred thought it was a ghost fleet. It sent shivers down my spine too. When it passed in the dead of night it was as if we could reach out and touch something close which wasn't there at all. I thought oars would made more noise, so we dismissed our thoughts. But I know it was Gutti because he was ordered to return to Flegg and the open seas."

"How can you be so certain? You know more about him, don't you?"

"Gutti may have been hired by the rebels for I know Hastein's men sell themselves as mercenaries in Francia and Brittany ..."

"Hastein? You mentioned him earlier. He's one of the Brothers, isn't he?"

"I think he is, but his base is on an isle where the Loire meets the western ocean – it's south of Brittany. He's not with the Brothers on Thanet Isle. And I know Hastein has called Gutti's liths to aid him in Francia."

"Then we are fortunate indeed!" Ric exclaimed.

"My friends had no part in the uprising. We were spared greater loss at North Burgh because Alcuin sent the Hethel Ceorl to Southwic."

"Why was he sent there?"

"He learned Gragus was in the area." Lee explained.

"And why is he so desperate to find him?"

"He doesn't know. But it worked in our interest. Alcuin's rebels had been gathered at Merholt Hall for some days in readiness to strike - and they may have succeeded in capturing North Burgh but by chance Alcuin went south the same day Lok arrived in Blythburgh where Edmund was waiting for him."

"Why was that? I never quite grasped why Edmund went north."

Lee explained about the slavers and her adventure at Icanho. He smiled but her seriousness was not broken.

"The oarsmen are very skilled at keeping themselves informed. They only lose battles in Francia when they are misinformed or careless. They like to be swift and certain. I expect Gutti did not like the delay and, therefore, did not join the rebels. He will regret not taking his mares."

"What!" Ric cried. "Not those in your mead?"

"Yes, they belong to him. When he came for them. I told him to wait for I thought they were close to foaling – but I was wrong for they have not foaled yet. Fortunately, he was with more gentle kin who held him back – I do not want to meet him again. He would kill me without thought."

"The game you play is too dangerous, Lee."

"I will send word and transport the mares to Flegg, and I'll avoid him - I promise," she said as she turned away. He laid his hand on her shoulder.

"You must keep away from them all," he warned.

"I cannot tear myself from Gragus. I truly love him, Ric."

"Gragus and Frith are perhaps to be trusted but Os has always had his doubts about Ædwine hasn't he? Without Gragus holding him back he will be as dangerous as Gutti, don't you think?"

"Of course, not. He would never harm me. He went with Gutti to fetch his wife and children," Lee revealed.

"Children? He can be no older than me."

"They have to marry young because they all die before they are thirty," Lee replied gloomily.

Their journey continued in silence, and at the camp they bade each other goodnight. Lee continued to think about Ædwine far away on stormy seas. How would he find peace with a man like Gutti?

During the night, Eth called for her, so she sat by him into the early morning when, at last, he fell into a restless sleep. She was tired when she said farewell to Ric. Eth had difficulty in mounting his horse and did not descend agaiin until late in the day. He neither ate nor drank anything.

Although it was late when they arrived at the forge at Sygelsmer, the steward was keen to inspect the metal strips and searched in vain for his blacksmith to come and give his opinion.

"He must have grown weary with the waiting. He wanted to know what quality they are. You can't be too careful these days. I had to send some back at Easter. How is your father, Eth?"

"He's well." Eth was brief for he wanted to be on his way, but the steward was keen to talk.

"He hasn't been down for several weeks," the steward continued.

"He's very busy at the Hall and Beodrickworth."

"And is this your young lady?"

"She's my sister," he said wearily.

Lee knew Eth wanted to press on to be home before dark.

"You have no sisters Eth – I know that much."

"He teases you, kind sir," Lee intervened. "I am Pip's sister from the Hellesden. We must be on our way for it is late."

"You might see the blacksmith up the valley side, he's staying at the hall near the donkey pasture."

"Isn't it where they found the mares?"

"Why, yes … "

"Come on Lee," interrupted Eth. "We'll never get home if you try to solve that old mystery."

"We'll look out for your blacksmith. What does he look like?"

"Like nothing you've ever seen before. He has braids all done in bands and like so."

He demonstrated how the man's hair was tied back and Lee laughed.

"It's very wild. I might do mine the same way."

"Hurry up Lee. I don't care how your hair is tied."

Eth began to drift and barely caught the blacksmith's name, Brand. Lee got back upon her horse, and they followed the lane as it wound up the hillside. They had not gone far when she sensed Eth was about to swoon. She drew her horse to a sudden halt and jumped down in time to steady her friend as he slid from the saddle.

"Go to the hall down the track," Lee urged the junior thegns. "Ask for some herbs for bruises to rub on his wound. It has ailed him all day."

The thegns saw how pale Eth was and hastened away to find help.

"I feel very sick. My head is thumping."

"You have drunk so little that is why," she reprimanded. "And you are faint through lack of nourishment. Why do you have to be so stubborn?"

"I am in such pain," he moaned and lay upon his back but then sat up again. Lee steadied him as he was very sick and trembled violently.

"Try to fix your thoughts on something and don't wander from it."

Lee did not know what to do to comfort the lad, so she covered him with her cloak and brushed her hand across his brow. It was not long before the junior thegns returned.

"He said you must wait here and not try to go any further."

"Does he have some herbs?"

"Yes. He's bringing his pack."

"Help me back on my horse Lee," Eth moaned. "We are almost home. What will Father say if I abandon my men? He already thinks I cannot be trusted. He said I was no more than a hot-heated cowherd. Not like a thegn at all. He said it was a disgraceful thing to hit a fellow thegn. He said he would have me dismissed if I failed in this."

"Don't fret Eth," Lee said. "We will tell him how brave you have been to bear up under such pain."

She held his hand and looked to the two lads who nodded in agreement. Lee closed her eyes and prayed for her friend.

"What has happened to Eth?" Someone asked. "Did he fall?"

Lee turned and was thankful help had arrived.

"He had a severe blow to his ribs, and we thought he had recovered but a few days ago one of his brothers jumped on him and it has flared up worse than before. He insists he can get home."

"Let me see the wound, Eth," he requested as the lad lifted his shirt.

"It's terrible!" Lee exclaimed.

"It's hot and he shivers. I have a roaring fire at my hall. We must take him there."

"I must get Lee and my thegns home," Eth protested.

"They can go home on their own," the blacksmith insisted.

"Lee can stay with you. Come now, lean on me."

Eth struggled to his feet.

"Shall we go to the tower for help?" A junior asked.

"No," Lee said as she looked at the man who lifted Eth and put him back on his horse. "We know Brand. Go and tell Pip I am on my way to Ældor Hall."

They parted company at the way to the derelict hall. The entrance to the narrow lane was overgrown and Eth had to bend down to avoid the branches. He moaned loudly.

"I must go and summon his father," Lee insisted.

"You take the horses to the meadow and come back here."

Lee obeyed. When she entered the shabby hall Eth was laying on some furs in front of a blazing fire and her friend was preparing a poultice to apply to the wound.

"I've seen this sort before," he commented. "If the bone is splintered it might damage his lungs. It's very likely it has bled inside - but his chest has a good feel about it. If he's no worse tomorrow, you can travel on to his hall."

"I cannot stay here with you."

"I thought you trusted me?"

"I do."

"Eth must lie quietly until the herbs ease the pain. Where have you been?"

"We've returned from Bures with the semi forged blades."

"I've been waiting for those. Did you know I was here?"

"How could I have known? Frith said you were far away. Does he know you are here?"

"Yes, but he is not pleased. He ordered me not to send word to you."

"Why not?"

"Why did you leave Gragus in North Burgh? If I had been strong enough, I would have rowed you downstream to Flegg."

"We both agreed it was not the right time."

"It will never be the right time, Lee. You must make up your mind."

"My thoughts are settled. When Gragus and Kadlin return, I will invite them to meet my kin. Frith will help me – so don't make trouble."

"It is just what he said to me. You have no time to wait Lee. The Chief Thegn has left his wife in Mercia - and he has the evidence he wants to discredit Gragus."

"I told you Edmund will say nothing to him about the maps. I trust my king and you ought to trust your brother."

Ædwine was silenced and threw more wood on the fire.

"Why didn't you keep watch over the lad and rest on the way?"

"I didn't know he was in pain," she protested. "I am weary Ædwine and I have to face his father - and he already blames me."

"For what?" Lee did not answer. "Did you injure Eth?"

"As good as," Lee confessed for it was useless trying to hide the truth from him. "I stirred him up and he hit the Thegn you mentioned, and there was a terrible struggle."

"You promised Gragus you would occupy yourself quietly at your hall. You have upset the wrong man – men."

"And you promised Kadlin you would rest. Have you recovered enough to work at the forge?"

"It's hard work but it does me good."

"You needed to rest longer on Flegg. Edmund's men saw you boarding Gutti's longship three days after we parted company.

"I had to find a way to Thanet. The rumours were true; my woman had disobeyed Hastein's orders and left his camp."

"Then why are you here?"

"Valr thought I would challenge her man to a duel and end up like father. He sent another to find out more. I must wait here until Gragus returns even though it offends Frith."

"He is trying to protect his position – he loves Kadlin - and she belongs here. Besides Edmund does not like you," Lee said bluntly. "Nor does Os, nor Eth's father."

"He does not like Gragus either. And neither will your brothers."

"My brothers?"

"Frith told me Edmund has sent word to them requesting their permission to allow you to marry."

"And I mean to be patient and wait for their reply."

"It is not a matter of patience. Your king wants you to be lulled to sleep," Ædwine protested.

"What do you mean?"

"He wants you to forget – and I know how this kingdom dulls the senses. You see, I am prepared this time. Let me take you to him Lee," he whispered. "I know where he has gone. We can leave tomorrow."

"But I have promised Edmund I will wait."

"Have you eaten?" Lee shook her head. "Have some bread and then you must rest. I will put another mattress down beside Eth's."

They said no more and when Lee had finished her supper she lay down and pulled the covers over herself.

"Are you angry with me?" She asked Ædwine.

"No, and things have changed. The Brothers are making haste to gain an advantage here. It has surprised me. I am sure Edmund already knows Frith is stranded here. And he will keep you from crossing the divide."

"Is Edmund in danger?"

"No more than I am," he complained.

Ædwine was determined to keep his wrath hidden because her king had the advantage in the battle for her heart; a battle he had vowed to win.

Lee turned away and was soon asleep and he sat watching

460

over her. He was weary but did not lay down to rest until the fire had burned low. He lay next to his jarl's maiden and fell asleep.

Lee stirred at the sound of rain beating upon the thatch and wondered where she was. It was dark and the place smelt musty and damp. Not far away she heard water dripping into a bowl as the rain seeped through the worn-out thatch. She listened to Eth's steady, but rasping breathing and turned to see if he was well covered with blankets.

Later Lee heard him stir and asked him if the pain had eased. "I'm very thirsty," he whispered. "Is Ædwine here?"

"Yes, he's asleep," she replied as she filled his cup and helped him sit up. Eth groaned loudly as the pain surged through his body again. Ædwine woke up and came to help him.

"Let him rest longer," Ædwine said.

Lee lay down beside the fire. She could not sleep for fear Eth might die and neither did she desire further conversation with Ædwine. He was like tinder from below fir trees, highly volatile and likely to flare up at the smallest spark. And yet, as he dozed, Lee thought how gentle and peaceful he looked.

"Wake up my fair maid," he whispered. "I hear horses drawing near. I'll go to greet them."

He bent down, kissed her, and left. Once more it took a while for Lee to recall where she was but when she did, she feared it would not please Edmund's Thegn to find her there.

It was cold and Lee shivered as she left the hall and found her horse. She was careful to avoid Eth's father who was out of sight across the courtyard and silently led her horse to the end of the lane where she mounted and raced away. Ædwine heard her horse and knew at once what she had done. He was not pleased but it was her way.

"Thank you," Eth murmured as he left.

"You take care, lad. And rest," Ædwine said as they parted.

He worked until midday and then rode towards Pip's, for

he knew he could no longer delay his task. When he entered the Hellesden Coppice he was immediately lost in wonder for it was no longer open with light pouring in through swaying branches; it was a dense thicket with tall grasses and herbs. The yellow sword irises shone as he approached the fallen willow, and his heart was moved. It was a beautiful place and he understood why she loved it so much.

He found Pip in the courtyard. He looked up and smiled.

"She is home then?" Ædwine asked.

"In time for breakfast," Pip replied laughing. "I was about to ride over to tell you. Did you find your way through the Hellesden? She was sure you would lose yourself."

"I nearly did. It is so changed. You need to trim those leaves back from the orchard tower," he advised.

"She's been too busy in the garden to be concerned about that folly. She means to make you work like a slave, you know, so I advise you not to step into the pightle yet. Come and see the new foals first," he urged. "They were all born when she was away."

"She thought they would be born when she was in North Burgh."

"They were very large with foal but now we know why. Their foals are the largest I have seen, and one had twins. Can you believe it?" Pip said as he opened the gate.

Lee watched her brother take Ædwine across to the mead. They did not stay long for Ædwine was eager to see her other mares. Win joined them and there was much merriment as Ædwine set the mares to work. It was more than she had hoped for – to have Ædwine back again. Gragus did not seem so far away, and her heart was full of joy.

Frith called in time to join them for supper, and he was pleased to see how they had welcomed Ædwine. His brother seemed to be restful again and Frith began to think he had recovered from the shock of his torture for he had certainly been very troubled by it until now. After supper Lee took Ædwine to see her garden and later they walked towards the pond where she shut in the geese for the night. On their return, they stopped to sit in the stable shelter and watched the young mares in the mead.

"It was a stealthy escape you made this morning," he said. "You should have taken my cloak. I was worried you would be cold."

"It wasn't too bad. I rode fast so the horse was warm. Did Edmund's Thegn hear me leave?"

"No. But he knew. He said very little. You were right, he is a very angry man. Let's hope Eth recovers quickly."

"I would like to go and visit him, but my presence will upset his father and I do not want him to complain to Edmund."

"Come with me tonight Lee before he reports I am here."

"Where will you take me? To Thanet?"

"Yes, to Thanet."

"What will your wife say?"

"Why would she care? She is with child – his child." Lee sighed for she had hoped Ædwine would find happiness with his wife again. He read her thoughts and continued. "There was never any chance we would renew our vows."

"So, you were married?"

"Vows are not the same."

"I thought your vows were totally binding – for fear of your deities."

"Some are and some are not."

"How confusing. Name some which are binding."

"Vows between brothers, battle brothers are very binding and ones that are said in the presence of such brethren." He hesitated.

"And those easily undone?"

"Any vows made between a man and a woman are not as binding, and hardly at all if no one else hears."

"That's very expedient if you are a man but very tiresome if you are a woman. If I were a man, would you love me more?" Lee asked without thinking.

"How can I love you more?" He whispered as he turned from her.

"Our ways say let 'yes' mean 'yes' and 'no' mean 'no'," she continued as she had not heard what he had said. "We are advised not to make vows."

"So, you do not get married either?"

"Of course, we do. But if I say yes, it is forever. I must never change my mind. I have said yes to Edmund; 'Yes, I will wait for him to write to my brothers.' I cannot break my word, even though there was no oath."

"Do you love him more than Gragus?"

"He is my king! Edmund does not make his loyal followers swear any oaths for he trusts our word. But stubborn ones he deals with differently. I understand why some would think an oath is binding for you heathens - but if you consider we are unworthy equals, the oath does not stand. Is that it?"

"Yes. You have seen our hearts and judged aright."

"And you do not consider Edmund as worthy as Gragus?"

"I know he is," Ædwine unexpectedly confirmed. He knew Edmund was as important to her as Gragus was to him. "But Lee you must come with me, for I am afraid we will lose you if you stay here any longer."

"I promised Gragus I will leave, in September, but not now."

"Four moons? That is a long time," he said wearily.

"Do they mean to overpower us before then? Is that what you truly fear? Gutti warned me all our mares would be his by winter."

"Gutti is anxious to please his men. They came here to

seek battle for they thought Salamon was secure in Brittany, but something is amiss in Francia, and he must settle his thoughts about returning before he decides how to intervene here."

"We have received a few reports about his part in the Merholt plot."

"He is raving with anger Lee. He was promised much but when words were broken, he feared the worst. My capture and torment rewarded Edmund well, for it delayed the uprising and Gutti left."

"Edmund did not desire your suffering. He saw the pit."

"I know."

"And I could have prevented it."

"I was captured through my own folly. It was not your fault," he replied.

"I should have intervened - but I was ..."

"You were offended?"

"It was not offence," Lee muttered. "It was, I mean, I was shaken by ..."

"The way we live?"

"Your world and mine are far apart. But not so with Frith. He is not like you or Gutti. And even Gutti has a lovely sister and gentler brother."

"Lindi despises me."

"Why?"

"Because I have never treated women well – not since Gragus ..."

"You cannot judge us all because of one maiden's wicked deed."

"You are wrong. She is only one of many who have tried to defeat us by trickery," he muttered. He moved away from her. Lee knew he was troubled by what had been said so she returned to the mares and their foals.

"I'll send payment for the mares to Gutti," Ædwine offered.

"They will be quite a challenge to break in; especially the twins."

"It's just what Os said when I saw him last – though he might have meant me," she laughed.

"Are you Pip's twin then?"

"Didn't you know?"

"I thought he was much older than you."

"He is aged because I have been such a burden to him."

"Sæwara was my twin," he said sadly. "She has been in my thoughts much since I was laid low. I have been told I was a gentle happy child, much like Frith, until she was taken. I know I was ... "

"How old were you when she was lost?"

"Thirteen summers."

"We were thirteen when mother and father died. We had each other and could not be parted. It is easier now but then it was impossible."

"You understand then, why I feel so alone? Part of me has stood still since then. Then there was the sorrow which washed over me when my brothers died. It has been Gragus who has held my head above the waves all these years. And now, my fairest maiden, it is you who holds back my anger. You make me feel joyful and I want you to be with us."

"I cannot leave my hall yet," she sighed.

"Then I must return to the forge and wait for you to see sense." He moved away from her again but this time he turned back sharply causing all his braids to dance. "Do not disappoint me, Lee. I ask because I don't want Gragus to lose you to ..."

"Look your brother is here," Lee whispered.

"You must tell me what the Chief Thegn did to offend young Eth another day. Take care when he is near. Remember he is a wolf. Vows may not constrain him."

Frith walked in through the open door of the stable and said it was late, and he was ready to leave.

"Pip does not want you here," he rebuked as he walked away with his brother. "Lee is trying her best to gain permission to marry Gragus, so stay away from her."

"But I cannot brother; not because I desire her, for I do not," Ædwine declared. "They are lulling her to sleep! And I will not watch helplessly from a distance as you do. I will be awake and ready with my sword when they stand between her and Gragus."

"Do not stir up trouble before Gragus returns, that is all I ask. They have questioned me at length about how you came to be here and would have arrested you had you not been such an exceptional blacksmith."

The two brothers left in silence.

Early on Monday Frith visited Ældor Hall. Flæ was distraught because Eth had been very sick again. Frith went to his room.

"Lee sent some honey cakes – I left them in the kitchen. Has the physician seen you?" Frith asked.

"He has been sent for. Where is Lee? Hasn't she forgiven me?"

"She doesn't blame you. Ædwine says her heart is heavy because you are hurt, and she feels the loss of your father. If only they would lay aside their stubbornness and agree to meet. How can I bring this about Eth?"

"Father has not spoken to me either. It was all silence yesterday. I overheard him arguing with mother. He was saying terrible things about Lee and mother was defending her. He knows she was there with Ædwine. But she did no wrong. She would not leave my side - just like Gragus would not leave you. She ran off because she didn't want to offend father! But he won't listen to me."

"Then I will speak to him. Is he at Edmund's Hall?"

"He's gone to the minster to pray and will not leave for days. He thinks he has failed."

"Failed?"

"He thinks God is angry because he has not kept Lee safe and pure."

"Lee has done nothing wrong. Ædwine can be wild but he guards her for Gragus, not himself. I will go to the monastery today."

"He will not see you," Eth warned. "Please urge Lee to visit me."

"I will. You must rest. Did you like my brother's hair?"

"I did," Eth sighed.

"Then ask Lee to put braids in yours and see what your father says."

Eth smiled and closed his eyes. He was very tired.

Frith entered the hall of the god he did not know. At the far end he glimpsed Edmund's Thegn on his knees before a simple altar table. Two flickering flames dimly burned either side of a plain wooden cross. The humble Thegn heard the footsteps but did not turn aside from his prayers. He thought it was one of the brothers who served there, and his eyes remained shut until the man who had knelt beside him began to speak in a foreign tongue. He turned and saw the oarsman's gaze fixed upon the simple cross; his tears were heightened by the gentle radiance from the candles.

"I want to know him and follow him, sir. I do not know where to begin. What must I do? I miss my dearest Kadlin, and she believes, and Lee never turns aside. I feel like a man standing far away but Lee stands at his side. She has done no wrong, sir, and she misses you. You must go to her, and I must come to your Lord, but I do not know what to do."

The Thegn's heart was moved, and he embraced the younger man.

"His message is simple enough – his call never changes. He says save yourself from this corrupt generation and turn from doing wrong and believe in him. He is the only one who can forgive sins and all our wickedness," he said plainly. "It is simple enough, believe and be baptised. Has Kadlin told you what he did, how he lived and the manner of his death?"

"Yes, and Lee has explained how he rose from the dead - and all the evidence is written in your Scriptures. Lee is helping me with the texts. There is something deep in me which knows these accounts are true. But my brother has a friend who has been baptised many times and he feels nothing. He is convinced it is all lies, or worse."

"There is no magic in baptism Frith. It is our response to show others we have decided to follow Jesus and live by his ways. Nor is it the end. It is the beginning. Once we lay our lives at his feet to love and serve him, he will send his Holy Spirit, the one whom he calls a counsellor, to be with you forever. He is the Spirit of truth, which is why your brother cannot accept him, for those who do not seek him do not see him or know him. But you have sought him Frith and he will not forsake you. Lee was wise to tell you he rose from the dead. He was able to do that because he had done no wrong and death could not hold him. We all deserve death because we do things our conscience tells us not to, and fail to do good when it is in our power to do so. When we ask him to forgive us, he cancels our debt, and we are free. Although we die, death will not hold us because he has paid our redemption price. After death we will be re-clothed in a body which is eternal. We will be with him in his kingdom. For now, the Holy Spirit lives in our hearts and strengthens us. He walks alongside and convicts us when we do wrong, and I have done much wrong in these past few weeks. It is why I have come aside to this place. I have been unkind and harsh with my wife – my precious wife."

"I love Kadlin dearly. I did not think I would miss her so much. She has not pressed me in this matter. I am here because I desire to understand and know him - but I have done much wrong. I have lied and mocked good people and taken lives in battle without thought. I have stolen and laid waste to much which was precious to others. I was eager to follow wicked men whose gods are far away, but your Jesus is calling me, I know it. I will follow but I am afraid and feel my ignorance for I do not know your ways though I see them in Lee and your Eth."

"You do not have to understand everything my son, just tell him what you have told me, that you have heeded his call and want to respond. I will pray for you."

The two men prayed, and Frith responded to the call. Great joy and peace filled his heart.

Dusk drew near and Lee stood in the courtyard watching the swallows feed their young in the wood store. When she saw Edmund's Thegn approach, she hastened into the store, hoping he had not seen her. He had probably come to complain about her conduct again.

"You have rightly turned your back to me," he said. Lee turned and embraced him.

"I am sorry Eth was hurt because I would not forgive Greg. Why is it so difficult to live how our Lord asked us to? I am trying not to demand my own way. I love Gragus and Frith and Ædwine. If we do not love them, how will they ever know our Lord's ways?"

A swallow flew past so low it brushed its wings against her hair.

"Do you know the psalm about swallows? What does it say?"

Lee thought and then replied. "'How lovely is your dwelling place, Lord of Hosts. I long and yearn for the courts of the Lord; my heart and flesh cry out for the living God. Even a sparrow finds a home, and a swallow, a nest for herself where she places her young near your altar ...'" She continued until she reached the last lines, and he joined her. "'I would rather be at the door of the house of my God than to live in the tents of the wicked. For the Lord God is a sun and shield. The Lord gives grace and glory; he does not withhold the good from those who live with integrity. Lord of Hosts, happy is the person who trusts in You!'"

"You have set your heart to do right my child. They have seen it, and Frith has chosen to answer. The Lord called him into the kingdom today."

Lee looked astonished.

"I thought he was annoyed with me because I spent too long out with Ædwine!" Lee exclaimed.

"You know I am not happy he has returned. Frith fears you think you know and understand Ædwine when you do not. The psalm is for you. Do not go to the tents of the wicked Lee. You must stay here. Ædwine is a very fearful man and he will not be easily resisted if he is determined to take you across the grey sea to Gragus."

"He is beginning to love the lanes and woods which surround us. He only saw the bare autumn bones when he was here before - and he is very taken by the beauty of our meads."

"They will not hold him here Lee. An injured wolf may seek solitude for a while, but when he feels fit enough, he will return to the pack. He is set against our ways," he warned.

"And I do not blame him. He has seen the false pomp and hypocrisy in Christendom and has rejected it. Our Lord reviled hypocrisy, didn't he? He was very severe with those who said they had life but lived in darkness - those who had the keys to knowledge of the Way but would not let others in. How many in our kingdom truly walk in His ways? In certain places, there is hardly a worthy man amongst the clergy. They are blind ..."

"And so are you, Lee. Do you think Ædwine will return the compassion you showed him - he will not! He is determined to break you and I will not stand by and see it happen. Tell him he must leave."

"We have to act wisely, sir," she pleaded. "For some are waiting for a reason to strike us and I must show Ædwine our loving kindness because they are watching him."

"Who are watching him?"

Lee faltered.

"Those on Flegg."

"And who are they?"

"I don't know. But they have gone south."

"Then send him back to them. Don't we have enough enemies from Mercia living amongst us?"

"Edmund has wasted too much time trying to reason with the Mercians. He must regulate their trade in the Borders."

"I agree we must defend our independence but if we expel the Mercians from Elmham North they are very likely to hire oarsmen so they can master us again."

"You are right sir those same oarsmen are hired as mercenaries in other kingdoms. Not just for attacking rivals – some use them to defend their liberty. Which is exactly what Salamon has done – and he is a Christian."

"Edmund will not put his confidence in oarsmen."

"Nor in Mercia. Greg will show us what they are really like now he has allied himself to them."

"His alliance will provoke them if he seeks annulment of his marriage."

"Surely it has not come to that already?" Lee interrupted. "Edmund must make him go back to her! Let me speak to him."

"It is not wise, Lee, to speak to our Chief Thegn."

"Nothing I do or suggest is wise, is it?" She complained.

Eth's father realised he must not let Lee fall into despair and added.

"We must be thankful Frith has chosen to do what is right. It is a new beginning for him, and you and Eth must help him."

"And you must pray for Ædwine," Lee urged as he turned to

leave. "He does feel at home here, I know it. He may not be ready to turn from his gods yet for he has long been bound to them. We must pray he will understand what Frith has done."

The two knelt to pray and Lee determined to tell Ædwine what had happened to Frith. She did not have to wait long because as Edmund's Thegn went on his way Ædwine walked through the orchard.

"It is late," she said in a whisper.

"I had to work until the furnace gave up its heat," he replied.

"Then you should be resting in your hall," she reprimanded.

"You know what a bare, miserable place that is. I need to speak with you. I could not rest yesterday, though I had nothing to do. I need to know what your Chief Thegn did to upset Eth and how things stand with your brother who came to North Burgh."

"Help me with the geese and then come back to the hall with me."

"We can talk at the stable," he suggested.

"I would rather go to the hall. I can find some supper for you. Pip and Win will want to know how your swords shaped up."

He agreed and she decided to go straight to the hall where he sat with Pip and Win. Lee then rushed out to secure the geese and returned to sit by the fire where he soon joined her.

"Pip said I can stay and leave in the morning, so tell me why you left North Burgh so suddenly."

"Edmund very wisely sent me home." She told him all about her journey to South Elmham and her stay at the healing halls which were no longer at Elmham because of the building works. Ædwine was not familiar with the river beyond the Stein Street crossing near Bunincga-Haye and listened carefully to her tale.

"Now tell me why Eth and the Thegn came to blows," he urged.

"The Thegn had told Æsc I was being corrupted by my association with oarsmen. He thinks I am ..." Lee searched for the right words. "Not pious enough." She knew he would not be satisfied with her answer.

"You did something foolish, didn't you? Frith would not speak of it. What did you do?"

"I put flowers in my hair."

Her answer was abrupt and was intended to make him laugh and stop his interrogation. He did not even smile. Lee stalled.

"It was more than flowers," he growled.

"The children put bluebells in my hair, and I did not want him to see me like that – because of Dummoc. I was with Gisla when the Thegn suddenly turned up at Edmund's Hall"

"Is Gisla intent on throwing you into his path?"

"I made every effort to avoid him."

"Tell me what happened!" Ædwine demanded so forcibly Pip looked up from the far side of the room and Lee met his gaze.

"I am weary," she complained.

"Weary or not Lee, you will tell me."

"I sought a way to escape, and if you insist on being so demanding then I will do the same now."

He did not want her to leave his side. Neither broke the silence and they sat with their eyes fixed upon the flickering flames until Pip and Win got up to leave for their sleeping quarters. Pip insisted Ædwine joined them.

Lee could not sleep. Not long after dawn she rose to begin her work. She hoped Ædwine would go to tend to the horses as he used to. When he arrived, her arms were full of hay which she arranged in the stalls.

"I went to the Shield Hall."

"I thought as much," he said coldly. "What happened?"

"It was just a friendly spar with Eth."

"And?"

"By mistake he caused me to swoon."

"He hit you?"

"Caught me hard with his shield edge," she admitted as she pointed to the place it had hit her head.

"Were you without your helm then?"

"Yes. I was without my helm!"

"And your senses, I fear."

"Do not humiliate me. Poor Eth made a mistake. Was it my fault?"

"The mistake was yours – and it not by chance!"

"Was it 'by chance' the Thegn was there when I fell? Eth would not let him give me aid and it upset my brother. I could not avoid his questions – everything turned against me."

"And you said it was not your fault. It was in your power to avoid going to the Shield Hall and you know it!"

"It was in your power to avoid the woman on the heath, but did you?"

He had not seen her so angry before and he stepped back towards the door. He hated angry women.

"How well you have proved your love for Gragus," he accused. "You could not remain quiet and blameless in your hall for a week!"

At breakfast Lee told her brother Ædwine had left and she did not expect him to return. However, the oarsman was determined not to lose her and merrily supped with them.

"Come away with me tonight," he whispered as they stood by the gate to Hilde's Mead. "I have packed all my goods. We can leave and be in Gipeswick by dawn."

"It is not what Gragus wants," Lee objected.

"You have ruined what he wanted."

"I have not!"

"Not yet perhaps, but your Thegn will not rest. He has left his wife and prowls after you like the wolf in your play. If you hear his cries you will turn. I beg you - come with me - I know where Gragus is."

"But I do not know where you are – that is my problem!"

He felt her words cut him down. He was unhappy at the forge for it reminded him of the past when he worked with Weland. They had been some of the happiest days he had known; together they had made all sorts of amulets and weapons and called upon their deities with enigmatic chants encasing luck and fortune in silver.

Without warning he took hold of the chain around her neck and drew the black disc to view. Lee did not like his mood and hastily removed the chain from her neck. She told him to keep it and he did.

"I can see where you are Lee," he called after her. "I've ridden the waves on a longship, and I always know where the shallows are. Waves break and crash where there is no depth. I see waters stirring in your eyes when they should be calm."

"If you see my tears before they fall then it is because I am afraid. I am not the one who has faltered and changed direction. When you stand on the shore you will see it is not the mightiest waves which reach the furthest. I will keep my agreement with Gragus even though I am weak."

When she saw Frith the next day, he was alarmed. The bonds between the two had been severed. However, he was thankful his brother had left peacefully. He did not know it was the lull before the storm broke.

CHAPTER NINETEEN

THE TEMPEST

On Thursday evening Lee walked over to Hilde's Mead with a bucket of roots and chopped herbs for the three mares and four foals. It was a cold evening for June, and she hastened back to the stable. Ædwine spoke from the gloom.

"I need to talk to you Lee. I left you standing alone at Dummoc, and I have always regretted it." He took her hand and kissed her braids. "I stood by and let the Thegn pour scorn and insults on you and did nothing to stop him. I cannot let it happen again. He has no right to debase my jarl or you. I will go to Kentforde – to his post and warn him before he muddies the waters further. I will not have you live in fear of him."

"You will not go to Kentforde." Lee hissed. "It will lead to more discord. I will be safe if I stay close to Pip."

"Safe!" He yelled. "Tonight, I could have been him. This is the place he caught you before."

"But he did not hold me captive for long, did he? Take your hands off me! I am not going anywhere with you!"

"Then I fear Gragus has lost you."

"Why? Are the oarsmen about to strike?"

"Yes."

"I don't believe you. Gragus would have remained here if he thought I was in danger from them. He will be back before the end of our harvest."

"Then let me keep you safe until he returns. I know many here who have wives who will give you shelter. Come with me before it is too late."

"Ædwine, I have explained many times what we agreed. You know Kadlin is to return to this kingdom to marry Frith. He's not leaving, is he?"

"He will follow me, or do you think he will bow his neck to your god? He knows what happens to people who do," he whispered. "I won't let him repeat father's folly."

"Frith is safe here. We don't force anyone to wear the 'white gowns' as you call our baptism. A man or woman is free to choose."

"But you are not free to choose, are you? If you were, you would be with Gragus. They will make some excuse to hold you here. Why wait until September when you can leave with me tonight? Let me watch over you."

"This is not watching over me. This is torment!" Lee cried.

"What do you know of torment? I suffered in the pit when you could have warned me. But your wretched piety stood in the way!"

"I was not being pious. I did not know who she was. You looked as if you enjoyed her company."

Lee did not like his sudden hostility.

"I hate whores," he cried. "And I did not lie with her!"

His directness shocked her, and she felt afraid.

"I will not keep arguing with you for I cannot bear all these harsh words," she sobbed. "Edmund has written to my brothers and has given them a fixed number of days to make their decision. I intend to honour that."

"Then Unnulfr has lost you and I cannot change fate," he murmured as he looked up at the starry sky. He pleaded with his gods in his own tongue for success – but the gods were against him. "And I have lost you too."

"Come inside and sit around the fire with us," she urged.

"What is the point in warming myself if I am going to get cold again? I will say goodbye here where I met you," he said icily.

Lee sadly watched the lone warrior slink into the deepening shadows. The flight of swallows had left him behind and he was isolated and confused. Lee thought she would never see him again.

The weary maiden wrestled with her misgivings and lay awake far into the night. She would go to the forge, give Ædwine the seaxe and tell him about his brother's choice. But she must not part with the precious knife. It belonged to Gragus, and she would not give it to another. It was pitch black when someone tried to shake her from sleep.

"Ædwine?" She whispered as if in a dream.

"Are you coming with me? Do not raise your voice or I will use my seaxe. Put what you will need in my bag and hurry."

"I am not leaving," she whispered. Lee was as determined as ever.

He took no notice, lit her lamp, and began to gather her things together. He emptied the contents of her box into his pack, and she hastened to put on her boots and over clothes. He thought she had given way to his will, but she played for time. She sat upon her bed and watched him complete his task. He would not take her! Tears fell upon the swirls and runes of the seaxe she held. It was a danger he had overlooked.

"Get your cloak," he commanded as if she were a slave.

Lee threw herself at him.

He had not expected such fury. Nor was he prepared for her battle cry. She knocked him to the floor where he took hold of her wrist to steady the hand which wielded the seaxe.

Meanwhile Pip had heard Ædwine's horse gasping in the courtyard and had dressed himself. He neared the place where his sister slept and, on hearing her wild shriek, burst into her room. His command stilled the two furies and they parted. Lee threw the seaxe upon her bed and moved as far as she could from the wild oarsman.

"Stay back brother," she warned. "He is not in his right mind. He is exhausted; they should have ensured he had recovered from his scourging before setting him to work from dawn to dusk. You must go home and rest Ædwine," she desperately urged.

"My name is not Ædwine!" He cried. "You know who I am."

"But I do not," Pip tried to intervene. The oarsman struck and Pip fell upon the bed. Lee stood between them.

"I gave you every chance to share life with us," the warrior scorned. "But you have cast us aside. I will make sure Gragus never sees you again!"

"But I love him."

"You lie! Your words were false from the start."

"I beg you to go and find him. Bring him to Flegg. I will wait here until he sends word."

"There is another place to wait if they count you worthy enough."

His voice seemed distant, and he no longer looked at her.

"Gragus promised to come back here Pip," she explained. "He told me to wait, and this man says I must go with him. What if our paths never cross again? Gragus called for me before and I was not here. If it happens again, I will lose him forever!"

"It is not true Lee. Your paths will cross. I will make sure they do - but not here. There is no honour to be found here. When they descend upon your realm you must be out of reach, with me. I will send you ahead of fate to a place where Unnulfr will find you. We can find shelter with Hastein. There will be nothing left here for any of us."

"Lee is right my friend, you are exhausted. Nothing you say makes sense to me. I have spoken to Gragus. I know he willingly let my sister return to our hall to allow us time to make an agreement with our kin. And we count you amongst our kin - Lee has much to lose if she flees with you."

"I do not care about losing my lands or my horses," Lee interrupted. "But I will not break my word! Get him to lie down for I am sure he will settle himself. Where he is staying is cold and damp, the thatch leaks and it's all hemmed in. There is such a stench from the mire. Please let him stay here."

"What? Has his madness drawn you in? If I had not heard his horse one of you would have been killed with that," Pip cried as he pointed to the seaxe. "Take your cursed knife and leave!"

Before Ædwine could take the seaxe Lee threw herself at him and tried to cling to him but he discarded her as one who felt a horsefly bite and brushed it away.

"The knife was in her hand, not mine." He threw his pack over his shoulder and replaced the seaxe in its embroidered case. He backed towards the door and made his escape.

Lee called to him in his language. Pip did not understand what she said. She clung to Ædwine's leg as he sat upon his horse and continued to plead with him. He took no notice and kicked her away but, to Pip's horror, she ran after him towards the outer gates. The commotion had woken Win and he caught her before she had chance to cross the home pightle.

"He has gone Lee, don't cry."

"I did not want him to leave. He is hurt and I have driven him to the camps on Thanet. Gragus will never forgive me. You must stop him," she pleaded.

Win prepared for his departure while Pip watched over the distraught maiden. Dawn crept upon the household and much later Pip heard a horse return. He stepped into the courtyard to greet his brother. But it was not Win. It was Gisla accompanied by a man and woman he did not recognise.

"Is Lee in her garden?" Gisla asked. "I have some news for her."

"Win has taken her to see Frith," he lied.

Inside the hall, Lee had gone to the partition to see if Ædwine had returned with Win. Her heart sank when she saw her aunt and she knew what she must do.

The sun was at its highest point when Lee drew into the shady overgrown yard. She did not intend to stay long so she left her horse tied to an elm sapling.

The entrance to the hall was dark and everything which had belonged to Ædwine had gone. She pushed up the latch, went inside and a man on his knees leapt to his feet.

"Why are you here Lee? My brother is rampaging around in a maddened state - you must go home."

He did not move aside, and Lee knew he sought to conceal something.

"He is here, isn't he?" She pushed forward but Frith firmly barred her way. "Is he dead?"

"Do not look!" He demanded.

"Let me see him." Lee insisted. However, it was not a body Frith shielded but some sort of shrine. She caught sight of blue feathers from a jay's wing. They were those attached to the seaxe cover he had taken. Lee recognised the threads.

"Close your eyes to it Lee," he said as he lifted her up and took her outside. "Wait here and do not move. Edmund's Thegn is not far behind me. He has taken some men with him to the forge. I cannot let him see what is in there. Even if you don't care what they think of him, I do."

"I do care Frith. I begged him not to go."

Lee hung her head in shame while he returned to gather the items strewn around the makeshift shrine. He hid them in his pack. Outside the forlorn maiden waited for him with her head resting on her drawn-up knees. Her hair flowed down like gentle waterfalls, and he was reminded of the day she had bravely led the Thegn away from his hiding place up an oak tree.

"Come with me, my love," he urged. "We must go down to the forge and intervene on his behalf."

However, the Blackheath Thegn had not found Ædwine at work nor had anyone seen him. The forge steward was distressed he had lost the finest blacksmith he had ever employed. Lee explained about his children being lost and the steward thought he understood why the man had left.

Lee kept close to Frith's side until she reached Ældor Hall where he advised her to return to Pip. She wrote a quick note for Eth and left with three junior thegns. Frith promised to visit her the following day and hastily left for Chadsacre to examine the objects he had stumbled upon.

The junior thegns rode through the Hellesden quite a way ahead of Lee who was in no hurry to return because she did not want to face Gisla. When she reached the fallen willow, she looked up and saw a blue feather amongst the branches which grew from the trunk. It held her gaze, but she could not reach it without climbing the tree, so she dismounted. The junior thegns saw her standing amongst the sword irises and thought she had stopped to pick some flowers.

Lee gazed upon the golden blooms and buds scattered at all heights amongst the broad sword-like leaves. She caught sight of another feather and made her way through the undergrowth to the place she had hidden behind the roots of the willow. Once freed the feather floated down and settled on the sandy soil, where the tree roots had once been anchored. An arch made from two fern fronds caught her eye. The sand had been disturbed and smoothed between the fronds and a mark imprinted there like the one on the bag Fred had pulled from the furze. There was no raven, but a single golden flower lay above the votive outline anchored by a silver wire. Lee began to slowly scrape away the sand and unearthed Ædwine's black disc. It was broken into two; the thin silver inlay was stretched out and anchored the flower though it still attached the two parts. What could it mean? Below it she found one of her green linden and silvered braids she had cut from her hair after Dummoc. It was with one of his braids. She untwined them and dropped the items into her purse, flattened the soil and scattered leaf litter over the place.

The young thegns called for her and she forgot the other feather for her thoughts were all astir. It was a second shrine, and she was suddenly very afraid.

"You can't hide in the brambles any longer," Eth's brother called as she drew close. "He's not going to move on. He could see your horse."

Her heart leapt. She ran to the juniors to see where the fugitive was, but it was not the one she sought. Further down the grassy ride, the Chief Thegn stood beside his horse waiting for the band of travellers to catch up. He observed her look of dismay as she drew to a sudden halt. However, Lee quickly gathered her senses and slowly led her horse towards the man.

"Are you waiting for, sir?" She asked almost too politely. "I hope we haven't delayed you."

"Not at all Lee, I thought you had stopped to pick some of those irises, but I see you have none. You look very pale, are you not well?"

"Eth is very sick," she said not meaning to accuse the man. He drew close to her and took her hand in his.

"The best physician from the Borders is on his way to see him. I will do all I can to help the lad. The blow went astray Lee and landed too heavily. Do you think I would deliberately hurt a fine young thegn?"

"I know you did not begin the struggle, sir. I upset Eth because you do not consider Gragus worthy enough to live amongst us."

"It is my duty, dear child, to protect this kingdom. I had doubts about the men you assisted, and every week I hear news to confirm my thoughts. Your older brothers are wiser than Edmund in these matters. Wessex will have nothing to do with oarsmen. They exclude them – and all their traders. The man desires you as a wife to gain favour here. When we honour him and turn our eyes from the truth his fyrd will strike."

He sensed his words had wounded her, so he kissed her hand and walked silently by her side. Lee fought back tears and anger, and the rest of the journey to her hall was blurred. She faintly recalled passing through the bramble mead where she mounted her horse again. When they drew level close to the orchard, she turned on him.

"I once loved this place! It was peaceful and safe until you came here. I have never feared Gragus, nor Ædwine. He does not alarm me as you do!"

"If I alarm you, it is because you are burdened by guilt and fear being found out!" He called after her as she strode down the lane.

"I have nothing to hide, sir," she said. Then she turned. "We have been open in the matter of our betrothal - unlike you."

"I married one who is devoted to our Holy Church, and yes, she is quite unlike you, for she would not throw herself at some vile heathen!"

"You had no right to marry her without Edmund's permission. Her kin are Mercians!"

Lee strode away.

"At least they serve one God. Is it right to be united with one who serves so many? I command you to separate from these pagans!"

"Command me?" Lee echoed. "You are not my king. And I can no longer respect you – even though you are Edmund's Chief Thegn. Your pursuit of riches drove you to it! I have learned how wealthy her kin are."

Her words were meant to wound, and the Chief Thegn

paused but he did not face what he had done.

"You will not deflect me from the truth this time, you foolish maiden. I will never let you marry him. He is a pagan, and his companions are pagans!"

"That is not true."

"Then you are more deceived than I reckoned."

"Do you not know Frith is going to be baptised on Sunday?" She said loudly enough to defy him. "Did you know?"

"No," he admitted. He paused to consider what he had said but Lee's temper overcame her.

"While you have been fully occupied with your ambitions, others have been on their knees! How dare you accuse these men when you are heaping up riches and lands for yourself? Frith has forsaken everything!"

"Do not believe all you hear for they put on the baptismal gowns lightly enough," he sneered. "What has he lost? He has a hall and land, and knowledge to sell to his kin. The Mercians are wise enough to follow the ways of Francia - they baptise their kind and then behead them!"

"Then go and live in Mercia!"

The Thegn looked at her and was repulsed by what he had said.

"Frith is wise to separate from his brother," he said as gently as he could. "But listen my maiden. We will not allow you to leave our realm with pagans who bow down to trees and springs and worship images and seek protection from amulets. I know you have taken to wearing one. It is superstition of the worst kind."

"I returned his necklace," she protested.

"Good, you show some wisdom at last."

Lee gave way at last and ordered the juniors to take her horse to the mead and then angrily climbed the bank into the orchard. He knew he must not leave her feeling so utterly defeated. Instead of riding away some madness overtook him.

He left his horse and went back and ascended the bank. Lee had not gone far, and she heard him brush through the leafy hedge. Lee, determined to stand up to him, swung around. She was about to warn him if he threatened her again, she would have him exiled. However, he had much to establish too. Before she could find words to satisfy her anger, he took her into his arms and kissed her.

He saw her eyes ablaze with contempt. She was angry and shaken by his passion. He trembled at what he had done.

"Lee, you and I were never so far apart," he declared. "We thought we knew what we wanted but have discovered we knew nothing at all. Do you know what you want? Is he worth pursuing? Will you find shelter with him? Come with me, it is not too late, is it? I know it is not. I will give you everything you want, everything."

"Why did you marry her?"

Before he could explain Lee had fled. Very slowly he made his way down into the gloomy lane. At Stane Hall he found solace with his soft-hearted hound. Meanwhile Lee had thrown herself upon her bed and cried. When she woke up Pip was there. He kissed her.

"What a day," he sighed. "You did not find him then?"

"No. I went to see Eth, but he is so weak. His father searched all morning for Ædwine, but he has gone."

"Did you see Frith?"

"Yes, he is coming over tomorrow. Has Gisla gone?"

"She left before midday. I went with them as far as the Osier Meads. They decided to go to Gipeswick. I've been back a good while – it's very late you know."

"They didn't see me leave, did they?"

"No," he laughed. "We have all mastered avoiding one another today."

Lee thought about her clash with the Chief Thegn. Pip was

wrong.

In the evening before the light began to fade, she returned to the orchard for some grass for the mares. She looked up to the tower which had not protected her from the Chief Thegn. Her folly weighed heavily on her shoulders. She climbed the tree to seek a place of refuge. For a long time, she sat at the entrance staring at the scene which lay before her eyes.

The woven wall panels had been decorated with spear irises and on the shelf, lay a series of objects including her favourite stone, an amber pebble with two arching fern fronds sealed inside it. There was another small bowl like the one in the hearth at Ædwine's lodgings. When she looked closer she discovered why Frith had been so determined not to let her examine the shrine. The bowl was filled with blood! A lock of hair bound between two jay feathers from the seaxe cover tassel lay next to an old hazel twig which bore a tiny red flower and catkin. It was the one Gragus had given her when they had chased through the lane sparring with Weland's seaxe. Her amber stone had been placed on a sword iris flower and all the objects has been circled round with the silver chain from Erik's talisman.

Lee reflected on what she had briefly glanced at the first shine for it had also been encircled. Then she realised what she had seen there was the silver necklace from North Burgh. Ædwine had tipped the contents of her box into his pack and had used them as shrine offerings to false gods. She shivered and gathered up the flowers and objects but left the bowl which she carefully carried down to the base of the tree where she emptied it into a root hollow. A narrow silver ring fell out and she barely prevented it from disappearing down the hole. It was delicately patterned and of very fine workmanship. She guessed Weland had made it and clasped it to her bosom.

Later she undid the clasp on the silver chain and threaded both rings on it. Lee could not sleep. The moon was exceptionally bright and streamed though the shuttering under the eaves. As she listened to the sounds of the night she heard the geese call and horses neighing.

She entered the stable shelter by climbing in over the hurdles from the mead and climbed the steps to where the hay was stored. From there she would be able to hear if any foxes or oarsmen were prowling around. When she stood at the top step, she sensed someone else was there.

"Ærnbjörn," she called softly. "Are you still angry with me?"

She waited a long time before he replied with a weary 'no'.

"Did you see me with the wolf?"

"Yes," he whispered. She wondered why he said no more and moved closer to him.

"And you are not angry, even though I broke my word?"

"I am too weary to be angry."

"And I was too fatigued, in body and thought, to run. Did you hear what I said about Frith?"

"Yes."

"I have tried to explain what has happened, but every time I met you this past week we have argued," she faltered. "O Ærnbjörn, I am sorry I have failed you. I will go with you tomorrow."

"I am tired Lee," he half whimpered. "And cold. Draw closer, as we were in the hold at North Burgh."

Lee obeyed.

"No harm will come to Frith. How I wish Kadlin were here with him," she sobbed. "And I want to be with Gragus."

"You will be with him Lee – I have vowed to do it and it must be done."

His words were slurred by exhaustion. Lee thought it wise not mention the shrines. She wanted him to rest and wake in a steadier state of mind.

"I love you too Ærnbjörn - and Frith," she sighed and then

lay looking at the moonlight as it streamed in through the gaps around the upper doors.

He held her hand, closed his eyes and at last slept.

At dawn, she found herself alone. But she was content enough to know he had renewed his promise to take her to Gragus.

"You told Pip Ædwine was going to Thanet," Frith remarked when he arrived to join them for breakfast.

"He said nothing certain. He's been vague all week, hinting at this and that. I am sure when he has found his bairns he will return."

"Bairns?" Repeated Pip.

"His children." Frith explained.

"He has some children?" Pip cried in astonishment.

"Yes, I have three nephews. He is estranged from them and the mother. I look forward to meeting them."

"How long have you known?"

"Ædwine told Lee the morning we parted in North Burgh. When we arrived at the dunes in Horsye, north of Flegg, Gragus told me."

"Is this why he is so unsettled?"

"I've never known him otherwise, except when he worked with you last autumn. He said the Hellesden was a very peaceful place," Frith replied.

Lee revived because she thought everything would work for good – and so did Pip for her escort to Elmham arrived before noon.

At the Beleham Tavern Branda threw her arms around Lee's neck and kissed her. Their time for learning was upon them and Branda's excitement dispersed Lee's gloom and she began to look forward to the weeks they were to spend as novices at the healing halls. Os, who accompanied his sister was relieved to see Lee safe and well for he knew how much Edmund's Thegn loathed Frith's kinsman.

Frith decided to delay his baptism until his brother had been found or some word came from him. Lee reflected on their parting at Hellesden Hall. She had not told Frith about Ædwine's return but they had freely discussed the shrines though neither mentioned the blood. Frith thought the maiden had been spared the burden of understanding what his brother had done.

As soon as Lee and Pip set out on their journey to Beleham, Frith visited the shrines again and began to consider what the objects might signify. His old religion had been vague and diverse, and its followers worshipped all manner of tree spirits and places – so the location of the shrines were significant.

Frith pondered what had been in his brother's thoughts but all he could see was confusion. Unlike Ædwine, he had never heeded superstitions which was why many of his countrymen had been loosed from their beliefs. He knew things had been different in the past for their homeland was a place where seers and priestesses wielded strict control over temple complexes. Among the elite group of men and women were those who foretold the coming of one jarl who would rule all others. The prophesy heralded the struggles between jarls and forced many to seek and establish new kingdoms across the waters. However, in so doing the priests and shamans lost influence and could no longer control how each disparate group interpreted their old tales. What had his gods ever done but take revenge and outwit each other in the vilest of ways? He had always thought they were too busy arguing with each other, or worse, to have regard for his life and sorrows.

However, his brother had fallen under the influence of Hastein's prophets of war, who, like the Brothers, venerated Thor and his hallowed groves. Vows were sacred and prominent and needed no overseer from a temple to validate them. It led to many honour reprisals; thus, Frith concluded, the gods became no more than helpless onlookers as man struck down man.

Frith struggled to understand why his brother had made three shrines and used so many circles and flowers. Circles represented death and rebirth but why all the flowers and braids? After much thought, he found Edmund and explained some of his fears concerning his brother but did not mention the ritual sacrifices made at the shrines. Edmund, therefore, concluded Ædwine had gone to die on the battlefield and reasoned Lee was safe enough under the watchful eyes of Bishop's Hunberht's healers.

Lee and Branda gained a great deal of knowledge during their first week at the Bishop's Hall. Those who served there saw at once the diligent nature of the two maidens so sent them to gather herbs which grew near the mill on the river. Five maidens left with their baskets and travelled with a party of brothers who were taking a wagon to the mill to collect merchandise. Beyond the great wooden building, along the westward path lay the water meads and the cultivated beds of spear iris which would soon be dug up for their roots which made a fine blue dye.

The maidens collected herbs as far as Fisherman's Lane where they crossed the rickety bridge over the backwater creek. Here they reached the lower meads and rested under the shade of an ancient willow. Lee was engrossed by the beauty of the place and her eyes roved to and fro taking in the shapes of trees and texture of the barks. She spied something peculiar about a smaller sallow which had half fallen over the channel they had crossed downstream. On closer inspection, she saw it was a cleverly constructed crossing leading to the alder carr isle beyond the far bank.

Lee had so far resisted all temptations to explore her new surroundings as Os had warned her to be a good example since she was the eldest. Indeed, she had done very well thus far, and the brothers and older residents were impressed by her noble character and intelligence. However, it was the first day she had been allowed to roam outside the extensive hurdle bound gardens, and she had been dancing through the tall, robust ox-eye daisies and pale lilies with sheer delight. To keep her feet to the quickest way back to the Halls was simply too much to ask.

She climbed the steps to the point where the willow branch was broken and then crawled along it until she was about two thirds of the way across the channel. The girls cried out for her to return because they were sure she would fall into the weed-covered water. Branda hushed them and watched as Lee stood up and balanced. She had seen a rope hanging from the branches of the alder tree on the opposite bank and stretched up to reach it. As she drew it near, Branda stepped back to see what she was doing but it was too late. Lee had launched herself off the broken branch and swung through the air to land safely on the far bank.

"See, it was easy enough," she cried with satisfaction.

"And how are you going to get back?" Branda whimpered.

"You should have asked before I jumped." Lee laughed. "But don't worry, whoever made the crossing must have known another way. Keep together and wait there and I'll follow this path to see where it goes."

It was a dead end into the alder quagmire, so she returned to try another way. Eventually she found a path and returned. She told the maidens to cross the bridge and make their way back to the church because she had found a path. Lee was certain it would join the lane higher up the valley.

The four girls raced ahead to get there first but had to return because they had left their baskets of herbs under the shady willow. Later they were sure it was Lee ahead in the distance by the church enclosure. Exhausted by their efforts they rested in the covered gateway below the church.

Branda turned to see Edmund and his thegns leave the church.

"I presume my dear Lee has not been able to behave herself and is not free to roam the meads with you," the king observed.

Branda blushed and was afraid to mention what had happened. She did not want Lee to be sent home so she was not as direct as she should have been. After a brief exchange of greetings, she addressed the maidens.

"We must go and find Lee in the gardens. She will be waiting for us."

Branda picked up her own basket and the one Lee had earlier filled. Edmund kindly took a basket and walked with them to the Bishop's Hall. The other maidens respected Branda's decision to keep quiet about Lee for they had come to understand what she was like and quite expected her to surprise them all by being dressed in all her finery to greet Edmund. They were aware they looked weary and dishevelled and walked slowly some distance behind Edmund's fine thegns.

Branda immediately set herself the task of finding Lee but when she had looked everywhere, she went to one of the leading ladies to explain what had happened. The kindly lady did not appear to be alarmed and sent Branda to prepare herself for the supper feast with the king.

Edmund found her at her table braiding her hair.

"Why didn't you tell me Lee was missing?" The king's intenseness made the lowly-hearted maiden tremble.

"I've looked everywhere for her Edmund," she sobbed. "I thought she was playing her favourite game - you know the way she makes you get delayed, and she is there all the time waiting."

Edmund was not satisfied with her reply and pressed her to explain what had happened. It took Branda a long time to recount her tale.

"So, the last time you saw her was in the alder carr all the way down the lane to the river? How long ago?" Edmund pressed.

"The sun was about a third in its descent, sir. Please forgive my foolishness - I did not want Lee to fall into misfortune. She had been perfectly well behaved until she saw the willow tree. She had to conquer it - you must know what she is like."

"I do know Branda," he said gently for he saw how troubled the young maiden was. "And I do not blame you. There is something I fear more than her irresponsible ways and high spirits, information I cannot share with you."

"Do you think she has fallen in the river and drowned?"

"She can swim very well for a maiden. Did you see anyone else in the meads or on the river?"

"There were women gathering flowers, but we had long passed them. There was no one else except the lady by the church whom I thought was Lee ahead of us."

"Think again Branda, just once more. The last time you saw her, was she changed in her thinking. Was she anxious?"

"No, she was just the same as when she leapt, though her feet were all muddied from the carr waters. She was as full of mirth and wit as she had been all day. I am sure she had not met anyone, good nor bad. Has the Thegn carried her off again? He swore he would."

"When?"

"Not long before Lee left her hall. She was anxious to get away from him," the maiden revealed.

Branda heard footsteps and looked up to see who it was who had entered her room. She was not sure who he was.

"This is Lee's friend, Frith, from Holy Cross. We have travelled here to seek her and to await the arrival of young Eth. He is being brought by the river to the halls to seek help for his wound."

"Has he made no progress? Lee has been very worried about him."

"And now we are concerned about her," replied Edmund before he turned to Frith. "We must take our thegns and make a search of the isle – they will find where her feet sank into the carr and follow from there. I know it well, but it is very overgrown and treacherously boggy in places." Edmund sighed and indicated they must leave. "Pray for her safe return dear maiden and do not blame yourself. I should have arrived sooner, but I failed to listen to my friend here."

Edmund left with the search party and did not return until after sunset. They did not find Lee in the alder carr and there were no signs she had walked along the banks. They searched as far as the mill in one direction and the ford in the other. The light had quickly faded and they did not want to risk overlooking any evidence. He and Frith retired early so they could make a prompt start to their search the next day. Boats had been brought up from below the mill, but Edmund was unsure where he should begin.

"It is too bad Edmund the young maiden did not tell you sooner. We lost much time. But this is my fault. I should have seen further but I did not realise the significance of what he planned."

"Then tell me Frith - all you know - all your thoughts. Do not be afraid to tell me unspeakable things. I will not hold you responsible for your brother's deeds. Lee is precious to me."

"I have thought through all the parts – those things he left behind and those he may have taken. My brother left the copy of her play and a few other items at his lodgings. The parchment was folded at the final scene – which has worried me. I told you her sword was missing from the Shield Hall. I think my brother took it. I was foolish to overlook the play for he has taken much from it. The flowers he left in his room perplexed me from the start and when I checked I found many faded blooms cast upon Lee's compost heap. All lilies they were Edmund – those which grow along banks of rivers. It is not a simple thing he has prepared to do. Her play began and ended by a river."

"I did read the play, and it was pleasing enough if you like tragedies. A fair maiden who sought to save her king and was prevented from doing so because of a wolf - which I thought represented my future and the oarsmen who threaten our realm."

"It had many meanings," Frith murmured as he recalled the way Gragus had given chase to the maiden and thrown his seaxe at her heart.

"What do you mean?"

"My brother did not see you as her king. It was Gragus who was her jarl. And he is Ædwine's jarl too. He thinks she has failed in her quest to bring healing to Gragus because she refused to go to him. The place where the Swan Princess dies was under a willow ..."

"Is Lee to die Frith? Please say no!" Edmund called out in anguish.

"I think so. My brother no longer sees Lee. He has worked his magic to make her a swan maiden – not a princess. And they must die to reach those they love."

"I do not grasp what you say my friend. In the play, she is frosted and cold – she was frozen like an outcast because she was betrayed."

"No, when it was performed it was clearly the seaxe through her heart – but not my brother's seaxe."

"Then whose?"

"Edmund – I do not know how to say this. The one at Dummoc represented the one she had taken from Gragus the day they first met in the Hellesden. It was the enchanted one Fred described to your Chief Thegn."

"She took his seaxe?" Edmund cried and Frith nodded. "So, there was another seaxe – the one the Chief Thegn sought?"

"Yes. She had carefully hidden it in the Hornbeam Wood near her hall. When I returned, she said she had put it under her mattress. Of all the places Edmund. And in those few muddled days before my brother left, Pip found them fighting over a seaxe. Ædwine took it. I am sure it was the seaxe which belonged to Gragus for it had a covered case decorated with feathers from a jay. I found three of those at the shrine."

"Shrine? You did not mention it was a shrine he had made."

"I did not want to offend you, sir. Nor did I want you to cut him off from Lee. I hoped I would reach her before he did, but I have failed. He loves her dearly, Edmund. When Lee left Hellesden Hall she told me there had been two further shrines and I have struggled to see why. I assume there were three because three people are involved."

"You must reveal what I do not understand. What did Lee find at these shrines she could not tell me about?"

"She found the black disc – his talisman – the one he had asked her to wear. It was not superstition Edmund; he thought if she were captured by oarsmen, they would recognise it and not harm her. She returned it in anger last week when she refused to go with him to find Gragus. He had broken it in half and buried it at the shrine she found in the Hellesden. It may signify the end of their friendship. And then there was …" Frith paused for he also had a ring which was to remain hidden. "Locks of hair, and feathers and ferns and the three circles. These are all matters of our afterlife Edmund. and I do not want to think about it."

"Your brother is dreadfully lost in his ways. Pray with me so our Lord will reveal the place and grant we find her unharmed."

Before dawn seven thegns and two brothers from the Bishop's Hall journeyed to the river with Frith and Edmund. They checked under all the bridges and every suitably cold watery place. A chance comment from one of the brothers about a cold stone floor where he had prayed throughout the night caused Edmund to ask if there were any other stone floors in the locality. The Abbot's old church beyond the river had a flint floor.

The church stood in an isolated spot which was reached by following an ancient sunken way bounded by a thick hazel hedge. Anyone travelling along it would have been concealed from the river meads. It crossed the highway and continued up a hill and then changed course to face west. It was said it had been a great causeway from ancient times and was aligned with the setting sun and the old church stood upon ground which was sacred before the Christian message had been proclaimed in the kingdom. The hallowed building stood in a dell and had a circular ditch and bank around it much like the one at Sutton Church. Edmund and Frith entered it alone. The king did not want anyone else to witness the scene he had come to dread.

Inside the church the air was cold; Edmund shivered and looked at Frith. Beyond the nave, they saw lighted candles burning very low upon the altar. One was elevated on a stand and illuminated the green gem in the hilt of her sword. Lee was lying there, dressed in her white robe. Her hair was carefully spread out over the linen altar cloth.

"He has sent Lee to welcome Gragus when he arrives at the Great Hall," cried Frith. "It is what I dreaded."

"Will he kill Gragus too?" Edmund asked.

"My jarl must die honourably in battle so he can take his place amongst the heavenly warriors. Perhaps my brother is on his way to him, to lead him into the final conflict." Frith sank to his knees and cried as if his brother were there. "O Ærnbjörn, why did you do this? It was not the way. We have lost her forever. You were wrong, she was not a swan maiden. She was gentle and kind, but mortal – O dearest Lee, you loved and rescued me, but I could not save you."

Edmund laid his hand on Frith's shoulder. The king stared at the distant tragedy. An ancient sword pierced her heart, as if she were indeed the doomed Swan Princess.

... to be continued in Edmund's Kingdom Part 2 Hastein's Daughters

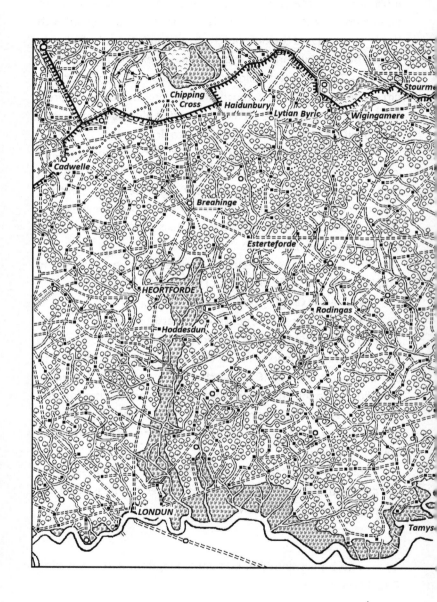

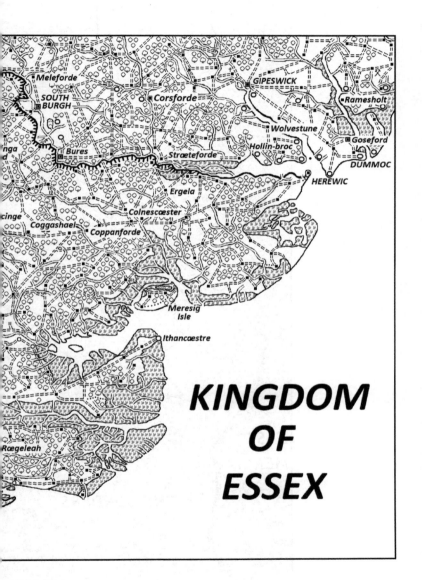

Meleforde

SOUTH
BURGH

Corsforde

GIPESWICK

Ramesholt

Wolvestune

Goseford

Bures

Stræteforde

Hollin-broc

DUMMOC

nga

HEREWIC

Ergela

cinge

Colnescæster

Coggashael

Coppanforde

Meresig
Isle

Ithancæstre

KINGDOM

OF

ESSEX

Ræegeleah

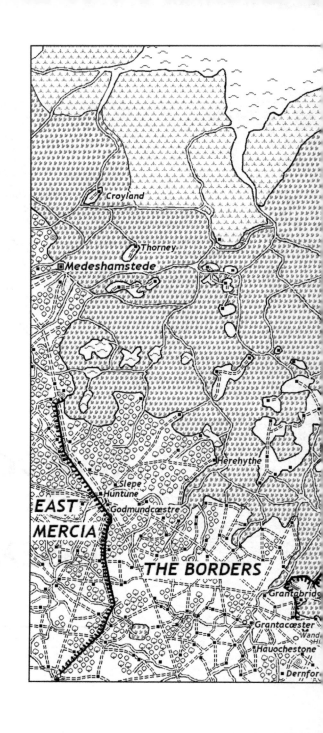

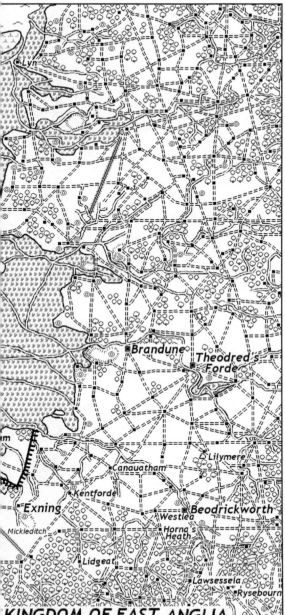

Lyn

Brandune

Theodred's
Forde

Lilymere

Canauatham

Kentforde

Exning

Westlea

Beodrickworth

Micklediitch

Horna's
Heath

Lidgeat

Lawsessela

Rysebourn

KINGDOM OF EAST ANGLIA